THE FIVE TIMES
I MET MYSELF

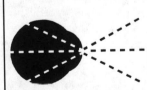

This Large Print Book carries the
Seal of Approval of N.A.V.H.

THE FIVE TIMES
I MET MYSELF

JAMES L. RUBART

THORNDIKE PRESS

A part of Gale, Cengage Learning

GALE
CENGAGE Learning·

Farmington Hills, Mich • San Francisco • New York • Waterville, Maine
Meriden, Conn • Mason, Ohio • Chicago

GALE
CENGAGE Learning

LIBRARY OF CONGRESS CATALOGING-IN-PUBLICATION DATA

Names: Rubart, James L.
Title: The five times I met myself / James L. Rubart.
Description: Waterville, Maine : Thorndike Press Large Print, 2016. | © 2015
    Series: Thorndike press large print Christian mystery
Identifiers: LCCN 2015041035| ISBN 9781410485731 (hardback) | ISBN
    1410485730 (hardcover)
Subjects: LCSH: Large type books. | BISAC: FICTION / Christian / Suspense. |
    GSAFD: Christian fiction.
Classification: LCC PS3618.U2326 F58 2016 | DDC 813/.6—dc23
LC record available at http://lccn.loc.gov/2015041035

Published in 2016 by arrangement with Thomas Nelson, Inc., a division of HarperCollins Christian Publishing, Inc.

Printed in Mexico
1 2 3 4 5 6 7 20 19 18 17 16

For Taylor and Micah.
What father could be more proud?

"The best thing about dreams is that fleeting moment, when you are between asleep and awake, when you don't know the difference between reality and fantasy, when for just that one moment you feel with your entire soul that the dream is reality, and it really happened."

— *James Arthur Baldwin*

"In my dreams I never have an age."

— *Madeleine L'Engle*

CHAPTER 1

May 10, 2015

The dream had come again last night, just as it had sliced into Brock's subconscious the night before that. A dream now dominating a significant portion of his waking moments. He had to talk to someone about it — someone with at least a smattering of psychology. Someone he could trust. His best choice was Morgan. His only choice, really.

Brock crossed Seattle's 4th Avenue and looked up at the sky as it surrendered to dusk. Not long till the spring evenings would hold the light till after nine o'clock. He reached the other side of the street, strode up to the front door of Java Spot, yanked the door open, and stepped inside. Three-quarters full. The perfect number of people. Not so many that newcomers would turn away, but enough to tell people it was a place to be. Morgan had to feel good having that many customers at six twenty.

Brock glanced around at the 1940s motif. Posters of Rosie the Riveter and Ted Williams, an old Coca-Cola sign, and the famous shot of the sailor kissing a nurse in Times Square hung on the walls. Definitely captured the hope of a post–World War II populace. Or maybe Java Spot simply appealed to those who wanted an alternative to the corporate giant that had more coffee shops sprinkled throughout Puget Sound than 7-Elevens.

On one side: a cluster of what looked like college students, a few couples, and some solo acts. The opposite side: three people hunched over their Mac laptops, and a large group of midfortysomethings laughed and pointed at each other in rapid-fire succession. What Java Spot put in its drinks was obviously the right concoction, which made Brock smile again, because he'd developed those concoctions being consumed in all fifteen of Morgan's locations as well as the rest of the country and overseas.

Brock took one more glance around the coffee shop, then strolled behind the counter and said, "Not a bad crowd for a Monday night."

"You can't come back here."

"Deal with it."

"Nope. Employees only. Get out. Now."

Morgan Myers lugged his sizable girth toward Brock and grinned. When he reached Brock, Morgan grabbed him by both shoulders and shook him like he was a stuffed animal. Yeah, maybe Morgan had put on more than a few pounds since their college days, but even after thirty-one years, he hadn't lost any of his linebacker strength.

"Amazing," Morgan said. "You actually have the hint of a tan to go with your slightly graying mane. A vacation you call work — but at least you got some sun."

"It was work."

"Uh-huh. A week in Costa Rica sipping coffee and checking out beans. Brutal. How did you survive? What, you were probably slaving away three, maybe four hours a day before you hit the beach?"

"Four and a half." Brock grinned at his friend.

"When did you get back?"

"Five days ago." Brock lowered his voice. "That's when they started."

"When what started?"

"When you get a moment, I need to talk."

"The doctor is in." Morgan tapped his chest.

"A degree in psychology you never used makes you a doctor?"

"I use it every day." Morgan waved his paw of a hand at the crowd. "Spill it. Problems with Karissa? Tyson? Work?"

"A dream. More like a nightmare."

Morgan beckoned with his finger and led Brock to the back room and into the office. After they settled into the small space, Morgan beckoned again with both hands. "Let's go. Tell me about dem cah-razy dreams."

"Strange dreams, not necessarily crazy." Brock glanced at Morgan's office door to make sure it was shut.

"You said nightmare."

"Not exactly. I'm not sure how to describe it — I'd almost call it spiritual but not in an uplifting way."

"Like a God dream?" Morgan's eyes were expectant.

"What do you mean?"

"I mean God dreams, where you know he's trying to tell you something." Morgan leaned forward and opened his hands. "Where he's talking to you through the dream, warning you, or letting you know something is coming, something to get ready for."

"God does that?"

"Um, yeah."

"It's not like that, I don't think. It's more . . . You ever have one of those dreams that's so real you can't tell if it's a dream or not, and when you wake up, you know intellectually it had to have been a dream, but you're still not one hundred percent sure?"

"Yes." Morgan's voice grew softer and he repeated his earlier request. "Tell me about the dream. In detail. And why it's freaking you out so much."

"My dad is in it."

"Oh boy, here we go."

"The dream isn't just a dream." Brock leaned back and focused on the ceiling of Morgan's office. "Yes, it's a dream, but Morg, I know it was more. My dad is young, early thirties I'm guessing, in the days before his nervous breakdown. The days before he started hating me."

"He didn't hate you."

Brock ignored the comment. "The light in his eyes is like fire. And he wears a jet-black fedora straight out of the fifties — so now I finally realize where the name of the company came from. He never wore a hat like that in life, and yet it was more him than anything I ever saw him wear." Brock glanced at Morgan. "You get that?"

Morgan nodded.

Brock paused. "You know how most dreams have elements of fantasy in them? Things that couldn't happen in real life?

This wasn't like that. Everything was as it should be. And it would take the push of a feather to convince me it really happened. That I was truly there. It was more real than real life."

"Go on."

The memory of the dream engulfed Brock and he lived it again, for the millionth time.

"Brock," his dad rumbled as they sat next to each other in Brock's boyhood backyard on a summer evening, both of them facing west, the sun starting to set.

"Yeah?" He gazed at the Douglas fir tree in the northwest corner. The tree he'd climb to the top when he was nine and ten and eleven and twelve to get away from his father.

"You need to listen to me." His dad held a small rectangular box wrapped in brown paper, which he tapped on the armrest of his chair. He pointed to the box and raised his eyebrows. "You see this? It's important."

"What is it?"

"Pay attention."

"I am." He turned to face his dad.

"No, not listening with one ear out the door like you always did." Dad beckoned with his finger right next to his ruddy cheek. "Right here. In my eyes. That kind of listening."

"Okay." The air warmed and his father's

eyes grew more intense. Brock had the urge to bolt from his chair, but his body wouldn't move. "I'm really listening."

"Good. You need to. Yeah, you really, truly need to." He turned the box over in his hands. "You have to make peace with Ron. Have to."

"Peace with Ron? Yeah, sure, Dad. Peace with a brother who's a year and a half younger but acts like he's three years older? One with a life mission to beat me in everything he does?"

"Same mission as yours."

"I'm not as bad as —"

"He's your brother."

"No, he's my business partner." Brock clutched his chair's armrests as anger rose inside. "And you gave him fifty-one percent of the company, which he lords over me every moment."

His dad turned away and gazed out over the darkening horizon. Once again he tapped the rectangular box in a slow rhythm on the armrest.

"It's coming, Brock, turning toward you just like the rotation of the earth. You can't stop it. It won't be easy. Definitely not easy. But good. You probably won't believe me, but it's good."

"What's coming, Dad?"

"Embrace it, Brock, even though it will be difficult. Face the truth, though it will be painful, for the truth will set you free." His dad leaned over and smacked his palm into Brock's chest so hard he caught his breath. "You need to get ready."

Brock pulled back. "Why'd you —"

"If you don't, it's going to bury you. If you don't, I'm going to bury you. Got it?"

"What's coming?"

His dad rose and grabbed Brock's shirt with both hands, yanked him out of the chair, and shook him hard. "Get ready!"

"For what?"

"Get ready!"

Louder this time.

"Tell me what's coming, Dad!"

Brock's dad pulled his face so close their noses touched and his voice dropped to a whisper. "For —"

But each time the words left his dad's mouth, the colors around them swirled and buried Brock, and he woke, breathing hard.

Brock stared at Morgan and whispered to his friend, "I have to get control of that dream. Get rid of it. My dad scares the snot out of me every time, and I'm tired of it."

"What's coming, Brock?"

"I don't know. I wake up every time before he tells me."

"You've had the dream more than once?"

"Five times in the past five days."

"Wow, someone wants to get your attention." Morgan leaned back and put his hands behind his head.

"This is God's way of saying hello?"

"What does Karissa say about it?"

"I haven't told her."

"Why not?"

Brock closed his eyes and let his head fall back onto his chair. "I don't want to get into it right now."

"Why not?"

"Morg?" Brock cocked his head and opened his eyes. "Give me a break."

"No worries." Morgan held his hands up. "What did you see and feel in the dream? Not with your mind, with your spirit."

Interesting question. On the surface there was nothing more than what he'd told Morgan. But underneath, there were layers he couldn't put into words.

"Like I couldn't stop whatever my dad says is coming, and yet I have to try."

"What else?"

"It's as if I was higher . . . I don't know how to describe it . . . The dream was clearer than it should have been, if that makes any sense. It gave me hope and fear at the same time."

"Yes." Morgan smiled. "Now we're get-

17

ting somewhere."

"I was there. I saw my dad, but not only saw him, I saw deeper. As if I was seeing the true self that was buried while he was alive. The dream was the most normal scene you can imagine. But it felt like I was touching the past and the present and the future all at the same time. And what he told me didn't come from me or my subconscious, it truly came from my dad. Do you understand, Morg?"

"It was like he was alive. In the present."

"Yes."

"But he looked young. In his thirties."

"Yes."

"And you're thinking he's talking to you from heaven."

"No. It was just a dream." Brock's head lulled back. "I mean, I don't know. It's why I'm talking to you." He clenched his fists. "So what he said . . . Was that a warning from God like you suggested? Or only a chemical reaction inside my head as I slept? And if it was a chemical reaction, could God have his hand on it? Maybe he orchestrated it?"

Morgan said in a sing-song voice, " 'The place where dreams and reality intersect, where the dream is immersed into the reality and is no longer a dream. A place where the infinite reaches us beyond the limitations of our mortal coils.' "

"What?"

"It's a quote from a book I read six months back. Thought I told you about it." Morgan twisted in his chair, stood, and scanned the bookshelves that ran across the back wall of his office. He shuffled a few feet to his left, reached for the highest shelf, pulled out a thin volume, and tossed it to Brock. "Here."

Brock caught it and looked at the cover. *Lucid Dreaming: Turning Dreams into Reality.*

"What's this?"

"Read it. Amazing stuff in there. Keep it, don't need it back. It's yours."

"What's lucid dreaming?"

"Read it. It might help you deal with the dream. Figure out what God's doing."

"Do you know what my dream meant?"

"Maybe." Morgan's eyes narrowed. "If I'm right, you're in for a ride."

"Why do you think that?"

"Just a feeling. Read the book and see where God leads you."

Brock tightened his grip on the steering wheel as he wove through the darkening streets toward home. Why were there always more questions than answers when he talked with Morgan? He supposed it was the price of friendship with a man so well read and probing.

Morgan's intuition was rarely wrong. Which meant the coming weeks would be a roller coaster without any chance to get off. As if he didn't have enough tension pumping through his veins at work, and even more on the home front.

CHAPTER 2

Brock slid his key into the lock of his east-side home on top of Newcastle with its view of Bellevue, and Lake Washington and Seattle in the distance. All the lights were off, which meant Tyson wasn't home. He knew his son wouldn't be, but it also meant Karissa was out somewhere with someone without telling him about it. Again. He went into the kitchen, set his briefcase and keys on the black granite counter, and called her. She picked up on the fourth ring.

"Hi."

"You're not home."

"I'm out, obviously."

"With?" He rubbed his eyes, then slid on his reading glasses and pawed through the mail that sat on the counter.

"Ruth."

"Oh." Brock wandered into the dark family room and flipped on a light. "Didn't know you were going out tonight."

21

"It was last minute. Ruth called and said she needed someone to talk to." Karissa paused, then answered the question she knew he was going to ask next. "Sorry, I forgot to let you know."

"No problem."

But it was a problem. It was a symptom of her slow pulling away from him, which he felt more than he could verbalize. It was a good marriage. A solid marriage. They loved each other. Even still liked each other. Most of the time. At least some of the time. Did he wonder what life would be like a year from now when Tyson headed off to college? Of course. Karissa certainly did, based on the number of conversations they'd had on the subject. But it didn't worry him. They'd be fine. Karissa had her interests, he had his, they had theirs together. At least they used to, and they could get them going again. Their life was okay. Used to be okay. Brock sighed and admitted for the first time since they'd started to make serious coin that money had become a salve that covered a lot of unspoken wounds.

"What time do you think you'll be home?"

"I don't know." Her tone said she was irritated by the question. "Don't stay up."

"Okay." He considered telling her to be

safe, but she'd think it was cliché. "Wake me up when you get home?"

"Sure."

But he knew she wouldn't.

Brock slipped into bed early and picked up Morgan's book. He meant to read just a few chapters but found it impossible to put down till he finished it. Morg was right. Fascinating. Lucid dreaming was a way to control his dreams. Which meant a way to grab hold of the one terrorizing him, wrench it from his subconscious, and destroy it.

He glanced at his watch. Twelve twenty-one. Still no Karissa. He considered texting her but knew she'd be annoyed. Checking up on her, she'd say. He pushed the worry from his mind and prayed the dream wouldn't come as sleep carried him away.

Brock slept solid — with no dreams, thank God — till he woke the next morning to the sound of the shower running. He opened his eyes a crack and stared through the half-open bathroom door. He didn't need to look at the clock on his nightstand. Had to be just after seven.

Same routine Monday through Friday for the past twenty-seven years. Karissa took an eight-minute shower every weekday morning starting at exactly seven a.m. Plus two minutes for her to dry off, which meant he had less than ten minutes to get to the kitchen, make coffee, and have it ready for them to drink a cup together. If she decided she had time.

Five minutes later, Karissa strolled around the corner of the hallway into the kitchen, drying her thick dark-brown hair with a light-green towel. Karissa sauntered up to him, kissed him on the cheek, and sat on the stool beside him.

"Sorry I didn't let you know I was going out last night." She gave him her scrunched-up-face grin that never failed to make him smile. At least in action, if not in heart. Could she see through his acting? Maybe the same way he saw through hers.

But it would be okay. They just needed time. He needed things at the company to stop being so volatile. Needed his sparring with Ron to subside. Needed to spend a bit more time with Tyson, which Karissa loved seeing him do.

"Tyson get off to school okay?"

"He was already gone by the time I got up at six."

"Student council stuff?"

"No. He's practicing his speech in front of two of the teachers." Karissa slid off the stool, scooted over to the refrigerator, and pulled out her caramel macchiato creamer.

She called to him over the top of the door. "You didn't bring over my creamer."

"It masks the flavor of the coffee."

How many times had they had this argument?

"It's the way I like it." She returned to the stool and shook her head at him.

"What speech?"

"Come on, Brock. How can you not remember? Dinner last week. The only time the three of us sat down together." She sighed and shifted her body away from him. "You were here for that. Correct?"

"Yes."

"But you don't recall him telling us about being voted by all the teachers and the entire senior class to give the commencement speech at graduation?"

"Yes, I do." Brock closed his eyes for a moment. "A lot going on at work."

"As there always is, as there always will be."

"It won't always be this intense, Karissa."

"And the sun won't always rise. But it will for a long time to come." She slipped off her stool and strolled away. "Are you in the office all day?"

"Yeah. I'm outta here in twenty minutes."

She waved without turning around. "Hope your day goes well."

Brock waited till she reached the bottom of the stairs that led to their bedroom. "Have you decided if you're coming Friday night?"

Karissa stopped but didn't turn. "Do you want me to come?"

"Like I told you, it's your choice. Either way is fine."

"That's what you said, but you'll resent it if I don't."

"No, I won't."

"Yes. You will." She rotated till she faced him, her face a mask of indifference. "I've been to three of your reunions."

"In other words, you don't want to go."

Karissa stared at him, eyes now frosty. "If you want me to come, I will come."

"Don't come. I'm completely fine with that. You'd be bored out of your mind."

"All right. Thank you." She turned and strode away.

"But if you do end up wanting to come, I'd love to have you there."

Karissa was already around the corner. If she heard him, she didn't respond.

CHAPTER 3

"Remember," Lennie said, "you have to give a speech at the reunion. Darby isn't coming and you were class VP, so you have to do it."

Brock laughed into his Bluetooth. He sat at his desk on the seventeenth floor of the Lincoln Tower One building in downtown Bellevue on Monday afternoon and stared at the floating span of concrete that bridged the eastside to Seattle. "Uh, no. No one wants to hear me talk."

"Yeah they do. At least I do, and since I planned this thing, I left a spot in the program for you."

"You'd be so much better than me. I'm not a good speaker."

"Are you kidding? You speak all the time for Black Fedora. TV, interviews, ads —"

"That's to a camera, or one reporter, and it's short sound bites —"

"You give talks to crowds —"

"Only when there's no way to get out of it. Gotta go, Lennie. I'll see you Friday night."

"But —"

Brock ended the call, pulled off his Bluetooth, and set it on his desk next to his Mac Pro. He refocused on an e-mail from a client wanting to develop a promotional video for their new set of stores. He hit reply to craft a response, but before he could type a word his intercom buzzed. Brock pushed the button.

"Hey, Michelle."

"Want to take a wild guess what I'm going to tell you?" Bright voice as always. Nothing ever seemed to bring his executive assistant down.

"Your husband just scored a six-album deal with Sony Music, they're giving him millions, and you're leaving me high and dry for the Bahamas tomorrow morning."

"Ehh! Wrong answer. Want to play again, double or nothing?"

"Someone should give him that deal. He's supremely talented."

"Thank you for coming all the way up to Arlington see him." Brock heard a smile in Michelle's voice. "You don't know what that meant for his confidence."

"I'm just glad they let a middle-aged guy

in the door."

"You don't look middle-aged."

"But you're admitting I am."

"By the calendar only." Michelle laughed. "Back to my question . . ."

"You want to let me know I have a meeting with Ron coming up in three minutes, and if I want to get there on time I should probably get going."

"Now you're a winner."

"What if I don't want to be on time? What if I don't want to go at all?" Brock released the button, stood, strode over to his office door, and opened it. "What do you think about you going for me?"

Michelle smiled and her eyes disappeared into her dark skin. Only twenty-six, but already the most accomplished assistant Brock had ever worked with. She shifted on her chair and waved fingers with bright blue nail polish through the air.

"You know how much I'd love to, but I would never consider depriving you of the chance to spend time with your favorite brother."

"At times your kindness astounds me."

"I try." Michelle bowed her head.

Brock loped toward Ron's office with a goal of finishing their talk in under ten minutes. He would be shocked if the meeting wasn't completely unnecessary. When he reached his brother's open door, he knocked on the door frame once, then stepped inside.

Ron Matthews stood at the far end of his office with his back to Brock. At his feet were six or seven golf balls, TaylorMade Tour Preferred X most likely. Brock couldn't see it, but there was of course a putter in his brother's hands. Either a Scotty Cameron hand-milled Fastback or a replica of Calamity Jane, Bobby Jones's putter. Bobby Jones, the greatest amateur golfer who ever lived, and Ron's hero.

Their CFO, Richard, stood fifteen or so feet to the left, both arms wrapped around a thick binder. Beside his shoes was a brass putting cup.

Ron glanced at the CFO before lining up one of his golf balls. "Anything else you need from me?"

"No, I'm fully prepared." He sniffed. "I'll implement the changes right away."

Ron drew the putter back and sent the pristine ball toward the cup. The ball slowed, crawled up the short ramp, and dropped into the center.

"Thank you, Richard."

"Of course."

Their CFO turned like a marionette on

strings, then waddled toward the door. When he was within a few feet of Brock, he nodded but didn't look into Brock's eyes.

"Brock."

"Richard."

As soon as the CFO stepped into the hallway and closed the door behind him, Brock strode toward Ron. "What changes?"

Ron rubbed his thick, short dark hair, then pulled another ball in front of him. His trademark business attire was black slacks, black shoes, and long-sleeved business shirts that were some variation of blue. Light blue, dark blue, checkered blue, blue stripes. At least he didn't wear ties.

Brock would come to work in nicely pressed jeans and T-shirts if he could get away with it. But his brother didn't embrace the casual look, so Brock donned the proper clothes when he was in the office. But on his frequent trips along the equator — visiting the coffee farms where Black Fedora's beans came from — his myriad T-shirts reigned supreme. Maybe he'd start dressing up someday. But at fifty-three, he didn't think the dog would be learning any new tricks.

"What changes, Ron?"

Ron sent the ball at his feet toward the brass ring. He missed left.

Brock's brother sighed and set the putter against the back wall. "Saving eight million dollars a year."

"By doing what?"

"We're going to change our buying patterns for a few cycles."

"You can't be serious." Brock held out his hands and shook his head. "You mean we're going to start buying beans from companies that employ slave labor to harvest their crop."

"Let me explain."

Heat rose in Brock, but he forced his voice to stay calm. "By purchasing our coffee from independent, worker-owned fields, we give them freedom. Their prices are five percent higher than what we would pay from other suppliers, but the extra money allows them to purchase land and change their lives. Radically."

"I know what the program does."

Brock ignored him. "The average yearly take-home wage for a worker harvesting beans is $1,200. But once they own just fifty acres, their yearly take-home jumps to $9,500."

"Brock? I was there when you set up the program."

Brock snapped his fingers. "Just like that they jump off the treadmill of barely making enough to survive. They make enough to save, to buy a small home, to send their children to school."

"Let me repeat: I know what the program does."

"I don't think you do. If you did, you wouldn't be suggesting we scrap it for even one day. What we do for the people down there is one of the foundational values of this company."

"We don't have a choice."

"What?"

"We need to switch. Just for a few cycles. Then we'll get back to —"

"Are we in trouble?" A chill wound through Brock.

"Nah, not bad. Things are thin, yes, but just because of our recent expansions." He walked toward Brock.

"Don't mess with me, Ron. What's going on?"

"Brock. Relax." Ron opened his hands. "Things are fine. But we just laid out six million for expansion into the Philippines, and another eight for Japan. Return on those investments will be substantial, but they won't start to trickle in for five, maybe even six quarters. And I am not one to let this company skate along on anything less than five hundred thousand in reserves. It's the way Dad always did it, it's the way we'll always do it. That way we avoid the places where the ice gets dangerously thin."

"Turning our back on the heart of this company isn't who we are."

"A few cycles, Brock. That's all."

"What about the workers down there who can't wait a few cycles?"

"They can wait."

"No, they can't."

They stood and stared at each other just like they had from the time Ron was old enough to stand. Both of them absolutely determined to win. When they were little they proved themselves with fists, then sports, and now the corporate arena. After thirty seconds, Ron broke the silence.

"We are making this *temporary* change, Brock." Ron glared at him. "I asked you for this meeting to inform you, not to ask your permission."

His brother turned and strolled back toward his putter.

After a late dinner and an even later cup of coffee, Brock went to bed ready to try lucid dreaming. It was a great excuse to get his mind off his meeting with Ron, and he wanted to be ready the next time his dad showed up in his dreams. Throughout the day he'd practiced the conscious techniques that should give him control of his subconscious world. Time to see if they would work.

Sleep came quickly and so did a dream. He sat in his kitchen, but it wasn't the right color. The beige was too dark, and the chair he sat in was a recliner, not a table chair. What had the book said? Right. Look at a tangible object, like a clock. He did, and the one on the wall shimmered, then faded, then vanished.

Yes! This was it. There was no doubt in his mind he was fully conscious, but this wasn't real. Clocks didn't disappear in the real world. This was definitely a dream. Next step, try to create something out of nothing.

He focused on the table and imagined a slice of Black Forest cake with a dollop of white-chocolate macadamia-nut ice cream on the side. Instantly the ice cream appeared, then started to fade. Brock breathed in deep — was he really breathing? — and focused on the image of the dessert. Again, the cake and ice cream appeared and this time they stayed solid.

He took a bite and knew he was ruined for real Black Forest cake for the rest of his life. This dream-cake version was perfection. He lifted another bite to his mouth and started to chew, but suddenly the taste overwhelming his taste buds wasn't cake, but squash — the food he loathed most in the world.

Brock spit the yellow mass of mush out of his mouth, pushed away from the table, and tried not to retch. A moment later he woke, his eyes watering. Obviously this lucid dreaming would take some work.

The next night he flew himself into a wall of the Grand Canyon, but hey, he flew! And controlled it. Mostly. The night after that he couldn't find the lucid state, but on Thursday night he found his way in again, and after he arrived he upped the stakes. If he was going to be able to control the dream with his dad, he needed to practice interacting with people — people that would set his adrenaline pumping. Strange thing was, since Morgan had given him the book on Sunday, the dream about his dad had not returned.

He recreated a scene from college where he'd been jumped by three frat boys during the fall of his junior year. The whap of their tennis shoes on the gray pavement behind him sounded like tiny firecrackers, but before they reached him, he imagined a thick walking stick in his hand, and it appeared. He spun and whipped the stick in a tight circle.

"It's not going to happen this time, boys."

"What's not going to happen?" the tallest of the three said.

"You're not going to bruise two of my ribs and borrow my wallet."

"What?" The stocky kid to the right looked hurt. "We wouldn't do that."

The third, the kid in the middle, grinned. That's when they attacked.

Brock focused and the three thugs moved toward him in super slow motion. By the time they reached him, he had strolled out of the way, then watched them spin and stare at him in amazement.

Stocky kid gaped. "How did you move like that?"

Brock started to answer but woke before the words could leave his mouth.

The sound of robins outside his bedroom window ushered him into morning. The dream wasn't perfect — it would have been nice to stay in it and figure out how to subdue the thugs — but it gave Brock the belief he'd be able to do something the next time his dad invaded Brock's dream world.

CHAPTER 4

The next evening, Brock pulled into the parking garage of the Sheraton hotel in downtown Seattle where his thirty-fifth high school reunion was being held, shut off the engine, and tried to push the meeting with Ron a few days back from his mind. Not easy. Something felt off. Even more difficult was ignoring the frustration he felt toward Karissa for making him go to the reunion alone. Wrong. She would have come. But he'd coerced her into too many corporate events over the years; he couldn't blame her for bowing out on this one. In truth, he couldn't blame her if she never joined him for another event the rest of their lives.

Thirty-five years since graduation. As he stared out the windshield of his silver Lexus at the semi-familiar faces moving toward the garage elevator, he marveled at the fact high school had happened that long ago. Didn't feel like it. The people going to their fortieth, forty-fifth, and fiftieth reunions probably said the same thing.

Brock glanced at his watch. A gift from Ron on the day three years ago when Black Fedora had hit twenty-five million in annual sales. Last month they'd hit fifty-three. So why did they have to pull their worker-funding program? The business side of Black Fedora was certainly Ron's, but the sense that storm clouds were gathering on the horizon made Brock wish he were more skilled at forecasting the proverbial weather.

Time to get in there. Smiles, everybody. Smiles.

The moment he stepped through the doors of the reunion room, he saw a face he hadn't seen since the first reunion back in '85; a face he could have waited to see till their class's two hundredth reunion: Mitchell Green.

"Whoa, baby!" Mitchell strode up to him in an Armani suit and a drink in both hands. "Brock Matthews, baby, I was going to die if you didn't come. Perfect timing. Here."

Mitchell handed him one of the drinks.

"Hey, Mitchell. Long time."

"Too long." Mitchell flicked Brock's shoulder. "We might not have been buds in high school, but times change and I'd like to propose a toast."

"To what?"

"You and me, rocking the business world down to its foundation." Mitchell raised his glass against Brock's. "I've seen what you're doing, you seen what I'm doing? Went public a year back, baby. You saw it, right? Score city. Yeah, I expected the IPO to jack up my net worth a few points, but fifteen million? Nah, didn't think it'd be that high. We're just a tiny little company, you know?"

Brock didn't know. Yes, he'd heard that Mitchell was part of a company that was doing well. And he'd heard the company was going public. But he didn't know exactly what they did other than some kind of venture capital investing.

"Talk to me. Time for your story." Mitchell punched Brock in the arm. "I've been tracking Black Fedora. Amazing how a nine-hundred-year-old commodity can stuff such copious amounts of filthy lucre into a man's pockets. But you guys know marketing, and that's what it's all about. Tell a good story, get the glory."

"We're doing fine, thanks."

"Fine? Fine!" Mitchell turned around in a slow circle, lifted his glass again, and spoke loudly. "This man and his brother run a fifty-million-dollar company, one that

Forbes says could be to coffee what Apple is to tech products if they worked a little harder. He says they're doing 'fine'? Watch out!"

Brock waited till Mitchell spun a second time and finished the rest of his drink in one gulp. "Are you married? Kids?"

"No, no. Don't try to change gears while the bike is in motion. When are you guys going public? Crazy that you haven't. The private stock thing you guys have going, not the way to go. Get out of the Dark Ages, baby."

"Not in the cards."

"How can it not be? You ever need any help, call me. I can launch you higher into the stratosphere than you knew a company could fly. I have the connections. I'm wired, baby, like no one knows."

"I'll keep that in mind."

"Hey, just saying you better do something. Or someone like me is going to swoop down!" Mitchell made a motion with his palm like a bird in flight. "Swoop down, grab all that private stock, and take over your company, and there'll be nothing you can do about it."

Brock didn't answer. With Mitchell's blood-alcohol level undoubtedly climbing like a rocket, the man wouldn't remember the conversation twenty minutes from now. Brock eased away as Mitchell pointed at him and grinned. "You and me, it's business destiny."

As soon as he made a full turn away, Lennie Buck's grinning face filled his vision. Lennie Buck had been a good friend since their sophomore year of high school, but they lost touch after Brock became — in Lennie's words — a Jesus freak. They'd reconnected after Lennie's fifteen-year career with the New York Rangers ended and he moved back to the Seattle area. He'd been a bruiser in the pro hockey world, and even though he was of average height, he still looked like he could body check a player twice as young and twice as big across the room.

Lennie, dressed in a black suit and high-top Converse sneakers, grabbed Brock by the shoulders.

"Did you hear me?" Lennie shook Brock's shoulders. "She's here. Can't believe she came. First one she's come to. Wild, yeah? And man, she is looking fine. So fine. Fireworks could happen, I'm telling ya."

Brock laughed and gave Lennie a quick hug. "You want to clue me in as to who and what you're talking about?"

"Sheila! Your Sheila. She walked through

the door five minutes before you did. Asked me about you. Smiled big when she said your name. I'm telling ya." He wagged his thumb at Brock. "When's the last time you saw her?"

A surge of anticipation coursed through Brock and he scolded himself — as if he could have stopped the feeling.

Sheila Waterson had been his high-school sweetheart. College sweetheart as well. And when they broke up — and even though Brock had been the one who did the breaking — she walked away with a piece of his heart. That wasn't a secret, at least not from Karissa. He'd never seen Sheila after they went down their separate paths, not even when connecting with old friends via social media became the rage. He'd never looked for her and was grateful she'd never looked for him.

"Hey, I'm talking here. Listen up, buddy." Lennie poked Brock in his stomach. "Whoa. Hold the presses. Nice abs, no BSG on your early-fifties frame. Steel abs, just like me." Lennie patted his own stomach. "She'll like that."

"BSG?"

"Big Sweaty Gut!" Lennie burst out laughing.

"You always did have a beautiful way with

words, Len."

"Right?" He laughed and grabbed Brock by the shoulders again, then ran the back of his hand down the front of Brock's sport coat. "Looking fine, so it's gotta be candy time. So tell me, how long since you've seen her?"

"It's been a while." Brock set his drink on a tray carried by a waiter who strolled past them. "But that's not why I came to the reunion."

"How long is a while? Years?"

Brock gave his head a light nod. "Not since we broke up."

"What? Serious?" Lennie rolled his head. "The love of your life still looking almost as good as she did in high school and you haven't been in touch?"

"See this?" Brock held up his left hand. "It's called a wedding ring. Part of it symbolizes that you've given your life to someone and you'll never betray them, that you'll stay with them through thick and thin."

Lennie grinned. "I probably should have figured that out during the time I was hitched."

"Yeah. Might have helped."

"And the time before that." Lennie grinned again and glanced around the room. "Okay, let's find her."

"We don't have to find her."

"Sure we do."

Brock's pulse tripped along faster than it should have as he glanced over the crowd. Nervous? Why? He shouldn't be. Yeah, right. He hadn't seen her in more than thirty years, and that little piece of his heart he'd never gotten back was calling out to him. Lennie might be looking for Sheila so she and Brock could connect, but Brock was looking for her so he could avoid making contact. Then her voice, exactly the same as it had been thirty-five years ago, floated over his shoulder.

"Hi, Brock."

He spun faster than he should have and lost his balance for a half second. He did a half step-hop to his right and steadied himself. "Sheila. Hi."

"You okay?"

She smiled and Brock thought about how hearing songs from years back often flooded his mind with memories from the days when he'd first heard them. Sheila's smile wasn't a song, but a flood of biblical proportions. When Lennie said she looked good, Brock had thought his old friend was exaggerating. He wasn't. Sure, there were lines, her skin not quite so smooth, her blonde hair

45

not quite so bright, and the years had stolen a bit of the beauty that youth gives so liberally, but no stranger would put her age past the midthirties. And one thing hadn't aged a day. Those sea-green eyes. Still captivating as a summer morning.

"Yeah. Fine."

She laughed and more memories flooded in. "A little too much to drink already?"

"Not a drop yet. I guess I'll never make it on the ice-skating circuit."

"You look great, Brock. Really."

"So do you." It sounded lame coming out of his mouth, but if it was, Sheila didn't let on.

She tilted her head. "Can we go somewhere to catch up that's a little less noisy?" She turned and gazed at their old classmates clustered together in groups of threes and fours as if scouting for a path through them.

"Sure."

"All right, fun times again." Lennie patted them both on the shoulders and nodded. "Be good, you two."

Sheila gave Brock a sympathetic smile, took his arm, and they slalomed toward the back of the room past a few winks and smiles from faces Brock knew, but their names were lost. The Eagles played too loudly overhead, but they saved him from

46

having to speak.

She released his arm after they emerged from the crowd on the other side of the ballroom, then clasped her hands in front of her as she glanced along the back wall for a quiet spot. "Good to see Lennie is still Lennie after all these years. He looks like he's doing well for himself."

"Would you believe he owns a company that builds high-tech docks for Fortune 500 companies all over the world?"

"Lennie?" She smiled. "Not in a million."

"Me either. And I didn't think our senior class pres would wind up working long hours at Home Depot."

"Scotty Anderson is working at Home Depot?"

"Just goes to show those 'Most Likely to Succeed' polls we took for the yearbook were a complete guessing game."

They wandered through a door that led to a long hallway, which led to an empty bar, except for a bartender with spiked hair and droopy eyes that made her look comatose. They settled at a table in the middle and she meandered over a minute later.

"Get you two anything?"

"Yes." Sheila smiled at Brock, then looked up at the bartender. "If you can do it, we'd love two butterscotch milkshakes, with an extra splash of butterscotch. Maybe two extra splashes."

The bartender's face contorted as if to say, "You're in a bar, not a drive-through," but she stayed silent and moseyed back to the bar and started making their milkshakes.

Brock couldn't stop a grin from breaking out. "You remembered."

"Of course. Every couple has a drink and a song, right?" She gave him a mock scowl. "Our first date, spring of our junior year, we went to the Ranch Drive-In in Bothell on the way back to my folks' house. 'September' was playing? Earth, Wind & Fire?"

"Wow. That takes me back." Brock shifted in his chair and smiled again. "I didn't think we ever decided on a song."

"We did. You didn't ever like it."

"Which means you decided."

She laughed. "I suppose it does."

The bartender returned with their drinks, and they lifted the shakes in unison.

"What should we toast to?" he asked.

"This is so cliché, but to memories of a simpler time, and of a love that was simpler as well."

Brock knocked his glass against Sheila's. "Well said."

They drank, and after staring at each other

48

to the point it was almost awkward, Brock opened his palms toward her. "So, are you going to catch me up on the past thirty years, or should I go first?"

For the next fifteen minutes they talked about careers and kids and mutual friends they'd lost touch with. But at sixteen minutes, like the clock striking midnight, Sheila's face grew serious and she touched Brock's hand like a feather — removed it an instant later.

"Forgive me if this is too forward, but have you thought about us over the years? What might have been?"

It *was* too forward, and yet it felt like the most natural thing in the world, so Brock didn't hesitate. "In the early years, yeah. Before I met Karissa, and during the first few years after. I used to have dreams about you, about us. Quite a few, actually. But not for a long, long time now."

Sheila nodded. "From what I've seen on Facebook, you two are a great couple."

Brock cocked his head. "So you've been stalking me."

"Not really." She smiled. "I don't even have an account. My kids do, so I jump on theirs every now and then and pull up your profile. You don't have it blocked, so anyone can see what you have up there."

"I should probably fix that." He returned her smile.

She took another drink of her milkshake as her face grew serious. "Can I go deeper?"

"Sure."

"I loved you as much as a twenty-one-year-old woman can love." She placed her finger on the rim of her glass and traced a slow circle till she reached the starting point. She looked up. "It took me a while to get over you; to get over us. More than a while."

She held no animosity in her voice, no bitterness toward him. Her eyes told him what he already knew — she wasn't asking for his apology, or even a response, but he gave both anyway.

"I'm sorry I hurt you."

"Don't be." She smiled without a hint of sadness. "The point is I did get over you. Got on with my life and it's been a good one. Very good."

Now pain did slide across her features — so fast most people would have missed it.

"What is it?"

"What do you mean?" Sheila looked down and picked at the corner of her tan coaster.

"Your words say it's been good, but your face disagrees. I saw it."

"Caught in the act." She looked at the

ceiling and let out a soft laugh. "Crazy how you never stop knowing a person once you've shared deep time with them."

"True." Brock paused, not sure if he should press or not. "So?"

"I lost my husband three years ago. I loved him so much. It still hurts. Not all the time, but it's always there at the back of my mind. My kids keep telling me it's been long enough, to go date someone, but I can't imagine ever marrying again. He was perfect for me."

"I'm sorry."

"Don't be. We had an amazing marriage."

Sheila wrapped her lips around her straw and took a long drink of her milkshake. "Are you still a Jesus freak?"

"Yeah." Brock smiled. "That'll never change."

Sheila returned his smile and laughed. "Me too."

"What?"

She pointed to the tiny cross around her neck. Funny he hadn't noticed it.

"You always said there was a difference between being a churchgoer and being a full-on follower of Jesus. I did play-time Christianity when we were together, and you even told me that's what it was, but I didn't understand till my late twenties."

51

"What happened?"

Sheila sat back and the same sadness he'd seen earlier flitted across her face. "That's what broke us up, isn't it? My lack of true surrender."

"It was a factor."

The bartender shuffled up to them and took their empty glasses. "Do you guys want another?"

"Probably shouldn't," Brock said. "I'm driving."

Again smiles between them and the years vanished more fully. They were just two eighteen-year-old kids having another milkshake and dreaming about the unquenchably bright future.

"How big?" Sheila's eyes were serious again.

"How big what?"

"A factor."

"You want a percentage?"

"Sure."

"I was kidding." Brock held up his hands in mock protest.

"I know." Sheila touched his hand for a moment, then pulled it away. "We had some golden days together, didn't we?"

Brock leaned back in his chair.

"I'd love to meet Karissa sometime."

"I'd like that. So would she." Brock

rapped the table. "Let's make it happen."

It wouldn't happen. Just like a yearbook promise to be friends forever.

The rest of the evening Brock enjoyed himself. He connected with old friends and even gave a lame speech toward the end of the evening. But it made Lennie happy and that was reason enough to have done it.

As he walked across the empty parking lot toward his car, a voice stopped him.

"Brock?"

He turned. It was Sheila. She eased up to him, her eyes darting around the lot. "One more thing."

She stepped closer as if she were about to speak, then hesitated.

"You okay?" Brock tried to read her eyes.

"Yes."

Without warning, she pulled him close and kissed him lightly on the lips. Before he had time to react, she pulled back and shook her head.

"Sorry." She looked down and turned away. "Good-bye, Brock."

As he drove home close to eleven thirty, sipping a cup of coffee to keep him alert on the road, the kiss and his conversation with Sheila seemed to be on perpetual repeat. Brock tried to push the guilt off his shoulders. Why should he feel guilty? He'd done

53

nothing wrong — feelings were amoral, right? It's what you did with them that counted in the end. So why did his mind keep screaming he'd done something horrid?

Because in his mind — and maybe even in his heart — he had.

CHAPTER 5

Twenty minutes later, Brock trudged toward his bedroom, hoping Karissa wouldn't ask about the reunion, but knowing of course she would. She was in bed reading a mystery novel when he slumped through their bedroom door. "Hey."

She set the book down on her chest and stared at him over the top of her dark-blue reading glasses. "So how was the reunion?"

"Fine."

"That's it?"

"Basically." Brock shrugged. "It was an evening of seeing people I don't want to see more than once every five years, but still fun to be there."

"Bump into anyone surprising?"

"Ran into Sheila." Brock tried to give an innocent smile.

"Really? Your old girlfriend, Sheila?" Karissa pulled down her reading glasses.

"Yeah."

"How was that?" Karissa set her novel on her nightstand. "You were really in love with her."

"It was good to see her." Brock unbuttoned his shirt and kicked off his shoes. "Saw Lennie Buck too. Goes by Len now, but he'll always be Lennie to me. He must have told twenty people about the time I knocked his teeth out in eighth-grade ice hockey and he called me Rocky."

"Hang on, let's put the car in reverse and back up a few feet." Karissa sat up in bed. "Was it weird seeing your old girlfriend after all these years?"

"Yeah, it was." Brock finished undressing and slipped into light sweats and an old Seahawks T-shirt.

"Is she happily married?"

"Her husband passed away three years ago."

"I'm sorry to hear that." Karissa looked away, but her tone of voice didn't match her words. "Are you still fond of her?"

Brock didn't respond, because he suspected what was coming next.

"Do you regret not marrying her?"

Bingo. He turned to her and looked her right in the eyes. "Not a chance. I love you. Not Sheila. I also have fond memories of my 1979 Toyota Celica, but I don't wish I was still driving it."

"Some men find their old cars and fix them up."

"Not this man."

"Promise?"

He came around to her side of the bed and leaned against the wall. "Why are you bothered by this?"

Karissa slid back down under the covers, picked up her novel, and opened it. Brock gazed at her, trying to find the right words. "If you're going to pretend to read, you should at least move your eyes back and forth."

"Shut up."

"Seriously. Talk to me." Brock sat on the edge of the bed next to Karissa and rubbed her arm. "Why would you ever worry about Sheila?"

"You have to know why. You're one of those weird men who actually have a few perceptive bones in their bodies . . . so you tell me."

Brock leaned back with his head against the wall and stifled a sigh. Of course he knew. And even before this détente, he knew that she knew. They'd hit the still waters, which were much different from calm waters. No wind meant stagnant sailing. It had been a long time since a robust wind had blown through their marriage to stir things up in a good way.

"There's no wind." Brock stared at the framed picture of their wedding vows, which hung over Karissa's dresser. "It's not blowing these days."

"What's that supposed to mean?"

"There was always wind to keep our sailboat in motion, but during the past six years — maybe longer — the wind has died down to nothing. So we're sitting stagnant. And on top of that, the sailboat needs to be repainted, and the sails need to be replaced, and the food in the galley is getting stale, and —"

"I get it."

"And you think I'm going to get a new sailboat, thinking that will fix the wind problem in my life and —"

"Brock!" Karissa tossed her book against the wall. "Didn't I just say, 'I get it'?"

Yes, she did just say it. In the same tone of voice he'd grown used to. *Calloused to* was the better description, because his heart had hardened and he didn't know what would soften it. Without question, hers had grown hard as well. She likely didn't have any solutions either. Karissa sat still for a few moments before sliding off the bed and onto the floor. She picked up her book and set it on her nightstand, then ambled around to his side of the bed.

"I'm sorry. I'm losing it too often these days."

"No you're not."

"Yes I am. I see it in your eyes that you agree." She crawled into bed beside him and rested her head on his chest. He stroked her hair. "What's going to happen to us? I don't want to lose you, lose us. I don't want you running off with some old girlfriend."

"I'm not going anywhere."

"Even if you don't, what will life be like when Tyson leaves? I don't want to be one of those cliché stories that everyone tells during their Thursday night get-togethers when we're not there. Where they pretend it isn't gossip because they'll 'pray for you.'"

"We won't be that couple."

"How do you know?"

"The wind will come up again."

Karissa repeated herself. "How do you know?"

He didn't.

After brushing his teeth, Brock crawled under the covers and picked up Morgan's book again. *Lucid Dreaming: Turning Dreams into Reality.* He turned to the back to review the steps to creating a successful lucid dream, but before he could start, Karissa interrupted him.

"I still don't get what lucid dreaming is, or why you're studying it."

"It's not that complicated."

"Then explain it to me in a way I can understand. And more than your typical three-word answer." Karissa propped herself up on an elbow and poked at his book. "Come on."

Brock sighed and closed his eyes. "After a stressful meeting with Ron still bothering me, and then the reunion, and our little flare-up, I just want to review this, then get to sleep and try to make the ideas in the book work, okay?"

"Okay. Wonderful." For the second time in ten minutes, Karissa tossed her book. It smacked the edge of her nightstand and thunked onto the floor. She reached over, snapped off her light, yanked the covers toward her, and turned her back to Brock.

"Let's not do this." Brock sighed and set his book down. "I'm sorry."

"Whatever."

He was tempted to bury himself in the book, but this was at least a chance to look for the wind. Who knew? Maybe she'd get as interested as he was.

"A lucid dream is any dream where you

know you're dreaming. You're conscious inside your dream. It's like you're awake, even though you're not. Aristotle said, 'Often when we're asleep, there's something in our consciousness that tells us that what we're seeing is a dream.' In other words, you're aware everything you're experiencing is happening in your mind, that there's no real danger, and that you're asleep in bed."

"What's the point of doing it?"

"If you get good at it, you can control your dreams."

"What do you mean *control*?" Karissa turned back over.

"You can decide what happens in the dream. People, places, conversations, outcomes. It's like being the director of a movie where you're also the lead actor, and you're in control of the other actors. And you can control the extraordinary things that happen in dreams."

"Like make yourself fly, or instantly travel from one place to another? Or talk to people from your childhood?"

"Exactly."

"Limited only by your imagination."

"Yes. The laws of physics no longer apply. And yet every one of your senses is working. Touch, taste, feel, sight, hearing . . . you can't imagine the Black Forest cake I ate."

"But again, what's the point?" Karissa stretched out her legs. "Why write a whole book on it? Why try to do it?"

"It's a tremendous tool for creativity. For healing fears. For problem solving. People with nightmares can end them by getting proficient at lucid dreaming. People learn to become public speakers, get better at sports, dance, even painting. Brain activity during the dream is the same as it would be during a real-life event — the neuron patterns needed for any skill can be embedded into the brain while sleeping, and you won't lose them when you wake up. Emotions too."

"You didn't answer my question." Karissa's voice grew intense. "Why are you doing it? You."

He stared at her for a few moments before answering. "Because I've been having dreams where my dad shows up, and I'd like to be able to make them stop."

"Tell me."

So he did, and when he finished, Karissa took his hand. "I'm sorry."

"It's okay."

"What's he trying to tell you?"

"I don't know."

She surprised him by not pressing the issue, and surprised him even more with her next suggestion.

"If you get good at it, maybe it could be our wind." Karissa turned over. "Good night."

"What did you say?"

"Nothing."

"You're saying I should try to bring you into one of my dreams." A shred of hope rose inside. "Interact with you."

"Your idea, not mine. Good night, Brock." Karissa slid the pink earplugs into her ears to mute his snoring when it fired up. "Happy sailing."

Brock lay with eyes open, mulling over the idea. What if he were to try to go back to their beginning and relive the emotions they had when they first dated? Wasn't that technique supposed to rekindle long-dormant feelings between couples? Plus it would take his mind off his worry about Black Fedora and might be an excellent way to dampen his emotional encounter with Sheila as well.

There was no guarantee he would slip into a lucid dreaming state tonight, but it wouldn't hurt to try. He scanned the page of steps, set the book down, and closed his eyes, then slowed his breathing and shot up a quick prayer.

Karissa's right, Lord. This might be the wind we need. Take me there tonight? Please?

CHAPTER 6

As soon as the dream started, Brock knew he was in control, and although the edges of his vision were hazy, as if looking through water, the rest was clear. By the looks of what lay in front of him, God had done a perfect job setting the scene.

He sat with Karissa on the west end of the vast lawn next to Woodland Park Zoo in north Seattle. It was the spot where he'd given her a promise ring during the summer of '86 after they'd been dating for eleven months. Too soon for an engagement ring, but he'd decided to make it clear he wanted to veer onto the road of serious relationship.

"Hey, are you with me?" Karissa leaned forward and tapped him on the nose.

A moment later the scene faded and he found himself standing at the fifty-yard line inside the Seahawks' stadium. He watched them score a touchdown on a screen pass that caught the other team napping. He shook his head. *C'mon, you can do this!*

"Brock?"

The zoo and lawn and Karissa undulated as if they were in a wave pool. "Yeah, I'm here. But feels like I'm dreaming."

He concentrated hard, and everything around him came into even clearer focus. Though Brock knew he was inside his own dream, the experience felt as real as it had the first time. As he stared at her, all the emotions and memories of that day streamed back into his consciousness. His frayed nerves at whether she'd even take the ring, his effort to figure out the right moment to give it to her, the hours he'd taken to make a little box out of wood to hold the ring. And now she held it, eyes bright.

"Me too. Dream come true." She raised her hand and let the sunlight play on the amethyst ring. "It's perfect."

He stared at her dark-brown hair and the curve of her cheeks as they flowed into her neck. Skin so smooth, and those eyes. For Brock, it had always been about Karissa's eyes. Three different shades of amber, depending on the light and her mood.

"You trying to get serious with me?"

"Without question." He settled onto one elbow on the park's thick grass. "Want to hear something crazy?"

"Sure."

"This really is a dream. This day happened, but a long time ago."

Karissa frowned. "What do you mean?"

"But I'm so glad I'm reliving it. I think you might be right. This type of dreaming might be able to bring healing. Because right now? I'm remembering how in love I am with you."

"You're not making a lot of sense." Karissa shifted on the lawn and frowned.

"Probably because I'm fifty-three years old." He laughed at himself. "My mind was a little more supple at twenty-four."

"You're fifty-three, huh?" She pulled her head back a few inches.

"In real life, yes, but not here. Here I'm young again. Pretty nice, actually."

Karissa's frown was now tinged with fear. "This isn't funny."

"Sorry, forget I said anything." Brock rolled onto his back and closed his eyes. "But I'm going to do this again. Come back into the past and visit us. It's definitely a good thing."

"Why are you doing this?"

"I just told you." Brock turned his head, opened his eyes, and squinted at her through the sunlight framing her head. "To remember what it was like."

He let his head settle back down on the warm lawn and closed his eyes again. So easy to forget where they'd come from. What a gift to be able to go back and re-pour that foundation. When he woke up he'd have to call Morgan and thank him.

"Here." Something landed on Brock's stomach and he opened his eyes. He lifted his head and spotted the box the ring had come in. He picked it up. The ring was back inside.

"Keep it a little longer, okay?" Karissa stood and brushed off her shorts.

"What's wrong?"

"Nothing." She slipped on her Disneyland sweatshirt and gave him a plastic smile. "I need to go."

"What are you doing?" Brock clambered to his knees, then to his feet.

"I'm fine, I just need to go."

"Is it something I —"

"Yes, absolutely it's something you said." She waved her hand at the spot where they'd sat. "All your talk of being old and not really being here, and it being a dream, and bringing back what we once had makes me uncomfortable, okay? I'm not ready to talk about us being married in the past tense. I don't know if I'm even ready to talk about us being married in the future. Can we slow this down?"

It was a rhetorical question, so Brock didn't respond. She gave an exasperated sigh and shook her head. "I'll be fine, but be back to being Brock next time I see you, okay?"

Karissa turned and trudged off.

"Karissa, I didn't —"

"We're good, don't worry about it. Really."

As Brock watched her go, he realized there was a great deal he needed to learn about lucid dreaming. But interacting with the Karissa from his past was a great way to practice, because the feelings of being with her again in the early days had certainly created a welcome breeze. If only he could figure out a way to keep it blowing.

CHAPTER 7

May 16, 2015

Early morning light angled through the kitchen windows as Brock stirred a rich concoction of hollandaise sauce and glanced at the eggs simmering on the stove. Every Saturday morning from the time Tyson was young, Brock had made his own special concoction of eggs Benedict. Karissa had never been into cooking beyond the basics, but Brock couldn't remember a time when he hadn't enjoyed exploring the vast landscape of what could be created in the kitchen. He had a gift for it. It wasn't much different from what he did for Black Fedora. But cooking offered so much more variety than developing new flavors of coffee.

Tyson sauntered into the kitchen and flopped into a chair next to the table. Looked like he just got a haircut. Short, neat, all hairs in place. Went well with his perpetual smile.

"What're you making, Dad?"

"Do you have to ask?" He glanced up and winked at his son.

"Nah. I could smell it all the way upstairs. But I would've known even if I couldn't smell it."

Brock smiled and turned back to his creation. Slice the ham ultrathin and overlap the pieces so you barely had to chew it, lay it on a lightly buttered English muffin, then the egg, drizzle on the sauce, sprinkle a few capers on top — not enough to steal the flavor, just to enhance it a bit. Next, give it two — sometimes three — slices of fresh avocado, and place a half spoonful of finely diced tomatoes on the side.

Finally, serve with a flourish and say something stupid like, "Voilà!" and watch your son roll his eyes at you, but know underneath that he won't ever stop loving the way his strange father serves up Saturday-morning breakfast.

"Is Mom joining us?"

"She was still asleep when I came out."

"Why does she sleep so long on Saturday mornings these days?"

"Tired I guess." Brock shrugged.

"From what?"

It was a good question without concrete answers. It wasn't that many years ago that

Karissa and he would get up at the same time on Saturday and Sunday mornings, grab coffee, and sit out on their back deck, rain, shine, or fog. They would review the week that just ended and talk about the week coming up. They'd read Oswald Chambers or *God Calling* — what Karissa called the Green Ladies because of the two authors and the color of the book's cover — and then spend a few minutes praying together.

Wasn't that more than a few years back? Yeah, it was. At least six. He couldn't remember why they'd stopped, just that there had been a slow slide from doing it five mornings a week, to three, to just on Saturdays, till they didn't sit down at all.

These days, Karissa slept till almost nine most Saturdays, and Brock had gotten used to having coffee alone. More than grown used to it, he probably would be irritated if Karissa walked into his den as he geared up for the day.

They had always said they wouldn't look at each other once the nest was empty and ask, "Do I even know you anymore?" But today Brock knew he'd be asking once Tyson left, and he had little doubt Karissa would be too.

"You know, if you don't sell your recipe to

some restaurant, you're an idiot."

"What?"

Tyson's comment brought him back to the present.

"Write the thing up, show it to a few nice Seattle restaurants. Sell the thing. Don't be stupid."

"I think that's a compliment."

"Yeah, it is." Tyson threw back a glass of orange juice and poured himself another half glass. "Wake up and do it."

"I cook for you guys, for myself, not for other people."

Back in his midthirties, Brock had considered pursuing cooking more seriously, but he never wanted it to turn into a job. It was his escape, and he'd always worried that if he attached dollar signs to the thing that brought him a river of joy, the joy would seep away till he was standing in a dry creek bed.

"I get that." Tyson dropped his fork on his now-empty plate and it clanged like a bell. "I'm just saying you could make some money if you let a few more people in on your secret sauce."

"Then it's not secret any longer."

"There's this cool verse in the Bible about not exasperating your kids. I think you should look it up."

"Thanks for the tip."

After breakfast, Brock went to his den to check the number of hits on Black Fedora's new website. Yes. Traffic was up again for the fourth straight month.

An hour later, Karissa strolled into the room, combing the tangles out of her long hair.

"I think I missed breakfast again."

"I made you an eggs Benedict. It's in the oven."

"Thanks." She stood and stared at the floor for a few seconds. "So? Did it work?"

"What? Dreaming about you?"

"Yeah, did you do the lucy dreaming and talk to me inside your dream?"

"Lucid, not lucy."

"I know." Karissa smiled. "Just trying to interject a puff of humor-wind into the sails. So, did you?"

"It was amazing." Brock leaned back from his monitor.

"Really? Tell me."

He smiled and shook his head. "It was so real. And you were so beautiful. It was the day I gave you that amethyst promise ring at Woodland Park Zoo."

"That was a weird day." She frowned as if trying to remember.

"It was a great day. It was the pre-engagement engagement ring."

"Yeah, but there was something about it that was strange, wasn't there?"

"Sunshine, warm weather, sub sandwiches, a few games of cribbage, and me giving you the ring . . . nothing strange that I recall."

"It's funny." Karissa gave him a puzzled look. "I thought you . . . wow, it's been so long, but I thought you gave me the ring at dinner the next night, not on the lawn."

"No, it was on the lawn."

"Doesn't matter." She waved her hand in dismissal. "But did it work? Did it bring back feelings?"

"It did." He smiled, stood, and wrapped her up in his arms. "We're going to make it."

"I hope so." She gave him a light squeeze back. "Are you going to work today?"

"Just for a few hours."

She blew out a long breath and bit her lower lip.

"What?"

"It's *Saturday*. You've made it, Brock. Black Fedora is everything you've ever dreamed it could be. More than what you dreamed. Far more. When are you going to slow down so we can enjoy the life it's given us?"

75

"We do enjoy life."

"Not like we should."

"I love that company. It's given us so much."

Karissa turned and as she walked away she said, "And taken as much as it's given."

That night, Brock sat in his den gazing at a photo of his dad and him taken years earlier.

In the picture, they stood on the dock of the Talon Lodge fishing resort up in Alaska, a king salmon in each of their hands, big stupid grins on their faces. One of the best days of Brock's life. The beauty of southeast Alaska had turned out to be stunning in late July, and the lodge was a genuine log cabin, but what made the trip unforgettable was it was the first time he and his dad had gone somewhere, just the two of them, since Brock was eight years old. They'd started to chip away at the ice that had been their relationship as long as he could remember.

His dad had asked him to go again the next summer — wanted to make it an annual trip, and Brock had too — but when July rolled around he'd backed out. Work had been insane.

He'd tried to come up with a few more things to bolster his excuse for not going, but there were none. The third year he'd again promised to go — and again broke his commitment. The summer after that his dad didn't ask. Then a heart attack struck him in early November of that year, and he was gone.

Brock lifted the photo off the wall and drilled down on every detail of the picture. The matching grins on their faces. The slightly whiter skin around their eyes where their sunglasses had shielded them. And their arms around each other.

"You still beating yourself up over that?"

Brock looked up to find Karissa standing in the doorway, arms folded.

"Hey, dear. Didn't see you."

"Are you?"

"A little bit, maybe."

"Maybe? Long past time to let it go."

"I know." Brock slid the photo onto his desk and sighed. "Not that simple though."

Karissa let the silence linger, but after a minute she said, "You should try it again."

"Try what?"

"Your lucid dreaming thing. Try talking to yourself this time. Young Brock. Tell him about Alaska. Why he should go. It won't change anything, but it might make you feel better. Get it off your chest, you know?"

"Myself?" He hadn't thought of that.

"Sure. If you can control your dream, why

not dream yourself into the past and have a conversation with the person you used to be?"

"That would be crazy." Brock touched a finger to the frame. "But wouldn't hurt anything to give it a shot."

CHAPTER 8

July 1985

Seconds after falling asleep that night, Brock found himself staring at the entrance to Morgan's place, Java Spot. Exactly where he wanted to be. As he stared at the door he willed the year to be 1985. Instantly the door swirled like a whirlpool. When it stopped it had morphed into the one Morgan had replaced when he took over the shop from his dad in the early nineties.

Brock drew a deep breath and stepped inside. If he was right, he was about to have an extremely strange encounter.

Brock glanced around. Two-thirds full. In one corner was a cluster of what looked like college students who seemed familiar. A few couples sat next to the windows. Three people sat alone, hunched over notebooks and textbooks, glancing from one to the other as they scribbled notes to themselves. He smiled. It seemed so archaic to study that way. But it would be another sixteen years before laptops would start taking over the computing world; ten before they'd be drinking his coffee in here.

He scanned the shop looking for . . . There! His heart pounded as he stared at the early-eighties version of himself winding his way to a table in the back. Brock had no video of himself from that time, only photos, so it was a strange sensation to watch himself in motion. It seemed like he moved faster, which shouldn't have been a surprise but for some reason still was. His hair was thicker, darker — almost black — and he twirled a pencil around his fingers like a miniature baton as he settled down at an empty table. Brock smiled. He stopped doing that with his pencils years ago.

He stared for a few more seconds, then juked his way around the tables and eased up to his younger self. If he was controlling the dream, then he should be able to talk to himself without much problem.

"Excuse me."

"Yeah?"

"Mind if I join you?"

The young version of himself looked up and gave a quizzical smile. "You are?"

"A friend."

"Uh, sure, why not?" He motioned to the

chair across the table.

Brock sat and spread his hands on the table and stared at the wrinkle-free complexion, the expectant, believing eyes. So much hope. The days when he had all the answers.

His younger self spread his hands on the table in an almost exact mirror of Brock's.

"What can I do for you?"

"I so wish this was really happening," Brock muttered.

"What was happening?"

"I need to tell you a few things." Brock sighed. "Just to get it off my chest, you know?"

"Not really." Young Brock glanced at Morgan, who stood behind the counter drying coffee mugs, then pushed his chair back a few inches.

"If this was real, I'd tell you so many things."

"If it was real." The younger version of himself raised his eyebrows.

"Yes." Brock stared into his own eyes. The moment felt as real as the dream in which his dad told him to embrace the painful truth because it would set him free.

"I'd tell you about obvious things to do differently and then ones that are more subtle, the ones under the surface of life. As the years wear on, they float up and demand you look at them. And if you don't pay attention to them now, you won't like the cloudy water you're left with."

"Should I be taking notes?"

"Great idea." Brock smiled to himself. He'd never been one to keep a journal. Wished he had. So many moments lost from memory.

"Who did you say you are?" Young Brock pulled his hands tighter across his flat stomach.

"And love your wife. Don't let the wind die down."

"Morgan put you up to this, didn't he?" Something shifted in his younger self's countenance as if he knew this was a practical joke and decided to play along. "So I'm getting married, huh?"

"Yes."

"What's her name?"

"Karissa."

Younger Brock leaned in and whispered, "So when should I let my girlfriend Sheila know about this?"

"When it's time."

"You're not going to give me the date?" Young Brock bobbed his head side to side as if taunting him. "Want to get the moment right."

"I don't want to spoil everything for you."

"Right, can't do that." Young Brock scooted his chair back, stood, and stuck out his hand. "Great to meet you, but I gotta go."

"A couple more things." Brock took his younger self's hand but didn't let go. "Stop beating yourself up over the fact that Royce stopped following Jesus. Not your fault."

Young Brock's face went pale as he pulled away from Brock's grip and sat back down. "How do you know about that?"

A slew of possible answers spilled into Brock's mind, but in the end he decided on the truth. It would make the dream more fun.

"Okay. Why not?" Brock smiled. "I'm you, thirty years from now."

"How do you know about Royce?" A sliver of fear hung in his younger self's eyes. "I'm serious." His younger self glanced in Morgan's direction, and when he turned back, his face had relaxed. "Wow. Right on. Finally you're here. What took you so long? Did you get here in a DeLorean or on a moonbeam?"

"I'm serious too."

"Oh yeah, I can tell you are." Young Brock brought his fingers together, formed a square, and peered through it at Brock as if it was a frame. "Not really seeing the resemblance between you and me."

"Trust me, gravity and gray will catch up with you."

"Uh-huh." Young Brock pointed at him. "How much did Morgan pay you to do this? He's making fun of the fact I think *Back to the Future* is the movie of the year, right?"

"No. I really am who I say I am."

"Cool." Brock snatched a scrap of paper out of his back pocket along with a pencil. "So lay it on me then, Future Me. Stocks to buy, Super Bowl winners to bet on, the exact date I meet this Karissa gal, friends to avoid, all of it. Gotta write it down so I don't forget."

"The problem isn't me being real, it's you. I so wish you were."

"I'm not real?"

As the words left his younger self's mouth, he blurred for a moment, and when he came into focus again, he wasn't Brock. In his place sat Mr. Hammond, Brock's fifth-grade teacher — and basketball coach.

"When you want to accomplish something, you don't try to do it, you do it." Mr. Hammond poked the table. "You don't try to practice, you practice. You don't try to get better at your outside shot, you put in the hours that will make it happen. Right,

Brock?"

"Right."

Brock closed his eyes and concentrated. When he opened them, Hammond was gone and Young Brock was back.

"Wow. That was strange."

"It's strange that you think I'm real?" His younger self shook his head.

"No, what just happened. I'm asleep at the moment, but aware I'm asleep, and controlling this dream, but I lost it for a second."

"So like I said, I'm not real."

"Correct. I've created you out of my mind and memories."

"I'm a figment of your imagination."

"Essentially, yes. All from my subconscious."

Young Brock knocked his head rapidly. "Hello? McFly? Anybody home?"

Brock stifled a laugh.

"What's funny?"

"I forgot how much I quoted from that movie after it first came out."

"What? You don't like *Back to the Future* in the decades to come, Future Man?"

"Not true." Brock smiled. "I own the trilogy."

"Trilogy? What trilogy?"

"You know how it says To Be Continued

at the end? Zemeckis makes the next movie and a third one at the same time. But the second one doesn't come out till '89. All three DVDs together don't come out till 2009."

"DVD? What's DVD?"

"You've seen CDs, right?"

"Yeah. Expensive."

"And you rent movies on VHS."

"Or Betamax."

"Right," Brock said. "I forgot about those."

"Betamax is far better than VHS."

"True, it was, but the better product isn't always the one that wins in the marketplace."

"You're getting off track."

Brock leaned back in his chair and smiled. He liked himself. Even though this wasn't real, and he was fully aware he was asleep right now next to Karissa, it still felt completely authentic and surprisingly fun.

"A DVD is a movie on a CD."

"A CD can't hold that much information."

"It will. By the summer of 2003, DVD rentals will pass VHS cassette rentals."

"Thanks for the uh, future history lesson." His younger self pushed back from the table and stood. "Like I said a few minutes back,

I gotta go. Anything else?"

"Yes, the most important thing."

"Lay it on me."

"Years from now, when your dad asks you to go on that second fishing trip, don't turn him down. Go. The year after that, when he asks you to go a third time, go on that trip too."

"I'm not exactly a fishing kind of guy. And my dad and I aren't exactly —"

"Go on the trips. Trust me. I promise it'll save you a great deal of regret. No matter how insane life gets, don't miss the trips."

His younger self laughed as he ambled away from the table. "Sure, Future Brock, why not?"

"One more thing."

"Yeah?"

Before he could respond, the floor of Java Spot tilted forty-five degrees, and Brock slid backward till he slammed into the wall and woke up. A combination of hope and regret filled his stomach. It had been therapeutic to talk to himself, but it hadn't done a thing to ease his regrets about not going on the Alaska trip.

CHAPTER 9

May 17, 2015

As soon as Brock woke the next morning, he stretched his arm out to feel for Karissa. She wasn't there. Probably already in the shower. Yep. The water was running along with the fan. He turned over and opened his eyes a crack and peered into the slice of light coming through the window curtains.

He rolled over, closed his eyes, and toyed with the idea of trying to get back to sleep, but he knew it would be futile. An instant later the dream from last night hit him. He'd done it, controlled his dreams to a greater degree than ever before. And it had felt so real talking to his younger self. Just as real as the dreams of his dad.

Brock opened his eyes for the second time and reached for Morgan's book as he sat up on the edge of the bed. He stared at the cover of *Lucid Dreaming: Turning Dreams into Reality,* blew out a long breath, then tucked the book under his arm and went to make coffee.

Eight minutes later, Brock shuffled into his den, set his coffee and the book on his desk, and wiggled the mouse to wake up his computer. As it fired up, he glanced at the photo to his right and faced the bittersweet memory of being in Alaska with his dad. The instant he looked he cocked his head and frowned. What in the world?

There wasn't a photo of his dad and him on the wall. There were three. Three framed pictures of them holding king salmon almost too big to lift.

"Morning." Karissa walked into his den, her dark-brown hair still wet from her shower. "How'd you sleep?"

Brock whirled and pointed at the photos while his eyes stayed locked on Karissa.

"What is this?"

"What is what?"

"Did you do this? And if you did, why? And if you didn't, who did?"

"Do what?" Karissa strolled over and looked in the direction Brock pointed.

"Put up two more photos. Of my dad and me."

"What are you talking about?"

"Maybe I'm losing my mind, or maybe it's my eyesight, but I'm seeing three pictures of Dad and me from that trip we took to Alaska."

"Yes." Karissa gave him a funny smile. "One photo for each year you went seems like a pretty good use of wall space to me."

"What did you say?" Heat seeped into Brock's face. "Each year?"

Karissa shuffled over to the leather chair next to Brock's desk and settled into it. "Are you okay?"

"I only went to Alaska with my dad once. In 1986. I didn't go again."

"What are you doing?"

"What do you mean —"

"Those trips are three of your most treasured memories. A time where you really connected with your dad." Karissa's face grew concerned. "Again, are you okay?"

The dream from last night washed over Brock again. The conversation he'd had with his younger self. Brock gave tiny shakes of his head. Not possible.

"Am I still dreaming?" He rubbed his eyes and blinked.

"I don't think so."

"It's the only answer."

"To?"

"I went only once. There's never been more than one picture of Dad and me on that wall."

"There've always been three." Karissa lightly touched his hand. "What's going on, Brock?"

"How is this possible? That conversation I had . . ." Brock let his head flop back against his chair. "How could it have worked? It wasn't real. It was just a dream."

"What worked? What's not possible?"

He sat up straight and took Karissa by the shoulders. "A lucid dream. Last night. I talked to myself last night, Karissa. In my dream. I told myself to never miss an Alaskan fishing trip with my dad, no matter how crazy life gets."

"Are you saying you don't remember going on those trips? That you only remember going on one?" Karissa pulled away and stood.

"Yes."

"And you think what you told yourself in a dream changed things?" She looked at him like he was crazy.

"Yes! I mean no." He fixed his eyes on her. "I don't know."

"You're scaring me." Karissa's breathing quickened. "I think you need to drop the lucid dreaming thing. Give the book back to Morgan."

"I'm not losing it here. I'm fine. But I swear I didn't go on two more trips."

91

She looked at him for ten seconds before responding. "I'm not saying you're nuts, but it probably wouldn't hurt to talk to a doctor."

Brock stared at her as a slow smile rose to his face. "That's exactly what I'm going to do. Try to talk to the only doctor who won't think I'm crazy."

"What doctor?"

Brock picked up the lucid dreaming book that sat next to his coffee. "The one who wrote this."

CHAPTER 10

May 18, 2015

"Dr. Thomas Shagull's clinic, may I assist you?"

The woman's voice sounded bored and slightly exasperated.

"I'm calling for Dr. Shagull, please."

"He doesn't work here any longer."

Brock frowned at the website on his laptop. "Isn't his name on the shingle?"

"Yes."

"And he owns the company?"

"Yes."

"That kind of implies he works there."

"John Hancock's name is on the John Hancock Insurance building, but that doesn't mean Johnny works there."

"Good point. My mistake." Brock sighed. "Any idea how I'd be able to reach the doctor?"

"Dr. Shagull is retired. He's officially the chairman of the board, but that's about it."

"I need to speak with him."

"I'm sorry. Dr. Shagull is a bit of a recluse these days. He's not real open to hanging out with fans."

"I'm not a fan."

"Exactly what all the fans say."

"I need his help." Brock decided to go for broke. "I've been having lucid dreams where I go into the past, and it's changing my present."

The woman on the other end of the line was silent for what seemed like five minutes. "Can you describe to me what you think has changed?"

"I'd rather not."

"It's your choice." The woman sighed. "What's your name?"

"Brock Matthews."

For some unexplained reason, Ms. Ice thawed a bit. "While I don't know if he'll respond, I can relay a message."

"Thanks, I appreciate it."

Brock gave the woman his cell number.

"And Mr. Matthews?"

"Yes?"

"Are you involved in the coffee industry?"

"I am."

Her voice moved from neutral to warm. "I read an article on you a year or so ago."

"Is that right?"

"Are you really the person at Black Fedora who develops all the flavors?"

"Guilty."

"I love your coffee. My favorite is that macadamia-nut-flavored concoction."

"That's one of mine as well. Thanks for mentioning that."

"I sure hope you don't leave your business like Dr. Shagull did."

"Believe me, I'm going to be there for a long time."

Brock's cell phone rang seventeen minutes later. The caller ID was blocked, but Brock guessed it was Dr. Shagull.

"Hello?"

"Are you the Brock Matthews who grew up in the Seattle area?"

"Yes."

"We don't know each other."

"No."

"Remarkable." The caller blew out a sharp breath. "Tell me what happened."

"Dr. Shagull?"

"I think you already know it is, so let us not waste one another's time." The doctor's voice was firm, but not unkind. "Tell me."

So much for introductions.

After Brock described the encounter with his younger self in his dream, and how it seemed to have changed things only he remembered, the doctor stayed silent for at least fifteen seconds.

"Are you there, Dr. Shagull?"

"Only one encounter so far?"

"Yes."

But the moment the words came out of his mouth, he remembered the odd conversation he'd had with Karissa after he'd dreamed about being at the zoo with her, giving her the ring. He described how Karissa recalled the day differently the next morning. Again, the doctor went silent. When he finally responded, his words held a tinge of excitement.

"I'd like to get together."

"You're in the Seattle area?"

"Are you available day after tomorrow? Say two in the afternoon?"

"Yes."

"Good. Let's meet at Robinswood Park."

"Am I losing my grip on reality? Have you ever heard of this happening before? What should I do before we meet?"

"Try it again."

"Talking to myself."

"Yes, what else would I be referring to?"

"Anything else?"

"Don't be late for our meeting."

Dr. Shagull hung up without waiting for a

response.

Try again? Why not? Brock didn't believe he'd truly changed things in the present by talking to himself in the past, but there was no way he was going to walk away from what was happening. Deep inside, he knew this experience was part of his dad's message, and he was determined to unwrap that brown package no matter what was inside.

He had the distinct impression he'd be visiting himself again that night, and when he did he would do a simple experiment to test whether he truly was talking to his younger self. But first, he needed to get into the office. His stomach kept telling him something at Black Fedora was boiling to the surface, and everyone near the pot was about to get scalded.

CHAPTER 11

When he reached his office, Brock tossed his keys into the kava bowl that he'd brought back from Fiji two years ago and tried to figure out why Ron would sacrifice the worker-funding program.

Brock sighed as he powered up his computer and flipped on a stream of instrumental acoustic guitar. Five minutes later the sound of Michelle arriving at her desk floated through his open door. He gave her a few minutes to settle in, then called out to her.

"Is my schedule today full of the normal amount of insanity or do we have an extra batch tossed in?"

She didn't answer.

"Michelle? You out there?"

"Yes." Michelle's normally chipper voice was quiet and held a somber edge to it.

Brock rose and strolled over to his door and leaned against the frame. "You okay?"

"Extra batch." She didn't look up.

"Excuse me?"

"Extra batch of insanity."

"Oh?"

Michelle pulled her upper teeth across her lower lip, glanced up at him, then turned back to her computer. "On my way in this morning, Ron asked me to block out some time for you and him this afternoon starting at four."

"About what?"

Ron and he communicated nearly every day, but typically through e-mail, or a spontaneous two or three minutes in the hallway. They only sat down once a quarter. Ron setting up a formal meeting was not the kind of sign from the heavens that the meeting would be positive.

"He thought you'd be finished by six thirty."

"Two and a half hours?"

"I suppose."

Brock studied Michelle's profile. Not like her to avoid looking at him. He repeated his earlier question. "About what, Michelle?"

"Company stuff, you know." She busied herself with straightening papers that didn't need to be straightened.

"No, I don't know." Brock closed the distance to Michelle's desk and settled into the maroon chair that sat parallel. Michelle finished with the papers and focused on her computer screen, but Brock doubted she saw anything.

"What's going on, Michelle?"

She finally turned and looked at him with eyes that pleaded with him not to press for an answer.

"It's not good, is it?"

She shook her head. A feeling in Brock's gut said it was worse than not good, that the cash flow issue Ron had mentioned the other day was more like a total drought.

The rest of the day passed in a daze as the certainty grew that his meeting with Ron would be a game changer.

At three fifty-nine, Brock stared at his brother's dark-wood office door. The door was rarely closed, if ever. Brock couldn't remember the last time he'd seen it shut. Not a good sign. He pushed it open and expected to see Ron either sitting at his desk banging away on his laptop — back ramrod straight, eyes in glare mode — or on the phone pacing back and forth in front of the floor-to-ceiling windows like a caged panther.

But all he saw in the dim light of a gray-skied Seattle afternoon was a desk piled with files and papers. Also unusual. Ron's desk never had more than one file on it at a time. Brock turned to the right and spotted his brother slumped back into one of the two facing chairs in the corner of the office. A legal-size file folder rested on his leg.

"Hey."

"Hey." Ron's head settled onto the back of the chair and rolled to the side. His eyes were vacant, his face pale in the dim light of the lamp to the left of his chair. Brock's stomach knotted.

"What's wrong?"

Ron stared at him before answering. "It's not good, bro."

"What isn't?"

"This." Ron held up the manila file.

"And you're holding . . ."

"The lawyers sent it over this morning."

Brock eased forward two steps. "That's who you've been meeting with for the past two weeks."

Ron nodded and tossed the file onto the floor next to his feet. The knot in Brock's gut cinched tighter.

"What does it say?"

"I don't know how to even start." Ron raised his hands as if in total defeat.

"Start anywhere." Brock's hands grew clammy.

Ron motioned to the chair across from him and Brock stood behind it. Ron glanced at Brock, then at the file, then out the window, then back to Brock. He closed his eyes and jammed his lips together as he gave little shakes of his head.

"Ron, talk to me. What is in there?"

"Walking papers."

"For who?"

"Us." Ron blew out a long breath. "I wish it contained a lifeboat. But women and children first, right?"

Brock asked the question even though he knew the answer. "What are you saying?"

"I should have told you earlier so you could have come up with a final flavor." Ron sat up with a sick expression on his face and pointed at Brock. "We'd have called it Titanic Morning."

A bowling ball appeared in Brock's stomach. "I asked you about this."

"Yeah, you did."

"What exactly, and I mean *exactly,* are you telling me?"

"I'm selling my company."

"You're what?"

"Selling my company."

"*Your* company?"

"Right. Sorry. Our company." Ron gave a dismissive shake of his head and pushed a stack of papers to the side of his desk. "Doesn't matter at this point."

"Yeah, it does matter." Brock leaned forward, his hands resting on the back of the chair. "You want to explain to me what's going on?"

"Sit." Ron stood, then flicked his finger at the chair across from him. "It's not my choice."

"At least you have that part straight; it isn't your choice. It's our choice."

"Relax, Brock. Yes, it's our choice. What I'm trying to say is there isn't much choice left. At this point we can take one of two paths. Either sell for less than pennies on the dollar, or file for bankruptcy, which we wouldn't climb out of. We're right in the middle, right at the crossroads." Ron ran his hand over his head and slumped into his black leather chair again. "Nah, we're not in the middle. We're at the end . . . and we lost. I lost. We sign papers in three days with an investment firm that's going to take over."

"Let's back up. Way back. How did I not know about this?"

"I know." Ron shrugged. "I should have told you earlier."

Brock picked up a bag of their coffee and shook it. "For the past year and a half you've told me things are as solid as they've ever been. Better than solid."

"I wasn't entirely forthcoming."

Brock didn't respond.

"If it makes you feel any better, my house is gone. Or will be. I put it up to get some working capital. Yacht is gone, all but one car is gone. My vacation home is gone. You could put your houses up, but at this point it wouldn't help."

"Again, what you talking about? This is ludicrous. Our sales have never been better. Crazy good. We're adding new clients every month. Reviews of our coffee have never been this strong. We've launched three new flavors this year and each one of them is pegging red on the in-coffeepots-everywhere meter."

Ron rose and went to the full-length windows that looked out over Lake Washington. The setting sun put him in silhouette. "The outside looks peachy, but the fruit is rotting on the inside."

"What does that mean?"

"It's my fault." Ron turned and wandered back over to Brock. He sat, leaned forward, and straightened the four issues of *Golf Digest* magazine that sat in the center of the table between them.

"Tell me what happened, Ron."

Ron flashed Brock a sick, lopsided smile. "Do you remember when we were kids, and we used to play Monopoly with Vince Capastano and his sister? Remember how Vince always seemed to have more cash than he should? How he was stealing it from the bank when we weren't looking?"

"I remember how you beat him up when we found out."

"He never cheated again." Ron pushed back his hair. "Wish I could do the same thing right now."

The truth washed over Brock like an icy wave. "Who stole our money, Ron?"

"I don't know."

"How can you not know?"

"It's not there. No trace of where it went. We can't find it. Our IT guys say the hackers were brilliant."

"When did this happen?"

"When do you think? While you were off gallivanting around the world in China, and Costa Rica, and Japan."

"Working. Not gallivanting."

"Whatever you want to call it."

"Are we going to start in on this again?"

"No." Ron slumped forward, head in hands. "I'm sorry."

"You're sorry? Why didn't you come to me?" The words came out louder than

Brock intended.

Ron blew out a long breath and turned his head toward Brock but didn't respond.

"We're going to find a way out of this."

"There isn't a way out, Brock."

"There's always a way out. We're going to battle this insanity with everything we have. Right?" Brock leaned forward and tried to keep his breathing steady. "Right?"

"I told you, it's over. I've *been* fighting it with everything I have. I've pulled every string. Called in every favor. We are finished."

"Then let me ask again, why did you keep this from me? Why didn't you tell me this was going on?"

"This was my war to fight, not yours."

"That's an asinine answer." Brock slammed his fist into his chair. "I've given my life to this company. Everything I own, everything I am, is wrapped up in Black Fedora. It goes down, so do I."

He'd told Karissa for years to wait just a little longer and the breakthrough would happen. And it had. The past six years had been stellar. This coming year was supposed to be even better, the one that would set them completely free. But now the dream was crashing and burning with the power of a nuclear warhead.

"The company was my life too."

"And you leave me out of the greatest battle it's ever faced? For the third time, why didn't you come to me?" Brock stood and paced on his brother's tan carpet.

"Like I said, this was mine to fight."

"Tell me the real reason. The deeper reason. Time to get real, brother."

"You're the artist, the one with heart and a palate that creates coffee flavors the world loves. The one who talks to the media, the spokesperson, the face everyone loves."

"I never wanted to be the spokesperson. The PR firm said it should be me, and you agreed, and even then I said no."

"But once we talked you into it, you learned to love the limelight, didn't you? Made you feel good. Made you feel needed. Told you you were worth something."

"What does that have to do with what's going on right now?"

"I have to spell it out? You're the face and heart of the company, I'm the mind and the strategist. I don't spend a lot of time in your part of the company and you don't spend a lot of time in mine."

"Nice try. Once more. The real reason."

"What do you want?"

"The truth."

"No you don't. You never do. You just

want this company all for yourself. And it ticks you off that you never have been the true owner. The fact I've held that itty-bitty two percent over you galls you so bad. You taste it every morning along with your three cups of coffee. And it torques you something fierce that I'm your baby brother and the one who is really in control."

"Oh, we're going to talk truth? How 'bout if I'd focused on the business side I'd be better at that part of the company than you could ever be."

"Now we're in fantasyland." Ron flicked his fingers in dismissal. "Enough."

The reality of what was about to happen to his life settled on Brock like a thick fog.

"What will we have left when this is over?"

"Nothing. I already told you that."

Brock's stomach clenched. They'd just bought the big house two and a half years ago. A nice vacation house too. When Tyson applied to colleges last fall they told him private college wouldn't be a problem. And he'd been accepted at Gonzaga. Shelling out $75,000 per year? No problem. Now suddenly it was.

"Does Shelly know?"

Ron nodded.

"You told your wife before you told me."

"Now you get to tell Karissa. Get over it."

"How many other people know?"

"Richard. The lawyers. No one else." Ron rubbed his forehead. "Yet."

"When is it going to leak?"

"It wouldn't surprise me if it hits the web by tomorrow morning. Tomorrow afternoon at the latest."

"Wow. Thanks for giving me so much lead time."

"You're welcome."

"I want to look at all the financials. Everything. There has to be a way out of this."

"I knew you'd say that, and knew what you'd want to do. So I've prepped it all for you. It's all ready to go." Ron pointed to a stack of papers on the corner of his desk. Two silver flash drives sat on top of the papers.

"I'm going to find us a way out of this."

"With your vaunted business skills?"

"Whatever it takes." Brock rose, picked up the papers and flash drives, and strode to the door. "There's always a solution if you dig hard enough."

"Not this time, brother."

When Brock left his office at nine thirty that night, a large part of him admitted Ron was right, on two counts. First, he didn't have the skills to find an answer. Second, from what he could understand, Black Fedora was drowning in red ink so deep he couldn't see the bottom.

As he pushed through the lobby doors of their building, despair stabbed at him. But it wasn't over yet. He refused to believe this was the end of the company he'd given his life to and loved like nothing else.

He trudged toward his parking lot two blocks away, wracking his brain for an answer, for even a shred of hope, but nothing came. Brock rounded the corner on Cherry Street and smacked into a man, who crumpled to the sidewalk as a muffled grunt escaped his mouth. Brock bent over and took the man's shoulder.

"Are you all right?"

"I'm fine. How are you?"

"Good."

"Sorry about that."

His matted hair was the color brown that looked like it had dust in it. His skin was dark and his thin green coat and pants clung to him as if they were a size or more too small. A backpack that might have been bright red once upon a time leaned against the building.

"Whew." The man shifted from his knees onto his backside and wrapped his arms around his legs. He glanced up at Brock. "You used to play football?"

"No."

"I did." The man patted himself on the chest. "Made it too. Cornerback. Played five seasons for the Rams back when they were in Los Angeles. Not a starter every game, but still made good coin. You should look me up."

"What's your name?"

"Robert."

"You need money?"

"Could always use a buck." The man grinned.

Brock looked at him. "That's all you want? A dollar?"

"If you can spare more, God will bless you."

"Oh he will?"

"Most assuredly." Robert looked at Brock with eyes that were as defiant as they were defining. This man might be living on the street with his entire world packed in a duffel bag, but it was clear he respected himself.

"Man makes his plans, but the Lord directs his steps." Robert opened his eyes wider as if to ask whether Brock accepted that as true.

Two thoughts struck Brock as he stared at the man. First, most people were probably closer to life on the street than they believed they could be. Here he stood, looking down both figuratively and literally on a man who could conceivably be himself in the short future. And second, his dad's words from his dream were coming true.

"What kind of food do you like?"

"Thai food." Robert smiled.

"Good choice." Brock extended his hand and the man took it. Brock pulled him to his feet.

Robert gave a shy smile. "I used to make it for my family."

"Really." Brock studied the man and wondered how much of this meeting was orchestrated by God. "That's interesting. It's a dish I've cooked a time or two for my family."

"Hard to do much cooking these days." Robert's eyes grew intense again and Brock turned away after a few seconds.

Brock opened his wallet and found two hundreds, a fifty, and three twenties. Depending on how the next week went, this might be the last time he could give stupidly for a long time. "Take this."

Robert opened the wad of cash, then slowly lifted his gaze. "I can't. Too much."

"I want you to have it. Maybe help you get a leg up." Brock pushed Robert's hand away. "The Lord gives, and I have a feeling the Lord is about to take away in great measure. So take this while you can."

Brock took the long way home, hoping Karissa would be asleep by the time he arrived. His wish was granted. Her soft rhythmic breathing was soothing in a way as sleep took him amid the torrent of anxiety.

CHAPTER 12

May 19, 2015

The malaise felt like a drug fogging his mind when Brock woke the next morning. It was almost like a dream, but he wasn't dreaming. He glanced at the clock. Two minutes after seven. Good. Karissa would be in the shower for at least another five minutes, which would give him time to escape to another part of the house where she wouldn't immediately find him. He needed time to process the explosion that was about to rock their world. Time to surface from the despair. He gave a sad laugh. Five minutes wouldn't be enough. Neither would five months if they truly were going to lose everything. And he'd seen it in Ron's eyes. They were.

He rolled out of bed and half walked, half jogged across their bedroom and through the door. Just in case Karissa finished early. Brock snaked into the kitchen, poured himself a cup of coffee, and started to head for the media room, but stopped to stare at the rain that squiggled down the windows. He put the coffee down and shuffled toward the French doors leading to the back deck and, beyond that, their lush green backyard.

He pulled the doors open and stepped onto the rain-soaked deck. The coolness of the water pelting him didn't snap him out of his trance-like state, but deepened it. Brock slogged over to the red brick push-of-a-button fire pit they'd put in five years ago and dropped into one of the seven plush patio chairs that ringed the pit. The water on the chair instantly soaked his back, but Brock barely noticed. He closed his eyes, tilted his head back so the rain would fall directly on his face, and asked God a question he doubted would be answered.

"Why?"

He sat there for minutes, or it might have been an hour. He didn't know, didn't care.

The squeak of the doors opening filled the air.

"Brock?"

Brock didn't open his eyes. Didn't turn. Didn't answer.

"Brock?" Karissa asked again. "Have you lost your mind?"

Again, he didn't answer. He should have,

but all that escaped his lips was a six-second sigh. The doors shut and he opened his eyes and glanced at them. Good. She'd gone back inside. Would leave him be, give him the time to do whatever it was he had to do. If only he knew what it was.

But half a minute later the doors squeaked again and he heard the rapid-fire patter of rain against Karissa's umbrella. He opened his eyes and listened to her soft footsteps across their cedar deck, almost drowned out by the sound of the rain. When she reached him, he motioned toward the chair across from him. She didn't speak. Just stared at him with a mixture of concern and worry.

"Care to join me?" Brock sat up a bit and motioned again to the chair next to him.

"What are you doing out here?"

"Taking a shower." Brock lifted his palm and let the rain patter down on it. "Nature's way."

"What happened?"

"Nothing." Brock wiped the rain off his eyebrows. "It's all good."

"All good? You're sitting outside in a deluge with a look on your face close to the one you had the day your dad died."

Brock stood and stared at the gathering blackness in the heart of the clouds.

"I should have gone to business school. I

should have been the one running the business side of the company, not Ron. If I'd gone to business school I could have convinced my dad to give *me* fifty-one percent of the company."

"What happened?" Karissa's eyes narrowed.

Brock turned to face her. "We're losing the company."

"What do you mean, *losing*?"

"Our lives are about to change."

The dark-blue umbrella slipped from Karissa's hand and fell slowly to the deck. She blinked against the rain now peppering her face. Blotches of rain spread across her shoulders.

"What are you talking about?" Karissa's face went pale. "How did this happen?"

"Someone hacked into our accounts. Stole the money. We're broke."

"And Ron didn't catch it."

"He trusted our CFO."

"He's the one who's doing this?"

"No, but the CFO should have seen it. He got snowed. Whoever did it covered their tracks. I don't understand that stuff. I just know the money is gone and whoever did it is good. We can't find them."

Karissa stared at him with utter despair on her face and gave slow, tiny shakes of her head.

"I should have done something." Brock raked his hand through his hair. "Made him show me the financials. Sat down with him on a regular basis, learned the basic skills at least."

"Don't sign." Karissa sat down hard and crossed her arms across her chest. "Fight this."

"I'm trying, believe me, but in the end I might have no choice."

"You always have a choice."

As Karissa walked away, Brock asked himself for the fifteen hundredth time why he hadn't gone to business school. The question haunted him the rest of the day and was still on his mind that night, when he slipped into a dream that called upon every one of his newly acquired lucid-dreaming skills.

CHAPTER 13

"What's wrong with you?"

His dad stood at the top of the stairs in a home that looked similar to the one he'd grown up in. It had light-brown shag carpet, and the walls were painted gold. "Wonderful World" by Sam Cooke poured out of a nearby stereo.

Brock stood on a linoleum landing and tried to run as his dad clomped down the stairs, but he couldn't move.

"What's wrong with him?" His brother Ron leaned on the railing above Brock to the right. He held the same brown package his dad had held in the earlier dream, but this time part of the wrapping was torn off and Brock saw hints of a blue box underneath. It stirred a memory deep inside. But before the memory could land, his dad's voice sliced through the air.

"He's an idiot, that's what's wrong with him."

Brock focused. *Change it! Get out of here!* But nothing changed. Nothing shifted, except the air grew thicker.

"I think your brother's right. You think you should have gone to business school? Nah, not a good idea."

"Why?" The word eked out as if Brock couldn't stop it.

"You know the truth. Do I have to say it?" His dad's face grew stony. "Ron, a business man? Yes. You? No."

"You didn't think I could cut it."

"You said it, not me." His father stopped halfway down the stairs.

"But if I wanted to run Black Fedora when you retire, I should have gotten a business degree."

His dad slowed his cadence to a crawl as he glared at Brock. "I never said you had to work for my company."

"I wanted to, Dad! Don't you get that?"

"You just wanted to beat your little brother." His dad stared at him with unblinking eyes. "And now it's going to destroy you. 'Cause it's coming."

"What is coming? Tell me!"

Brock woke seconds later, covered in sweat. He eased out of bed, careful not to disturb Karissa, took a shower, grabbed a cup of coffee, then went to his den to practice his lucid-dreaming techniques. Now more than ever, he needed to find his younger self again and test the idea that what he said to himself in the past truly could have an impact on his present.

He returned to bed an hour later and immediately returned to the land of dreams, but this time he was in control.

When the dream started, Brock immediately knew where he was. He stood four and a half miles north of the North Cascades Highway's Rainy Pass on a section of the Pacific Crest Trail. No idea why his subconscious had brought him here, but it was a spectacular spot to converse with his younger self.

This section of the PCT ran along the eastern edge of the Cascades and through the Pasaysten Wilderness. The lack of any snow told him it had to be at least mid-August, maybe as late as mid-September. But if he was about to bump into his younger self, it had to be September 1986.

That was the date of his first solo backpacking trip, and he'd been more nervous than he let anyone see. But he'd made it to Manning Provincial Park in British Columbia with no major incidents, touched the marker, then made the trek back to road

5400 at Hart's Pass, where Morgan picked him up.

A sweeping fir-lined valley spread out before Brock. Behind him was a series of switchbacks that led to the top of Cutthroat Pass. An ache of regret welled up in him. He'd promised himself that if he ever had a son, he'd take him on this trail, but he and Tyson had never made the trip. Brock had never even mentioned the idea.

He smiled at the memory of a man he'd bumped into nicknamed Yukon.

"I'm California born and bred, but I'm a Washingtonian now. Folks up here are kinder than warm snot on a cold day."

Brock didn't want to understand the analogy and didn't ask for an explanation.

"Yeah, I might not have a home, but I'm not homeless." Yukon spread his arms wide and gazed over the vast array of mountains. "Got everything I need on my back, and this is my front yard, backyard, living room, and kitchen. No mansion on earth can compare."

Brock pulled himself out of the memory and gazed up at the jagged peak of Golden Horn in the distance. A moment later he saw movement on the trail one hundred yards away. A royal blue backpack moved along in quick rhythm. It took Brock only a few seconds to know it was himself. Brock strode toward his younger self, amazed at how real the dream felt. Not only what he was seeing, but feeling as well. The cool breeze, the strain on his legs as he pushed forward to catch himself.

The scene morphed, and he stood on the beach in front of a home down on the Oregon coast while a storm raged out over the ocean. But he pulled it back in seconds. He was definitely getting better at controlling these dreams.

When he got to within thirty yards, he called out. "Brock!"

His younger self stopped, turned, and stared. "Yeah?"

Brock closed the gap. "Can I talk to you?"

"Do we know each other?" He stared at Brock with a puzzled expression.

"Not really."

"You are?" But recognition swept over his face. He pointed at Brock with an incredulous look. "What in the world? It's you, isn't it? The bizarre guy from Morgan's coffee shop last year. Unbelievable."

"You remember me?"

"With that act of yours, you're kind of hard to forget." His countenance was full of caution. "It's hard to forget a guy who predicts you'll meet a girl named Karissa and then it happens. However you did it, that was a nice trick."

"How long have you been dating?"

It would be interesting if the dream version of himself would give the correct date they started seeing each other.

"You tell me, Future Brock." His younger self pulled off his pack and leaned it against a large boulder on the side of the trail. "What in the world are you doing up here?"

"Looking for you."

The look on Young Brock's face said that wasn't the best answer. He understood why. Even inside a dream, his younger self would react in a realistic way. Bumping into himself at Java Spot was one thing. Seeing each other on a remote trail in the Cascade Mountains seventy-five miles from the closest town was another.

"Without any kind of a pack? Water? Who are you really, and why are you stalking me? And tell me the trick. How did you know I would meet a girl named Karissa? Lucky guess?"

Brock twisted his head and felt for a daypack. Nothing. "I'm not stalking you."

"You're just a hiker out for a stroll, huh?"

"Something like that."

A marmot skittered across the trail as his

124

younger self laughed and said, "Sure you are."

"I am."

"Where'd you come from? Rainy? Are you trying to get back there before night? That's another twelve miles, so unless you're planning to jog the rest of the way, I'd turn around."

"I'm in a dream, remember?"

"Oh yeah." Young Brock gave his forehead a mock slap. "Right. And I'm just a part of that dream. Not real."

"No, you're not."

His younger self picked up his pack and cinched it up. "This is weird, I have to tell you. You coming up here, finding me."

"Don't worry, I'll leave as soon as I tell you something."

"Fine." Young Brock hoisted his pack higher on his hips. "Then get yourself back to the highway."

"Will do. First, you changed things. You went to Alaska two more times than I did."

"I did, huh?"

"Yes. Thank you."

"Is that it? Are we done?" His younger self turned to go.

"I want to try an experiment if you're up for it."

"Oh sure, Future Me, anything to help

125

you feel like you're living like Doc Brown."

"In 2003, Steve Miller is going to release a more comprehensive collection of his band's greatest hits. I bought his first greatest-hits album, but never this updated version. Buy it for me, all right?"

"Again, why not?" Young Brock pointed at him and grinned. "I've always kind of liked Steve Miller, and if it makes you happy, F. B., I'll do it."

CHAPTER 14

Brock's sky-blue '74 Volkswagen Super Beetle sputtered as he threw it into third gear. Two emotions fought for his attention. The first, excitement about his date with Karissa; the second, his frustration over not being able to stop thinking about the old guy who claimed to be him in the future. That was impossible, so then who was he? And why had he targeted Brock?

At the park, Brock stretched while he waited for Karissa to show. She arrived a few minutes later wearing dark-blue spandex, a purple windbreaker, and that radiant smile that soaked him in warmth every time he saw it. No makeup, hair tied on top of her head, and still stunning. She grabbed him around the waist, squeezed tight, then released him and jogged away. "What are you waiting for? Let's go."

Brock grinned and broke into a run to

catch up to her. When he did, she yanked on his sweatshirt. "Think you can keep up with me today?"

"Gotta keep hope alive."

"Good." Karissa picked up her pace. "I need a full workout and I don't want any weak links in the chain holding me back."

"We're chains?"

"A chain of fools."

"You're too young to know that song."

"So are you, but you still know it."

"That's because I was forced to play it in my high-school rock band days. Morgan loved it, and since he was the leader . . ."

They buzzed past walkers and slower joggers down the Burke-Gilman Trail — built over the top of an old Eastern Railway corridor — which ran from Seattle's Gas Works Park all the way out to Lake Sammamish twenty-seven miles away.

Cyclists decked out in sunglasses and bright form-fitting tops and shorts zipped past them, calling out, "On your left!" as they sped by. Women pushing baby strollers ambled past them going the other direction. The trail was bordered on each side with an ample assortment of maple trees, thick with huge green leaves that filtered the sun.

When they passed Matthews Beach, the right side of the trail opened to opulent houses that sat on the shore of Lake Washington, and that's when Brock broached the subject he'd hesitated to bring up.

"I have something to tell you" — Brock sucked in a breath and tried to talk without gasping; Karissa might get the impression he was winded — "that's on the far side of bizarre."

"Oh?" Karissa glanced at him with eyebrows raised and slowed her pace slightly.

"I recently had an, um, interesting conversation with an extremely strange man."

"Where did you meet said man?"

"First time? Last year, at Morgan's, before I met you. Second time when I hiked the PCT a few weeks back." Brock hesitated, then dove into the deep end. "He says when we met, he wasn't really there, he was dreaming. And that I wasn't real, just part of his dream."

"Okay, I'm starting to get the bizarre part." Karissa glanced at him with narrowed eyes. "Who is he?"

They passed a pair of young girls who struggled to stay upright on their roller skates.

"I don't know."

"He didn't tell you his name?"

"Not exactly."

"What's that mean?"

"That's the even more bizarre part." Brock pointed his finger at his head and tapped it. "He says we're related."

"How?"

Brock waited till they passed a man riding a recumbent bike so slowly it seemed a miracle he stayed upright.

"He claims to be me."

Karissa jerked her head toward him and laughed. "He what?"

"That's what he says, that he's me. Me from the future."

Karissa wiggled her fingers. "How exciting."

"He's serious."

"Me too!" She grinned, maneuvered closer, and punched him lightly on his arm. "I've always wanted to talk to myself in the future. Can you ask him to send me back next time? I know I'd be up for it."

"Good news. I still have all my hair."

It helped to joke about the subject, but the anxiety inside still churned like an avalanche.

"Wonderful. I like your hair." Karissa's smile faded. "I can tell this is bothering you. Who is he really?"

"I honestly don't know."

Brock fell in behind Karissa for a few paces as a slew of cyclists approached from the opposite direction and whizzed past them.

"I'm thinking riding this trail might be more fun than running it."

"Why don't you just tell me you're out of shape and can't hack my torrid pace?"

"Can't admit that. Twenty-four-year-old males are required to maintain their macho image at all times. No weaknesses allowed ever."

"What about late last summer when we did the Crystal Mountain Summit run?"

"You mean me throwing up at the top?"

"Umhmm."

"That was to make you feel better."

Karissa smiled and slowed to a steady jog. Brock's breathing grew more rhythmic and his lungs stopped burning with the fires of Hades. "Will I ruin your image of me if I say thank you?"

"Not in the slightest." Karissa slowed a bit more and gave him a serious look. "Can we talk a few more minutes about this future you?"

"Sure."

"When he showed up last year at Java Spot, did Morgan talk to him too?"

"No, I'm sure Morgan saw him, but the place was busy and he didn't come over to the table."

"Why haven't you told me about it till now?"

"Because I thought he was some harmless wacko, but the more I think about it . . ."

"You don't anymore? You think he's dangerous?"

"No, not dangerous. I actually kind of like the guy." Brock paused to breathe. "It's just that . . ."

"What?"

"There's no way he should know some of the things he knows."

"In other words, Morgan is playing one of his practicals on you. The Joke Master strikes again."

"Exactly what I'm thinking."

A few paces later, the trail opened up on their right to the parking lot for Log Boom Park. Twenty or so cars dotted the concrete. Halfway to the end of the lot, Karissa slowed to a walk and Brock followed her lead.

"You ready for a break?" Karissa glanced at her watch. "We've been doing seven-and-a-half-minute miles for forty-five minutes now, and I'm feeling the burn."

"Sure, if you need to." Brock stopped and grinned as he leaned forward with both hands on his knees and drew in deep breaths of the crisp September air.

"I'm getting the distinct feeling this guy's knowing things he shouldn't know is the precursor to a serious conversation."

"Could be."

"Then let's go out to the end of the dock and have a serious conversation."

They strolled out to the end of the pier that jutted two hundred feet into Lake Washington. Only a few boats dotted the water.

They reached the end and sat with their legs hanging over the water.

"I can't get some of the things he's told me out of my mind." Brock glanced at Karissa. "Like I said, impossible for him to know them."

"You're not serious." Karissa pulled back and narrowed her eyes. "You don't actually think this guy —"

"No way. Of course not."

"You do!" She laughed.

"No, I don't."

"Why would you even entertain an idea like that?"

"Probably because of Paul."

"Paul your cousin?"

"No. Paul in the New Testament, the one God took up into heaven to take a look around." Brock turned and faced Karissa. "If God can do something like that, or take

Enoch up without him physically dying, or take John into a vision where he's a time traveler, seeing the future, why couldn't he do something like this?"

"I'm not saying he couldn't, but even with bringing God into it, you do realize how completely insane you sound?"

"Without question." He grabbed a splinter of wood that had come loose from the dock and tossed it into the water.

"And you also realize you can't talk to anyone about this, right?"

"I didn't even want to talk to you about it."

"Just so you know . . ." She took his hand. "I don't think you're crazy to consider all possibilities."

"Thanks."

"So when do I get to meet your imaginary friend?" Karissa giggled. "Sorry, I couldn't resist."

"Not funny."

"I thought it was."

"Okay, it was a little funny." Brock sighed.

"So what's the biggest thing this guy knew that he shouldn't have known? The thing that keeps you from letting it all go?"

Brock studied Karissa's face. She still thought it was a joke, he could tell, but this might push her out of the world of humor.

And that wouldn't necessarily be a bad thing.

"At the first meeting, he told me I was going to break up with Sheila and start dating a girl named Karissa. This was a whole month before I met you."

Karissa's eyes went wide. "Okay, that is definitely weird."

"I realize it was probably just a lucky guess, but still . . ."

"What else did he say about us?"

"He apparently thinks a great deal of you."

Karissa smiled and told him with her eyes she knew what that meant. She was definitely a treasure, without question the greatest thing in his life. And by the time the Pacific Northwest leaves dropped from the trees next year, he would ask if she wanted to commit to going through the rest of their earthly existence together, forever and ever amen.

He took Karissa's hand and she squeezed it tight. "Your older, wiser self seems to be saying there's an extended future for us."

"Apparently, yes." Brock drew her face to his and kissed her deeply.

When they pulled away, Karissa took Brock's face in both her hands and peered deep into his eyes. "I think I like Future Brock."

"Yeah, I thought you would."

"So you really think Morgan set this whole thing up?"

"That's what I'm going to find out tonight."

CHAPTER 15

That evening, Brock sat at his usual table in Java Spot, waiting for Morgan to close up his dad's business, and tried to make sense of his two encounters with the old guy who claimed to be him. The guy's hair had thinned and was going gray, but the color still showed a healthy amount of the dark brown it must have been earlier in his life. Same color as Brock's. Then there was his amber eyes. Again, the same color.

And there was a quality about the man that mesmerized Brock. Confidence? Maybe. But it was more than that. The man carried himself in a way that reminded him of . . .

He shook it off and stopped trying to figure it out. He glanced over at Morgan as his friend wiped down the reclaimed-wood countertop. Morgan was the answer. Had to be. All this was one of his friend's strange practical jokes. What other possibility was there? If only he could get rid of that infinitesimal shred of doubt. No, there was no doubt. There were only two possibilities: Morgan had set him up, or the old guy was crazy. But the old guy had been over-the-top sincere, which is the part that weirded Brock out the most. That and the things Future Brock knew.

A few minutes later, Morgan finished up and sauntered over to him with a ceramic mug full of coffee.

"Why the night visit and not out with Karissa?"

"I saw her earlier today."

"What else? I see it pushing to get out."

Brock motioned toward the chair across from him, and Morgan plopped into it.

"Last year, I had a strange encounter with a man right here in your shop. I blew it off. Wasn't worth mentioning to you, although now I wish I had. But then he showed up again during my hike on the PCT a few weeks back. Just wondering if you had anything to do with the guy."

"Do with him?"

"Like putting him up to messing with my mind."

"How is he messing with you?"

There wasn't a hint of playfulness in Morgan's eyes. Didn't surprise Brock. In the

138

years they'd played poker together, his friend had never shown any tells. Stone Face was the nickname Brock and his friends had given Morgan.

"Is this the moment where you tell me you had nothing to do with my two meetings with the guy?"

"I had nothing to do with your two meetings with the guy."

"He put on a masterful performance. Did you coach him on what to say?"

"Who is *him*?"

"You serious?" Brock tilted his head forward. "You didn't set this up?"

"I didn't set up anything." Morgan stared deep into Brock's eyes. "You're a little freaked, pal. I can see it. What's going on?"

If Morgan hadn't set it up and Future Brock wasn't crazy, then someone was playing him. Someone who knew more than most people did about Brock's life. But who? And more importantly, why?

"You know what he told me?" Brock shook his head. "Told me he was me, thirty years from now. I guess it would be twenty-nine years at this point."

Morgan's thin smile grew into a full-out grin. "You have got to be kidding."

"No. Told me I was going to meet Karissa a whole month before you introduced us."

"This guy should call himself Amazing Brockdini." Morgan pulled the towel off his shoulder and wiped the maple-wood table. "That it?"

"Told me the first time we met I should go on a fishing trip with my dad, then the second time told me I'd done it."

"But you haven't done it yet, because it's still in your future."

"Right."

"But he's saying it's his past, because he's from the future."

"Makes your brain spin, doesn't it?"

"But it also makes total sense that you would travel back here from the future to talk yourself into going on a fishing trip." Morgan shrugged. "Because you like fishing so much."

"Yeah, total sense."

"Why are you so worked up about an imaginary self from the future?"

"He says I'm the imaginary one. That I'm part of his dreams."

"Describe the guy to me."

"I'm surprised you didn't notice him a year ago. We sat at the back of the shop, but still, we weren't that far away."

"Sorry, don't remember. Describe him."

"A little shorter than me, graying brown hair. Amber eyes, still fairly lean. One hundred eighty pounds or so."

Morgan took a drink out of his large ceramic cup, thunked it back down on the table, and tilted his head to the side. "Lemme ask you something, Brock-O. You think maybe your mind is trying to tell you something?"

"Like?"

"You know who you just described?"

The question struck Brock like a ten-foot emotional wave, and he admitted what he'd felt from the first time he'd met the older gentleman. But Brock had ignored the impression and pushed it down where he wouldn't have to deal with it.

"I'm right, aren't I?" Morgan leaned in with expectant eyes.

"Thanks for asking."

"You're not going to say it, so I will." Morgan poked him in the chest. "You just described your dad."

"No I didn't." Brock answered too quickly, but Morgan already knew he was lying.

"Oh shut up, you did too. I see it written all over your face. All's I'm saying is, maybe you're trying to work some things out."

Brock stared at Morgan's table. Too many hot drinks had started to crack the finish. "What things?"

"I think you want a relationship with your dad."

"You think wrong."

"You don't hate your dad."

"Oh that's right. I don't. Not at all. Never have."

"You gotta give your dad a break. He's not the same guy he was before he started doing the religion thing. He changed. Genuine change."

"It's called following Jesus, or being a Christian. Not 'doing the religion thing.' "

"Right, I keep forgetting your cool lingo." Morgan raised his hands toward the ceiling and shook them. "How can I get saved and keep mah soul from the comin' hellfire? Speak to me the truuuuuth, Brother Brock!"

Brock laughed. "You better be careful. You don't have much time left, pal. I've called down the hounds of heaven on you, and they're coming."

"Woof." Morgan grinned and popped Brock's shoulder with his fist. "We're getting off the subject. If you can't see that your dad isn't the same guy he was when we grew up, then maybe you're blind."

"Still doesn't explain who sent the guy and why whoever sent him."

"I'm just saying you should stay open.

And next time the guy drops in, ask him if Minnesota ever wins a Super Bowl."

CHAPTER 16

May 20, 2015
Finally. Meeting day with the doctor. Brock kissed Karissa good-bye and walked out the front door toward his car. As soon as he slipped behind the wheel of his Lexus and fired it up, a song pounding through the speakers stopped him cold: Steve Miller's "Jungle Love." Impossible. He popped the CD out of the player and stared at it. *Young Hearts.* The "complete greatest hits" album he'd never purchased.

He pulled out of the garage and called Karissa as he sped down the street toward 405.

"Forget something?"

"Steve Miller's *Young Love* CD is in my car."

"Uh-huh. You're surprised by that?"

"Do I own his first *Greatest Hits* CD, or only this one?"

"I don't know. I think only that one. Why?"

"Unbelievable."

"What?"

"It happened again." Brock came to a stop on 8th Street and waited for the light.

"What happened?"

"I met myself in a dream and told my younger self I was going to do an experiment. I told him to buy Steve Miller's second greatest hits album."

"So?"

"I never bought this album."

"Sure you did, I remember you doing it. You said you were thinking of getting it for yourself for Christmas, and I told you to buy it. I think it was Christmas 2003."

The car behind him laid on his horn, and Brock looked at the now-green light. He accelerated and tried to slow his breathing.

"No, I didn't."

"I'm pretty sure you did."

"This is too strange. It can't really be happening. How would you remember that and not me?"

"I don't know, but I do know I have to go. Tyson needs breakfast."

Brock hung up, laughed at himself, and popped the Steve Miller CD back into his player. Did he really believe he could go to sleep and somehow communicate with the person he was thirty-plus years ago? And

145

that their conversation would change the present? No. It was ludicrous. But his laughter faded as he pressed his lips together and tried to come up with a rational explanation for what had happened. He couldn't. There was only one explanation that made sense, and it made no sense at all. His meeting with Dr. Shagull couldn't come soon enough.

Brock sat on a bench near the front of the park and looked at his watch; the doc was twenty minutes late. No cell number to call the good doctor on. He'd wait another ten.

Nine minutes later, a man approached. Brock knew it was Dr. Shagull. Maybe it was the way the man sauntered toward him as if studying a lab rat. More likely was the fact that no one else in the park stood a chance of being the doctor.

Brock stood and extended his hand. "Dr. Shagull, I presume."

The doctor sighed as he shook Brock's hand. "If you knew how many times I've had to endure that opening line, you'd beg me to forgive you for using it."

"Sorry. I'll ask for your forgiveness even without knowing." Brock bowed his head. "I'm Brock Matthews."

Dr. Shagull's pale face looked like it had

146

melted slightly years ago, then hardened into a perpetual expression of expectation. He was the type of lean that made him seem taller than he really was. Brock guessed his height at six three, but he probably wasn't much taller than six feet. His sparse gray-blond hair waved in the light breeze and his thick glasses couldn't hide bright eyes that flitted from left to right to up and down — as if there wasn't anything worth looking at for more than a quarter second. He smelled of pipe tobacco, and the effect of all his apparent quirks gave the impression that either he was playing the role of an eccentric professor in a community theater stage play or he'd stepped out of England in the 1950s. The only thing missing was the British accent.

"Thank you for taking the time to see me."

Dr. Shagull tilted his head down and looked over the top of his glasses. "I rarely meet readers of my book. Close to never."

"Thanks for making an exception in my case, Dr. Shagull."

The doctor continued as if Brock hadn't spoken. "But in your case, I wanted to. More than that, I feel it's a necessity." The doctor's eyes seemed to laugh as he motioned toward the path to their left. "Shall we?"

They made their way down the trail toward the lake.

"And by the way, call me Shagull, or Thomas, but don't call me Dr."

"All right."

They settled into a slow walk along the edge of the water and for a time didn't speak. Shagull was the one who broke the silence. "Are you a man of faith?"

"Yes." Brock glanced at the doctor. "Are you?"

"Yes, I would call it that. Some wouldn't describe me that way. Which is fine." Shagull reached into his pocket and pulled out a pipe. "Do you mind?"

Brock shook his head. The reality was, too much pipe smoke would bring on a pounding migraine, but outside he rarely had a problem with it. As long as he and the doctor stayed on the path and the breeze blowing into their faces continued, he'd be okay.

"There is an intelligence behind everything that occurs in this universe, and I believe that intelligence is God. As you know, *God* isn't a name any more than *president* is a name. It refers to a position only. I'm more than content to call this intelligence God."

"What about Christ? Was he the son of this Intelligence?"

"The most brilliant man who ever lived."

"Man?"

"Of course he would be the brightest mind in history, yes? I suppose that comes with being God and all."

"So you believe Christ was the Son of God?"

The doctor stopped and smiled. "Is this really why you wanted to see me?"

"No."

"Then why don't we get on with it."

"Am I time traveling?"

"I don't think so."

"Then where am I going? Everything in my dreams is from the past. And the younger version of myself doesn't think it's a dream. For him, it's real. My dream is happening in his reality, in his present and my past."

"How do you know that?"

"Because I'm changing things! I'm talking to this younger version of myself, and those conversations are making him do different things than I did the first time, and when I wake up there are differences. If I wasn't really back there, truly talking to him, nothing in my present world would shift, correct?"

"Does anyone else notice these changes?"

"What do you mean?"

"When you wake up and things are different, are you the only one that thinks things have changed, or are there other people who think reality has shifted?"

"I still don't understand the question. Of course I'm the only one who thinks reality has shifted. When the younger version of me changes things, then it changes for him and everyone around him from what happened the first time. Their time line is —"

"If you're the only one who thinks the present has changed, then how do you know all the transformations you seem to be going through are real? How do you know all the supposed world shifting isn't happening only inside your own head?"

Brock stopped stone cold and stared at the back of the doctor's head as he continued to stroll down the path. A numbness overtook him and seemed to freeze his mind. Impossible. Things had changed even if he was the only one who knew it. But how could he know that for certain?

"What are you saying? That I'm nuts? That I've made up this whole thing in my mind?"

"I'm only asking the question."

"If that's true, then I'd be certifiable."

"Most people would come to that conclusion anyway."

"So what do I do?"

"You have choices. If you are indeed practicing lucid dreaming, you can stop. The next time you encounter yourself, wake up. Or shift the dream in a different direction, away from your younger self."

Brock watched three ducks fight over bread being tossed to them by two children.

"I don't want to stop. I want to change things."

"Most people would. Tell me, then, what would you change?" The doctor winked at him. "If these changes weren't just occurring inside your own mind. What would you do with this power if you really, truly had it?"

"Two things. I'd figure out a way to have a relationship with my dad, and I'd figure out how to go to business school instead of getting a degree in marketing."

"Then why not try to do those things?"

"Because a large part of me doesn't believe this is happening."

"If that is the case, what do you have to lose?"

CHAPTER 17

November 3, 1989
The sun woke Brock at five thirty on Friday morning. Five more days in Costa Rica and he'd be on a plane heading back to Seattle. After getting a cup of coffee, he strolled out onto the veranda of the villa where he was a guest and stared at the coffee fields. But after a few seconds he wasn't seeing the fields any longer. His gaze turned inward, to a question Karissa had posed the morning he left for this trip.

"What if your dad dies earlier than later?"

"What in the world made you think of that?"

Karissa ignored the question. "Would you regret not trying harder to have a relationship with him?"

"I'm working on it."

"Really? How hard?"

Not hard. Not at all. She was right, and the time to do something about it was now.

His dad was a horse, would probably live forever, but Brock should probably make an effort soon. He wandered back inside the villa and looked around his room for something to write on. He spied a postcard and pen on the desk in the corner of the room. Brock picked up both, intending to ease back outside to one of the wicker chairs and start a note to his father. But the light on his phone was flashing. The front desk said mail had arrived for him, and he went to pick it up. It was one envelope. From his father. Brock shook his head. God had to be laughing. He took the envelope back to his room and opened it.

Hello, Brock,

I suppose I could have sent this letter to your Seattle home, or dropped it off with you at work, but my thought was to get it to you at a time when you were alone and away from any distractions.

Don't worry, this won't be long, but I suppose it's inevitable that at fifty-three I'd start thinking about my mortality.

With that in mind, I'm wondering if we can get together before the leaves are fully gone from the trees. Can we try again? Can we have a cup of coffee together? Can we have a laugh or two and see where it takes us?

Your father and, hopefully,
friend

Brock leaned back and breathed deep. His dad, his friend? He felt like his soul split in two. One part desperately wanted to jump on a plane and have that conversation — the part that still felt eight years old and longed to fall into his dad's arms before the dark years came. But he wasn't eight anymore. On the other hand, his dad was trying.

Brock wandered out onto the veranda with pen and postcard in hand and wrote a quick message.

Dad,
   Got your letter. Thanks. A cup of coffee sounds good. I'll be home from this trip in five days. I might even beat this postcard back. I'll call you then, and we'll pick a time and place.

Brock

Now if he could just get up enough nerve to mail it.

Brock watched a flock of clay-colored thrushes glide over the coffee fields and prayed that his relationship with his dad

154

would take flight just as easily. Just after midnight, Brock slipped into his bed, pulled the thin blue comforter over his body, and prayed for his calloused heart to soften, for the courage to send off the postcard, and for a new beginning.

Just before sleep took him, the cordless phone rang.

"Hello?"

"Hey." It was Karissa. "Sorry. I woke you, didn't I?"

"No. I mean I was just falling asleep, but I'm glad you called."

"Really?"

"Yeah." Brock settled back on the bed and closed his eyes. "What's up?"

Brock heard her pull in a sharp breath. "I have a strong feeling you need to start building a relationship with your dad." She hesitated. "He called me. Told me he cared about me, about us. Wants us to be happy together. Has always thought I was the right one for you. That he feels close. It was very sweet. Tender."

He didn't respond, and she let the silence linger. She undoubtedly knew he needed a moment to collect his thoughts. To wrestle with the idea that his dad was tender toward her and not toward him. But . . . his dad's letter did express a longing for restoration.

"Feels close? We've already been married a year and a half and he's hardly spent any time around you."

"Which says a lot, doesn't it?"

"Yeah, so does the letter he sent me."

"At the hotel?"

"Yeah. Wants to have coffee."

"God is in this, Brock."

Brock stood and eased across the room and through the villa doors onto the balcony overlooking the field of coffee beans. The moon threw splotches of light through the clouds onto the plantation.

"I know he's in it. I'm just not sure if I'm ready to pull down the wall. Those bricks have been there a long time."

"Which is why you need to do it now. It's a chance for healing, and while your dad might not be able to say all the words he wants to, I believe you'll see in his eyes what he's truly telling you. Meet with him. You need this."

Did he? Probably. Definitely. But it wasn't that easy.

"You ever get to a spot where you've always wanted to stand and then realize you're stuck on the edge of a precipice and there's no turning back, but there's no way across?"

"There's a bridge there if you'd only open

your eyes to see it. He cares about you. Don't you see that you've shut him out as much as he's shut you out? Can't you see that you two are so much alike, you're acting like magnets who get too close and shove each other apart?"

"I was never good at science."

"Go talk to him, Brock. This is one of those moments that you can't ever get back."

"I have no idea what I'd say."

"You don't have to. He asked you. So you listen to what he says, then trust that God will bring you the right words."

"And if the meeting is a disaster?"

"Then you go down in flames knowing you at least tried."

Forty-nine percent of him said stay behind the wall. Fifty-one percent said take a sledgehammer to the bricks and see what remained when the dust cleared.

"All right. I'll do it. I'll mail a note in the morning."

"Can I tell you something else?"

"Sure."

"I think you need to come home early."

"I'll only be down here another five days."

"I think you need to come home tomorrow."

"Why?"

"I just do."

"Five days. I promise I'll talk to my dad the moment I get home."

"Okay."

After they hung up, Brock turned and walked back inside. *I'll talk to my dad.* It felt good to say the words. Now he was committed. And hope surfaced, unbidden and strong. Yes, he'd kept his dad at arm's length, and yes, he'd tried at times to reach out, but why did his dad always give up so easily? Brock would go home and have the conversation, but he needed time to get ready for it. Prepare mentally, emotionally, spiritually. And Costa Rica was the best place in the world to do that.

Brock spun through his meetings the next morning and afternoon in a daze. He was glad for his habit of taking detailed notes, because he couldn't recall even a tenth of the conversations as he lay in bed that evening. His dad's note and his conversation with Karissa kept pushing out all other thoughts. It was time. Within six days, he'd have the conversation he longed for and dreaded at the same time.

The next day was the same, and the next. God might be in it, but the process was exhausting. By nine that night he was ready for bed. It was early for sleep, but he was ready to slip into a world that didn't involve visions of coffee on his father's luxurious deck overlooking Puget Sound. He tried to compose his part of a talk that might finally close the gulf between them, but the words didn't form in his mind.

When sleep came that night it came hard. He slipped into a dream where he stood on the stern of a boat as it crested a massive wave and then descended like an out-of-control roller coaster into the trough of the next wave. As he glanced at the star-strewn night sky the clanging of the ship's bell grew louder. A warning? Of what? Should he go below deck? The bell increased in volume. Then it wasn't the bell but the phone in his room shattering the dream and pulling him back into the conscious world.

Brock fumbled for it on his nightstand and knocked it away. He leaned over and fished the phone off the hardwood floor. His sheets were covered with sweat, as if his body knew something his mind didn't. He squinted at his watch. Three forty-five a.m.

"Hello?" Brock turned and let his head fall back onto his pillow.

"It's me. Sorry to wake you."

"It's okay."

Brock listened to Karissa's labored breathing for a few seconds and heard the catch in her voice. The temperature in the room instantly rose ten degrees. "What is it?"

"Your dad."

Brock asked the question he didn't want to ask. "What happened?"

"I'm so sorry, Brock."

Karissa's sobs came through his phone in waves as Brock closed his eyes and covered his face with his damp palm. His dad couldn't be gone. Not now. They were going to start to build a real relationship. Heal the past. He couldn't be gone. It wasn't possible. Brock needed to wake up. This was part of his dream; his nightmare.

Brock felt four years old again. He was sitting on his dad's lap in the days before the breakdown. Good days before the pieces of Brock's heart had been shattered all over the floor.

"He's not gone, Karissa. He can't be. We . . . there are things we have to say."

"I know, Brock. I know."

After he hung up, Brock went out on the balcony and let the numbness of the moment soak into him. He watched the sky turn gray, then red with the early morning light. Why would God do this to him? Why couldn't he let his dad live another week? That's all it would have taken. Even just three days.

CHAPTER 18

November 18, 1989

Brock and Ron buried their father two weeks later on Saturday morning at Lake View Cemetery. The pastor and a few others must have said profound and heart-wrenching things about his dad, because when the funeral ended, friends and extended family told Brock how moving the service was and how beautiful the eulogies were. But his mind had been too numb to take any of it in. He couldn't remember anything but snatches of his own tribute.

His mind was too buried in the guilt of not having that conversation with his dad years earlier — the one that would have fixed everything. He allowed himself a sad smile. It probably wouldn't have solved everything, but it would have been a start.

After the service ended, as he studied the people who moved away over the grass, Karissa slid her arm inside his, pulled closer, and held his arm tight. "Should we go?"

He didn't answer, but Karissa didn't ask again. Part of him wanted to leave, and part of him wanted to stay right here until his dad somehow spoke to him from heaven and said everything was okay; that someday, when Brock took the same journey his dad just had, there would be restoration between them. But the only sound came from a finch high in the weeping willow tree to his right. Finally Brock squeezed her hand and said, "Go? I suppose we should, but . . ."

He watched the last of the mourners shuffle away. Their muted conversations swirled around his ears but he couldn't make out any of their words. In a few minutes, Karissa and he would be completely alone at the grave.

"I have an idea." She slipped her arm free and faced him, her bright eyes searching his face for a connection point. "Why don't I go on ahead and give you some time here alone? I can get a ride with Ron and Shelly."

"He's already gone."

"No, I asked him to stay in the parking lot for a bit — just in case. I thought you might want a few minutes of solitude."

He loved her for knowing him so well. It's exactly what Brock wanted, but given how torn up his emotions were, even he hadn't known that till the moment she said it.

"Yeah, if you don't mind." He took her hands and stared at them.

"Take all the time you need." Karissa kissed him on the cheek and whispered in his ear. "He loved you, even though you have a tough time believing it."

"I know."

"No, you don't know that at all, but someday I believe you will."

Brock watched her stroll away over the grass, the late-afternoon sunshine lighting up her hair like burnished gold. Life would be a devastating journey without her.

Brock closed his eyes and focused on the sun warming his face. His dad was gone and he'd blown it, but this, too, would pass, wouldn't it? Maybe. At some point he'd face his dad's death and the fact neither had been able to breach the rift between them.

His dad would say Brock had only gone through the motions, that there had been many times where he could have made more of an effort. Probably true. No, it was true. No point in trying to justify his actions now that his dad was gone. He would need all his energy going forward to deal with the guilt of not being the son his father wanted.

CHAPTER 19

June 1987

Not long after he fell asleep the night after his meeting with Dr. Shagull, Brock found himself standing on lush green turf with the dew of morning still lingering on its blades. The smell of early summer combined with gasoline floated past him. The scene started to swirl and shift to the side of a mountain, but Brock brought the dream back to the lawn. Something was familiar about this place, and he waited for more of the surroundings to come into focus. A few seconds later, the sound of a small-engine plane firing up filled the air. Of course. He knew where he was. Harvey Airfield in south Snohomish. He'd spent two years here after college while working on his post-grad marketing degree, working on planes and studying for his pilot's license, which he never ended up getting.

He walked toward the shed and willed his

younger self to come out into the midmorning sunshine. Seconds later, Young Brock appeared carrying a cup of coffee. Midmorning break, perfect timing. Which of course it would be, since he was the director of this mini play.

The younger version of himself looked up when Brock was twenty feet away. He stopped, shook his head, then came on as if resigned to the fact he wouldn't be left alone.

"Future Man." His younger self lifted his cup when he reached Brock. "Good to see you again. How are the hover cars working out for everyone? Did the Cubs ever win another World Series?"

"You again remember our earlier talks."

"Of course. Since it was you that created them, and you created me, we'd both have to remember it, right?" Young Brock winked.

Strange to be playing mind games with himself with such conviction.

"Good to see you too." Brock shoved his hands in his pockets. "Can I join you?"

"Sure." Young Brock motioned to a picnic table a few yards away, and they both sat.

"Do you really think you're a time traveler?" Young Brock grinned. " 'Cause I've always wanted to do that."

"Only in my dreams."

"So you're only crazy in your head then?"

"Probably."

He glanced around at the field and the three white Cessna six-seaters lined up to their right, and then gestured to the coffee in his younger self's hand. "It has to be later than the spring of '87."

"Why do you say that?"

"That's when I started drinking coffee."

"How'd you know?" Brock frowned, then waved his hand. "Right, I keep forgetting you're me."

"I can't remember what made me finally give in."

"Give in?"

Brock sighed. "I promised myself I'd never drink coffee because it was my dad's business, then I ended up working there."

"I end up working for my dad?"

"Yes."

"That's not going to happen."

"It does, and Ron is going to drive the thing into the ground."

"So you're telling me not to go to work there."

"That's not what I want to talk to you about."

"What do you want to say?"

His younger self drained the last of his coffee and crushed the Styrofoam cup in his hand. Brock glanced at the cup and smiled.

"Not many people use those anymore."

"Cups? What happens in the future? Do you drink out of your hands? Mainline the coffee right into your veins? Take a pill instead?"

"We don't use much Styrofoam. Protecting the environment is a big deal in the future. Everyone is going green."

Young Brock stared at him with an I-don't-care expression.

Brock chuckled. "If you want to make some money, get on the green thing before anyone else does."

"Got it. Will do."

Young Brock waggled his thumb behind him at the area reserved for packing parachutes and training new jumpers in the art of leaping from a perfectly good airplane.

"Do I ever do that?"

"Fly like an eagle?" Brock smiled as he looked at the training area.

"No, drop like a rock until the chute opens."

"Yes, you do."

"Even though I'm scared of heights."

"You never get rid of the fear, but you learn to control it. Good life lesson."

"Listen, I gotta go, break time's over." His

younger self pushed off the picnic bench and grinned. "Any new words of wisdom from the future? Was there something you wanted to talk about?"

"You need to talk to your dad about your relationship, Brock."

"My dad and I —"

"Do you want a relationship with him?"

"We have one, it's just not that close."

"Not that close? Miles apart is 'not that close'?"

"We have our issues."

"Do you want a better relationship?"

"Look, I went fishing with him like you asked. During the trip things were okay, but I . . ." Brock's younger self flicked his coffee cup with his forefinger. "It's not going to happen, Future Me. My dad and I . . . well, let's just say someday that might be a place I'll go, but not yet."

"You have to."

"No. I don't."

Brock stared at him for a few seconds before turning away and staring out across the airfield. So much for having complete control of this dream.

"Relax, Future Brock. Most fathers and sons have issues. Probably ninety-five percent. I'm not unusual. But we're okay. He changed when he became a Christian. He figured things out. And we get along these days. My past with him isn't that big of a deal."

"It is a big deal." Regret surged inside Brock. "You have to talk to him soon."

"No!" Young Brock laughed as he smacked his fist onto the table. "Like I said, maybe someday, but not now."

"There is no tomorrow."

"Apollo Creed, *Rocky III*."

"Yes, and it's true."

"Lookit, Future Me." His younger self smiled wide. "I kinda like you. More than kind of. You're entertaining — I mean, come on, the idea of yourself coming back from the future and hanging out . . . it's cool. But since you won't tell me who you really are, or the true reason you're interested in me, I'm probably not going to be swallowing many of your golden nuggets of advice. Cool?"

"You don't believe me."

"Not exactly." His twenty-five-year-old self raised his eyebrows. "Feel like finally telling me your real name?"

Brock zeroed in on his younger self's face. "Brock Lee Matthews."

His younger self's face went white. "How do you know my middle name?"

"Mom and Dad certainly had a sense of

humor, didn't they?"

"No one knows my middle name." Young Brock staggered backward.

"Except you." Brock pointed at his head. "You know it."

"How'd you find out? Who put you up to this? Was it Ron? It *was* Morgan, wasn't it?"

"This is happening, Brock. I don't know how, but it's real. It isn't just a dream. And I need to talk to you about something else."

"Yeah?"

"Business school."

But his younger self just laughed, then turned and strode toward the hangar and Brock woke up.

CHAPTER 20

May 21, 2015

That night after work, Brock slid behind the wheel of his Lexus and ground his teeth. The dashboard clock read ten fifteen. Far later than he wanted it to be. If he had something to show for it, he might feel okay. But all he'd accomplished that day was confirm there was nothing he could do about the volcano about to explode under Black Fedora. And from what he could glean from Karissa and Ron, nothing had changed between his dad and him. So his younger self had done nothing.

Brock glanced at the time again. Should check in with Karissa. She didn't pick up so he hung up and called again. This time she did, a heavy distance in her voice.

"Where have you been?"

"The office."

"Working late again."

"Yeah, trying to build an ark."

"The flood is coming, isn't it?" She went silent for a few seconds. "And there's nothing you can do to stop it."

"I won't quit trying till the waves bury me. I'll figure out a way. I promise."

"Okay."

Brock turned onto the freeway. "How are you?"

"I'm good."

Her tone said the opposite.

"I don't believe you."

"No, don't worry about me, I'm fine."

"Liar."

"Don't worry about me, please." The sigh that sailed through the phone told him not to push it.

"Okay."

"How soon will you be home?"

"Twenty minutes." Brock pulled onto 405 and merged into a light flow of traffic. "What are you doing?"

"Tyson's out. So I'm just sitting here. Thinking."

"That's what worries me." Brock laughed. She didn't join him. "See you in a few."

The line went dead without her saying good-bye, and Brock tried to steel himself against a conversation he guessed was coming. One he'd already had with her a million times; one he wasn't up for having again right now. The talk about the nest going empty when college stole Tyson away from them, and what she would do with her life now that her identity as a mom was vanishing. He knew she needed to process it, also knew he didn't need to do much more than just listen, but with the pressure of Black Fedora pounding down on his brain, he wasn't up for another spin through the same water they'd rowed through so many times before.

He put in the *Young Hearts* CD and tried to enjoy the music, but even "Fly Like an Eagle" didn't help his mood.

He turned onto Sutherland Street, which offered glimpses of Lake Washington, and slowed down. Lights on a smattering of boats far out on the water winked at him as if they knew something he didn't. A few minutes later he pulled into the garage and sat with his hands on the wheel, and sent out a silent request. *I'm tired. But she needs me. Your strength, your understanding, your wisdom.*

Brock pushed through the door from the garage into the kitchen and squinted into the darkness. No lights were on, Karissa's usual Jeff Johnson music wasn't playing, and the TV wasn't on either. Just silence. Not a good sign. He stopped in the kitchen and poured himself a glass of wine, and one for her as well.

"Karissa?"

Brock strolled to the bottom of the stairs and called her name, but there was no answer. He clomped up the stairs to the halfway point and called her name again. Again no response. Brock descended and ambled past his den. Next he tried their media room, but why would she be sitting there when he couldn't hear anything coming from the TV speakers? Where was she? He went back past his den to the stairs and climbed them two at a time.

"Karissa?"

He called louder as he went down the hall, then into their bedroom, but there was still no answer. On the veranda? No. He went back downstairs and was about to go into the kitchen when he heard a faint noise from behind him. Did it come from the den? He spun and walked back and glanced again at the lamp that was on in the corner. Wait. He'd missed it the first time. That lamp was on? He never left that lamp on.

He stepped inside and caught movement out of the corner of his eye to his left. Karissa. She sat in the shadows in the brown suede love seat she'd bought for him three Christmases ago. Her legs were tucked underneath her, shoulders slumped. Her hair was tied into a ponytail and she wore his ancient University of Washington Huskies sweatshirt.

Both her hands were wrapped around a cup he'd bought her ages ago during a trip they'd taken to Victoria, BC. The soft glow from the lamp across the room didn't provide enough light to tell him what her expression was, but her body language shouted the answer. Her gaze was straight ahead.

"Karissa?" Brock stepped into his den and set their wine glasses on his desk. "Didn't you hear me calling you?"

She nodded and kept staring out the window at the light rain splattering against the glass.

"Why didn't you answer?"

Her only response was to take a sip of her tea.

"What's going on?"

Still silence.

"Do you want to be alone? You're thinking about Tyson going off to school, right?" Brock slid out of his coat. "Do you need to talk about it? You're going to make it, you know."

Karissa shifted and set the cup down, glanced at him, then focused on the window again. She wiped her cheek.

"It's going to be okay. He'll be home for weekends, home for Christmas, spring break. And you'll find new hobbies and —"

"It's not that."

"Then what is it?"

She turned and stared at him for a long time before answering. "Money is like gold leaf covering wood that is rotting underneath. And our gold leaf is blowing away."

"What are you talking about?" Brock took two halting steps into the room.

"Our money has kept me alive. It's allowed me to do things for Tyson and other people. Allowed me to buy things I want and go on trips I wanted to go on." Karissa drank more of her tea. "It's a salve for us. For me. It's been an ointment that numbs the truth, keeps the pain from registering. Allows us to trudge on down the path, never noticing the gangrene spreading in our feet. Without it . . ."

Brock settled into the chair across from Karissa and waited, but she didn't continue.

"We're going to survive. Even if I can't save this company, I promise. We will figure out a way to keep most of our lifestyle, and even if we go totally bust, I can start over, rebuild, create —"

"You don't get it, do you? Didn't you hear

176

what I just said? It's not about our lifestyle."

"Then help me understand what it's about."

The silence stretched out, but Brock stayed quiet. Finally Karissa spoke.

"I had coffee with Britt today."

"Oh?"

"She asked me a question and it uncovered something deep I didn't even know was there. Or didn't want to admit was there."

"What was the question?"

"It was simple." Karissa glanced at each wall of Brock's den. "We were talking about how we've supported our husbands' hopes and dreams and careers, and Britt asked me, 'How does Brock support you and your dreams? What does he do to keep you going? How does he really show he appreciates everything you've done for him over the years?' "

"What did you say?" Brock rose and made to join her on the couch.

"No." Karissa jabbed a finger at his chair. "You stay there."

He sat back down and repeated himself. "What did you tell her?"

"The truth." For the first time since he'd entered the room, she looked him in the eyes.

"And that's when the gold fluttered away,

and I saw what was underneath. The thing I'd never seen before. Or seen but never admitted it to myself."

"Is that what's been bothering you?"

"A lot of things have been bothering me. It's just another on the list."

But he knew it wasn't just another item on the list. It was *the* item.

"I'm sorry."

"You're sorry? Wow, thank you. That makes it all better." Karissa shifted in her chair. "You gave your heart to that wretched company."

"So we could have —"

"What about my life, Brock? The things I dreamed about doing? I put my entire existence on hold for twenty-seven years so you could build that company, and what do I have to show for it? Soon it's going to just be you and me. And you have your career. You're a rock star of the coffee world — and like you just said, you might be able to rebuild even if you can't save Black Fedora, but me? What do I have?"

"I thought you wanted to be a mom."

Karissa smacked her teacup down on the saucer and a smattering of tea spilled onto a stack of papers. He was smart enough not to react.

"I did want to be a mom. It was my dream

to be a mom and pour myself into Tyson, and I did, but you drained me. So many ideas, so much pressure for Black Fedora to break out, so much time hearing about your battles with Ron, all the dinners and parties and grand openings. Events I loathed going to, but I still went. Every time. I'm worn out, Brock."

"I remember asking you once what you wanted to do, and you told me you weren't sure. I would have supported you —"

"How many times, Brock? Once?" Karissa turned in the love seat, held up a finger, and fully faced him. "You asked one time! Then you checked it off your list and moved on to the next hobby, or dream, or big idea on your list. It's always been about you. And about that company. I never worried about you having an affair with another woman, because your mistress was right in front of me all the time. Black Fedora is the love of your life, not me."

"Not true." Brock again tried to rise and go to her, and again Karissa stopped him.

"I asked you about your dreams every day. I encouraged you, believed in you, listened to you as you told me about your and Ron's plans to turn Black Fedora into a company far beyond what your dad ever dreamed it could be. I put up with the seventy-hour workweeks, the vacations you always put off."

Brock stayed quiet as the truth seeped through his defenses. What could he say? Anything that came to mind seemed stupid.

"What do you want to do? You can do it now. Take classes, learn how to —"

"You are such a man. The years are gone, Brock."

"Start now. It's never too late."

"Really?" She poked her legs. "You think I can become a dancer at my age?"

"You . . . I didn't . . ."

"Didn't know?" A sad little laugh escaped her mouth. "Because you didn't ask about my dreams. Because there was only ever room for yours."

She looked at him with eyes of sadness, which was worse than accusation. When she turned away to stare at his wall of achievements again, she spoke in a whisper.

"I was always the wind. You never were. And I have no wind left."

CHAPTER 21

Brock tried to watch *SportsCenter,* but he couldn't get his mind off Karissa's words. Was he that bad? Was it his job to pull her dreams out of her? After wrestling with his thoughts for an hour, he shuffled upstairs intending to go to bed, but something stopped him before he stepped into their bedroom. A distinct feeling shot through him. He couldn't name it, but definitely an impression that he needed to go up into the attic.

He eased down the hall and entered the empty bedroom next to Tyson's. He walked into the room's closet and pulled the cord that released the ladder that led up to their attic. He plugged one ear against the screech of the metal ladder as it opened up. Obviously it had been a few years since either Karissa or he had been up there.

His dad's words from the recurring dream streamed across his mind's eye as he gazed up into the attic: *Embrace it, Brock, even though it will be difficult. Face the truth though it will be painful, for the truth will set you free.*

The rungs groaned as he climbed. When he reached the top, Brock fumbled for the string, found it, and pulled. Light filled the eight-by-eight-foot space. He'd carpeted it years ago and put in shelving to store all the memorabilia he couldn't part with. He'd forgotten about the chair he'd brought up. A black leather chair brought up in pieces and assembled by a friend of his who used to work at an upholstery shop. If they ever sold the place, the chair would stay.

Brock settled into the chair and glanced around the small space. So many books he'd never get around to reading. Hot Wheels cars from when he was a kid, old pictures of the football and baseball teams he and Morgan had played on. He picked up a photo from 1980 and smiled. The only year he played hockey, after being talked into it by Lennie Buck.

There he stood, with Lennie's arm around his shoulder, big stupid grins on both their faces. Lennie missing a tooth. Brock had kept all his teeth. Lennie claimed that showed Brock wasn't serious about the game. He pawed deeper into the box and found an old puck, scarred by too many games outside on the street. He sighed. Why had he hung onto all this junk for all these years? He hadn't missed it. But now that he saw it, he was glad he hadn't tossed it out.

He glanced at his old yearbooks. He pulled out the one from his senior year and opened it. Seconds later his fingers found the page Sheila had signed. Her note and the drawing took up most of the page. It'd been years since he last thought of the image she created.

She'd drawn a picture of a lion's head and a unicorn's head next to each other in semi-profile. Brock had forgotten how talented she was. The animals' faces were strong, their eyes pulsing with strength and purpose. Lion and unicorn. That's what Sheila had said they were.

"Amazing," he'd told her as they sat on the back deck of her parents' house going through their yearbooks together right after graduation. "I'll keep this page of my yearbook forever."

"Glad you like it, because that's just the warm-up."

"What?"

Sheila rose from the picnic table, sauntered into the house, and returned a minute later holding a picture frame with its back to him. She smiled and slowly spun it around till the front faced him. It was the lion and unicorn again, but this time twice as large, and with such detail it was hard to believe it wasn't a photo. In the lower corner she'd signed it, just below a line that said, "Forever."

Brock closed the yearbook and glanced around the attic for Sheila's piece. He squinted at the small space between two sets of boxes to his right. There. Brock rose, stepped over to the boxes, reached behind them, and pulled out Sheila's framed drawing.

Karissa asked why he kept the picture, and he had never given her a good answer. Probably because he didn't know why. Now he did. Time to get rid of it.

He turned it over. Brock didn't remember Sheila writing anything on the back, but it wouldn't hurt to check. Nope. Nothing. Wait. The upper corner of the backing was torn, and he thought he saw writing underneath. He set the picture down flat on the ottoman and ripped back the paper. Bold, fluid script covered the back of the white mat. Sheila's handwriting.

Brock blinked twice and read.

Dear Brock,

Do you want to know my silly, Disneyland, fairy-princess dream? That on our wedding day, I'll peel back the paper and show you this note. Am I crazy? Probably. But I love you and can't imagine life apart. Do you feel the same? You tell me you do, but how can we really know when we've only just graduated from high school? I don't know, but at the same time I do know. Don't you? Please tell me you do too.

Please tell me when we go off to our separate colleges, the distance will only make us grow closer. Tell me that the next four years will fly by like an eagle and our spirits will carry us together during the time we're apart. Tell me our graduation from college will be here in an instant and we'll get married two months later on a hot July day. Tell me?

But if you're reading this alone, and I'm not beside you, please know that this eighteen-year-old girl loved you with everything she had inside. If you have discovered what I wrote here, and I'm not beside you, I hope you are happy. I hope you've found someone who makes your life complete and loves you like you deserve to be loved.

And if you're reading this years from now, decades from now, and we're not together, maybe you'll look me up and see what I'm doing, and what I've become, and you'll tell me what you've become. Because once you give a person part of your heart, they have that piece forever, don't you think?

So you have a piece of me now, and a year from now, and thirty years from now. Keep that piece of my heart safe, okay? Just like I'll keep the piece of your heart you've given me safe.

All of my love, now and I so hope

forever,

Sheila

Brock fell back into the chair and took in a long breath. Did she have a piece of his heart still? He didn't need to ask the question. Yes, she did. He'd made the right choice to break up with her, hadn't he? There was no question he had. But if there was no question, then why was he asking it? What if he'd waited to see if she would turn her life over to the Lord? What if he'd broken up but not been so quick to rush into a relationship with Karissa? What if, what if, what if . . .

He had to stop. The only roads this type

of thinking would lead him to would take him over a cliff.

"God, need your help here. Tempted to go down some pretty dangerous paths."

But no help came.

CHAPTER 22

May 22, 2015

The first e-mail Brock opened on Friday morning at the office stopped him cold.

Dear Brock,

I've been debating whether to e-mail you for five days. But I think I need to, so here goes.

I'm sorry. I never should have kissed you at the reunion. I don't know what came over me, but it wasn't right. Forgive me? Please? And yet at the same time, if I'm honest — and I need to be — I don't regret doing it.

When I saw you again, all the emotions that we used to share came rushing back. All the memories, you know? I know you do, because I saw it in your eyes.

I'm not saying I want to see you again. That's not fair to you and Karissa.

I guess I'm just trying to say what if. What if I'd become a Christian earlier? How differently would our lives have turned out? If we could turn back the clock, what would my life look like now? What would ours look like? Do you think about that?

Maybe I shouldn't have even written this e-mail to you. But now I have, and I'm thinking I'll probably have the courage to hit send.

With love, and thoughts of what might have been,

Sheila

Brock hesitated, then deleted the e-mail. No response was the only response that made sense. In his mind at least. His heart screamed something different and images rushed into his mind that he could stop, but didn't. Karissa divorcing him. Being alone. Seeing Sheila, just for a casual dinner, then things progressing to . . .

"Stop it!" He pushed himself away from his desk and pounded a fist into his leg.

It didn't matter what he felt. He wouldn't go down that what-if road, because he knew where it ended. He'd traveled over it in his mind too often since the reunion. He and

Karissa would make it. So would Black Fedora.

If only he believed those things were true.

Brock spent the rest of the day going over the company's financials again. It was hopeless. After he pushed the papers to the side and minimized the spreadsheets on his laptop, Brock pulled up ESPN on his computer to find a story on the Seahawks and the experts' predictions on their coming season, anything to distract him.

A few clicks later he landed on a series of interviews with ex-pro quarterbacks who were asked what they'd do differently if they could play their career over again. A few said they wouldn't have changed anything. A couple of others mentioned investing their money more wisely, but the last QB locked Brock's gaze on the screen.

"Honestly, I wish I could go back in time and talk to my younger self. Convince that kid to take business classes instead of majoring in doing just enough to pass. When you're that age you think you'll play forever." The QB smiled. "But the good news is, I'm awake now. I'm taking classes, I'm learning those skills, but it's too late to save for a few things I'd like to have."

Brock closed his eyes. He had to try again to talk to his younger self about business school. Could it be more obvious? For the first time in an age, he felt hope. If the show on ESPN wasn't a sign from God, he didn't know what was. It was as if God was speaking to him directly through that interview, telling him that as crazy as it sounded, he had to dream again, and this time convince Young Brock to go to business school. Chance of it working? None, most likely. The idea was ludicrous, but why not try?

Up till now he'd doubted, wondered if this whole thing of talking to himself in dreams wasn't just his brain sliding off the table of sanity, but when night came, he would lock himself into this rocket ship, follow God's lead, and ride it into the heavens.

Brock's cell phone interrupted his thoughts. It was Ron. Interesting timing.

"What?"

"Reminder. We sign papers this afternoon at four."

"We need to talk about that."

"Nothing to talk about. Please, get that through your thick skull."

"We can't sign, Ron."

"Yeah we can. And we will. Today. Four."

The line went dead. Brock buzzed Michelle.

"Do you know where Ron is?"

"Working from home today. Won't be in

191

till just before the signing."

Brock snatched his keys off his desk and strode out his door. No way would he sign without taking a shot in the world of dreams.

When Ron's wife, Shelly, opened their door twenty-five minutes later, she gave Brock a grim smile.

"Things okay between you two?" Shelly asked.

"Sure."

"Lying doesn't become you, Brock."

"No, I mean, a few things aren't great, but a few are." He shrugged. "We're brothers. That's how brothers are. It always turns out okay in the end. You know how it is between us."

"That's what always worries me."

"Where is he?"

"Take a wild guess." Shelly tilted her head to the left.

Brock motioned to the side with his thumb. "I think I'll just walk around instead of going through your house."

"Have fun."

Brock strolled around the side of his brother's home, across the lush grass, and down the slight incline that led to the back of Ron's sprawling estate. His property was just shy of ten acres — at least till the bank came and took it away — and the backyard took up nine and a half. And of those, eight were used for three short, immaculate par-three golf holes.

The scent of freshly cut grass surrounded Brock. A hint of wind off the lake toyed with the flags. Ron waved with a golf club, then turned back to focus on the ball teed up at his feet. He drew the club back, made a full turn of his shoulders, then started slowly back down, accelerating as the club got closer to the ball. Then *thwack!* The white orb rocketed off the tee toward the green 125 yards away. Brock hadn't seen many smoother swings than Ron's. Ron teed up another ball as Brock reached his brother.

Ron motioned toward the ball. "Care to hit a few with me?"

"Hardly." Brock scoffed. "Even with those lessons you bought me a few years back, I've never come close to figuring out this game."

"So what? Doesn't mean you can't get out on the course with me. Have some fun."

"It's not fun."

"What isn't fun? Having to put a leash on your ego because I'm better than you at golf? Admitting that you'll never, ever beat me?"

"Not now, Ron."

His brother turned and gazed into his eyes. "I'm just saying someday I'd love to play a round of golf with you. Share the experience. Not as competitors. Just as brothers."

"Yeah, sure. Maybe in our next life."

Ron turned back and sighed. Then he loosened his grip for a second, regripped, and sent another TaylorMade golf ball skyward. It seemed to hang in the air longer than physics said it should, then dropped from the sky and settled fifteen yards to the right of the pin.

"Nice."

"I don't know what's wrong with my swing." Ron kicked the grass. "Everything's headed to the right these days."

"That wasn't a good shot?"

Ron shook his head, a little smile playing on his lips. "I know, I should loosen up about it. But golf does that to you. That little voice in your head says, 'I can get better' and you're never satisfied."

"Why didn't you ever try to turn pro?"

"Real pro?"

"Yeah. You're amazingly good."

"But not amazingly great." Ron teed up another ball, and seconds later it soared toward the green. It stopped five yards away.

194

"The pros are so far beyond me. I'd get on the courses they play and maybe come away after four rounds of my best golf five over par. Meanwhile, the winning score would be sixteen or seventeen under. Plus the amateur tournaments have a purity to them that the cash tourneys don't."

"Like Bobby Jones."

"Something like that." Ron grimaced.

"We need to talk about the signing, Ron."

Ron pointed at the three-tiered putting green dotted with eight tiny flags in the center of his spread. "Let's talk and putt at the same time."

They strolled the twenty yards to Ron's putting green in silence. When they reached the fringe, Brock said, "I think I have a way to fix things."

"We've been over this."

"Give me the weekend."

"Today. Four o'clock. We sign."

"I have a plan that will let us keep the company. We won't have to sell."

"Enlighten me, then." Ron folded his arms. "What's the plan?"

"I can't explain it."

"Yes, you can." Ron put his hands on his hips. "If I'm going to make an excuse, I want to know why I'm making it. Every delay puts more power in the buyers' hands.

And just in case you've forgotten, Dad gave me fifty-one percent of this company. This is not a democracy. If I have to sign without you, I will."

"That will make things more complicated for you."

"Which is why I'll give you the weekend as long as you tell me your plan."

"Trust me." Brock eased over to the fringe of the putting green. "I truly can't explain it."

"Then trust me, I'm signing this afternoon."

From Ron's perspective, there was no reason to wait. They had a deal that would keep them from total disaster. But a ten-cents-on-the-dollar buyout wasn't much of a solution.

Yes, waiting another day always gave room for the buyers to change their minds or decide to squeeze Black Fedora harder. But it was more about Ron lording his fifty-one percent over Brock's head. It was about winning, just as it had always been between them.

"Okay." Brock opened his hands in resignation. "Here's my plan. I'm going to convince my younger self to go to business school so that when 1989 rolls around, Dad will give fifty-one percent of this company to me instead of to you. That way you never fly the Black Fedora plane into the tarmac at five hundred miles per hour, and we won't even be having this discussion."

"Funny." Ron gave a mock smile. "You still on that kick that you could have run this company better than me?" Ron's head fell back and he gave a bitter laugh. "I would like to have seen you try. We'd have been working in a bowling alley store a year after dad died if you'd taken control."

"Really."

"You develop coffee flavors, Brock!" Ron tossed his putter ten yards to the right. "You work on marketing campaigns. You schmooze with our buyers and give wonderful media interviews. Those skills have helped make us both a very comfortable living, but those skills are not the same needed to navigate the world of business. You'd have been chewed up so badly there wouldn't be anything to spit out."

"The natural ability is there."

"So you want to take over now? In the fifty-ninth second of the eleventh hour? Yeah, why not, Brock? I'll give you your extra time, even if you won't tell me what your plan is, just because I want to watch you implode." Ron yanked off his golf glove and shoved it into his back pocket. "You want the reality? Just between you and me?"

"Oh yeah, that's exactly what I want. Your version of reality."

"Dad saw the truth from the time we were kids. All growing up. Then in our twenties when we started working here. He watched us! He knew you didn't have the skills to run Black Fedora. I did. So he chose me. And you've hated him and me ever since."

It would have been far less painful if Ron had slugged him in the gut. Brock went quiet and fought to keep his emotions from spilling over.

"Dad was blind." Brock tried to breathe steady. "He never truly saw my gifts, never saw me for who I am. Never believed in me the way he believed in you. It wasn't fun being the black sheep."

Ron's face softened. "Yes, he chose me to run the company. It doesn't mean he didn't love you."

"I agree. It just means he loved me less."

"Don't believe that lie, Brockie." Ron's voice was quiet.

Brock blinked. Ron's childhood name for Brock. Ron hadn't called him that for years. It was his brother's way of reaching out, but too much had passed between them.

"I gotta go." Brock shifted his weight but Ron held up his hand.

"I think there's more to say."

"There isn't."

"Why not?"

Why? Because the conversation had already ripped off too many layers of Brock's heart. Brock turned his face toward the sky. The clouds had covered the sun completely and a light rain began to fall.

"I gotta go." He strode off the green across the backyard toward his car.

Ron caught up to Brock, then stepped around in front of him. The hard veneer had returned. "You need to face this. Need to know how Dad truly felt about you. Yes, he and I were closer than you two, but that doesn't mean —"

"Let it go, Ron. This is over."

"No, we're not done." Ron jabbed a finger at Brock. "Talk to me. I know it's been years for us, but we are flesh and blood. Why won't you believe Dad loved you?"

"You want to break me down? Want some true confession time? Fine. You're right, Dad breaking my heart is exactly what this is all about."

Ron shifted his weight and Brock could tell his brother was fighting to stay kind. "Okay. I get it. Like I said, he and I were closer."

"Closer? He and I were never anything

but worlds apart."

Ron continued as if he hadn't heard Brock. "And yes, he wasn't the greatest dad when we were younger. But think about his past. He's an only child. His mom says to his father, 'Leave him alone, he's mine. And then Dad's physically and emotionally abused by her? No siblings. No cousins. No one but our psycho grandmother to teach him about life? He's in his midthirties on the outside but a little boy on the inside, trying to raise us without a clue how to do it. Can't you comprehend that? Emotionally he was younger than we were."

Brock scowled. "I get it, but it doesn't change what he did to me. You weren't as old. It didn't affect you anywhere close to the same degree."

"I know his nervous breakdown did serious damage to you. But give him some credit. He beat the illness. He got his mind back and started living out the things he was hearing at church. Made a commitment to the Person instead of the institution and lived for God the rest of his life. Major life shift, or don't you remember?"

"Remember? Do I remember?" Brock snorted. "You really truly don't understand, do you, Ronnie? Being two years older meant I saw and went through things that didn't even touch you. I had to be strong for you. For Mom. I shielded you when the bombs went off all around us."

Ron rubbed his face. "I've never really thought about that. But still —"

"Nope." Brock walked around Ron and strode away. "There's no *but still,* there's only changing the past."

"You do that, Brock. Change the past. Go have a great conversation with yourself. But Monday you're coming back to the land of reality and we're signing the papers."

CHAPTER 23

Brock wove through traffic toward home as he tried to squash the dread rising in his throat. He had no option: he had to dream tonight and find his younger self. Convince him to go to business school.

He pushed the thoughts from his mind and tried to concentrate on his upcoming dinner with Karissa. *Out* to dinner. Not at home. He'd suggested it as a way to reconnect, put some wind in the sails. Earlier in the day when he'd talked her into the dinner she'd been aloof, more than usual, and he'd thought the dinner suggestion would do the opposite. He couldn't make sense of it.

Ten minutes later he jogged toward Cutters, which overlooked the sound just west of Pike Place Market. Brock scrunched up his shoulders to keep the rain from running down the back of his neck and glanced at the sky. Patches of blue were visible between the rain clouds. The sun might still break out in time for reds and golds to be splashed over the Olympic Mountains.

He stepped into the crab house and glanced around the lobby. Karissa wasn't there. Probably already at their table. But as he was halfway to the restaurant's front desk, she emerged from the ladies' room. Were her eyes red? Hard to tell in the muted light. She spotted him and blinked multiple times as they approached each other.

"Hi." He leaned forward to give her a kiss and she offered him her cheek.

"Hi." She gave him a weak smile.

The maître d's feet slid along the carpet right up to them. He nodded. "I can show you to your table."

"You ready to sit down?"

She shook her head. "Not really hungry. Are you?"

He hadn't thought about it, but now that he did, Brock realized he was famished. He'd skipped lunch, and breakfast had been coffee and a bagel smeared with strawberry cream cheese.

He smiled. "No, I'm good."

"Don't lie, Brock. You do it too much as it is."

"Fine. I'm hungry." He lowered his voice. "Your turn. Is this a conversation we want to have in a restaurant, or in private?"

Karissa hesitated for only a moment. "Private."

Brock turned to the maître d', apologized for the last-second cancellation, and offered to pay a bit of restitution, but the man refused.

When they reached the street, Brock motioned to the right. "Rain has stopped. How 'bout we walk down to the waterfront?"

"I was thinking Golden Gardens."

"Okay. Do you want to drive together?"

Karissa shook her head again. "Let's meet there."

"Why?"

"I'll see you there."

All the way to the park, Brock fought the feeling of dread swirling around him. The fifteen minutes it took to get there felt like hours. Finally they reached the park and Brock pulled in next to Karissa's Honda and got out. She already stood ten feet in front of her car. Neither of them spoke till they'd reached the end of the park and settled onto a green bench that was still dry enough to sit on and looked out on the water.

"I have to talk to you about something," she said.

He gazed at her hair, the curve of her ears, her petite nose, her olive skin. And her eyes, which he'd lost himself in from the first day they'd met. Karissa blinked and glanced furtively at him, then pulled on her earlobe. "I can't do it anymore."

Brock's hands went cold. It didn't take a genius to know where this was going. "Do what?"

"I need some time."

"I don't under— You're not serious, are you?" But he knew she was deadly serious.

"This is harder than I thought it would be. Way harder." Tears pooled in her eyes.

"We can work this out, Karissa."

"I'm sure we can." Karissa took his hands. "I'm not saying I want a divorce, just some time."

"What does that mean?" A boulder dropped into Brock's stomach.

"I want a separation." Tears spilled onto her cheeks. Karissa stood and walked to the edge of the sand. She slumped forward as small sobs escaped. He didn't speak. Finally she turned and came back to him, her cheeks wet.

"Why?" Brock tried to breathe steadily. "I don't understand."

"I need you to decide if you want us, Brock."

"What are you saying? Of course I do."

She bit her lower lip and gave infinitesimal shakes of her head. "No. First, you want to save Black Fedora and continue to rule the coffee world. Second, you want to beat Ron. I come third, Tyson comes fourth. I need you to decide if you can make your family first."

"It's not true. You and Tyson come first."

"You need to go." She snatched her purse off the park bench. "I need to go."

Karissa spun and scurried to her car and slipped inside. Her brake lights flashed red as she exited the parking lot, and in that instant a resolve exploded inside Brock and filled him. He would dream that night, and in it, he would fix everything.

CHAPTER 24

August 1987

Brock pulled off the headphones connected to his Walkman cassette player, spun, and glanced behind him. No one stared at him from anywhere on the vast expanse of grass in Bothell's Blyth Park. No one lurked in the shadows behind the line of Douglas fir trees that stood where the lawn met the forest with their gaze fixed on his movements. But it felt like it. What was his problem?

None of the dozen people spread out on the thick grass having picnics and throwing Frisbees in the late May sunshine were the least interested in him — unless Brock counted the golden Lab that cocked his head and looked quizzically in his direction. Brock turned back to his *Seattle Times*, focused on the sports section, and tried to ignore the sensation of someone watching that continued to pepper his mind.

Looked like the Seahawks' schedule would

be a decent one in the fall. As long as Knox figured out how to get Dave Krieg to quit fumbling and Largent kept hauling in passes. With Curt Warner slicing through defenses, the Hawks had a good chance of finishing near the top of the AFC West.

There it was again, the feeling that eyes were zeroed in on the back of his head. He concentrated, trying to picture in his mind the exact spot behind him where the feeling came from. Center. No, a little left of center. Close by? No. It came from behind the trees, past the swing set and near the trail that wound through the forest to the east.

He closed his eyes and tried to keep from laughing. This was ridiculous. Who had the ability to figure out the spot where a non-existent person stared at him? It was all in his head. But the image of a person who stood two hundred yards behind him, shielded between two hemlock trees, stayed burned into his mind's eye.

Brock dropped his paper, whirled, and fixed his gaze on the spot he'd seen in his mind. Yes. There! Movement. He stood, squinted, and this time hit pay dirt. Was it him? Yes. It was the guy who claimed to be an older version of himself. Now the guy was stalking him? He rose to his feet and strode toward Future Brock.

■ ■ ■ ■

Brock stood between two hemlock trees on the edge of the lawn and stared at his younger self. There were so many things he wanted to tell himself, but he couldn't say too much. If he really could influence his present by talking to himself in the past, he needed to choose his words carefully.

The solution was simple — get himself to go to business school instead of getting a post-grad marketing degree — but convincing his younger self he had to go wouldn't be easy.

Young Brock whirled and stared directly at him before Brock had time to react. He'd been spotted. Time to engage. He walked out from behind the trees and toward his younger version, who had risen and came toward him. His younger self stopped when they were five yards apart.

"Why are you stalking me?"

"I wasn't. I'm not."

"So hiding behind a tree, staring at people, is normal behavior in the future?"

"How did you know I was there? In the trees."

"I felt you." A mocking look and a wiggle of his fingers. "I suppose since we're the same, your presence alerted my subconscious mind. Wooooooo."

"I don't expect you to believe me, but I want you to listen."

"Sure, why not? You're entertaining and you're harmless so far. Most people would've slapped a restraining order on you." Young Brock playfully pointed a finger at Brock. "But we're not most people, are we?"

"No, we are not."

"So what can I do for you, F. B.?"

"I need you to change something else in the future. Last night, God confirmed exactly what it is and what needs to be done."

"This ought to be good."

"Last time we talked, I told you Ron had let our coffee company nose-dive into the ground. Do you remember that?"

"It was just two months ago that you stalked me at Harvey Airfield."

"Just two months?"

"Nice!" His younger self slapped his jeans. "I didn't know I had that talent."

"What talent?" Brock frowned.

"Incredible acting." Young Brock rolled the sports section into a tube, held it up, and dropped his voice. "I'd like to thank the Academy . . ."

"I'm not acting."

"Right, right. Forgot." Young Brock cocked his head and winked.

"Ron and I start running the company and things go well, extremely well. But it turns out someone stole all the money out from under us, and now we're going down like the *Titanic.*"

"What does that have to do with me?"

"You have to go to business school. You can fix it. Prevent it from ever happening. You need to run the company, not Ron."

"I hate to be the Needle Man here, Brock Senior, but I gotta." His younger self squeezed his thumb and forefinger together and jutted them in Brock's direction.

"You're going to pop my balloon."

"Exactly. Sorry. No biz school in my future."

"It's the only way to change things. It's my only shot left. *Our* only shot."

"Yeah, well, like I just said, business school and Brock are never going to happen. And if you really are me, you know why."

A stray Frisbee landed at their feet, and Young Brock picked it up and slung it back to three teens forty yards away.

"It doesn't matter. You have to go. Just like you went on those fishing trips."

"Just one trip so far, Future Me. A fishing boat's an up and back. Business school is the slow boat to China with a captain who wouldn't want me on board."

"What does that mean?"

"Why do I have to explain this to you?" Young Brock settled onto the lush lawn and plucked a long blade of grass. "Ron is the one Dad wants in business school, not me. Or did you forget? Plus, I'm not built for it, and I have no desire to study business."

"Business is not accounting." Brock sat and leaned in. "It's not all facts and figures. In truth, it's very little of that. Business is people — knowing them, understanding them, motivating them — and you're good at that. Better than you know."

"Wow! Another talent I didn't know I had."

Brock wasn't making any headway, and he had no idea how much longer the dream would last.

"Hey, Future Brock. Wake up." His younger self snapped his fingers. "Can we talk about something else? You're not convincing me to go to business school, so how 'bout we drop the subject?"

"It's the only reason I'm here."

"Then how 'bout I go back to my newspaper and you go back to the future?"

Not much time left. His body was stirring, trying to wake up, and he knew he wasn't going to have another chance. *Lord, help!*

Brock glanced around the park, searching for inspiration. Yes! There it was. He turned to himself. "Give me three more minutes. Then I'll be gone."

"Okay, lay it on me, F. B." Brock leaned back in the thick grass, resting on his elbows.

Brock waved his hand over the park and leaned close to his younger self. "Picture yourself on this playground at four years old. Imagine you're that small again. Can you do it? Your little heart pounds with anticipation of what an hour in the park will bring, but not an atom of hesitation as you traipse from the concrete of the parking lot onto the thick grass. You stare at the merry-go-round and think of the speed that comes from sitting on the very edge and hanging over the ground as your friends spin you as fast as they can. Then you spot the swings, and the rush of how high they've taken you in the past fills your little mind.

"But then the tiniest hint of fear inside you starts to grow, and everything else on the playground melts away — because now you've spotted the slide."

He pointed over Brock's shoulder at what had to be one of the longest playground slides in the country. At least fifteen feet high and forty feet long.

"Picture that slide, but three times as long as it is now, and three times as high. Because that's the perspective you'd have if you were in your four-year-old body. Can you feel it drawing you in like a superpowered magnet? But there's another part of your younger self that wants to hold back, stay safe. The part that begs you not to risk the scraped knee if you crash coming off the slide. The part that wants to hide from the fear you'd feel standing at the top. The part that wants to keep your little four-year-old soul from feeling like it was standing on top of the world's highest building, wind whipping through your hair, your stomach squeezed like a walnut in a nutcracker and your heart hammering in your little-boy chest. But when you were young, you never gave in to the fear. You always launched yourself over the edge.

"And yet the slide in your own life right now stirs great fear in you. Because it is now higher than it ever was in your childhood. So you don't climb. You stay in the shadows at the base of the slide and watch in safety the rare man or woman who ventures to the top, then goes over the edge.

"You're standing on the edge right now, Brock. Deep inside there's a desire to grasp the brass ring of Black Fedora. To put yourself in a position to run the company. To best your brother in the arena of business. But your fear strangles you. What if Ron does better at business school? What if you give everything you have, and your dad still chooses Ron to run the company?"

His younger self's mouth opened slightly, his breaths came a hair faster. This was working.

"You are the older brother. It's your birthright, not Ron's. And if you do this, you'll shift the course of your relationship with your dad. It will grow. You'll have that connection you've longed for. It's time to choose, Brock. Choose to face the fear, and step into what you were meant to do, or stay in the shadows for the rest of your life."

Brock finished his lengthy monologue by squeezing Young Brock's shoulder. It felt as though strength flowed out from him into the younger man's core. Then he gazed at his younger self till he looked up.

"I know ninety-nine percent of you doesn't believe I'm who I say I am, or that this can be truly happening. Much of me feels the same. But if God has given us this gift, then we must take it and run with it like the wind."

"Anything else?"

"Yes, the most important." Brock fixed his gaze deep into his younger self's eyes. "Karissa."

"What about her?"

"Love her well. Put her first. Before the company, before your drive to best Ron, before everything but God."

As Brock uttered those final words, the piercing sound of his phone alarm shattered the dream, and he woke under a shroud of fear as to where he would find himself when he opened his eyes.

CHAPTER 25

September 2, 1987

Wednesday morning at ten thirty, Brock walked into Java Spot, pulled a packet from under his arm, and tossed it on the counter in front of Morgan.

"What's that?"

"Copy of a business-school application." He sat on one of the stools and grinned. "Mine."

Morgan pulled the packet closer and opened it. "UW?"

"Yeah."

"I hear it's big bucks to go there. And tough to get in."

"Right on both counts. But it's one of the best."

"Makes sense then." Morgan pointed at him and gave a fake smile.

"I'm picking up a smattering of sarcasm in your voice."

"You think?" Morgan leaned forward,

tapped the packet, then pushed it back across the counter. "That's not you."

"Maybe it is. I'm thinking about going."

"Why?"

"Because someday my dad is going to retire, and he'll hand over the reins of the company to Ron and me, but one of us will have to be at the helm."

"You can't run it together?" Morgan turned and poured them both a cup of dark roast.

"That's the plan, that we do run it together, but one of us will have control. Dad doesn't believe in an equal partnership. Says ultimately one of us has to be in charge so when we can't agree on which way to go, someone will be able to pull the trigger."

Morgan opened a bag of breakfast blend and sniffed it, then set it to the side. "And you think your dad will choose Ron?"

"Of course he'll choose Ron." Brock toasted Morgan and took a drink of his coffee. "Unless I change things."

"Have you talked to your dad about it?"

"Oh yeah, sure. He's one hundred percent behind me going to business school. Been begging me to do it."

"Speaking of sarcasm." Morgan sighed. "So maybe your dad doesn't see you as the business type. Is there even the slightest possibility that he's right?"

Brock snatched the packet off the counter. "Thanks for the massive support."

Morgan shrugged. "What does Karissa say about it?"

"That's where I'm headed now."

"She's not going to like it."

"I know, which is why I'd ask you to pray for me if you were a praying man."

"Can't say I'll pray, but I'll wish you good luck." Morgan clapped him on the shoulder. "You're going to need it."

"I need to talk to you about something."

"Okay."

Karissa and he sat overlooking Lake Sammamish. The sun had broken through the clouds, and Brock thought it the perfect setting to talk to her about the new direction he was about to take.

"I bumped into Future Me again."

"Oh yeah?" Karissa laughed. "So this guy still claims to be you."

Brock nodded. "He got pretty passionate about something I need to do."

"What's that?"

"He says I have to go to business school."

"What?" Karissa's tone grew serious. "Business school?"

"Yeah."

"That's not you."

"Exactly what Morgan said." Brock scowled. "Why isn't it me?"

"Are you kidding?" She drew her legs up and sat cross-legged, her hands resting on his knees. "You're only a few units away from getting your marketing degree. You really want to tack another three years of school onto your to-do list? Doing something you've never shown any interest in?"

"Maybe."

"And do you really want to get into competition with Ron? Both of you going to business school? That wouldn't be about business school; it would be about you beating your brother."

"He needs to be beat."

Karissa groaned. "Come on, Brock. Don't give in and take even one step down that trail. It's wide, Brock, and will lead to destruction."

"How can you say that?"

"How much have you prayed about the idea of business school?" She lasered her gaze on him. "Were you even going to talk to me about it?"

"I'm talking to you right now." Brock raised his voice more than he wanted to.

"Let me ask again, have you prayed about it?"

"I'm just thinking about going to business school. It's not like I've made a final decision."

"Final?" Karissa cocked her head and narrowed her eyes. "You've already turned in an application, haven't you?"

Brock rolled his head back and forth and avoided her eyes.

"You haven't made a final decision, huh? Yeah, right. You won't decide till you get accepted, then the decision will be made for you."

"I can beat him, Karissa. Dad will see it, I'll prove it to him, and when it comes time to hand the company over to Ron and me, he'll give me the controlling interest."

"And will that finally tell you your dad loves you?"

"Don't go there."

"Where does that put us?"

"We might be delayed for a bit."

"So we wait another three years to start our life together?"

"Three years isn't going to make a difference when we're talking about the rest of our lives. And if I'm running the company, our lives will be very, very good."

"This isn't right, Brock. I feel it."

"And I feel it *is* right. So who has the direct line to God, and which one of us isn't hearing straight?"

Karissa repeated her question for the third time. "Did you pray about it?"

"I don't need to. This is the path I need to go down. The one we need to go down."

Karissa stood and Brock started to join her.

"No." She pointed at the dock. "Stay here."

She jogged off and Brock watched her till she reached the end of the path. She didn't look back.

CHAPTER 26

May 23, 2015

The alarm on Brock's cell phone woke him Saturday at seven, but it wasn't his alarm. It was Ron. Brock stared at the photo of Ron on the screen and was tempted to ignore it, roll over, and go back to sleep. But Ron wouldn't be calling at this ungodly hour unless it was serious.

"What's wrong?" Brock flopped back on his bed and shut his eyes. "You okay?"

"Me? You're the one who should worry about being okay if you're not two minutes from getting here."

"Getting where?"

"Funny. How close are you to the gate?"

"Gate?" Brock rubbed his eyes and opened them. "Yeah, listen, I realize I just opened my eyes, and my mind is still booting up, but I'm not exactly following you."

Brock rolled out of bed and staggered to his feet. He glanced at Karissa's side of the

223

bed. Empty of course. He'd begged her to come home, but she was resolute that their separation would last at least a month. Wait, the shower was running. Was it possible? Had she come home last night after he fell asleep?

"I gotta go, Ron. I gotta check on Karissa."

"Again, you're funny. Really, my stomach hurts, but Alaska Airlines is leaving for the great white north in twenty-seven minutes with or without us. I'd prefer it be with."

"What are you talking about?" Brock rubbed his eyes again and glanced at the clock on his nightstand. Six and a half hours of sleep, but it felt like he'd slept only three.

"What is wrong with you?" Ron's voice came through the phone ten decibels louder. "The plane is leaving."

"What are you doing at the airport?"

"You're serious, aren't you?"

"Yes. What are you doing?"

"The same thing we've done every year since Dad died. We get on a plane. We fly to Alaska. We go fishing in his honor. We try to get along for most of the trip. We catch fish. We eat them. We toast Dad. We take a few pictures. We come home. Then we plan for the next trip."

As Ron spoke, the heat inside Brock grew

to flammable levels. The dream! Had it worked? *Oh please, yes.*

"What about the company?" Brock sat up straight.

"Ours?"

"Yes, ours!" He spat out the words stronger than he meant to.

"What is your problem?"

"The buyout. Did we sell?"

"Are you always like this at seven a.m.?"

"Just answer me."

"Wake up, Brock." A sigh of disgust filtered through the phone. "Profits of twenty-three million last year weren't enough for you? You think we should sell the company and start something else?" Ron laughed. "Just because pot is legal in Washington doesn't mean you have to smoke it. Duuuuuude!"

Hope exploded inside Brock. As insane as it sounded, even to himself, it had worked. It must have worked. His younger self must have gone to business school. Karissa was in the shower because she'd never left. There was no separation. He laughed and threw his head back.

"Yes!" Brock shook his fist in triumph. "It worked, brother. It actually, insanely, unbelievably worked."

"What are you talking about?"

There was no way to explain to Ron what had happened. He wouldn't believe it. It would be tough enough to come up with an excuse as to why he didn't remember the trip. Best to ride this wave as smoothly as possible.

"Sorry, finally waking up. Really strange dream, you know, still kind of caught up in it."

"In other words, I have to see if I can get us on a later flight."

"Yeah. I blew it. Sorry."

"You're truly bizarre sometimes, bro."

"You don't know the sixteenth of it."

"You're paying for the change fee."

"Without question. I'll be there as soon as I can."

Brock shook his head as he hung up and laughed again. It wasn't possible. But it was possible. His younger self really, truly had changed things. Obviously. He must have gone to business school. It had worked. He had no doubt that when he arrived at the airport an hour from now, Ron would confirm that Brock was running the company and held fifty-one percent of the stock. And best of all, he and Karissa were back together. Wait, not *back* together, simply together.

As he made his way to the overstuffed

chair in the corner of their bedroom and sat, waves of giddiness washed over him. Had he really done it? Yes! He needed to stop asking the same question.

So unless he was still in the dream — which he knew he wasn't — he'd done the impossible. Wait till he told Dr. Shagull. Brock grinned wide and let more laughter spill out of his mouth as his head fell back on the chair. Things were going to be okay. More than okay. Far more than okay.

Brock glanced at the timer on his phone and then at the bathroom door. He'd talked to Ron for four minutes, thirty seconds. Which meant Karissa would be strolling out of the bathroom door, probably within the next minute. It would be tough not to grab her in a bear hug and smother her with kisses. The wind had returned and their sails would soon be full.

The shower shut off a few seconds later. She'd wrap herself in a towel, step through the door, and head straight for the coffee machine. He'd stand, take her hand in his as she strolled toward the kitchen, celebrate the dawn of a new day even if he was the only one who truly knew why.

When the door opened, two thoughts shot through his mind simultaneously. He was about to black out, and he was extremely grateful he was sitting down. Because the woman who stepped through the doorway and glanced at him wasn't Karissa.

CHAPTER 27

"Are you all right?"

Brock drew in sharp breaths and blinked three times. He breathed deep twice more before he could focus. A cold cloth was on his head. He reached for it as he stared into the eyes of the woman who obviously put it there.

"Sheila."

Her brows were furrowed. "What happened to you?"

Brock closed his eyes and opened them slowly as if doing so would make Karissa appear in Sheila's place.

"Don't scare me like that." Sheila rose to her feet and folded her arms. "You going to be okay?"

The sensation of blacking out again washed over Brock, but this time he didn't succumb. Part of him wished he could. He tried to sit up, but his body felt like lead and he slumped back against the chair and glanced around the room.

"This isn't my bedroom."

"Yours? No, it's ours."

Brock pressed his hands against his head.

"Easy." She knelt back down and squeezed his forearm. "Give yourself a moment."

"Sheila, what are you —"

Brock didn't finish the sentence. First, asking what she was doing there would make no sense to her, and second, he knew exactly what she was doing here. He'd changed things. Everything. But the shock of seeing her in flesh and blood kept his mouth shut.

"We're married." The words slogged out of his mouth.

"Uh, yeah."

"Karissa and I got divorced." Sweat seeped out on his forehead but it felt cold.

"Hope so." Sheila stood and rolled her eyes. "I'd hate to think I've been married to you illegally for the past four years."

"We've been married four years. I can't believe it." Brock's mind spun.

"Yeah, me too sometimes." For the second time Sheila stood and pulled her arms tight across her teal robe.

"How could he do this?" Brock muttered to himself. "Why would he leave her?"

"Do what? And who is her?"

"I didn't think there was any way he'd go. But he must have."

"Hey, I'm talking to you." Sheila stood over him now, hands on hips, eyes dark.

Brock stared up at her scowling face. "He went to business school."

"Who?"

"Me."

"What are you talking about? Of course you went to business school."

"I didn't really believe talking to myself could change things. I don't even believe it now. Part of me wants to believe I'm still in the dream even though I know I'm not." Brock looked up and frowned at Sheila. "But it happened. I really changed things. He went to business school. And that sets the dominoes in motion. I'm so stupid. One change affects all the others."

"You're making absolutely no sense." Sheila sighed. "Normal."

"Where's Karissa?"

"Karissa again?"

"Is she married?"

"You want to tell me why you want to know where your ex-wife is? And you want to know if she's married? Hello? Did blacking out destroy the remaining part of your brain?"

"Just tell me where she is right now."

231

"How in the world would I know that?" Sheila pulled back and glared at him. "What's this sudden obsession with your ex-wife? And it better be a detailed explanation with a good reason behind it."

Brock had an overwhelming urge to tell Sheila exactly what was going on, but he resisted it.

"I had a dream, one of those dreams so real you can't be sure that it isn't. I was still married to Karissa, and when I woke up, and it wasn't her that walked out of the bathroom, I —"

"You really are starting to worry me. You need to get checked out. I don't want your mind to go."

She gazed at him with expectant eyes.

Act normal. He had to act normal till he could get control of the panic pounding up from deep inside. "Thanks, I appreciate the concern."

Sheila turned and strode back toward the door. "I'm not concerned about you. I'm concerned about your money."

Brock sat in his bedroom trying to stop his mind from spinning out of control. What else about this version of his life was going to turn his world upside down? And what had his younger self done or not done to create it? He had no bearings, no perspective, no idea what role he played with anyone.

One thing he did know: he wasn't going to Alaska.

"I can't go," Brock repeated for the third time.

"You what?" Ron's frustration poured through the phone.

"You heard me the first time. And the second."

Brock stood and pushed through the French doors at the back of his bedroom onto the veranda. The sight stunned him. He definitely wasn't in Bellevue anymore. He apparently lived in a cliff-top home with unobstructed views of Puget Sound. He glanced to his right and left. The home was massive, easily 7,500 square feet at a rough guess.

He glanced down to find a huge swimming pool. A pool in Seattle? Didn't make much sense to have one in a place that got only two solid months of summer, but it fit with the drowning feeling that now swirled around in his mind.

"Brock, you there?" Ron's voice brought him back to the problem at hand.

"I can't explain it, but . . . it's not good timing."

"No, it is good timing. You need this break. You need to get away from everything in the Lower 48 — turn off your cell, your e-mail, your everything, and get some soul restoration going."

"I need more than that."

"What is going on with you?"

"I can't tell you."

As soon as Brock hung up with his brother, he called Morgan, the one who'd started this whole thing with the book and hinted at knowing what God was doing with the dreams. Brock needed answers.

"Brock-O. Talk to me."

"I've been dreaming, Morg. Lucid dreaming. More vivid than you can imagine. I met my younger self, talked to him, and he changed things. Radically. I need your help. You said you knew what the dream with my dad meant, and that we'd talk after I read the book."

"Hey!" Morgan's laughter boomed through Brock's cell phone. "Who is this and what have you done with my friend?"

"I need you to get serious."

"Okay, then tell me what on this planet called earth you're talking about."

Heat flooded Brock's head. "The book on

lucid dreaming. You gave it to me after I
—"

"I don't even know what lucid dreaming
means, so I'm not thinking I gave you a
book on it."

"Come on, Morg. Not time to be messing
with me. You talked about God dreams and
—"

"Sorry to interrupt, but truly, Brock. I
don't know what you're talking about. I've
heard of Christians who interpret dreams,
but that's not me. Probably won't be unless
God forces it on me." Morgan paused. "You
okay?"

"No, I'm not."

Brock hung up the phone as waves of
despair washed over him. What else had
changed?

He spent the rest of the morning and early
afternoon discovering that he was indeed
the CEO of Black Fedora, that the company
had gone public sixteen years ago, that he
was worth seventy-six million dollars and
his brother was worth fifty-six million, but
it hardly mattered.

After searching his phone and finding a
number for Karissa in it, he tried calling
her, but there was no answer and he didn't
leave a message. What would he say? "Hey,
just discovered we're divorced because I

talked to myself in a dream, but I realize I really love you."

Brock called Tyson's cell phone as well, but his son didn't answer either.

He finally wandered downstairs into the media room and turned on the TV to try to take his mind off the insanity his world had become. But he didn't see any of the stories. His mind was too fixated on how soon night would come so he could get back to sleep and somehow, some way, fix the mess he'd created.

The door from the kitchen into the garage slammed. Brock wandered into the family room. As he started toward the kitchen, the sound of heels clicking across the hardwood floors in his direction filled the air.

"What are you doing here?" Sheila stormed into the family room and put both hands on her hips. "Aren't you supposed to be in Alaska by now?"

"I canceled the trip. I'm not going."

"That much is obvious. The question is why."

"I need to work some things out."

"And I need you to be out of the house." Sheila tossed her purse onto the sofa next to him.

"Thanks."

"Why aren't you on a plane?"

"I already told you."

She turned to go, then spun back. "I suppose Tyson will cancel going to his mom's and be here this weekend then?"

"Will he? I don't know."

"Well you better get on it, because if he's here, then I'm not. And I'm not leaving. So you better figure out where the two of you are going."

"What is your problem?"

"My problem? Tyson is my problem. What stint is he on now? Number three? Four? He's been sober what . . . three weeks now? I give it another ten days max, because that will be a new record for him being clean. When is he going to burn the house down? When should I expect him to bring a few of his pals over to steal a few more of my things to finance his habit while you chant, 'It's going to be different this time'?"

"Tyson is on drugs?" The blood drained from Brock's face and he lurched forward.

"You're an idiot if you think that's funny."

Brock's stomach tightened. He'd been so wrapped up in what had happened to him and Karissa and Sheila that he hadn't considered what might have happened to Tyson.

"Where is he?"

"Tyson? Are you serious? That's like asking where one of the FBI's ten most wanted is hanging out."

"Answer me. Do you know where he is? Any idea?"

"You know what else is my problem?" She pointed out the door of the media room toward the kitchen. "That's my problem, because you make it my problem by messing it up all the time with those weird dishes you like to cook. It stinks. Want another problem? Seeing four grand leave our checking account every month to go to your ex. But those things are minor compared to the real problem around here."

Brock's voice rose. "And that is?"

"You. But I'm seriously considering fixing that unless things change around here." She pulled a business card from her back pocket and tossed it at him. "She's a really good attorney, so you better get ready."

By eight o'clock that evening, exhaustion had settled on Brock like a thick November fog, and he lay out on the couch in his den, begging sleep to take him. He had to dream — find his younger self once more and now convince him to not go to business school. Insane.

Sheila came home a little after ten and went straight upstairs. Brock didn't get up.

He closed his eyes and tried to relax. Wasn't happening. An hour or so later, the tentacles of sleep had started to take him when a sound crashed into his mind. It sounded like the door from the garage into the kitchen bursting open and slamming into the wall behind it. Brock tapped his cell phone and glanced at the time. Almost eleven thirty. Either thieves or Tyson. Brock bet on the second option. He struggled into a sitting position, rose, and lumbered out of the room.

It was Tyson. But the young man standing across the kitchen looked nothing like his son. His hair was dyed jet black and lay plastered against his head and face. Guyliner surrounded his eyes, and his fingernails were painted black. His face looked like bleached copy paper, and his eyes were sunken. Three or four silver chains hung from his neck, and the black jeans and black T-shirt that hung on his skeletal frame made his whole appearance look like a clichéd Halloween costume of a Goth druggie.

"Tyson?"

"Yeah, I know, don't say it. I look like baked feces with a glaze finish. Right?" Tyson staggered over to the couch in front of the big screen and collapsed into the cushions. "And yeah, you've probably already heard from that princess wife of yours, the wagon hit a bump when I wasn't looking and I'm not exactly really riding it anymore, you know?"

Despair clutched at Brock's throat.

Tyson flopped onto his back and threw his arms wide. "But I'm not giving up. No way, huh-uh, going to get back on that sled and figure it out this time. Gonna get clean! Stay clean. This time it's gonna be different! Yeah, baby!"

Tyson's voice rose and fell like a roller coaster. It was obvious he was sky high. " 'Cause if I don't you're going to kick me out for good, right?" Tyson grinned at Brock with yellowed teeth.

"I need to talk to you. As gut-level honest as we've ever been."

"Oh really?"

"Yes."

"Sounds good." Tyson tapped his stomach with his fist. "Gut-level honesty, yeah, baby. Love it. But Dad? You should think of a different intro for your heart-to-heart talks with me. That one is getting old."

With considerable effort, Tyson pushed himself off the couch and wobbled toward the stairs.

"Tyson, you know how you say you're going to try again? Right now, I'm going to try again, to speak from my heart in a way I haven't done before. Then I want to hear from yours."

Tyson's eyes cleared, and Brock thought he would sit back down. But Tyson turned and stumbled away. For a minute, Brock did nothing. But apparently that's what he'd been doing with his son for most of his life in this time line — and if he was honest, in every other time line he'd lived. There's no way he would let it continue.

Brock rose and followed Tyson into his bedroom. His son lay on his bed, forearm covering his eyes, heavy-metal music playing through his speakers, just loud enough to hear. Brock stood in the doorway and tried to figure out what to say.

"Really, Dad. Not now." Tyson turned onto his side, his back now to Brock. "I feel bad, I just want to rack some hours and try to forgive myself. I'll even pray about it, I promise. I'm going to get into my Bible again, the whole thing, but just right now, lemme catch some z's, okay?"

Brock eased into the room and took a stack of heavy-metal CDs off the chair in front of Tyson's desk and sat. The chair creaked and Tyson turned his head and opened one eye.

"You still here?"

"All I need is you to give me your thoughts on a few things, and I'll let you sleep."

"In the morning."

"Now."

"Morning, Dad. I'm sure my answers will be much more coherent."

"No matter what you've done, I forgive you. I'm here for you. I'll walk whatever road you're going down if you let me."

"Forgive me? No you don't. You say that a lot, but you don't mean it." Tyson rolled over and stared at the wall. "You want gut-level honest, Dad? I don't know why you had me. I know why Mom did, but why did you? Your life is Black Fedora. Always has been, always will be. You love that coffee, and yeah, it smells fine. I even drink it sometimes. But it's your rainbow, your pot of gold at the end, and you're never going to take your eyes off of it."

Sleep had to come soon. And with it, dreams. It had to.

The next hour dragged by like a century — having that half cup of coffee earlier in the evening probably didn't help in his quest for slumber — but as two thirty a.m. rolled around, Brock felt sleep finally reaching out for him. As it did, he promised himself he would dream and find his younger self.

When he succumbed to the subconscious world, his hope rose, because he had the distinct feeling it was a promise he'd be able to keep.

CHAPTER 28

As the dream swept him away, Brock was back at Java Spot and stood just inside the door. Morgan placed mugs on the tray next to the espresso machine and watched a young barista prepare drinks for a group of four girls who looked like they were in college. Morgan's hair was shorter than last time his dreams had taken him here, and his friend had gained a few pounds. More than a few. Maybe fifteen?

Brock glanced at the tables, searching for a newspaper. Looking over the shoulder of a squat middle-aged man with a large bald spot, he spotted a copy of the *Seattle Times*. Brock squinted to see the date. August 11, 1989.

Two years after the last time he talked to himself. Not what he'd expected.

"It's been a while."

Brock whirled at the voice and found himself staring into his younger self's face.

Young Brock had filled out in a good way and seemed to be half an inch taller. Had he grown that much in his twenties?

"So once again, you remember me."

"Yeah, I remember you, F. B." A puzzled smile came over Young Brock's face, and he waved his thumb toward the back of the room. "Want to sit down and catch up? Love to tell you what's happened since our encounter at Blyth Park, because you were so right."

"I want to hear all about it."

"Great." His younger self pointed at a table in the farthest corner of the coffee shop. "I'll grab us a couple of drinks. What do you want?"

"Why don't you grab me a grande white-chocolate mocha cut once?"

"A grand what?"

Brock smiled inside. Right. Back in the mideighties Starbucks was still getting ready to take over the world. Few people had heard of the million and one concoctions the company would later create and everyone else would copy.

"Maybe I should describe it to you and you can tell Morgan and his dad and they can beat Starbucks to the starting line."

"Who is Starbucks?" A wave of recognition splashed across his younger self's face.

"Oh, yeah. Those guys down at the market who make the burnt coffee."

"Yep, that's them."

"They're a fad. Morgan says they're never going to go anywhere."

"I wouldn't be so sure about that."

"Oh yeah, you know something, Future Man? Does Starbucks take over the world?"

"Just about."

"You just snag that table before someone else does. I'll snag us some drinks — I should know what you'd like — and you can take a sip of yours and tell me if I'm right about your taste buds."

It wasn't till Brock reached the table that the utter hopelessness of the situation hit him. Young Brock had just said going to business school was the right choice. So he'd already started down that path. Of course he had. It had been two years since their last talk. So what could he do at this point to change things? He could try, that's what he could do. He could talk to Brock about Karissa. And he could plead for the Lord's help. *Guide me, please. I'm out of control once more.*

Brock settled into the chair against the wall and watched his younger self and Morgan interact. He could tell there was some debate about the two drinks, but he couldn't decipher what it was about. A few minutes later, Young Brock arrived with two vanilla lattes.

"Looks like you and Morgan were arguing about these concoctions."

"Yeah, he was acting weird. Let's just say for some reason he didn't think you should have a drink too."

"Why?"

"No idea. Thought one drink should be enough for the both of us." Young Brock toasted and they knocked their cups together.

"To you, Future Me. I thought you were crazy that day in the park, but I have to give you at least a twenty-one-gun salute. You were right. Absolutely right. Thank you."

"No, it wasn't the right call. That's why I'm here."

"What?" Young Brock laughed.

"Going to business school. It wasn't the right path. It changed things in the future. Not in a good way."

Young Brock leaned back and grinned. "So you're still on that you're-me-in-the-future kick?"

"I don't know if this is a dream or if this is real, but trust me, you need to —"

"Hang on, my turn." Young Brock leaned in, elbows on the table. "I trusted you last time, whoever you really are, and went to business school. So now it's your turn to trust me. When I say you changed my life, I don't mean just my career. Turns out I'm quite good at business. More than good. My professors see it, and more importantly, my dad sees it. For the first time ever, he and I have something to talk about. We're getting along. More than getting along. I'm only twenty-seven, but I'm already a vice president at Black Fedora. Dad is talking about Ron and me running the company together fifty-fifty when he retires. He's never said that before. Trust me, things are working out like I never dreamed. I've fallen in love with Black Fedora."

A boulder landed in Brock's stomach. He had to try a different tack.

"If you're getting this good at business, take a job with another company. Or start your own. Why tie your future to a company you have to run with someone else?"

Young Brock leaned back, took a long drink of his coffee, and shook his head. "Do you want me to repeat myself, or do you just want to play the tape in your own head again? Yeah, my dad and I have a long, long way to go, but there's something I can't fight inside. Something I don't want to fight. So I'm laying down my gloves, because deep inside I do want a relationship with him. So if he ever asks, I'll go on those trips to Alaska just like you want, and in the meantime I'm going to pour my heart into Black Fedora."

It was an argument Brock had no answer for. He wasn't going to convince Brock to leave the company. No chance for that now, but what about Karissa?

"Tell me about Karissa."

"How do you know I'm still . . . ah, right. You're me. Uh-huh. Whatever." Brock gave a mock smile. "Doing a little spying on me?"

"No." Brock grimaced. "Are you still together?"

"We're still seeing each other on a fairly regular basis."

Brock clenched his hands. By the time they were twenty-seven, he and Karissa had been married for more than a year.

"Are you serious with her?"

"It's not exclusive if that's what you're asking. We're both seeing other people."

"Who else are you seeing? Sheila?"

"Love to hear why you think that's any of your business."

"Are you seeing Sheila?"

"Yeah, from time to time." A smile and recognition washed over his younger self's face. "But don't worry, it's just friends."

"You're not right for each other."

"I told you, we're just friends."

"Keep it that way."

"Again, why is my love life any of your business?"

"Because I love Karissa. And she's no longer in my life. And I don't want to live without her."

Young Brock stared at him for a long time before he leaned forward and pushed his coffee cup into Brock's and slid it toward the edge of the table, then pulled his own cup back.

"What are you doing?"

"You tell me, since you are me." Young Brock looked up from under his eyebrows. "It's a metaphor."

Brock took a breath and held it. He did know. "You're putting distance between you and me."

"Very good."

"Why?"

"You think maybe it's about time you tell me who you really are?"

"It's impossible, but I've stopped saying that, because obviously it is possible. I am you, at age fifty-three, and I want to save you from —"

"Okay, I think we're done here." Young Brock stood and opened his palms. "Unless you want to come clean on why you're doing this, and what your real name is."

Brock stared up at his younger self and willed him to sit back down. But his younger self didn't.

"I can prove it."

"How?"

"Ask me anything. Something you've never told another soul."

"I'm not playing that game."

"If I am you, then I'd know that you're the type of person who would have a hard time backing down from a challenge like this. Because I also know there's an infinitesimally small part of you that believes me, as insane as it sounds, a part that thinks it's possible this is really happening."

Young Brock squinted at him for ten seconds. Twenty. Thirty. Then he sat back down.

"All right. I'll play." Another ten seconds. "When I was eleven, I went to basketball camp. Things didn't turn out the way I wanted them to. After I came back, I hung up my shoes. I've never told anyone the reason. So why don't you tell me what it was."

The question stunned Brock. Maybe because it was the one memory he refused to let himself visit. So why would his younger self bring it up to someone he thought was a man sliding off the end of his rocker? But again, it was the perfect question. A memory so deep and protected no one would know about it and what it did to him.

Within the dream, the memory of that day washed over Brock.

CHAPTER 29

July 1973

Brock stood flanked by a row of boys along the side of the court, Adidas basketball shoes on his feet that his mom bought the week before he left for the basketball camp. New basketball shorts. New shirt. Ready to take on the world.

The camp's head coach was teaching the fundamentals of zone defense. The man stood at midcourt in a white T-shirt and black sweat pants. A thick silver whistle hung around his neck on a thin leather cord. Four of his assistant coaches stood twenty feet away, two on each side of the key.

He smacked the basketball in his hand again and again with his palm in a slow cadence.

"Now stay with me, men. I'm guessing most of you have only played man-to-man up till this point in your young basketball careers. But when you get to high school, you'll need to know zone defense."

He bounced the ball once and barked, "Okay, let's do this right. I need a volunteer." The coach's gaze swept the line of boys. Every hand shot into the air and Young Brock strained hard, as if he could make his higher than anyone else's.

The coach's eyes stopped. "You, come out here and help me demonstrate this."

Brock pointed at his chest.

"Yeah, you." The coach jabbed his finger at Brock. "This your first year at camp?"

"Second," Brock squeaked.

"What?"

"Second," he said louder.

"Perfect." The coach nodded once. "Name?"

"Brock Ma—"

"Let's go, Brock." The coach wiggled the forefinger of one hand at Brock and pointed to a spot on the court with the other. "Get out here and help me demonstrate this."

Brock sucked in a quick breath and sprinted out to the coach, who tossed him a basketball, then guided him by the shoulders to stand five feet away.

The coach's voice sounded loud behind him. "One more volunteer." A pause, then, "You. What's your name?"

"Ben." A kid with stringy blond hair that

hung over his eyes rubbed his hands on his shorts.

"Get to the baseline, Ben. Now."

The coach pointed to a spot on the baseline and turned back to Brock.

"All right, Brock, think about how you're going to find the best passing lane to get the ball to Ben. Go, let's run this."

Passing lane? Had they talked about that during the past three days? No, he would have remembered. He wrote notes every night in his bunk about what they'd been taught, and there was nothing about passing lanes. Not last year, not this year. But he couldn't stand there and do nothing.

The coaches moved toward him and bobbed on their toes. Brock dribbled toward the coach on the right side of the key, but he'd only taken three steps before he pulled up and held the ball. He'd frozen. Stupid. He didn't have a clue what to do. So what? Fake it. Trying something was better than nothing. A whistle shattered the mumbling from the other kids on the side of the court.

"Brock!" the coach said. "What do you think you're doing?"

"I, uh . . ."

"Can you do this?" The coach smacked his fist into his palm.

"Yeah, but I'm thinking maybe I need to

figure out . . . I mean I need you to tell —"

"Then don't talk about it, do it."

The coach blew his whistle and shouted, "Let's run it again. Go!"

As before, the coaches moved toward him like a wall. Run what? He had no idea what he was supposed to run. But like before, he couldn't stand there and do nothing. Brock dribbled to his right and tried to spot Ben down by the basket, but the coaches towered over him and seemed to move like lightning.

Even though part of him screamed not to pick up his dribble, he couldn't stop himself and did it a second time. The whistle tore through his ears again and he lifted his head to the coach. He glanced at Brock with disdain and waved his hands like he was getting rid of a swarm of flies.

"Get off of my court." He turned to the other coaches. "Can you get me someone who has the slightest clue what they're doing?"

A few of the older kids snickered. Six or seven kids raised their hands and as they did Brock tried to talk to the coach. "I'm sorry, but I didn't know what you wanted. I didn't understand what you were asking me to do."

The coach ignored him and jerked his fingers toward a kid who loped out of the crowd to take Brock's place. He put the kid in the same spot where Brock had stood.

"I'm sorry, Coach, I tried but I —"

"Yeah, I'm sure you did, but I'd like to get this done before lunch, so let's move on." Brock stared at the coach for a sign of compassion, a shred of kindness, but the coach's face was stone. "You got cotton in your ears, son? Move!"

This time the majority of the kids broke into full-out laughter and the rush of blood to Brock's face felt like fire. He turned and stared at the spot in the line where he'd come from. The kids stood there with folded arms and stupid grins on their faces. Brock wove his way back to them, not sure where he should stand, wanting to sprint from the gym, pack his bag, and leave forever.

He struggled through the rest of the practice, pain eking out of every pore in his eleven-year-old face. Finally practice was over and he grabbed his bag from the bleachers and hoisted it over his shoulder. He trudged alone toward the gym doors and pushed them open as if there was a heavy wind buffeting them.

He took only three steps before the doors opened behind him. Brock turned and froze. It was the head coach, walking straight toward him.

"Uh, Coach?"

"Yeah."

"About what happened in there? I'm sorry —"

The coach slowed, but didn't stop. Brock hesitated, then shuffled along the dirt path that led back to the cabins.

"I'm not understanding you, son." The coach glanced at Brock, then picked up his pace, so Brock picked up his pace as well.

"In there, the practice, I didn't run it right and —"

"Oh, you were the one who kept screwing up my practice?" The coach gave a dismissive grin. "Forget it. We got it fixed. Some people aren't cut out for basketball. Don't beat yourself up over it. Find something else to do, kid. Trust me, you'll be better off for it."

Brock swallowed hard as the memory faded. He'd never told anyone about the conversation with the coach, and he'd never picked up a basketball again.

His younger self's voice broke through his thoughts.

"Hello? Future Brock? You going to give me an answer? Tell me why I stopped playing basketball? Or don't you have any idea?"

Brock gazed at his younger self for a few

moments before responding.

"That coach was a father figure. He took the place of Dad, and when he crushed you, you vowed to never play again or have anything to do with the sport. Walking away from basketball snuffed out your floundering relationship with Dad, and you've felt guilty about that ever since."

His younger self went pale. But he didn't move except for a tightening of his jaw. Then a slight nod. Then he rose from his chair and reached into his pocket. He dropped twelve dollars on the table and tilted his head toward Morgan. "Can you see that Morgan gets that? And stay away from me."

As soon as the words left his mouth, the dream ended, and Brock woke to a sound that seemed familiar but was completely out of place.

Chapter 30

May 24, 2015

Had it worked? Had his last dream convinced his younger self to stay with Karissa? He turned over and opened one eye a crack, trying to brace himself against the possibility it wouldn't be Karissa next to him. But there was no one beside him. No shower, no sounds at all from the bathroom, and none floating into the bedroom from the kitchen. But there was that distant, out-of-place sound. What was it? He knew it but couldn't quite place it.

Brock opened his eyes fully, rolled out of bed, and froze. Not his bedroom. Instead, he found himself standing in a much smaller bedroom staring at brown paneled walls and windows covered with beige ruffled curtains that looked like they were straight out of the nineties.

He definitely wasn't in Sheila's and his opulent spread. Was it possible? Hope rose inside. Maybe his younger self had changed his mind and either moved off the business path or started his own company. Most importantly, maybe he was still married to Karissa.

A pang of longing for her shot through him, and he willed her to be in the next room, sitting in her favorite chair, reading a mystery novel.

"Hello?" Brock wandered toward the bedroom door and pulled it open. "Kariss—"

Her name died on his lips as he stared at the family room in front of him. There was no Karissa, and the room wasn't his — and yet it was. His books lined the beat-up bookshelves along the far wall. His desk was crammed into a tiny room. His collection of cookbooks were stacked on the small kitchen counter.

It wasn't until the subtle shift of the floor under his feet that Brock realized where he had to be. He stumbled to the back door, yanked it open, and stepped onto the narrow deck of a houseboat. He stared at the water lapping at the dock. That was the sound he'd heard in the bedroom. What was he doing here? He had an overwhelming desire to click his heels three times. But he knew it wouldn't take him back.

"Morning, Brock."

Brock spun toward the voice. It belonged to a robust woman who looked to be in her midsixties. She stood across the water on the deck of the boat that neighbored his. She had perfectly round wire-rimmed glasses too small for her plump face, and thick wavy hair that must have been blonde once upon a time. She held an oversized mug that gave off a healthy cloud of steam. She raised the cup to him in a toast.

Her eyes were on the nova side of bright, and her smile was the type that spoke of someone who had been through the valley and emerged from the other side with joy unstoppable. Brock liked her immediately.

"Good morning." He took a step toward her.

"Love the new blend." She raised her mug to her lips. "You need to let me pay you for it."

As Brock studied the woman, he decided to forgo pretending he knew her. He was too tired to try figuring out where he'd landed this time.

"I . . . I need your help."

"Is that so?"

Brock nodded and tried to figure out where — and how — to start.

"Finally my turn to help you, huh?

Thought you'd never ask." The woman strolled up to the railing that framed her deck and leaned her elbows on the maple-stained wood. "It's been tough, I know."

"That's the problem. You might know, but I don't." Brock grasped his own railing with both hands and squeezed. "I need to warn you, I'm going to ask a few questions that will sound very, very strange."

"After the questions I asked you all last year?" She took a quick sip of her coffee. "Don't think you're going to surprise this old dame with anything."

"I might."

"Not gonna happen, Spanky." She took another sip. "But hey, I was wrong once, way back in my teens, so let the games begin."

Across the channel from him, windows of other houseboats were turning gold from the rising sun. He glanced at them before turning back to the lady and giving her a weak smile. "What's your name?"

Amusement flashed on the woman's face, but for less than an instant, replaced by that grin that made everything all right. "You get smacked on the head?"

"When I woke up this morning, nothing was familiar."

"What do you mean nothing?"

Brock swept his arm in a slow circle. "I don't recognize any of this."

"Amnesia?"

"Not really. I know who I am, I know I'm in Seattle, I know my past — at least some of it — but the present is a bit muddled. I don't remember anything about where I'm standing right now."

Her amusement turned to concern. "We need to get you checked out."

"Don't worry, I'm fine, and I promise you I don't need to go to the hospital. Like I said, this is going to be strange, but I need you to help me down this path."

"Okay. But if you start doing the chicken dance I'm making the call."

"Agreed."

"Elizabeth Martha Townsend." She winked as if inviting him to play a game.

"But what do people call you?"

"Liz." She raised an eyebrow. "Or Lizzie. That's what my close friends call me."

Something in her eyes told Brock he was in a different category. "What do I call you?"

"Beth. The only one who does." She held out her cup of coffee to him, and even though he had no idea who this woman was, it felt natural for Brock to take it, as if they'd shared hundreds of mornings together, sharing their lives and sharing cups of coffee.

"Only one who's allowed to call me that. Or you call me Sis. Either one works. But never Big Sis. That doesn't work. Don't need to be reminded about my weight or my age." She winked for a second time.

"We're good friends." He said it more as a statement than a question. "Really good friends."

"I would say so."

Brock nodded and plowed ahead with his next question. "How long have I lived here?"

"You were living here when I moved in three years ago."

"I work for Black Fedora Coffee."

"Work for them? Well yes, I suppose. You own the company, but you don't spend a lot of time there these days."

"Why not?"

"You've made it. Reached the top before your midfifties. Money. Loads of money. Great product. Respect. And employees who like you and are good at running the company." She patted his hand. "They don't need you much. Sorry, you worked your way out of a job."

"If I have money, what am doing living in a houseboat on Lake Union?"

"These things aren't that cheap, pal."

"Yeah, probably true, but . . ."

"Too good for us, huh?" For a moment

her smile lifted the dark fog that was encroaching on his mind.

"Hardly."

"You're here because you like it here. It's smack dab in the middle of the city, but it can also feel like you're in the middle of nowhere. When the wind blows hard, your home rocks you to sleep like your baby days, and it's pretty sweet to watch the kayakers paddle along the channel like giant ducks."

"Tell me more."

Beth squinted at him as if she still wasn't sure Brock was serious about all this. "Sheila got the house in the divorce. And you're still paying a hefty chunk of cash every month to Karissa. So you came here. Decided you liked not having to worry about a yard. And it's close to the places you need to go frequently."

"Where do I go frequently?"

"Downtown."

Brock saw hesitation in Beth's eyes. "Seattle? Black Fedora's offices are now in Seattle? What happened to Bellevue?"

"You really don't know, do you?" Beth's eyes turned compassionate. "This isn't a game."

"No, it's not."

Beth started to speak, then let the words die on her lips. She hugged him with the

266

look on her face and sighed. "I think we've had enough questions for one session, don't you?"

Brock knew immediately what the look meant. "Tyson."

Beth bit her lip and nodded.

Brock drew in a sharp breath. "Where is he?"

"I'm not the one to tell you this."

"I need to know, Beth."

"Yes, if you really truly don't know, you do need to know." Beth's countenance grew serious. "Call Karissa."

"Thanks, Beth. You'll understand if I cut our conversation short."

"Of course."

Brock turned to head into his houseboat, find his cell phone, and call Karissa, but then he spun back to Beth.

"What about Ron?"

"Yes?"

"What's our relationship like?"

Again, Brock saw pain on his new friend's face.

"At the risk of repeating myself, you really don't know any of this, do you?"

"No." Brock shook his head.

"You don't talk much about your brother."

"But we work together."

"No. Not really."

"Do I see him? Are we friends?"

"You told me everything changed after the accident."

"What accident?"

Beth eased down her deck till she reached the little gate, then pushed through it and stepped onto Brock's deck. She ambled toward him with her arms open wide, then took him in a long hug. When she released him, she took him by the shoulders. "I'm sorry to be a broken record, but you need to find that out for yourself."

Brock staggered inside, found his cell phone, scrolled through his contacts. Yes. Karissa was there. So were Ron and Tyson. He got voice mail for Karissa and Ron, a disconnected number for his son. Brock then went to the computer in the small office and scoured the Internet for clues to what had happened to Tyson and to Ron. But he found nothing.

By midafternoon exhaustion fell over him and he lay down on the couch intending to close his eyes only for a few moments, but sleep stole over him. When the dream started Brock's mind fought to wake up, because somehow he knew exactly who he'd be talking to — and he wasn't up for another conversation. Wake up! But he couldn't.

This had all the properties of a lucid dream, except for the fact he wasn't in control.

Once again his dad and he were in the backyard, the sun now straight overhead. Once again, his dad held the brown-wrapped rectangular box in hand. Once again, Brock tried to shift things to no avail.

"What's in the box, Dad?"

His dad stared at the rectangular box as if he didn't realize he held it. He glanced at Brock and fixed his gaze on the box again. "Nothing."

"Can I see it?" Brock held out his hand.

"No." His dad tossed the box behind him and before it struck the ground it vanished. "So tell me, Brock. Are you finished screwing up your life? Or do you have more work to do?"

"Why are you doing this to me?"

Brock's dad sat back as if stunned the question would be asked. "What about what you did to me?"

"I don't under—"

"No, you never did." His dad let out a disgusted sigh. "Never knew what you did to my heart."

"What are you talking about?"

"You really want to know?" His dad narrowed his eyes and didn't wait for an answer.

"When you quit playing basketball."

"I had to."

"Had to? You had to!" His father smacked his fist into his palm. "I wanted to teach you everything I knew about the game. You had the skill. The height and build for it. The brains. But poof! One day at the end of summer you just give it up without a shred of warning."

His father jabbed his finger in Brock's direction. "Yes, basketball was my thing, thought it could be our thing. But you dumped it all. Wouldn't talk to me about it. Wouldn't explain why to anyone."

"You abused me! Why would I come to you? I was terrified of you."

"You remember when you were fifteen? I score courtside tickets to go see the Sonics, get that pass to go to the locker room before the game to meet the players . . . you think I did that because I couldn't stand you? And you turn me down."

"Dad, I —"

"And now?" His dad rose from his chair and towered over Brock. "You're making things worse. So much worse. You need to fix things. Fix things!"

Brock woke up breathing hard. That wasn't his dad, it was just a dream. His dad had changed, his dad did love him, but the thought wasn't enough to convince his heart it was true.

CHAPTER 31

"I have to talk to you, Karissa. Call me back. Doesn't matter what hour of the day." Brock hung up and paced back and forth across the carpet of his houseboat.

It was the sixth message he'd left during the past twelve hours. In their life before he'd fallen into this new life, Karissa was religious about returning phone calls within five minutes if she was available. So she either wasn't available or was choosing not to call him back. Brock put his cash on the latter.

It was a few minutes after midnight. He'd have to wait till morning to try again. Brock lay down, but after thirty minutes he knew sleep would elude him till at least two. The dream with his dad had spooked him too much to easily fall asleep. He wandered out onto his deck and looked up. A light curtain of clouds moved across the sky, but the moon was strong enough to shine through them. When he was little he thought the moon burned through the clouds with its light. If only it could burn through the clouds he had created. But if Beth's silence was any indication, they would grow significantly darker.

He rose off his wooden chair, stepped to his door, and started to turn the doorknob to go back inside when the squeal of Beth's door stopped him. She stepped onto her deck wrapped in a tie-dye robe that made her look bigger than she was. Her gaze was fixed on the moon as his had been, but he had little doubt she saw him.

"You could use some WD-40 on that door." Brock wandered to his railing, which separated his house from Beth's by less than four feet.

"But then you might have sneaked back inside without me getting the chance to talk to you."

"True."

"You get ahold of Karissa?"

"Not yet. But you probably knew that."

"Why do you say that?"

"Because I think I tell you most of my stuff, and you probably tell me most of yours. And I think you know that Karissa avoids me like Ebola and she's never going to return my calls."

Beth settled into her jade-green camping chair, gripped her railing with both hands, and gazed up at the moon. "I just brewed up a fresh pot of coffee, you want some?"

"At this hour?"

"Coffee never keeps me awake." She motioned back inside. "Was just finishing when I stepped out here. Let me grab you a cup."

"I'm done drinking coffee for a long time. Black Fedora has screwed up my life so completely, I'm done. Until I get it fixed, no java on my lips."

"Okay. Be right back."

When Beth returned she set her *I think, Therefore I'm Beth* mug on the railing and said, "It's going to be okay, you know."

"What is?"

"Everything. Like you always say to me, God is the God of hope. And even though you're going through a storm right now, the calm waters are coming. I believe it."

Brock tried to believe it as well, even if for a moment, but he couldn't. How could Beth know everything would be okay? That anything would be, for that matter.

"If I wanted to talk to her, if I had to talk to her, where would I go?"

Beth smiled and hesitated for only a moment before answering. "I'd probably go to choir practice."

"She's singing in a choir?" Brock leaned on the railing with both elbows.

"Karissa leads the choir."

"Are you serious?"

"Of course."

"She sang in high school, but she's never taught a choir."

"This is an unusual choir."

"How so?"

"It's not easy to describe. It's one that's best heard, rather than told about."

"And where would I find such a choir?"

"They're practicing for their end-of-the-year concert."

"So the choir is made up of students."

"Yes it is."

"Karissa is teaching," Brock said, more to himself than to Beth.

"Just go see them, Brock. See her. Just don't tell her I told you anything."

"Done."

The next afternoon Brock pulled up to the address Beth had given him, parked his car, and wandered toward a two-story brick building. After he stepped through the double doors, an Asian woman who looked to be in her midthirties greeted him from behind a wide desk.

275

"Can I help you?"

"I'm here to see the choir."

She smiled. "Can't wait for the performance?"

"I'm friends with the director."

"You're fortunate then." The woman smiled. "Karissa is a special one."

"Yes, she is."

The woman motioned with her hand. "Down this hall, second right. That will lead into the auditorium. Head for the back and through the door on the middle left. I'm guessing you'll hear them from there."

Brock pushed open the doors of the auditorium and saw a small stage with forty or fifty light-tan seats on either side of a wide middle aisle. The place looked old and in need of paint, but bright banners obviously created by children hung from the walls on both sides and they gave the auditorium a warmth new paint and a remodel would never bring.

He ambled down the aisle and gazed at each banner. When he reached the last banner on the right-hand side he stopped and felt a sweet sorrow rise in his heart. It was a badly done portrait of Karissa that somehow captured a joy he'd not seen in her in years. It was signed with at least thirty signatures and at the bottom in bright blue letters was written, "We love you so much, Ms. Karissa."

Of course it would be her first name. When she taught school before they had Tyson, she had never let her students call her by her last name. It was always Ms. Karissa.

I need to reach her heart, Lord. Show me Beth is right, and there's hope.

As he stood in the silence, eyes closed, a noise he'd never heard before pricked at his ears. The sound was muted as if coming from a distance and was garbled. Was it a crowd of people shouting? No, not shouting — it was a kind of groaning that rose and fell in a rhythm. Almost a mutilated singing.

He eased toward the door at the far side of the auditorium, then passed through it into a hallway. The volume of the voices increased, and he followed the sound till he reached the door it came from. He took tiny steps up to the door and peeked around the edge. At the back of the room at least forty children between ten and fourteen years old stood on risers. Girls and boys mixed together, tall, short, all different races, all with faces shining, all with an unintelligible sound pouring from their mouths.

It was singing, but the most awful and most beautiful song Brock had ever heard.

There was no melody — and each student sang their own song with their own cadence, and yet somehow the sounds all intertwined with each other to create a symphony of resonance that buried Brock in its splendor.

But the magnificence was so much more than their singing. They didn't just sing with their mouths, but with arms and hands and bodies and eyes and faces as well.

And while their voices weren't connected by any kind of familiar harmony, their arms and hands and fingers flowed together in a symmetry that stunned Brock. No choreographed dance he'd ever seen held the fluidity of these students' performance. It was evident their guide had unleashed this beauty inside them. She believed in them, taught them, inspired them, and brought out a radiance few would fight to uncover.

Karissa stood with her back to him, her exaggerated movements guiding them as they sang with utter abandon. As she swayed, her long dark-brown hair moved back and forth across her back like a wave.

Tears came to his eyes as he watched her fully immersed in her glory — setting these students free in a way he could never imagine doing. A glory he'd been too blind to see, a glory he hadn't looked for. Even if he had somehow woken up to the truth that was right in front of him, would he have urged her to pursue it? Or would he have been so consumed in Black Fedora that her dream would have never stood a chance? Is that why she left in this time line? Or what had broken them up in the one before?

Brock tried to remain still, but he couldn't help moving to a music that was like nothing he'd ever heard. As he watched, a little boy on the end turned and spotted him. He nudged the Japanese girl next to him and she turned. Those two were enough to catch Karissa's attention. She stopped the performance and spun toward him before Brock could slip back behind the door.

Her broad smile faded like the sun on a rainy Seattle spring day. She turned back to her students and signed a message to her students, who signed back. Then she gazed to her right and spoke to a young African American girl who appeared to be in her midtwenties. The girl stood and came over in front of the students. Karissa turned and wandered over to him as if she didn't want to come but didn't have a choice.

"Hi, Karissa. I don't want to disturb you, but I called and you didn't call back."

She didn't answer.

Brock glanced at the children. "That was incredible. I didn't know deaf people sang."

"Yes, they sing, Brock." She drew her arms across her chest.

"I need to talk to you."

"I can't right now." She hesitated, then took a step closer. "Even if I could, there's nothing we need to talk about that can't be communicated via e-mail."

Brock glanced at Karissa's students again. "You've transformed them. It's mesmerizing."

"Thanks." Karissa gave a grim smile. "I need you to leave."

Brock gazed at her, trying to tell her with his eyes what he couldn't with his words. "I never knew you wanted to do something like this. Why couldn't I see it?"

A look passed over her face as if she accepted the fact he wouldn't leave without speaking to him.

"I don't know, Brock. It would have been nice if you did."

"I'm stunned at what you've accomplished."

"They are amazing."

"You're amazing. The way you must have worked with them. The way you've taken kids who can't hear and turned them into a choir that sings with a beauty I've never imagined."

"Thanks, Brock. I appreciate it." She

shoved her hands in her pockets. "And I'm sorry I haven't returned your calls. It's been busy. What can I do for you?"

"I don't want to bore you with the details, but I'm having a kind of amnesia, and there are a lot of things I can't remember."

"Amnesia? Since when?" She frowned, then glanced back at her students. Her aide gave them instructions, and they came down off the riser and walked toward a collection of backpacks.

"I'm forgetting things, Karissa. Important things."

"Did you have an accident? Hit your head?"

"No, I'm fine."

"But you can't remember things."

"That's right."

"Like what?"

"I remember most things, but there are some major holes missing. I asked Beth about one of them, and she said I should hear it from you."

"I like her, how is she?"

Karissa knew Beth? "Doing well."

Karissa took a light-blue coat off the wall where it hung on a wooden peg, pointed to the door, and walked toward it. "I need to be at another appointment, can we walk while we talk? Annalisa will take care of them from here."

"Sure. Of course."

Brock waited till they'd walked twenty paces and were out of earshot of Karissa's assistant. "Where's Tyson?"

"What?" She turned with a confused look.

"Where's our son?"

"You don't remember where Tyson is?"

"No. Where is he?"

"Do we have to get into that right now?"

"Where is he?"

"I don't understand. How can you not know that?"

"I told you, major holes."

Karissa hitched up her jeans and picked up her pace. She reached the door to the outside and shoved it open. A blast of cool air washed over them and Karissa zipped up her coat.

"Are you going to tell me?"

"You really don't remember?" She stopped and turned to him.

Brock opened his arms wide in surrender and shook his head.

Karissa sighed and resumed walking.

"Before I tell you, you need to know it wasn't your fault."

"What wasn't my fault?"

"What is wrong with you?"

"Just tell me."

"Tell you what?" She scowled. "That Tyson killed a man in a barroom brawl but he didn't mean to? That the fight the two of you had sent him to that bar?"

"I didn't have a fight with him."

"Yes, you had a fight. Yes, you told him to go drown his head in whatever would set it straight, but you didn't force him to go there, didn't force him to start drinking, and didn't force him to react like a junior-high kid when the other guy provoked him."

"Killed? Tyson murdered him?"

"Manslaughter isn't murder."

"How long?" Brock's breathing came in quick gasps. "How long has he been in? How long till he gets out?"

"When he went in, his lawyer said because of his age and the circumstances, that good behavior could get him out in as little as three years. Maybe less."

"So how long to go?"

Darkness fell on Karissa's face. "His behavior in there can't be described as good."

Brock tried to stop the panic sliding across his chest.

Karissa glared at him. "I'm still having a hard time believing you've forgotten this."

He started to speak but before he could, she continued. "At the same time, if I were you and was going to forget something, this would be near the top of the list."

"What happened inside? What's the bad behavior?"

Karissa's eyes watered and she swallowed hard. "He murdered another inmate. He's not getting out of there for a very, very long time."

Brock slumped forward and almost went to his knees. "My fault. It's my fault."

"No, Brock. No." For the first time since they started talking, he saw a hint of compassion on her face. "Like I said, it was not your fault, Brock. He wasn't a child. He was twenty-one years old. He had a choice to go into that bar. He had a choice."

"But if I hadn't argued with him, if I'd put down my own pride, he might not have gone. I have to go see him."

Karissa sighed.

"What?"

"Tyson agrees with you."

"That it was my fault?"

Karissa nodded.

"What are you saying?"

"You go down there all the time." Again the look of compassion. "But he rarely agrees to see you."

"I have to try."

CHAPTER 32

May 26, 2015

A guard who likely weighed in at over three hundred pounds motioned Brock to the window in the King County Jail. Brock handed over a slip of paper with Tyson's name and cell number. The clerk took it without looking up, scribbled the date and something else Brock couldn't make out, and handed it back.

"How long till we'll be taken inside?"

The guard looked up at Brock, then shifted his focus to the book in Brock's hand. "You can't take anything in there."

"Nothing?"

"Doesn't anyone read anymore?" the guard muttered. He pointed at a sign on the wall next to Brock. "What does that say?"

Brock looked at the sign. " 'No phones, no cameras, no money.' Basically nothing."

"That's basically right."

"What about this book?"

The guard's expression transitioned from boredom to exasperation. "Is that book something?"

"I suppose."

"So it's not nothing?"

"True."

"What do you think that means, then?"

"That I can't bring it in."

"Bingo."

"He needs it."

"Uh-huh."

The guard extended his hand. Brock hesitated, handed the book over, then sat with several other people on the long hard bench along the wall to the right. Everything in the waiting room was a shade of brown that looked like it was shipped in from the 1930s. The air was cool, almost cold, but taking breaths felt like being in a sauna. And the walls. Ugh. They weren't closing in on him. That's what his eyes said, but his brain disagreed. Odds were, Tyson's quarters were worse. Imagining Tyson living here — no, not living, existing — roiled his stomach.

A few minutes later a guard called for all those in the waiting room to join him at the elevator. Brock glanced from face to face. None of them carried any hope. He supposed his face looked the same. The elevator was crowded and smelled like a heavy antiseptic had been sprayed in a futile attempt to cover up the odor of wet rags. He stood behind a thin woman who sang to herself, not loud enough to make out the words. Next to him was a man with eyes like dark marbles and a pinched face that was too tan.

When they reached Tyson's floor, all of them went through security one by one. As Brock waited, he felt like he was on a river shooting him toward Tyson, and now that the moment was here, a large part of him wanted to head for the shoreline.

A few minutes later, Brock sat at the end of a gray, cafeteria-style table and fixed his eyes on the door the guard said Tyson would come through. A few minutes later, a stream of inmates meandered through the door. Only a few of them looked like they wanted to be there.

And then in a flash, Tyson stood on the other side of the table staring down at him. "Long time no see, Dad."

"Tyson." Brock stood, stepped around the table, and reached out to take Tyson in his arms, but his son yanked himself out of Brock's grip.

"What do you think you're doing?" Tyson scowled at him.

His voice was strained and matched the look in his eyes. Tyson's face was gaunt, and it didn't look like his gray jumpsuit had been washed in a week. A smattering of three-day growth lined his chin and upper lip, and his hair was long and matted.

"I'm going to get you out of here. I'm going to fix this."

"Oh you are, huh?" Tyson leaned forward and scoffed. "You and what army?"

"I promise you —"

"What are you doing here?" Tyson squinted at him. "Why'd you come?"

"I had to see you."

"Why?" Tyson glanced around the room as if looking for a way to escape.

Brock stared at his son and tried to imagine the type of father he must have been in this time line. Part of him wanted to rail against the thought that he could have ignored his son. But the truth won, and Brock admitted there were dark places inside of him capable of even worse things.

"Talk to me. Tell me what you're going through."

"Why do you care?"

"Please?"

Tyson shrugged and sat down. He picked at a stain on the table top. "I'm making it. I'm meeting all kinds of interesting people.

Good mix of inmates, you know? Lots of experience here. Different crimes, different ages, races. It's a fascinating microcosm of society."

His son glanced up, and for a moment Brock saw pain in his eyes, but then Tyson's mask slid back on and he focused again on the table.

"The thing about having killed someone is it gave me respect when I arrived. But the part that blows is every metalhead in here wants to test it. See if I'm really as tough as the rumors say." He unbuttoned his cuff and pulled up his sleeve. "This is my best souvenir so far."

A deep red scar ran from Tyson's wrist up past his bicep. Brock sucked in a quick breath.

"Impressive, huh?" His son flexed his arm and the scar turned white. "You like it?"

Brock swallowed and tried to speak.

"No?" He pulled his shirt back over the scar. "Can't move the arm so good, but the doctor says in another six months I should get eighty percent mobility back."

"I'm so sorry."

"For what?"

"The fight. The things I said."

"Don't sweat it." Tyson's words didn't match the rancor on his face.

"I pushed you. If I hadn't —"

"I said don't sweat it. I'm learning lots of stuff in here, know what I mean? Mad skills." Tyson gave a mirthless sideways grin that told Brock more than he wanted to know.

"You can't let this place take you over."

"Sorry, already done." Tyson made a check mark on the table.

If the eyes were the window to the soul, then lights had gone out inside of his son.

"You have to fight it."

"Fight what?"

"What do you mean fight what?" Brock motioned at the room. "This place is suffocating."

"Oh really?" Tyson gave a mocking smile.

"They allow you a Bible in here, right?"

"Grow up, Dad. Kind of done with fantasyland."

"I can't explain this in any way that is rational, but I'm going to change this."

"Shut up about fixing things. You fixed it that night. You destroyed my life." Tyson smacked his hands on the table and leaned forward close enough for Brock to smell his rancid breath. "And killing a guy in here earned me unlimited nights in my six-by-six mansion. I don't need you to try to make me think about the outside world or give

290

me stupid promises about fixing things. Got it?"

Brock tried to mute the sorrow that welled up inside. Karissa was right, he and Tyson had no relationship.

"Do you ever see your mom?"

"She drops by, yeah." Tyson stared at his hands. Dirt was wedged under his fingernails.

"How is she doing?"

"Ask her yourself."

"I saw her, but she's not exactly forthcoming about her life." Brock stared at his hands. "I'm not her favorite person."

"Just admit it's time to ram a Sherlock hat down on your head, Dad."

"What?"

"Hello? Follow the clues." Tyson gave him the wide-eyed why-are-you-so-stupid look, then drew out each word. "Maybe she doesn't want to talk to you because she hates you. After what you've done to her, can you blame her?"

Despair like a boulder pressed down on Brock.

"I love you, Tyson."

Tyson's eyes widened, and then he started laughing. The mocking peals from his throat grew louder and louder and didn't stop till the guard called out, "Time's up! Let's go!"

As Brock left the jail he knew what his next stop needed to be. Ron's house. It couldn't be worse than his encounter with Tyson. But something in his stomach said it would be.

CHAPTER 33

When Ron's wife Shelly answered the door that afternoon, the look on her face said she didn't want him there.

"Hello, Brock."

"Is he here, Shelly?"

Shelly stepped onto the patio and shut the door behind her. "I'm not sure it's a good idea to talk to him right now."

"Why?"

"What do you need to tell him?"

A breeze came up and the wind chimes sounded, as if to announce Brock's request.

"I need to find out what happened between Ron and me."

She studied his face as if trying to understand and fighting against an anger just below the surface.

"Is he here?"

"You're not going away, are you?" She pulled her arms across her chest.

"Not till I talk to him."

"Call him."

"I've been trying."

She opened the front door and nodded, as if accepting the fact he wouldn't leave till he talked to his brother.

"He's out on the dock fishing."

She walked through the house and he followed.

"Fishing? I thought for sure you'd say putting green."

The same confused look rose to her face, this time definitely laced with anger. She pushed through the French doors onto the deck overlooking Ron's large lawn, which gently sloped down to the lake. Shelly glanced over the deck to the right and then glared at Brock.

He looked down on the spot where Ron had once built his three-tiered putting green dotted with eight flags. It was Brock's turn to feel confused. The flags were gone, and the grass had grown so thick it was hard to tell where the green used to be. Weeds filled the green, along with brown splotches that made the green look like a mutated cow. It was the same with the three par-three holes Ron had built. The pristine mini-course had become a pasture.

"What happened to the green and the golf holes?"

Once more, Shelly glared at him, then turned and strode away. "Whatever you have to say, get it over with fast."

Brock eased down the steps, onto the lawn, and toward his brother. When he reached the long dock Ron sat at the end of, Brock took one step onto the walkway and stopped. Not that taking another minute would help him find a perfect intro to discovering the accident Beth had told him about, but it might help him craft a better opening sentence than, "Hey, bro, did I do something bad?"

When he was halfway down the dock his brother turned, glanced at Brock, then turned back to the lake. At least his brother didn't tell him to leave. Brock eased up next to him and waited a minute before speaking.

"I didn't think I'd find you here." Brock glanced behind him. "Why'd you let the putting green grow over and the par-threes go to seed?"

"If that's your attempt at humor it's not even close to working."

Ron cast with his left hand. His right hand was stuffed into the pocket of his windbreaker.

"Can we talk?"

"About what?"

"Making peace with whatever war is going on between us."

Brock stuck out his hand — hoping it could be the start of a goodwill offering — but the scorn on Ron's face told him his brother's hand wouldn't be offered in return.

"Are you drunk? Returned to hitting the bottle on a regular basis?"

"What?" Brock jerked his head back. He'd been drunk twice in his life. Once in college and once in his early thirties. He continued to hold his hand out to Ron. "I don't drink."

Ron glanced at Brock's hand, then into his eyes. There was venom in his brother's gaze. "What do you think you're doing?"

Brock lowered his hand. "Nothing. I was just —"

"You're sick, you know that?" Ron gave a disgusted shake of his head. "Peace? You go after peace with a grenade?"

"I'm only trying to —"

"What? Tick me off even more? Drive the rift between us deeper? We still have to at least pretend to work together."

Brock's temperature rose. "Knock it off, Ron. I was just offering to shake your hand."

"Oh yeah? That's all? Just a little handshake between brothers?" Ron lurched up from the dock and let out a bitter laugh.

"Great idea, love it. Let's make it into a photo op for Black Fedora. Yeah!"

Ron glanced over Brock's shoulder and waved as if welcoming a group of reporters to join them. "Over here guys, we're not only brothers forced to be in business together, we are absolutely the best of pals! And we're so excited about revisiting the incident that made us best buds forever!"

Ron looked down at his hand still stuffed inside his jacket and pointed his left hand at it. "Look, watch the magic, boys and girls."

The fabric bulged. Then with a flourish, Ron pulled his hand out of the jacket and shoved it at Brock with a sick grin. Only Ron's hand wasn't there. Just a blotched purple stub that ended at his wrist.

"Put 'er there, bro!"

Brock swallowed and staggered back a step.

"Come on, Brock, ol' pal, shake the stump. It's beautiful, isn't it?" Ron wiggled it. "Come on, come on, come on now, you've never done it. Never taken hold of it and felt the nub. You've always wanted to, haven't you? I know you have."

A twisted grin was splayed on Ron's face as he stepped toward Brock.

"Your hand . . . what happened?"

"I don't believe this." Ron shoved the end

of his arm back in his jacket pocket, reached down and snatched his fishing pole off the dock, and pushed past Brock. A few strides down the walkway he spun. "I thought we'd moved beyond this. Put it behind us to the point where we could at least function together."

Brock knew he should shut up and figure out another way to answer the question that pounded through his brain, but the words spilled out a third time before he could stop them. "What happened?"

"You've got to be kidding me. You think playing an idiot is going to solve anything?" Ron spat to his side into the water. "We are so not ever talking about that. Ever again. You hear me? You have a serious screw loose if you want to resurrect that nightmare." The pain etched into Ron's face seemed to deepen, and his gaze flitted to his right as if he struggled not to look at his missing hand. "Do you hear me?"

"I hear you." Brock's breaths came rapid fire as he stared at his brother. "I'm going to fix this. I'm going to get this whole thing straightened out. All of it."

"What?"

"I haven't dreamed for the past two nights, but I will again soon. I know it. And when I do you'll have your hand back to the way it was. I promise you that. And Karissa and I will be back together, and Tyson will be out of jail."

But what if he couldn't dream again?

"You're delusional." Ron turned, strode down the walkway, and left Brock staring after him.

Brock turned and staggered back over the dock, across the lawn, and finally around the side of the house. It was obvious Ron wasn't going to be his source of information. As he rounded the corner of the house onto the front lawn, Shelly's voice called out from the front porch. He stopped and whirled toward her.

"Looked like you had a wonderful conversation."

"Not so much."

She opened her hands and scowled. "What is wrong with your tiny little brain?"

"Tell me what happened." Brock took a step forward. "What happened to his hand?"

She stared at Brock like he'd just suggested finding a Glock and trying to pick off all the neighborhood kittens.

"Help me, Shelly." He clenched his fists. "Something is going on with me that I can't talk about. I truly don't recall what happened. I can't tell you anything more than that I've lost parts of my memory and can't get them back. And I've obviously lost the ones tied to Ron's hand."

"Selective amnesia."

"Believe me, I'm not the one who made the selections."

Shelly took long breaths in and out through her nose. No fire in her breathing, but definitely in her eyes. "Golf was his life."

"I know that. Which is why I have to be told about the accident."

Shelly stared at him as if frozen to the front porch. "Accident? Is that what you call it?"

"I don't know!" Brock popped his fists together. "I don't know what to call it because I don't know anything. Please, believe me."

Shelly's face softened, if only minutely.

"Was I there? Did I see it happen? Please, Shelly, it might help." He took another step toward her.

"If you truly don't know what you did, it won't put you in a better frame of mind to find out what happened."

"Please?"

"Trust me, Brock, you don't want to know."

"Please."

"Okay." Shelly marched into the house and returned less than a minute later holding a VHS tape. She clipped down the porch steps, marched over to him, and waggled it in front of his face. "I don't know why Ron's held onto this after all these years. Not the kind of home movie that stirs up the giggles."

"What's on the tape?"

"You both were such idiots, but you won the prize."

"What's on there, Shelly?"

"You still have a VHS player?" She slapped the tape against his chest and he reached up and took hold of it. But she didn't let go. "Last chance to leave it alone."

Part of Brock screamed at him to do exactly that. But a larger part had to know what had happened to his brother, because only a fool wouldn't be able to see he was an integral part of the horror that caused Ron to lose his hand.

Images of what could be on the VHS streaked through his mind all the way home and fueled a well-orchestrated plan of procrastination once he shut himself into the houseboat for the night. But by ten o'clock the scales tipped, and the pressure to know outweighed his trepidation. It took twenty minutes of searching, but he finally found a VHS player buried in a storage closet in one of the extra bedrooms upstairs.

After he hooked it up to his TV, he closed all the blinds, turned off every light, and pressed play. Thirty seconds later, as the images of Ron and him filled the screen, his mind screamed at him to shut the video off. But his hand wouldn't obey.

CHAPTER 34

The date stamp on the video said 08/12/1997.

"We really going to do this?" Brock bounced on his toes in a tight circle as Ron mirrored him.

They moved on a thick lawn, with what must have been a bright sun overhead. Ron's backyard if Brock had to guess. The camera angle shifted, and Brock caught the flash of one of Ron's golfing flags in the background. Definitely Ron's backyard.

"Is that your way of saying you want to concede before we even start?" Ron jabbed a finger toward Brock. "Go ahead, back down, hand me the cash, admit you have no chance, and it's over."

"No way."

"We go till one of us taps out, agreed?" Ron grinned.

"You better practice saying uncle, bro."

"Not needed. Never going to say it."

The two of them increased the speed of their circling, and both raised their arms and flicked their hands at each other as if to attack.

A voice next to the camera mumbled, "Idiots in the king's court. I can't believe they're doing this. Midthirties and still acting like they're sixteen. You'd think at their age, they'd give up acting like macho jerks who have to prove something to each other."

Karissa's voice. The sound of it shot a pang of longing through Brock, and he leaned closer to his TV screen.

"I can believe it. Completely." That was Shelly. "They have a disease almost impossible to overcome."

"What disease?"

"Being unfortunate enough to be born male."

"Hey! Are you filming?" Ron turned to the camera.

"Yes." Shelly raised her voice. "So the whole world can see how stupid you and your brother are!"

"A psychologist could make a career out of those two."

"Without question." Shelly giggled. "This will be wonderful play-by-play for them to listen to when they watch the tape."

"Unfortunately even if they listen, they

304

won't hear the truth in it," Karissa said. "Remind me when men are supposed to grow up?"

The two wives continued talking, but the action on screen took all Brock's attention. He and Ron had stopped circling and started grappling each other as if in the finals of Olympic wrestling. And while the women might have found the match amusing, the looks on his and Ron's faces said this was a deadly serious competition.

Why were they doing it at this stage of their lives? Sure, he and Ron had fought and wrestled like all brothers do growing up. Brock lost a couple of teeth over the years. Ron still had scars from some of their bouts. But by their early twenties they'd grown up enough to forgo the wrestling for more mundane forms of dueling. Obviously that wasn't the case in this time line.

By now Brock had shot for Ron's legs twice and missed both times. Unlike organized wrestling, it was clear in this match there were no breaks between rounds. After another forty seconds of each looking for an opening, Ron faked high, dove for Brock's legs, flipped Brock onto his back, and drove his knee into Brock's ribs. Brock grunted and tried to spin out of the hold before Ron could lock on. Not fast enough. Now Ron had Brock on his stomach and ground his elbow into the spot where he'd sunk his knee into Brock's ribs.

Brock shot his head back and cracked Ron in the face. His brother staggered to his feet and held a hand up to his now bleeding nose. After pressing it hard for a few moments, he dropped his hand to his jeans and wiped it off.

"Okay, that's enough. Game over." Karissa's voice was loud enough to snap both brothers' heads over in her direction. But just as fast they turned and locked their gaze on each other.

"We done?" Brock gasped out.

Ron pulled in a quick breath and wiped his nose again "Not . . . even . . . close."

"Oh come on you macho freaks," Shelly shouted. "Can't you just play chess?"

Ron turned and pointed a finger at her. "Keep filming."

"Remember what I said about them being idiots in the court? I take it back. They're royalty. The rulers of the Imbecilic Nation. Co-emperors of stupidity."

"I agree." Karissa raised her voice. "It's over, Brock. This is no longer a game."

Brock continued to move in a slow circle, his gaze flitting from her to Ron. "This was never a game."

"Then what is it?"

"Life."

"For crying out loud, you two are brothers." Shelly's voice.

Ron glanced at the camera. "Exactly."

Bouncing on their toes as they circled was long past. Each of them drew in ragged breaths as they staggered around each other in a slow arc. Ron had dominated the match, and as he lunged at Brock's legs, Brock held little hope that things would change. His brother had lorded his physical strength over Brock since the day he matched him in height and weight at age fourteen, and he'd done the same in their professional life. This match wouldn't end much differently than any of their competitions had ended, no matter what time line it was in. But as Brock stared, riveted to the screen, he realized he might be wrong. Something in his eyes on screen said this time the sands would shift in his favor.

Ron lunged for the second time since his nose was bloodied. Somehow Brock side-stepped the attack at the last moment and wrapped his arms and legs around Ron's off-balance body. They crashed to the ground, and their bodies tore into the sod. The thud of their fall was accompanied by a whoosh of wind out of Ron's lungs. But

Brock didn't let go. As Ron gasped for air, Brock grabbed his brother's hand and secured it in a hold that would cause excruciating pain if he tried to move.

As Brock stared at the screen he didn't have to imagine what was going through the mind of the Brock in the video. He knew. It was splayed across his face in a blazing display of triumph. Part of his mind was screaming to let his brother go, let him catch his breath before they continued, but it was drowned out by the voice shouting to give no mercy till his brother submitted. Finally, he would win.

Ten seconds later Ron had caught his breath and rocked back and forth in an effort to free himself from Brock's grip. As he did, Brock applied more pressure to Ron's hand.

"Arrrghhh!" Ron cried through gritted teeth.

"Cry uncle." Brock dug his feet into the sod and pushed all his weight down on his brother.

"No way," Ron spit out.

"Say it!"

Ron's only response was to growl.

"Say it now!" Brock squeezed harder. "I won."

"You'll never win."

Brock whispered, "Say it, little brother."

Again, a cry of pain shot out of Ron's mouth.

"Just say it, Ron. Admit it. I've won."

Ron's voice dropped to half its volume. Brock was surprised the tape picked it up.

"Maybe you won some stupid wrestling match, but I won the Dad Olympics and that's real world. You lost, bro. Forever."

Brock stared at the screen and knew what was about to happen before it did. Something inside him would snap, and he'd make a move he'd regret forever. Brock lifted off his brother six inches, then threw his entire weight down into his arm, into his hand, into his grip that held Ron's hand in his.

The snap of the bones in Ron's hand sounded like a set of miniature dominoes being knocked over at quadruple speed. It couldn't have been that loud, but the noise of his brother's hand shattering spilled out of Brock's TV speakers as if the sound was cranked to a hundred decibels. The cry of Ron's pain seemed to split Brock's ears open.

The camera went shaky a second later, and the view on screen was of the sky, the grass, and then back to Ron and Brock. Whoever was filming must have set the camera down on a chair or table but didn't turn it off. A second later Shelly and Karissa shot into the frame and rushed toward Ron and him.

"Get off him! Get off him!" Shelly popped Brock in the side with both hands, and when that didn't work, reared back and kicked him in the ribs with her cowboy boot.

Brock rolled off and landed on his back, his arms splayed to each side. His breathing came fast and as his eyes closed, Shelly punched him in the stomach, shouted, "What were you thinking!" then turned to Ron. "Are you all right?"

Karissa knelt between Ron's and Brock's heads. She glanced at Brock and scowled. "Happy now?"

"Are you okay?" Shelly asked again.

Ron's eyes were shut and he grimaced as if in agonizing pain. Which he assuredly was.

"We're going to emergency."

"I'm coming with you." Karissa glanced at Brock in a way that said he wasn't invited.

Brock tried to pull his gaze from the screen but it wasn't possible. On screen, Brock's face went pale, probably from realizing what he'd done. Shelly and Karissa helped Ron to his feet as Brock rose to his. Brock started to speak three times, but nothing passed his lips. As he started to speak a fourth time, Ron lasered him with a look of hatred, and Brock mouthed the words, "I'm sorry."

Ron turned away and hobbled toward the house. In three seconds he, Shelly, and Karissa were out of the frame, leaving Brock alone. He rubbed his face as a sigh came from the depths of his chest. He stood with head in hand for over two minutes before finally giving a start as he realized the camera was still on. He shook his head, walked up to the camera, and shut off the tape.

The video ended and the screen filled with black-and-white snow, accompanied by a hiss. In his houseboat, Brock didn't move, didn't bother to shut the tape off. No mystery what had happened. He'd destroyed so many bones in his brother's hand there was no way to rebuild it into anything close to usable. So at a certain point a doctor must have suggested amputating the hand in an effort to see if a prosthetic could give Ron some semblance of a normal two-handed life. But Ron's golf? Gone forever.

May 26, 2015
Brock lay in bed that night trying to sleep for two and half hours before he gave up. He was so wired after seeing the video that his brain refused to shut down. So what was

311

he supposed to do while he ground through the next day, waiting to dream again?

Easy answer. Try to reach Shagull. No idea if the doctor would be in this time line, but it wouldn't be hard to find out.

Brock got out of bed, walked into the living room and across it into the small den on the other side of the kitchen. He searched for a picture of his dad and him in Alaska. Not there. Not even one. Brock turned to the desk and tore through a pile of notes and papers. Nothing. Nothing in the top drawer either. Had he made contact with Dr. Shagull in this time line? He desperately wanted the answer to be yes, but evidence was mounting that said no.

He started to reach for one of the lower drawers of the desk when he saw a card lying on the brown speckled carpet. Shagull's. Yes. So he had contacted the doctor in this reality. Brock glanced at his cell phone. Almost midnight. Too late for the doctor to answer, but he could leave a message.

The phone didn't even finish the first ring before the doctor answered.

"Hello?"

"You're up?"

"Obviously. Who is this?"

"Brock Matthews. Do you remember me?"

"Yes, Brock."

"We've talked before." Of course they had. The card wouldn't be here if they hadn't.

"You don't recall?"

"I remember, but I didn't know if you would."

"Why is that?"

"I woke up in a very different place than where I went to sleep, and everything has changed, and I don't remember any of it. So I don't know what we've talked about from your perspective."

"I see."

"Do you?" Brock wiped his damp forehead. "Is this really happening to me?"

"I'm not sure I understand the question."

"How can you not understand the question? Am I really going into the past and talking to myself? Am I causing a younger version of myself to change things in the present? Am I living out that old movie *Back to the Future* in real life?"

"We talked about this before, but I will reiterate. I have no way of knowing if these things are truly happening to you. I have no context to judge against. All I can observe is what I see around me. You tell me things were dissimilar before, but evidence for that comes only from your words. There's nothing you can show me or anyone else that indicates things were at all different previously."

"You're saying I'm crazy? That it's all in my head?" Brock wandered back through his living room and out onto his deck.

"No. I am not saying that. I'm simply trying to explain why I cannot offer an assessment or even attempt to answer the question you just posed, which was, 'Is this really happening to me?' Is it happening in your head at the least? We can answer that question in the positive. Is it happening in the construct of physical reality? I don't know, and I don't believe it is wise to guess."

"All I'm asking is, is it possible? Or am I crazy?"

"I recall you mentioning in our first conversation that you are a man of faith. Am I correct in that?"

"Yes. I am."

"As am I. Consequently, we both likely ascribe to the maxim that with God, all things are possible, yes?"

"Yes." Brock stared at the dark sky. Rain was coming.

"Then I suppose you have to ask yourself if you believe that or not."

"I believe that, but not for something like this."

"Ah, I see. So all things are possible for

this God of ours except for the ones you decide are not possible. Have you given him a list to make sure he doesn't do anything you don't approve of?"

"This is science fiction. Fantasy."

"Some would say the same thing about the parting of the Red Sea, or dead and dry bones rising up and becoming an army. Some say those are simply metaphors, stories, not accounts of true incidents. What do you believe?"

"At least tell me how to get control of this insanity." Brock climbed his exterior circular stairs to the rooftop deck of his house and slumped into a chair. "I have to fix it. I have to go back again and do whatever is necessary to set things right."

"Have you ever considered the idea that you're not in control of any of it? And never have been?"

"If I'm not in control, then who is?"

"As I said a moment ago, I suppose you need to ask yourself what you truly believe."

"What's that supposed to mean?"

"According to the belief system it seems we both attempt to adhere to, either the Lover of our souls is in control, or the enemy of our souls is in control. You didn't really think you were, did you?"

"That's the whole point of your book!

That we can control our dreams. Are you saying that's not true?"

"I suggest we schedule an in-person rendezvous. When can you meet?"

"Right now."

Shagull laughed. "The soonest I can get together with you is day after tomorrow. Will that work?"

"Not sooner?"

"I'm sorry, Brock. I have other matters to attend to that prevent me from seeing you before then."

CHAPTER 35

May 28, 2015

"I haven't been dreaming, but when I do next time, how do I know I won't make it worse?" Brock clomped back and forth across the hardwood floors of Dr. Shagull's home. "How can I know what to try to change?"

"I don't know." The doctor studied him from his kitchen chair as if looking at a rare painting he might buy.

"Then how do I get things back to the way they should be?"

"And how should they be?"

The question was excellent. Did he want them exactly the way they were before this whole nightmare started? Not exactly, no. He wanted to have loved Karissa better, to have been more involved with Tyson. To have treated Ron as a brother and not an enemy. And a million other things.

"I'm not sure how they should be."

"It would be difficult to advise you on how to bring things back to a state of 'I'm not sure.' "

The doctor picked up a teacup and set it in the middle of a white sheet of paper. He moved it millimeters back and forth till he seemed satisfied it was dead center, then pulled out a mechanical pencil. He drew a circle around the cup, lifted it, then drew two more circles with the lines overlapping so there was a small space in the middle where the three circles intersected.

"See this?" The doctor glanced down at the piece of paper, then back up at Brock. He tapped on the spot with his pencil where the three circles intersected, then filled in the area with quick strokes so it was shaded gray. "This is the area I'm fascinated with."

"Why is that?"

"It's what all my research has led me to." The doctor drew a quick circle around the area. "It's the place where the past, present, and future meet. The place of dreams where there are never any barriers of time."

"You're saying that's where we're at when we dream." Brock pointed at the gray area.

The doctor nodded. "The place where life can be altered forever."

"The kind of altering I've been doing."

"Apparently."

"Altered forever, meaning I can't go back. Make things the way they were before."

"On paper." The doctor stared at the diagram and went silent. "I don't know if it's even truly occurring."

"What do you mean *on paper*?"

"I'm saying it's theoretically possible for you to be doing what you're doing, but highly unlikely. So you're either crazy, or . . ." Shagull leaned back and studied Brock for a long time. "For example, speaking of time travel, it is theoretically possible. But no serious scientist thinks it can actually be done. In the same way, I think you can access this plane" — the doctor tapped the paper again — "in theory, but not in reality. However, you might have proven me wrong."

"I don't understand. Let's pretend for a moment I'm doing what you don't think is possible — and believe me, I'm not sure it's possible even though it's happening to me — are you saying I'm not really there in my past?"

"No, you are there. But not in a way most people would understand."

"Yeah, most people. Like me."

Dr. Shagull pushed the paper with the three circles back in front of Brock and tapped the center once more.

"I'm saying you might be outside of this plane of existence."

"Ah, now it all makes sense."

"Good to see you still have a sense of humor." The doctor tapped the paper again. "I believe this is not only where the past, present, and future meet, it's also the place where the Father, Son, and Holy Spirit intersect. They are separate, yet One."

Brock shook his head.

"Stay with me, Brock. If you can believe that this truth is real, that there is a place where the past, present, and future exist together, and if you can believe the Father, Son, and Holy Spirit exist in that moment as well, then you can believe they can take you to a place outside of time where you can communicate with your younger self."

"I don't care where the place is, or what it is, I just want to know what to do when I get there."

"But I care where that place is, and your case has the potential to revolutionize my research. So in a way, that makes us partners."

Brock drove back to the houseboat more confused and frustrated than before he'd talked to Shagull. He didn't care about the science behind his dreams, and he didn't like how the doctor sometimes looked at him like he was a lab rat. And he still had no idea what he should attempt the next time he dreamed.

As he clomped along the dock to his houseboat he spotted Beth turning away from his door.

"Hey, Beth."

Her smile lit up the early evening air.

"Did you forget about me?"

"Umm . . ."

"We haven't missed a Thursday-night game in over two and a half years." She held out a cribbage board and a deck of cards. "I thought this might be the evening we broke our streak."

"No, uh, I didn't forget."

She laughed. "Yes, you did! But I forgive you." She motioned toward the rooftop deck. "On top as usual?"

"Yeah, perfect," Brock said. "I'll be right up."

Brock joined Beth three minutes later. He carried a bag of peanut butter–filled pretzels and a strawberry lemonade for each of them, then settled into the deck chair on the opposite side of a small wood table. He set down the drinks and pretzels and motioned for her to deal.

After getting skunked the first game and

beating her by nineteen points in the second, Brock watched Beth set the cards aside and drill him with those knowing eyes.

"Talk to me. What's the latest?"

"I need to dream again." He tossed a pretzel off the top of the deck into the water. Three ducks thrashed toward the treat.

"Excuse me?"

"I've ruined my life and the lives of the people I love. If I dream again, I think I can fix things. The problem is, I don't know what I should change."

"From what you've told me over the years, it doesn't sound like you need to think about sleeping, you need to celebrate the fact you're finally waking up."

"You're probably right. I'm finally starting to see."

"Yes, I believe you are." Beth winked. "Your eyes are opening."

"To what?"

"You want my un-Photoshopped answer?"

"Yes."

"I believe God is allowing your eyes to open to the chains that are wrapped around you, and the ones wrapped around Karissa. And I believe you have the power to cut those chains so you can live the life you were designed to live. One of freedom. He can give you new vision."

"So you're a doctor."

"No. He is the Surgeon, but I sometimes assist." Beth's voice grew soft and she leaned across the table. "And if you're willing, God will apply his laser technology to your eyes."

"Spiritual Lasik."

"Yes."

Brock sat back and folded his arms. "From the look on your face, I'm assuming God or someone else helped perform this type of operation on you."

"And I'll be eternally grateful that he did."

"And how did it turn out? Do you now see as clearly as you want to?"

Beth slid both hands around her lemonade, pulled it close, and stared at it for so long Brock wondered if she'd heard the question. Were those tears behind Beth's glasses? Brock couldn't tell.

"Yes. I do see clearly now. Too clearly, and often the light is too bright. In so many ways I wish I was still blind and I could shield my eyes from the truth, because my surgery came far too late in life. But if I could block out the truth, I wouldn't have been able to help the Brocks of the world, and pray for them, and encourage them to open their hearts and eyes wider than they knew was possible."

Brock wasn't sure if he should thank Beth or excuse himself gracefully and call it a night. But he needed guidance. He needed a clue about what to do in his next dream, and what to do until he dreamed again. Brock was a man hurtling down the highway without any lug nuts on the tires, and God was the only one with a tire iron.

"Let's say I'm willing to step into the operating room. What's next?"

"Sorry to break the news to you." Beth smiled and shook her head. "You're already on the operating table."

"Can I tell you something crazy?" he rose and walked over to Beth.

"Of course."

"Really crazy."

"Please."

"The reason I didn't know you the other day is because I've been having dreams where I talk to my younger self. Then he changes things based on our conversations, and when I wake up my world is one I don't know."

Beth glanced at the table. "What did you put in those lemonades?"

"Beth, I'm —"

"I know you're serious, Brock." She cocked her head and smiled. "And if you knew my history, you would know I believe you fully."

"Thank you." Brock breathed relief.

"But even so, I don't think your focus should be on dreaming again."

"Are you kidding? I can't live this life. It's falling apart. I need to dream. I have to fix this."

"What if you can't dream of your younger self again? What if these dreams have all been inside your head? What if this is your permanent life?"

"I can't accept that."

"You might not have a choice."

"Then what do I do?"

"If what you've told me is true, you created this time line. So for the moment, live in it. Live in the now. Take time to pray, to listen for the answers God is giving you. Think about what's most important."

"I already know that answer: Karissa."

"Even more important than Black Fedora, hmm?"

"They're both important."

"I see." She stared at him with the most serious eyes he'd seen from her so far.

"What do you know?"

"Nothing."

"If God is telling you something, I'd like to know what it is."

"I know." Beth patted Brock's hand like

325

he was a little boy. "You're going to want a lot of things in the days to come. Don't worry, I've been praying for you and will continue. I do know this: he is for you and will hold nothing back to set you free."

Beth finished her drink, stood, and walked toward the edge of Brock's roof. She started down the stairs, then turned and pressed her lips together as if deciding whether to speak or stay silent. She decided to speak. "I should warn you. When I've seen God take people down these kind of paths, it doesn't get easier at the point you're at. It always gets harder."

CHAPTER 36

May 31, 2005

Brock reached the summit of Mt. Pilchuck at four thirty in the afternoon. His lungs were in decent condition for a man in his early forties, but it had taken him longer to reach the top than he expected. It wasn't long, two and a half miles, and the grade wasn't steep, but still, it wasn't a beginner's hike. He was thankful the trail had been empty except for two hikers who passed him on their way back down, three-quarters of the way up.

"Anyone up top?" Brock asked as the hikers passed.

"Nope. All yours." The man gave him a quick salute. "Enjoy the solitude."

Exactly what he intended to do. He wanted to be alone as he created his own personal time capsule — one he might never find. Most of him still couldn't believe the man he'd met multiple times back in his twenties was who he said he was, but in case the impossible had happened, he wanted to get a message to that man. And since it had been more than fifteen years since Future Brock had shown up, Brock didn't think he'd get the chance to deliver the message in person.

Why hide the message at Pilchuck? He didn't know except to say it felt right. It felt like the place God had led him. And if God had led him, then he could somehow, some way, lead Future Brock to this spot.

It took only ten minutes to find the right hiding spot for the box and its contents. As he finished by placing a large rock over the box, the sound of boots scraping across rock floated toward him from his right.

A lean man with a small daypack stood ten yards away. He looked to be in his late forties or early fifties. He wore thick glasses and had a pale face and thinning blond hair.

"I'm sorry to have disturbed your solitude."

Brock glanced at the spot he'd hidden the box, then back to the man.

"Don't worry." The man waved a gnarled walking stick. "I'm not going to steal whatever you've hidden there. But I'll go if you want to relocate it."

Brock considered the idea. "Nah, there's

nothing in there of value to anyone but me."

The man nodded, turned, and ambled the thirty yards or so over to the ladder that led up onto the deck of the historic fire lookout. A minute later Brock joined him.

To the north, Mt. Baker, the Olympics to the far west. As Brock gazed at the splendor, he prayed: that the box would be found if it was supposed to be; that no one else would discover it hidden in the rocks; that the message would do its work if the time for it to be found ever came.

"Spectacular day."

Brock nodded.

The man turned to Brock. "Is this your first time to the top of Pilchuck?"

"Yes. You?"

"My seventeenth. Not sure why I keep ascending these particular slopes. There are other mountains. But this is the one that continues to beckon." He swept his hand out at the view. "This is probably why."

"It's stunning."

"I didn't expect anyone else up here so late in the day."

"Neither did I."

The man nodded as if he understood completely. "What do you do when you're not hiking mountains?"

"I'm an owner of a coffee company."

Brock leaned forward on the railing that faced the south. "What about you?"

"I'm a psychology professor at the University of Washington."

"That's where I went to school. Long time ago." Brock studied the man. "What's your area of focus?"

"Dreams and how the subconscious affects our waking world."

Brock whipped his head toward the professor. "Are you kidding?"

"That intrigues you?"

"Do you believe in God?"

"Yes."

"I came up here because I felt like God told me to in a dream." Brock gripped the railing hard. "And now you show up."

"I'm an answer?"

Brock gazed at the view of Rainier in the distance. "Do you mind if I tell you something crazy?"

"Please do." The professor smiled as if to say, *That's all I ever hear.*

"In my twenties, I met a man a number of times who claimed to be dreaming during the times we talked — and he claimed to be me thirty-plus years in the future."

"I see."

"You don't seem shocked."

"No. I'm not." The professor waved his

hand above his head. "The world of dreams is an unexplored territory. And anyone claiming to understand God and what he's capable of doing has not even begun to know him. Dreams plus God can equal a potent combination for conjuring up the unexplained."

"Then perhaps we were supposed to meet."

"I believe that is highly likely." The professor extended his hand. "I'm Thomas Shagull."

"Brock Matthews." Brock shook the professor's hand firmly.

"Is that why you're up here, Brock? To figure out what you believe about this man from the future?"

"No." Brock shook his head and gave a resigned smile. "I don't know if I'll ever figure that out."

"So what is the reason?"

Brock stared at the professor and tried to decide how much to tell.

"I came up here to leave a message for my future self. I have no idea if he'll ever get that message, but I'm going to leave it anyway. Because the part of me that believes he was who he said he was wants to tell him the most important thing I learned from our talks, and remind him of that lesson.

Because whether he was me or he wasn't me, he changed my life."

The professor studied Brock before responding. "Perhaps we'll meet again, Brock Matthews."

"Yeah, maybe we will."

CHAPTER 37

May 29, 2015

Brock leaned against a maple tree on the campus of Seattle University. The sun was warm, but not hot, and he couldn't ignore his longing for summer the way it used to be — with Karissa and Tyson.

What if Beth was right, and he had to stay in this time line for the rest of his life? Or worse, what if all his encounters with his younger self had all been in his head? Not only did that mean he was going insane, but he'd have to live with what he'd done to Karissa, Tyson, Sheila, and Ron. No, he refused to believe that there wasn't a way to change things. But he instinctively knew that chance wouldn't come till he talked to Shagull again. So in the meantime, he'd try to change the world he might be stuck in. And that meant somehow winning back Karissa's heart.

He glanced at his watch. Karissa's class

would get out in five minutes. He tried to think of a line that would break the wall of ice sure to be surrounding her, but anything more than a cliché wouldn't surface.

A few minutes later the door of the building opened and his stomach clenched in anticipation. But she wasn't there. Just a few students signing to each other as they clambered down the concrete steps to the walkway in front of the building. Then more students in bunches. And finally, Karissa.

She pushed through the door, her concentration on a woman with her who looked to be in her midtwenties. Not talking with her voice. Signing. Strange to see a woman he'd known the majority of his life communicating in a language he didn't even know she spoke until days ago.

As they reached the bottom step, whatever they communicated sent laughter through both women, and they looked at each other like old friends. Not surprising. Karissa was one of those magnet people everyone was immediately drawn to, and no doubt her students would be in love with her.

She wore tan boots with her blue jeans tucked in, and a light coat that flowed out behind her like water. There was a lightness to her he'd never seen.

Before he could approach, she turned and

spotted him, as if some kind of radar inside her warned he was there. The lightness in her step vanished. She fixed her gaze on him, shook her head no, and strode off down the concrete pathway with her friend beside her. As they clipped along she pulled out sunglasses and slid them on.

Brock pushed off the tree and jogged after her. As he approached, Karissa picked up her pace. When he reached her, she took her friend by the arm and took a sharp right away from him.

"Karissa."

"Stay away from me, Brock."

"I saw Tyson."

"Good for you, but that has nothing to do with me."

"I just need a minute."

She continued toward the center of the campus along with her friend at a fast clip.

"Just sixty seconds, Karissa."

Karissa stopped but didn't turn, her profile to him, and stared into the cotton white clouds overhead. Her friend lifted her hands and signed. Brock didn't need to understand sign language to know the woman had just asked if Karissa was okay. Karissa nodded and made a quick sign back. The woman looked back and glanced at Brock, then concentrated on Karissa again. Another sign, another response from Karissa. The woman took one more concerned look in Brock's direction, then walked away. Karissa turned and strode off, if possible, faster than her former march.

A few seconds later he fell into stride beside her. "Hey, can you slow down a minute?"

"What are you doing here?" She moved to the right to create more space between them. "You better have a reason. One that's really, really compelling."

"Can we have a cup of coffee? Just a few minutes."

"What?" She stopped and whirled on him. "A cup of coffee? Why would I have a cup of coffee with you? Reminisce about all the good ol' times?"

"Just to talk."

"About what, Brock?" Karissa pulled her arms tight across her chest and glanced around the campus as if students or fellow teachers might be watching.

"Anything. Everything. No agenda."

"If there's no agenda, then you don't need to talk to me." Her foot tapped the sidewalk double time. "I don't know why you keep pressing this. There's no going back, ever. It's over between us. It has been for nearly eight years. Why do you keep trying to resurrect it?"

"Because we were made for each other. I want to know what happened to us."

Karissa coughed out a laugh. "Let me ask, do you think people 'made for each other' are supposed to stick together no matter what? Fight for their marriage? Thick and thin? Sickness and health? Or were those just lines on our wedding day?"

"Yes, they are, that's why I'm here right n—"

"Really? Is that why you took that trip with Sheila to the coast while I still thought we were figuring things out, working to make things work? Before we even filed?"

The air was sucked out of his lungs as if he'd been punched. No. Impossible. He'd never have done that to her.

"I can't explain this, but I didn't do that. It wasn't me."

"This is going to be good." She yanked her arms across her chest. "Let's hear it."

"That was a different Brock. I wouldn't ever have done that."

"Oh, your clone slept with her?"

"It happened in another time line."

"Another what?" Karissa frowned and squinted at him, eyes on fire.

"Another time line. This isn't my time line."

"What are you babbling about?"

"I know it sounds crazy, but this isn't my life. I've been shoved into this time line, but I don't remember any of it because I didn't live it."

He stepped toward her but she raised a palm and he stopped.

"Good one." Karissa shook her head. "Next you'll be telling me that we're not really alive, that we're all just brains in a laboratory hooked up to wires that are stimulating our nervous systems."

She whirled and marched away. Brock caught up to her in three strides.

"I just want to talk. Ten minutes."

"No."

"Five."

"No." Karissa stopped and spun toward him. "Not four, not three, not two, not one."

"I need to try to explain what has been happening, even if it sounds like science fiction."

Karissa frowned and pointed at Brock. "On second thought, I think you're right. Let's do it. It'll be so fun. Should we invite Sheila and my boyfriend to join us, or just record the conversation so they can enjoy it on their own time? No wait, I have an even better idea. Maybe we can double date. Sheila and Rex can hang out at the other

338

end of the coffee shop while you and I have our little rendezvous, then the four of us can go have dinner. Maybe catch a play at the 5th Avenue afterwards. It'll be really special." She reached in her purse and pulled out her cell phone. "Let's give them a call."

"My heart is still yours, Karissa. Always will be."

Karissa jerked her head back and she blinked. "Shut up, Brock."

"I never saw it. Maybe glimpses of what we had, but not like I do now. And I never saw you like I should."

"Didn't you hear me?" She pulled on her ear. "I said shut up."

"And even though you're fighting it hard, I can see it in the back of your eyes. The fire might be almost out, but not completely."

"Then you're blind." Karissa pointed a finger at him. "Don't follow me."

She turned and walked away. Brock watched her till she turned the corner half a block ahead. She didn't turn back.

He didn't believe her. There was a spark, maybe dull, but he saw it. He had to find a way to dream again. Find himself again. Stop this insanity from destroying everything. A bitter laugh poured out of him.

Stop the destruction? It had already happened.

CHAPTER 38

June 8, 2015

Ten days of despair passed by accompanied by ten nights without dreams. What was wrong with him? Why was his subconscious world shutting him out? Brock sat in his houseboat on Monday evening trying to ignore the hunger in his stomach, not wanting to cook anything, not wanting to make the effort to go get food. Finally his stomach won out, and he drove to a Thai restaurant he'd found right after waking up on Lake Union. He had visited almost daily since then.

"Hello, Mr. Brock. The usual?"

Thai Won On had one of the cheesier restaurant names Brock had seen, but the food was far better than average. Plus, Aroon, who owned the place, clapped his hands and yelled, "Whoop, whoop!" every time a customer placed an order. That was strange enough to distract Brock from his current world if only for a few seconds. It even made him smile once or twice.

"Sure, the usual. Why not?" Brock set a ten-dollar bill on the counter.

Aroon spun on his heel, clapped three times, and shouted, "Mr. Brock takes a number seven, yah, that's the scoop, everybody say it with me now, a big whoop, whoop!"

Aroon's wife and their two sons joined in on the whoop-whoop part, and indeed, Brock smiled. Aroon handed Brock his change and then leaned in close to Brock's ear. "You smile when we put in order, but never smile when you step inside. Sadness is on you, no?"

"It is." Brock tried to smile again, but if he succeeded it had to be weak. "It's going to work out though."

"How do you know?"

Brock shrugged in response, which was no response, eased over to a chair along the side wall, and sat. He tried not to think about his fractured life and how it would work out, but it wasn't possible. He picked up a year-old copy of *People* magazine and stared at Robin Williams on the cover. It didn't exactly work out for Robin. What made Brock think things would work out for him? Because God was on his side?

Right. Not anymore. Every trip he took to converse with his younger self had made things worse. These days he couldn't even try. And making things better here in this time line was proving impossible.

Ten minutes later he pushed into the street door accompanied by the jangle of bells at the top of the door. Exhaustion hit him even though he shouldn't be tired. Actually he had every reason in the world to be tired. He slogged down the street toward his car, eyes on the concrete in front of his feet. But a few seconds later his gaze was pulled up by a voice he felt he should know.

"Brock?"

The call came from an unfamiliar face, but the man's countenance said they knew each other. The man was over six feet and wore his brown curly hair long. His eyes were bright and his flowing clothes looked like they came straight out of the Summer of Love. The man loped toward Brock with a wide smile and open arms.

"Yes."

Should he fake it? Pretend to know the guy? Probably. It would avoid a lot of questions and get him home much quicker.

"How are you?" Brock shifted his meal and offered his hand.

"Well beyond what I should be allowed to enjoy." He pointed at Brock's bag and frowned. "What is that?"

"Takeout. Thai."

"No! No! This can't be." The man closed his eyes, leaned back, and drew in a long smell through his nose. "Ah, just kidding. Aroon cooks a mean Thai dish."

"He does indeed."

"But you?" The man opened his eyes and frowned. "Takeout?"

"Yeah. Rough day."

"Why not whip it up yourself? Twenty minutes, max. It would be better than this, I mean, it smells wonderful, but with your skill —"

So the man knew he cooked?

"I'm not cooking much these days."

"Sorry to hear that. Any particular reason?"

"A number of different factors. Mostly just life, you know?"

"No, I don't know."

Brock let out a surprised snort. "The cordial thing when someone says something like that is to nod and agree."

The man laughed loudly. "Do you recall that you and I got to know each other a few paces beyond the student-teacher relationship?"

"Um, sure."

Had he taken cooking classes from the guy?

"Do you recall I'm not the best poser in the world?"

Brock nodded.

"Can you handle a serious moment?"

"Sure." Brock shifted his weight and looked deep into the man's eyes.

"You have real talent."

"Thanks." Brock looked down and tried to focus on the pavement, but he felt the man's gaze boring into his skull. He pulled his head up and looked into the man's eyes again.

"I'm serious. The majority of the folks who come through my classes are hobbyists, and some have true skill, but you? You're a cut above. A few cuts above. I would write a recommendation to any restaurant for you. Don't give it up."

The man stared at him as if waiting for an answer.

"Life has gotten complicated."

"Life is a tapestry of complications." The man swirled his hand through the air. "You're no different from anyone else. And the only failures in life are the men and women who stop weaving."

"Good to see you again." Brock shifted

his meal back to his right hand and nodded. "I appreciate the thoughts."

The man nodded back and walked off
without another word.

Brock ate his meal while he stared at the
ripples on Lake Union and waited for
another dreamless night to take him. His
next meeting with Shagull was still days off,
and he fought to believe this would not be
his existence for the rest of his life.

Each day that passed without dreaming
was another nail in the coffin. His mind
filled with the possibility that he'd never
win Karissa back, but he refused to let the
thought attach itself to his heart. He would
win her back. He had to.

Moments later, as if on cue, the memory
of how they met surfaced, and he relived
that day back in '85 when she'd stolen his
heart forever.

CHAPTER 39

August 13, 1985

"What are you doing on Saturday?"

The sun had just reached the midpoint in its arc across the sky. Morgan and Brock hoisted cans of paint up their ladders propped against the Quail Run apartments in north Kirkland. It wasn't a bad way to make money for grad school, and working with Morgan made the days move faster. Morgan's dad wanted him to work more than just at the coffee shop to understand what working for someone else was like.

Saturday? Brock had nothing planned. But the way Morgan asked told Brock it wasn't a casual question.

"Going somewhere with you?"

"I hope so. I need a wingman."

"For?"

"I have a date." Morgan glanced at Brock before turning back to the apartment building. He pulled his paintbrush back and forth

347

across the tan siding, turning it white. "Kind of."

"I love 'kind of' dates."

"It's casual, not sure if I want to take it to the next level, not sure if she wants to, but it's time to find out."

"What's her name?"

"Can't tell you. Don't want to jinx it."

"How is telling me her name going to jinx it?"

Morgan appeared to concentrate on the wall in front of him and worked on it with broad strokes. "I met her up at Western. She broke up with this jerk in April that treated her like dirt, and we've spent some time together. Just friends, but I think there might be something there. We've been writing letters since school got out, and last time I wrote I asked her to go to the waterslides and she said yes."

"Is that supposed to explain why you won't tell me her name?"

"I told you, not going to jinx it."

"Where is this Romeo and Juliet slip-and-slide encounter supposed to take place?"

"Up north. The Birch Bay Waterslides six miles south of the Canadian border."

"And you think you need a chaperone?"

"Nah." Morgan sighed. "I just don't want to be the only guy there, that's way awkward. She's bringing two of her roommates. Three against one. I need to you there to balance things out."

Brock dipped his brush in the can of white paint sitting on his aluminum ladder and worked on the drainpipe that ran up the wall for three stories. He'd be climbing to the top of the building before six o'clock rolled around. *College kid dies falling off a ladder three stories up. Film at eleven.*

He sighed and looked at Morg. Brock didn't want to take an entire day to drive to Bellingham and back, or pretend to be interested in two girls just so Morgan could make his move on one of his classmates. He'd just broken up with Sheila and didn't want anything to do with the opposite sex for at least twenty years. On the other hand, Morgan had traipsed along on Brock's numerous female adventures over the years.

"What am I supposed to do if I go?" Brock climbed another two rungs up his ladder.

"Keep the other two girls occupied while I see if there's any hope for me. Make sure I have the space to wield my irresistible moves."

"Does this mystery woman know your moves are irresistible?"

"Ha." A large dollop of white paint freed itself from Morgan's brush and splattered on the gray patio ten feet below. "So are you in?"

Brock pointed at the concrete. "You're going to want to clean that up if you don't want Gordy reducing the size of your backside."

"Yeah, yeah. In a minute."

"Hey!" At that moment, their boss, Gordy Daubenspeck, strode around the corner. "Brock is right, get that cleaned up. Now."

Brock snickered.

"What are you laughing at, Matthews?" Gordy pointed at the wall in front of Brock's brush. "How many times do I have to tell you to get enough paint on your brush? We want to cover the wall, don't we? Tan showing through is not good. So don't scrub, floooooow, you must floooooow when you paint. Got it?"

"Yes, sir. Right away, sir." Brock gave a mock salute. "Flooooooowwww."

Gordy strode off as he grumbled, "Rookies. Can't teach 'em anything."

Morgan watched Gordy lumber off, then winked at Brock. "So? Are you in?"

"Why don't you just ask her out, just the two of you?"

"That's what I thought this was when she said yes." Morgan lumbered down off the ladder, which protested against his bulk.

"Then she added her two roommates."

"Maybe she's sending you a message."

"I've never done anything that would make her think we're more than friends." Morgan spit on the ground and used a rag to wipe up the paint. "So that's probably why she invited them."

"Nice clean-up technique. There's this thing called water you might try using."

"I didn't want to make a move till this weekend, so now that she has friends coming, I don't want that to mess it up."

"She's on to you."

"What's that mean?"

"Women are human radar machines." Brock inspected his flow on the drainpipe and climbed another two rungs on his ladder. "I think they can pick up on if a guy is trying to cross the friend-neutral zone."

"She's not on to me."

"Okay."

"Are you in?"

"Sure."

"Thanks. You won't regret it."

"Sure I won't."

August 17, 1985

They pulled onto 405 north at eight Saturday morning accompanied by the sounds of Led Zeppelin blasting out of Morgan's Alpine speakers. An hour and fifty minutes later they pulled into the Birch Bay Waterslides parking lot. The lot was half full, with more cars streaming in at the lot's other entrance. They parked, got out of Morgan's Camaro, and leaned against the car as Morgan scanned the lot for his kind-of date. Ten minutes later, a late-seventies powder-blue Subaru pulled into the lot, and Morgan pushed off his car. A twinge of nervous anticipation washed through Brock as he caught a glimpse of the driver of the car and her passenger. Where did that come from?

The Subaru pulled into a spot thirty yards from Morgan and Brock. Two girls got out and glanced around the lot. A few seconds later they spotted Morgan, waved, then called out, "Hey! You made it!"

Brock glared at Morgan. "I thought you said there would be three girls. You set me up on a blind date."

"I didn't know. Swear! She said she was bringing both her roommates."

"Great."

"Here we go." Morgan flicked a hidden thumbs-up to Brock, then spun and moved toward the girls. He picked up his pace as he got closer, and by the time he was fifteen yards away he had broken into a slow jog.

Brock strolled over with the slow-boat-to-China approach. This would be a long day.

As he approached the girls, he tensed. The one on the right had dark-brown hair, brown eyes that made Bambi's look dull by comparison, and a playfulness in her face that was more than captivating. *Intoxicating* was the more accurate description. She wore a white tank top and dark-blue shorts that hugged long, tanned legs. Her gaze was fixed on Morgan and she pointed at him, then wiggled her finger toward the water-slides.

"This should be so fun."

"No doubt." Morgan reached the girl and gave her a quick hug, then nodded at the one on the left and said hello.

So the girl on the right was the girl with no name. No question why Morgan was enamored with her. A few seconds later Brock reached the three of them.

"Okay." Morgan put his sizable arm around Brock. "This is my best friend in the universe, Brock Matthews. Brock, this is Karissa, and this is her friend, Bonnie."

"Good to meet both of you." Brock thanked himself for putting sunglasses on. No way for Karissa to know he was gawking at her. It was her. Had to be. The one Future Brock had talked about less than a month earlier.

"You too," Karissa said, and Bonnie added the same.

"What happened to your other roommate?" Morgan glanced between the two girls.

"Something came up at the last second. Sorry about that."

"No, it's all good." Morgan turned to Brock. "You good?"

"I'm good." He ignored the hammering of his heart and smiled.

"We going to do this?" Karissa pointed again to the waterslides in back of her, and her smile dimmed the sun.

Brock had dated a lot of girls in high school and college and had enjoyed getting to know all of them. But none came close to the dream girl he'd held in his mind since his midteens. Until now. Stupid to feel this way. How could she be his dream girl after two minutes of knowing her? But the emotion was undeniable. How had the old guy known?

They made small talk as they bought their tickets and listened to the shrieks of fun coming from the slides. They passed through the gate and strolled into the park, which was filled with the smell of chlorine and overcooked hot dogs. After getting a locker key, Morgan and Brock headed into the men's bathroom to change into their swimsuits.

"Whaddaya think?" Morgan slid a key into the locker, opened the door, and held it as he waited for Brock's answer.

"Waterslides look great." Brock pulled his suit out of his bag, set his sunglasses on the small shelf of the locker, slipped off his T-shirt, and stretched his arms over his head. "Should be a fun day."

He glanced up at Morgan, who had somehow already changed. Faster than Clark Kent changing into Superman in a phone booth.

"Nice try, what do you think of her?"

"Bonnie seems really nice. I like her curly hair, good smile. Nice laugh."

"Do I have to hurt you? Don't want to, but I will." Morgan pulled his fist back and jabbed it back and forth.

"Karissa's cute, bright personality . . . I can see why you like her."

"She's beautiful."

"I agree."

"So you're good with the plan? Keeping Bonnie company?"

"Like white on rice."

They emerged from the men's bathroom and Brock took in the four huge slides that dominated the park. Two smaller slides were set to the left, and a six-story speed slide with a long line of people shot into the sky on their right. The park also boasted a kiddie pool with three slides, a giant hot tub, and the River Ride, which you could float down in single, double, or triple occupancy tubes.

After two or three minutes, Morgan turned his palms skyward. "Where are they?"

"Getting ready."

"How long does it take to put a swimsuit on?"

"For you, apparently eleven point five seconds. For them a little longer." Brock popped him in the shoulder. "Don't worry, Karissa probably just wants to make sure she's perfect for you."

"You looking to drown today?"

As Brock laughed he spotted Karissa and Bonnie exiting the women's bathroom. Karissa strolled toward them in a pale blue swimsuit that definitely accentuated her trim figure but covered enough skin that Brock didn't feel like he was leering simply by glancing in her direction. She'd pulled her hair into a ponytail, which dropped her age by five years but somehow made her even more beautiful.

They joined the girls at the edge of a grassy section of the park and laid down their towels. The four of them attacked each one of the four main slides with abandon. The banter between them was light and quick, and Brock tried to keep his answers brief as Karissa engaged him in questions about his major in college, and what movies he liked, and what his hobbies were. He kept wishing Morgan would engage, but his big friend was uncharacteristically quiet.

After an hour and a half, they meandered back to their towels spread out on the grass to the west of the slides and ate turkey sandwiches washed down with Dr Pepper and Mountain Dew. The sun grew hotter and Brock wanted to get back to the water. But this wasn't his show.

"Ready?" Karissa tossed her sandwich wrapper into a paper bag, bounded to her feet, and cupped her hand to her ear. "I hear the Hydrocliff calling. Free-fall slide with a sixty-foot drop, and that's the only one we haven't tried yet. We must go. Adventure awaits."

"Nah." Morgan patted his stomach. "Need to let the food settle for a few more minutes first before free-falling anywhere. Or even standing up."

"Bonnie? You ready?"

"Same." Bonnie squinted up at Karissa. "Take a few slides without me, 'kay?"

Karissa poked Brock's leg with her toe and flashed her megawatt smile. "How 'bout you?"

Awkward moment. Should he stay? Everything in him wanted to go, but this was Morgan's chance. His opening to get some time with Karissa alone. What was Morgan thinking? *Move, you big ox.*

Brock turned to Morgan. "Karissa's right. Adrenaline calls. Time to answer. Bonnie and I'll hold down the fortress and guard the blankets."

"Give me ten, fifteen maybe. Okay, twenty." Morgan settled back on his blanket, slipped his sunglasses on, and splayed his arms out to the side. "Maybe thirty. I try to promise I won't fall asleep."

Karissa laughed. "Am I the only one who thinks I can lie in the sun anywhere, but where else can I get massive amounts of water up my nose as I slide down those tubes totally out of control?" Karissa poked Brock again. "Come on, I can tell you want to go."

He did. So he went. For the next two hours Karissa and he whipped down the slides behind each other, rode double tubes together, and raced on different slides, starting at the same time to see who shot out into the landing pool first. They talked about everything and nothing as they climbed the stairs and waited in line for their turns. Brock couldn't ignore the playful, inviting look in Karissa's eyes every time she looked at him.

The day ended too soon, and the four of them stood in the middle of the parking lot saying their good-byes.

"That was too fun." Karissa smiled at Morgan and gave him a quick hug. "See you at Marcia and Scott's wedding in a few months, right?"

"Indeed you will."

She turned to Brock. "You're playing guitar in their wedding, from what Morgan tells me."

Brock nodded.

"Then I guess I'll see you as well." She stared at him a split second past normal, and Brock's heart felt it like a laser.

Brock nodded again. Minutes later, Morgan and he had slipped into the Camaro and were speeding down I-5 back to Seattle. Brock turned up Van Halen on Morgan's car stereo and as soon as he did, Morgan turned it down. "You good, my sunburnt brother?"

"Yeah."

"Liar."

"Some brother I turn out to be." Brock sighed and stared out the window to his right at the thick stands of trees whizzing by.

"What do you mean?"

Brock glanced at Morgan, then turned to gaze through the passenger window again. "Sorry."

"For what?"

"For what happened today."

Morgan grinned. "Tell me what happened."

"Me. Ejecting from the plane and leaving you with no wingman."

"English, Brock."

"Spending all that time with Karissa while you and Bonnie were on the grass." Brock pressed his temples. "For flirting with her . . . for —"

"For hitting it off with Karissa like a grand-slam homer?"

"Yeah." Brock rubbed his finger on a deep scrape on his knee he'd picked up on the River Ride. "I didn't mean for it to happen, but she asked if I wanted to go, and you didn't —"

"Let it lie." Morgan laughed and popped the steering wheel. "I think it's awesome."

"You do?"

"I knew if you guys ever met and spent more than five minutes together you'd hit it off like a sun going nova."

"If you knew that, then why'd you invite me? I thought you liked her."

"I do. For you." Morgan grinned. "You and your God-destiny stuff can make you extremely stubborn at times. If I'd told you what I was doing, you never would have come. You'd have said it's too soon after Sheila. You'd have said God would set you up when he wanted to do it, that he doesn't need my help. But if I told you I needed help, I knew you'd be there. And you were. So I figured I'd give God an assist on this one. Am I good, or am I good?"

"You don't believe in God."

"Answer the question."

"You're very good."

A smile rose to Brock's face and stayed there for at least five minutes. Eddie Van Halen continued to play his astonishing guitar solos, and Morgan popped him in the shoulder as if toasting the emotions coursing through Brock.

"So?" Morgan said after the song finished.

"What do you mean *so*?"

"What do you think? Gut-level honest."

A puff of laughter escaped Brock's lips. Honest? He'd only broken up with Sheila a month ago and had promised himself he'd be single for a long time, but he was head over heels for Karissa. It was stupid to say it, but he couldn't imagine life without her.

"You're right, I shouldn't even be thinking about it . . . but she's my dream girl. Everything about her."

As they tore over the freeway back down to Seattle, Brock had room for only one thought in his head: When could he see her again? He replayed her smile, her quick wit, her captivating eyes.

"I'm best man, right?" Morgan laughed.

"Shut up. I just met her."

"Just take it slow, she's been burned."

"How?"

"Don't ask me, I don't know what it means. Bonnie just said she's got the deer syndrome right now." Morgan glanced at Brock. "You know. A little skittish. That bad relationship I mentioned when we were painting. I'm guessing that's it."

Morgan continued talking, but Brock didn't catch any of it. *Hit it off* was the wrong description for his encounter with Karissa. Meeting a woman it would be tough to live without was more accurate. She'd yanked his heart out of his chest and said, "Hello, Brock, I'm your destiny."

■ ■ ■ ■

The memory faded and Brock shook his head. So vivid the memory, so real the emotions. But the smell of brewing coffee and the sound of kayakers on the water outside stole over him, and he remembered where he was. But though the scene faded, the feelings didn't. He'd never believed in love at first sight, but after August 17, 1985, he definitely believed in love at first day. Karissa had captured him lock, stock, and barrel with unquenchable visions of the future.

Less than three years later they were married and started living a life that wasn't a fairy tale every hour of the day, but twenty-three and a half hours out of twenty-four was pretty good. It was so cliché, but so, so true: you never know what you have till it's gone. And now the love that used to burn inside her for him had been completely snuffed out. And he was the one who had smothered the fire. But now he would grab matches and relight it.

CHAPTER 40

June 9, 2015

He found Karissa the next afternoon at the university.

"What do you want, Brock?" Karissa glanced at him, then back to her cell phone as she marched across campus.

Time to risk it all.

"I need to tell you in detail about something I mentioned last time we spoke."

"Send me an e-mail." Karissa typed on her phone as she glanced back and forth between the path and her cell.

"It won't take long." Brock waited till she finished with her phone. "But I need your full attention."

"How long?"

"Five minutes."

"Do it in three." She took a last look at her cell phone, slid it into her purse.

Brock held his hands out to his side and pleaded with his eyes.

"Fine, four minutes. Go."

"Do you remember me telling you I've been forgetting things? When I talked to you about Tyson?"

"Yes." She tapped her foot.

"That's not exactly true."

"Big shocker." Her tapping sped up. "Thanks for the confession. Are we done?"

"It's not that I can't remember, it's that the majority of the things in my life right now, the history of my life right now, didn't happen to me. Do you remember me telling you last time that this isn't my time line? That's what I meant. I didn't live this life."

"Wow, now we're dealing with reality. Good." Karissa sighed and hoisted her purse farther up her shoulder. "I gotta go."

"Please, two more minutes." Brock held up his fingers. "Just two. Something impossible has been happening to me. I don't know how, Karissa. But I'm dead serious when I tell you somehow I dreamed and talked to a younger version of myself. I told him things and he made different choices, and it changed things here in the present. Each time I woke up from a dream, the world had changed. Everything was different, and not in a good way."

She stopped tapping her foot. Her shoulders slumped and she slowly shook her head. Brock braced for her full dismissal of him.

"What did you say?" She took a tiny step toward him, an incredulous look splayed on her face as she repeated the question. "What did you just say to me?"

"That I'm somehow connecting with the Brock from the mideighties. In my dreams."

"This can't be happening." Her gaze moved past his head, and she put out a hand as if to steady herself, shuffled a few steps to the right, and settled onto a bench.

"Karissa?" Brock moved toward her.

"How in the world . . . it's not possible . . ."

"What's not?" He stopped three feet from the bench.

"This is so bizarre."

"What is?"

She frowned at him, disbelief on her face. "You told me about this. You did. It's all coming back to me."

Had he? In another one of the time lines? If he had, she wouldn't be reacting like this. "I don't think so. This is the first time I've —"

"Shut up, Brock. I mean you told me about it when we were young. When we were first dating. You told me you were having conversations with some old guy who claimed to be you. We were running on the Burke-Gilman Trail." She peered up at him with a look full of trepidation. "I blew it off at the time, and you did too after I started questioning your sanity. We joked about it for at least a few months after. But I could tell, there was a part of you that believed God was doing something extraordinary. A part that didn't just believe, but would take action."

"That Brock did take action."

"You can't be serious. You're saying that version of yourself did things differently?"

"In my reality yes. In yours, no."

"But even though I don't remember both time lines, you do?"

"No, I only remember the one I was in before I started dreaming. So each time things change, I'm flying blind. I'm trying to figure out what has changed, the chaos that version of myself has created."

Karissa's eyes narrowed. "Not the choices you would have made."

Brock was silent for a moment. "But I did make them. The capability to choose the wrong path is in me. And worse than that, I'm the one who set myself on that path."

"You're making my mind spin."

"Welcome to my insane world." Brock opened his palms. "His actions — my actions — changed everything. It's my fault, all of it. My fault."

"What is?"

"Didn't you hear me? I outlined a plan for myself and it changed my history. Things that I never wanted to happen, happened. And now all I want is to go back."

"Back to what?"

"You and me. There was never a divorce. I never married Sheila. Tyson never killed a man and went to jail."

"You really believe that, don't you?"

"I lived it. It was my reality for fifty-three years. What I've been going through for the past two weeks is not my life. Not your life. Not our life. It's a waking nightmare."

"Were we happy?"

The question tore at Brock because he couldn't lie, but he didn't want to tell her the truth. "We could have been."

She stared at him with cold eyes, but then the ice started to melt, and she didn't drop her gaze. It took only seconds for the final bit of frost to leave her countenance, and for the first time in years, in any of the realities he'd lived in, the real Karissa looked at him.

" 'My density has brought me to you.' " Brock smiled, held out his hand like George McFly did in *Back to the Future,* and finished the quote. " 'I'm your density. I mean, your destiny.' "

She tried to suppress her laughter, but he saw the last vestige of her resolve to shut him out shatter, and she laughed. Brock took a tentative step forward, then another, then he sat next to her on the bench.

"We can figure this out. We can turn it around, I know we can."

Karissa shuddered as if years of pain were falling off her. She turned away from him slightly and leaned forward as her hands rose to her face. Soft sobs floated toward him and he debated staying still or letting his arm wrap around her. He hesitated, then put his arm on her shoulders with the weight of a feather. With his other hand, he pulled two tickets from his back pocket and held them out in front of her.

"What's that?"

"Me being crazy." He hesitated as he glanced at the tickets. "It's two tickets to the Birch Bay Waterslides."

"You can't be serious."

"Want to go?"

"You're insane, Brock." Karissa turned her head, but not before Brock spied a hint of longing in her eyes.

"Do you remember that day?"

The veneer cracked further and Brock saw

the twenty-four-year-old Karissa that had fallen in love with him that summer day back in '85. And then he saw deeper, into the pain he'd caused her. It didn't matter that he hadn't really done it to her, because the choices he'd made had caused it to happen, no matter which version of him caused it.

"One of the best days of my life."

"Then let's go back." Brock held up the tickets again. "Please. Let's just try."

"Brock, I don't . . . I can't . . ."

"No expectations, let's just go."

Karissa shuddered again, then stiffened and pushed herself into the back of the bench. A moment later the mask was back up and set in place more securely than before.

"No, Brock. I'm not a kid anymore. Neither are you. Let it go. Let us go."

"I can't. I love you too much."

"I'm sorry. This is too strange." Karissa shifted her weight from him and scooted away. "Maybe a shred of my mind believes you. But even if it does, what difference does that make? We're still where we are. Now. Today."

He stared at her as his stomach clenched. "I don't understand."

"Don't you get it? You might not remember carving up our relationship with a serrated blade, but I do."

"I'm sorry, but that wasn't —"

"Listen! In my time line, you still made the choices you made, the scars you created are just as deep, and the memories just as painful."

Brock had no argument. She was right. He did get it. But that didn't quench his certainty that God was in this moment right now, and he wanted to breach the wall that stood between them.

"Don't shut me out. You felt it. I know you felt it. God stirred something inside you. Don't shut him out. Don't shut down what he's doing between us."

"Really?" Karissa tilted her head down, looked at him from under her eyebrows and pointed at the sky. "You're going to lay the God card on me? After what you've done to me? You've got to be kidding."

She tilted her head back and locked her jaw. The final brick in her wall snapped into place, and he had no doubt the Karissa who had sat on the bench next to him just a moment ago had vanished.

"Don't go, Karissa. Please."

"Stay out of my life." She surged to her feet, spun, then called out over her shoulder.

"You and I are dead. And resurrection isn't coming."

CHAPTER 41

Brock headed for Java Spot praying he and Morgan were still friends. He was the only person left. But what if his friend didn't know him in this time line? What if his younger self had blown up that relationship as well? But he was out of other options and needed to talk to someone.

When he arrived at Java Spot, Brock went around to the back and pulled out the key Morgan had given him years ago. If it worked in the lock that would be a strong sign they were still friends. He slid it in, hesitated a moment, then turned. The lock opened and Brock puffed out a sigh of relief. Yes.

He wove through the stainless-steel racks that held filters and syrups and boxes of Black Fedora coffee. He tapped a case of Colibri Ochre and smiled. He'd actually had to work a little to get that one right. Before he could leave the storage room, the two-way door was flung open. Morgan stepped through and jerked his head back in surprise.

"Whoa, Nelly!" Morgan did his horrid impression of that old sports announcer. "Ya talk about chur ding-dong-dandy breakin, give-me-a-heart-attack play. You trying to get yourself shot, son?" Morgan grinned and gave Brock a quick hug. "Where've you been, Brock-O?"

"We're friends, right?"

"No, sworn enemies as we've always been. Like Lex and Superman. You're Lex, of course." Morgan threw his head back and flexed in a bodybuilder pose that accentuated his biceps as well as his sizable gut. "Tell me, I know, I should change my name to Adonis."

"Without question."

Morgan relaxed and pointed to his mouth. "I sound just like him, don't I?"

"The impression's getting better." Brock held his thumb and forefinger a half inch apart. "You've moved it from a one to a one and a half on a scale of a thousand."

Morgan wiggled a finger at him. "I'm going to make money on that impression someday. Just needs a little more work."

"No one knows who what's-his-name is anymore."

"Wrong again. Everyone knows him. Keith Jackson is a legend."

"So was Howard Cosell."

"Who?" Morgan squinted.

"My point exactly."

"I know who Cosell was. I grew up with him just like you. That was a joke."

"I'm laughing inside."

Morgan grabbed a stack of napkins and a bottle of Italian-soda syrup and handed them to Brock. "Here, take this out, will ya?"

Brock followed him out into the shop. A few customers lingered, but the place was mostly empty. Morgan snatched two bags of Jamaican Azure and one bag of Karoma Brûlée off a shelf to Brock's right and plopped them on the counter. "People are loving your latest concoctions. They're gold."

"I need to talk."

"Okay, spill it." Morgan rested his large frame on his elbows on the counter. "From the look on your face, it's a whopper."

"I'm stuck here."

"Where?"

"I can't get out of this time line."

"Good, now you're making sense."

"This isn't my life." Brock swept his hand in a wide circle. "None of it. You're not going to believe me, I know, but I swear to you that I'm not making it up."

"Making what up?"

"And it's your fault."

"You want to start at the beginning?"

"Do you remember giving me that book on lucid dreaming?"

"A book on what?"

Brock rubbed his face. Of course not. Not in this time line. "Never mind."

"No way, you gotta tell me now."

As Brock laid out what had happened to him, Morgan's face morphed from amusement to concern to resignation.

"You really believe what you're telling me."

"I don't believe it, I know it. I swear I've had conversations inside my dreams with a younger version of myself. Told him things he should do differently. He did, and it's destroyed my life."

"Sorry to be blunt, Brock-O, but you did that all by yourself."

"Yeah, I did, just not in the way you think I did." Brock stared at the cup of coffee in front of him. He didn't have the energy to try to convince Morgan what he said was true. Even if he did, what would it accomplish? It wouldn't change anything.

"I went to see my brother yesterday."

"Any thaw?"

"I threw another six feet of ice on top of what was already there." Brock kicked at the floor.

"How?"

"The wrestling match from years back. I revisited what I did to his hand."

Morgan frowned. "Why in the world would you unearth that treasure?"

"Couldn't help it." Brock frowned at Morgan. "It didn't happen in my other time line."

"Of course it didn't." Morgan winked. "Talk to me, what do you need?"

"Right now, I need a liberal dose of Baileys added to this concoction. Do you have any in the back?"

Morgan frowned at him with the look of a scolding teacher. "Don't think we need to go there."

"What?"

"You better be joking about the drink or I'm going to have to smack you upside the head and see if there's any sanity left inside."

"What's wrong with me having a drink?"

Morgan stared at him, the scolding look now returning to one of concern.

"You okay?"

"Tell me why you're worried about me having a drink."

Even before Brock heard the answer, he knew his world was about to be rocked again with a revelation that would rip the cover off another dark part of his soul. Even though the three remaining Java Spot customers were well out of earshot, Morgan leaned forward and lowered his voice.

"I'm not that familiar with AA and the principles they sling around in their meetings, but I'm thinking that once you're set free from the bottled demons, you aren't supposed to pick up a glass ever again."

Heat washed through Brock as he recalled Ron's implication. "How long?"

"You telling me you don't remember anything from those years?"

Brock blinked.

"What you are doing, Brock?"

"Please."

"Are you telling me you don't have any recollection about being wasted six days out of seven for three years straight?"

Brock's only response was a shake of his head.

"You truly don't?"

"How long ago?"

Morgan looked up to his right. "You started drinking in 2000 and it went full-blown gonzo in 2001. Let's just say you started the second half of the decade in a way you'll never remember."

"And then?"

"By the summer of 2004 you figured it out, got help, and haven't touched anything that I know of since. And never been tempted since." Morgan let out a mock cough. "Till now."

"The drinking." Brock spun a drink coaster like a top. "That's what broke up my marriage to Karissa."

"It wasn't just the drinking, but the booze had to be a major contributing factor, yeah. No surprise there. You ready to tell me what's really going on?"

"I already told you." Brock stood and stared down at his friend. "Thanks for listening. And do me a favor."

"Anything."

"In three days I'm meeting with a man who might be able to help. Pray for that conversation."

Morgan laughed. "You're never going to let that go, are you?"

"Let what go?" Brock's body went limp. "You became a Christian at that men's retreat back in '98. I was there."

Morgan smiled. "Tell you what, Brock-O. If I ever do get religious, my first prayer will be for you."

CHAPTER 42

June 10, 2015
Finally. Time to meet with Shagull again. Within minutes of arriving at the Ballard Locks, Brock spotted Shagull leaning back against the railing. The doctor peered into the locks at the boats lined up for their turn as he stuffed what looked like three or four walnuts into his mouth. When he spied Brock he waved and chewed faster, and tossed the rest of his meal to the pigeons in front of him looking for a snack.

"Lovely day," Shagull said when Brock reached him, then guided them to a dark-green bench.

Brock gazed at the sunlight dancing on the leaves of the maples and drew in the faint scent of Puget Sound carried by a light wind. What the doctor said was true, but he hadn't noticed any of it till now. "Hard to see the beauty these days."

"Ah, yes." The doctor leaned his walking

stick up against the bench. "I can't imagine."

"You mean you can imagine."

"No." The doctor leaned in. "I can't for a moment conjure up the pain you must be going through. I have great empathy for you."

Brock leaned forward, elbows on his knees, "Karissa is gone from my life. Tyson is barely there. Morgan isn't a Christian. Please tell me there's hope for me dreaming again. I have to get back there."

The doctor answered by launching into a monologue.

"In its own way, the story of every man and every woman is a quest. A journey not unlike Bilbo's in *The Hobbit,* or Dorothy's in *The Wonderful Wizard of Oz,* or the Pevensie children in *The Lion, the Witch, and the Wardrobe.* Bilbo went with the dwarfs. Dorothy went down the yellow-brick road. Lucy, Edmund, Susan, and Peter stepped through the wardrobe and into Narnia. Alice went down the rabbit hole. Neo chose the red pill. You are on your own quest."

Brock leaned back and sighed. He wasn't up for a lecture about quests and destiny. He needed to know how to dream again.

"There's a point to this, right?"

"Most people refuse to face the truth.

They choose to stay where they think they're safe." Shagull sat back against the bench. "You've made choices, Brock."

"And look where it's brought me."

"Where is that?"

"You know exactly where. Tell me how to dream again so I can get back to the time before I, or he, made the decisions I influenced him to make. I have to turn this thing around."

"What if you never dream again?"

"I can't continue to live like this."

"Why not? You're the one who set this life in motion." The doctor folded his hands and tilted his head.

"Which is why I need to be the one to change its trajectory."

"I'd like to give you something." The doctor used one hand to open his coat, the other to pull out a long brown envelope. He set the envelope on his lap.

"What's in the envelope?"

"We'll get to that in a minute." The doctor tapped his lips. "Do you think God speaks? Talks to us?"

"Sometimes I think yes, sometimes I'm not so sure."

"Neither am I." The doctor chuckled. "But I'm starting to lose my balance on the fence and believe I'm falling."

"Which side are you coming down on?"

"That he does speak. If we're willing to slow down enough to listen. And if we're willing to act on what he says."

"You care to tell me what he said to you?"

"I think you might need to do something that was set in motion years ago. I think it's time." The doctor lifted the envelope. "It might seem a little odd, but I think God told me to make a suggestion."

"What?"

"It's just an impression, mind you, that it should be now. Might have been him telling me, might have been a stray idea that bubbled up from my subconscious without bidding."

"What should be now?"

Shagull handed Brock the envelope. "Open it."

Brock tore open the envelope and pulled out a sheet of paper with a picture of a mountain on it. Below the photo it read, *Despite its intermediate difficulty, Mount Pilchuck sees a slew of visitors in any given year as hikers flock to the trail for its grand panoramic views and historic restored fire lookout. Easily one of the most rewarding hikes in the area, its relatively short 2.7 mile, 2,300-foot ascent gifts you 360-degree views of Mount Baker, Mount Rainier, and the Olympics from its shelter lookout, which sits nestled on a summit that tops out around 5,300 feet. The journey is made possible by a high-elevation trailhead, which sets you off on your travels around 3,000 feet, cutting what would otherwise be an arduous ten-mile round-trip in half.*

"You want me to hike up there."

"Yes."

"And do what?"

"Northeast of the fire lookout — fifty or so feet — is a box hidden, covered by a rock two shades darker than any of the rocks near it. I want you to find it."

"Did you leave it there?"

"No, a friend of mine did."

"But you want me to open it."

"Yes. Trust me, my friend will be fine with that."

"Who is your friend?"

The doctor's eyes brightened, and his countenance betrayed a deeper knowledge of what Mt. Pilchuck would mean for Brock.

"What do you know, Dr. Shagull?"

The doctor rose and brushed off his slacks. "Nothing."

"Tell me."

The doctor clasped his hands behind his back and stretched his arms. "It would take considerable force to convince me that would be a wise decision. We'll talk again after your return."

Shagull tipped his hat, snatched his walking stick from where it rested against the bench, and strode away from Brock at a faster clip than a man of his age should have been able to generate. Brock remained on the bench for another ten minutes, wishing he was in better shape, because tomorrow he'd go on a hike that might be the key to the door of his salvation, and he wouldn't be able to get up that mountain fast enough.

CHAPTER 43

June 11, 2015

Within ten minutes of reaching the top of Mt. Pilchuck, Brock found the rock on the north side of the summit and shoved it to the side. Underneath was a wooden box inside a thick plastic bag, within another plastic bag, both yellowed with age. He opened the bags and slid out the box. His name was carved into the top. What? How was that possible? A friend of Shagull's had done this?

Brock lifted the box and climbed down the back side of the peak till he found a small alcove where he wouldn't be spotted by anyone who might appear at the top of the mountain. Even though he'd hit the trail at six thirty that morning, he didn't want to chance bumping into other early risers.

The box was simple but radiated an astounding elegance. Six or seven inches long by four inches wide. It looked like maple wood with multiple coats of a dark stain. Brock ran his fingers over the surface, almost expecting it be warm. It wasn't, but a sense of wonder and lightness filled him as he placed his whole hand on the box.

He lifted the lid slowly as if he didn't want the wonders inside to escape. The box made no sound as he lifted the lid. A thick piece of paper sat on top of the contents. He unfolded it.

May 31, 2005

Dear Future Brock,

Brock stopped and went to the bottom of the page to confirm what he'd just realized.

Your friend in dreams,
Brock

Heat raced through him. Incomprehensible. *He* was Shagull's friend, the one who had made the box and placed it on top of this mountain. Brock closed his eyes for a few seconds, then opened them and read the entire letter from the top.

May 31, 2005

Dear Future Brock,
If you're reading this, then you are who

you said you were all those years ago.

You changed my life through the things you said, and through things you didn't say.

Now, maybe it's time for me to change yours, or at least remind you of what I pray you already know and are living out every day.

I was going through some old boxes that Mom was going to throw out and found something I want you to see. I'm not going to tell you why, I get the feeling God will tell you what it's all about. And if you embrace what he tells you, it will set you free.

I think what you'll find in the box I made is the place where the circles intersect.

Your friend in dreams,

Brock

As Brock reread the letter, he tried to wrap his mind around the fact his younger self had written to him in this time line. He'd stopped trying to figure out how his present and past had intertwined to form a new reality, but this was a new twist. And how did Shagull know to send him up this mountain?

Brock turned the box over and his breath

caught. Carved into the bottom were the three overlapping circles Shagull had shown him. The place where the past, the present, and the future meet. And the place where the Father, the Son, and the Spirit intersect.

The top and bottom of the box were lined with what looked like white silk. A thin black border ran along its edges. The only thing inside was a small rectangular object wrapped in light-brown paper. Wonder surged through Brock. The package from his dreams of his father. He touched the torn corner as if it might shock him, hesitated, then tore half the paper away.

Brock sat stunned, staring at a relic from this childhood he hadn't thought of for forty years. Captain Action. The Ideal Toy Company's answer to G.I. Joe. Captain Action, who could turn into Batman, Spider-Man, Captain America, Aquaman, the Lone Ranger, and so many other characters.

Captain Action, the ultimate hero. One for Ron, one for Brock, Christmas 1971. His dad had been almost giddy that morning.

"Okay, last present, boys!" His dad had handed them the gifts and rubbed his hands together as he waited for them to rip off the paper and discover what was inside.

"Do you like him?" Their father grinned

and nodded as they gave their approval. Ron and Brock loved Captain Action.

How could he have forgotten the worlds he and Ron created together? Millions of late nights under their fort blanket downstairs, each of them with their Captain Action in hand, battling the forces of evil together. Their mom forcing them to come inside after another endless summer night of creating adventures under the trees in their backyard.

"Ronnie! Watch this!" Brock had launched himself out of the apple tree next to their above-ground plastic pool, Captain Action in Superman mode in hand, and belly-flopped into the water. When Brock recovered, Ron climbed the tree and flung himself down like his older brother, smacking the water even harder. Their stomachs hurt for two hours, but they didn't care.

Their dad built them a headquarters for the captains out of wood and bought them every issue of the Captain Action comic book. But in the fall of the following year, their dad had his nervous breakdown and everything changed. Captain Action left Brock's life. The figure reminded him too much of his dad. But that wasn't the case with Ron.

"Brockie! Come on, let's play." Ron had

held up his Captain Action and his Green Hornet costume on a Saturday afternoon full of rain and boredom. "You be the Phantom, and I'll be Green Hornet. And we'll save the —"

"Ronnie, I'm . . . I don't feel like it right now . . . I gotta do some other stuff."

"Whaddaya gotta do?"

"Practice basketball and school stuff."

"What about the code?" Ron's eyes pleaded with him. "We gotta follow our Code. Please?"

"Um, yeah, maybe after dinner tonight, okay?"

"Promise?"

"Yeah, sure."

But Brock broke the promise, and they never played Captain Action again.

Brock stared at the package and tore off the rest of the brown wrapping. He hesitated, then opened the top and pulled out the figure. Captain Action stared at him as if asking where Brock had been all these years. *Stupid thought,* he told himself. But it wasn't.

Taped to the figure was a piece of paper. Brock had no doubt what it was.

"I have an idea, boys." Their dad had put down a piece of paper and laid a thick black marker on top of it. "Every hero has a code.

How he's going to act. What do you think about coming up with a code for you guys and Captain Action? Because you two are heroes now."

Brock unfolded the paper as if it were two-thousand-year-old parchment. There, scrawled in Ron's and his eight- and nine-year-old writing, was their proclamation to the world:

OUR CAPTAIN ACTION CODE

Save the world!
Destroy the bad guys!
Rescue all the good guys!
Get the girl free!
Brothers till the end of time!
That's all that matters or will ever matter!

Brock sat on the granite boulder, overwhelmed with the truth exploding in his heart. The breeze picked up as if to confirm his feelings. The Code. So simple. So true. There was no line on there about making Black Fedora an idol. Nothing in the Code about being so focused on competition and winning it would become a god. No mention of ignoring your son.

Save the world. Free the girl. Brothers till the end of time. That's all that matters.

Brock read the Code again, and then for a third time before folding it and sliding Captain Action and the note back into the box.

He sat staring at the horizon as the sun made its way across the sky. Finally, he pulled out his phone and dialed Shagull.

"Hello?"

"We met before, didn't we?"

"Yes, Brock. We did. Ten years ago. In the very spot you're standing right now. And we met a few times after that as well."

"You talked to him — to me — about the three circles."

"Yes."

"Only ten years ago." Brock rubbed his face. "When you heard I'd called you, it must have been a shock."

"Quite. Especially when I realized you had no recollection of that earlier encounter. But part of me anticipated it based on what the other Brock told me."

"That's why you don't see readers of your book, but you agreed to see me. Why you've never charged me anything. You wanted to see how this would play out."

"And I wanted to help you."

"Why didn't you tell me?"

"You have to understand, this whole adventure has been almost as strange for you as it has for me, so I wasn't sure how much to say, and how much to leave unsaid. But one thing I was certain of: God is behind this, and with him in control, it is better to say less than needed, rather than say more."

"This explains why you're the only one who has stayed constant in every time line."

"It doesn't explain how it's possible, but it certainly explains why."

"What else do you know?"

"Nothing."

"Where do I go from here?"

"What was in the box? Did it give you any direction?"

"Yes."

"That's all you're going to say?"

"That's all."

When Brock pushed through the door of his houseboat at five that afternoon, he set the box on his kitchen counter and made himself his highly customized BLT. He took it to the roof and watched a pair of kayakers traverse the waters of Lake Union.

His younger self thought God would tell him what the box was all about, that he wouldn't need it spelled out. Uh, yeah. Nice understatement. A billboard across the sky wouldn't have been more clear. He'd forsaken the Code. Karissa? He hadn't set her free, he'd wrapped her in chains. Brothers till the end of time? Yeah, right.

It was time to be a true hero. Die to what he wanted and live to the Code. Time to fix what he'd done. Time to dream and set things right.

He slipped into bed that night begging God to let him dream again so he could save the people he loved. But sleep came and went without dreams and he woke after only four hours, with little hope left.

He glanced at his watch. Two a.m. He sank into the silence and closed his eyes, again asking for the chance to dream. After half an hour crawled by, Brock blew out a long sigh, sat up on the edge of the bed, and forced his body to a standing position. Pain shot down his neck where the tension of his life had taken up permanent residence. He massaged it as he rambled across the room and into the kitchen to make a snack and plan his next steps.

CHAPTER 44

June 12, 2015

Brock wandered onto his deck, settled into his chair, and wrapped himself in the blanket Karissa had given him during the early years of their marriage. Dawn wouldn't begin to creep over the mountains to the east for another two and a half hours, and it felt like it never would. He glanced over at Beth's place. No light on, of course. Nothing stirred at this hour except a few stray cars heading over the Aurora bridge and a few more creeping up and down I-5.

But time seemed to lose its meaning, and almost before he realized it, a thin layer of gray light grew between the horizon and the clouds. A few minutes later it turned into a streak of muted red, then hints of gold crept into the swath of color. He didn't pray, didn't let anything into his mind except the peace of the moment, a fragment of respite from the storm.

But he had to face the truth Young Brock had shown him. He'd forsaken the Code behind the insidious excuse that he was providing for his family, while the whole time he'd made work his god. A god that promised validation always inches beyond his grasp. And now the deception had been exposed, and the light of truth was scorching him.

Yes, there were noble reasons for wanting Black Fedora to succeed. For Karissa and Tyson. For Ron and his family. But those reasons paled in comparison to his ignoble need for validation and identity.

The creak of a door jolted Brock out of his contemplation. He spun to find Beth standing on her deck gazing out over the water.

"Hello, Brock."

"Perfect timing."

"Oh yeah?"

"I took a hike up a mountain."

"Tell me about it." She continued to look straight ahead.

So Brock did.

A smile formed on Beth's face. "And?"

"I'm figuring out what to do next."

"No you're not. You know what's next." Beth turned her gaze toward him and her smile turned radiant. "Keep following the

Code. You've been trying to free the girl
already."

"That's not going so well."

"Then what's your next mission?"

"Brothers forever."

CHAPTER 45

Later that morning, Brock walked into Ron's office and glanced around in surprise. This office was smaller than the one in the other time lines. But it made sense. In this world Brock was the majority owner.

"What are you doing here?" Ron glanced up from his laptop, then went back to studying his monitor.

Brock strode over to Ron and slid a package of papers across his desk.

"What's this?" Ron poked at it with his good hand.

"It's my shares in the company. All of them. And now they're yours. Just sign the papers and you own Black Fedora. Not me, not us. Just you."

"What is wrong with you?" Ron leaned back and put his handless arm behind his head. "Why are you doing this?"

"I want a relationship with you."

"Oh yeah? How exciting."

"Yes, it is."

"Any other reason?"

Brock rested his hands on Ron's desk. "The success of Black Fedora has been one of my gods. Another of my gods has been beating you. The third god in my trinity has been validating myself by being in the spotlight. And now, that life of serving other gods is over."

Ron pointed at the papers again. "Are you sure about this?"

Brock nodded.

Ron leaned forward, his face softer than Brock had seen it in years.

"Interesting timing."

"Why?"

"Because I just discovered we've been blindsided. Someone has been buying up shares of our private stock. All the board members deny any involvement. But it has to be one of them. And if we don't figure it out fast, the shares you want to give me will be worthless. And we'll end up having to sell the company for pennies, or file for bankruptcy."

"What?"

Brock's legs went to liquid and he stumbled. It was happening again. His business skills had not been able to stop it. Not hackers this time, but just as bad.

"It can't be like this. I don't understand."

"I don't either, but right now let's not worry about the shares." Ron stood and came out from behind his desk and nodded at Brock. "I appreciate the gesture. Truly, because I believe you mean it. But for the moment, we need to pour all our energy into finding out who is behind this."

For the next twenty-four hours, Brock worked without sleep trying to uncover the people behind the attack on Black Fedora. But he found nothing. *Think!* There had to be an answer, a way to find out. *Lord?*

Brock slept a few hours, then woke, headed back to the office, and dove back in. He and Black Fedora's IT team went after every lead, trying to identify the one behind the subterfuge, but all of them were dead ends.

Finally, close to eleven that night, Brock shut his office door and shuffled down the hallway of Black Fedora's eighth floor. Half the lights had been shut off, which made the office dim; places always lit now hid in shadow. It gave Brock an eerie feeling, as if he were the last one in the world. He'd never had a problem working by himself at the office late, but as he made his way toward the elevators, the solitary feeling

401

threatened to smother him.

Maybe because it reflected the truth that he was utterly alone for the first time in his life. Karissa was gone, Tyson was locked away for probably life, and his brother was little better than an enemy. Maybe after finding the mastermind behind Black Fedora's demise, he'd move to eastern Washington, build a home in the hills above Chelan, and live the life of a hermit.

He called the elevator, and it slid open immediately as if waiting for him. He stepped inside and pushed the button for the parking garage. He gave his head a shake as if he could toss off the feeling of hopelessness. But it hung on like a leech and continued to draw life out of him. Didn't matter. He felt dead anyway.

When he determined who the mastermind was, at least Ron and he could stare down the person or people who had destroyed them. Brock wouldn't give up till he confronted the man or woman who orchestrated the attack. It was all he had left.

The elevator opened to the gray concrete landscape of the parking garage and he slogged toward his car. The garage was empty except for a silver Astro van with a rack on top that made it look like a giant toaster.

Yes, he would dig again tomorrow like there was no tomorrow, but right now all he wanted was solitude and a movie on his big screen. A moment to forget the world, forget everything and everyone he'd lost.

The garage was still except for the echo of his shoes against the pavement and the sputter of a fluorescent light trying to hang onto its last few hours of life.

He slipped into his Lexus and tossed his briefcase onto the passenger seat. He fumbled on his keychain for his key, found it, and slid it into the ignition. But before he could start his car, a voice from the backseat shot a bolt of adrenaline through him.

"Don't do that. We're going to sit here in your car together for a few minutes, and I wouldn't want you to waste any gas. We need to have a nice little chat before you go home."

Brock's pulse spiked and he started to twist toward the backseat, but his temple smacked into the cold muzzle of a gun.

"Don't do that either."

His gaze shot to the rearview mirror, and the voice spoke a third time as a hand shoved his head forward and down. "Nope. That's not going to be an option for the next few minutes."

"Tell you what." The barrel of the gun

pushed his head hard to the left, and Brock's head struck the driver's-side window. "You keep your eyes on the wall there to the left. You don't even think about taking a look at me and you don't get shot. Deal?"

Brock nodded as sweat broke out on his forehead and palms. "What do you want?"

"Cooperation. Nothing more. No idea why you're acting like a fool, but we want to give you a little wisdom to chew on. Make sure we're playing well together."

When Brock glanced in the mirror he'd been able to make out nothing more than a figure dressed in a black ski mask and black coat. The voice was deep and not one Brock recognized. It was clear trying to look in the mirror again wouldn't gain him anything except possibly getting shot, so he focused on the windshield and tried to steady his breathing.

"What kind of cooper—"

"I'll ask, you answer, all right?"

Brock nodded again.

"What do you think you're doing up there in the office? You've turned into quite the amateur private detective, digging into all kinds of files."

"How do you know —"

The smack of the gun against his temple shot pain down his neck and into his arm.

A second later a tickling sensation told him the blow had broken his skin. He reached up and his fingers found a thin trickle of blood wiggling its way down the side of his face.

"I ask. You answer. I thought I made that clear. Did I or did I not?"

The man pressed the gun against the wound. The pain made Brock grunt and push his head back against his leather headrest.

"Are we clear now?"

The man's breath was hot on Brock's neck. He must have eaten a bucket full of garlic for lunch. Brock tilted his head to the left and nodded.

"One easy question. Answer it, and I leave, and you go home. All right?"

Brock nodded.

"Why are you digging into the takeover?"

"It's none of your business."

The man snickered. "The reason I'm sitting in the back of your car is because it's intimately my business. Now tell me why."

"I might be on the *Titanic*, but before the ship goes down I'm going to look whatever iceberg destroyed us in the eye and make them tell me why they did it."

"Are you on crack? Or simply idiotic? What, are you doing it for show? What kind of purpose could it serve?"

"I'm going to find out who is behind this. Expose them. Nail them for it."

"You're an idiot. Stop the charade. It won't bring any good to anyone." The man flicked the barrel of the gun against Brock's chin.

"Now, I'm going to get out of the car and walk away. You'll keep staring straight ahead for three minutes. Count it out like you're a kid again playing hide-and-seek. One thousand one, one thousand two, one thousand three . . . if you don't, I'll shoot you."

"I'm going to find you."

"Sure you are." The back door opened and Brock heard the man step out. "I've enjoyed our talk. I hope you have too. I trust we both have clarity on where we go from here." The sound of the hammer on the gun being pulled back filled the car. "One more thing. I assume you realize that if you don't take my advice, I'll visit you again. But it won't be to talk. I might even pay a visit to your ex. From what I've seen, you still have feelings for her."

The rear passenger door slammed shut, and Brock risked turning to watch the man stride away. Bad move. The man lifted the gun and fired. Brock ducked just before the passenger window exploded and glass rained down on him. He rammed his key into the ignition and twisted. The car roared to life, Brock threw it into gear and gunned the engine. The squeal of his tires wasn't loud enough to cover the sound of his rear window shattering.

For half a mile all Brock could do was gasp each time he drew breath and keep his speedometer from blowing through the speed limit. He could call the police, yes, but what would that do? They knew about Karissa, and undoubtedly Tyson as well.

At home Brock sat at his computer, exhausted but unable to sleep. He pulled up his e-mail for a distraction and that's when the answer came to him like a flash of lightning. There was an e-mail from his high-school reunion listing the people who had come and their contact information. At the top was Mitchell Green, and his words from the reunion came back to Brock: *Hey, just saying you better do something. Or someone like me is going to swoop down, grab all that private stock, and take over your company, and there'll be nothing you can do about it.*

Time to pay his old friend a visit.

Chapter 46

June 15, 2015

"Hello, Mitchell."

"Hello, Brock." Mitchell glanced to his right and left and pulled his light coat tighter as they stood on the beach at the west end of Discovery Park. "Why did you set up this meeting? And why here?"

"I need answers. And I don't want to get them in either of our offices with any other ears around."

"Not sure it's such a great idea for us to be hanging out together in any public place, no matter how private."

"Why?"

A lone jogger ran past fifty yards from where they stood. No one else was in view.

"Don't think I need to tell you that." Mitchell gave a half smile.

"Yeah, I think you do. Afraid the truth will come out? That you'll have to get honest about what's going on with Black Fedora?"

Brock shook his head slowly. "I think you're the one who sent that thug after me yesterday."

"Of course I did." Mitchell scoffed. "You were acting idiotic. Like you are right now."

"You wanted to kill me."

"Come on, Brock. I just wanted to shut you up. Stop you from digging. Scare you. I couldn't kill you, although you've made me want to over these past days."

"What?"

"I realize that for some reason you're putting on a show for Ron, but the way you're going at it, I was getting the feeling you'd go too far and tell him about me. So I wanted to put the brakes on without doing something asinine like calling you or meeting with you — as we're stupidly doing right now."

"I have no idea what you're talking about. But tell him about you? Yeah. Of course I'm going to tell Ron about you." Brock peered out over the sound, trying to quell his anger, before turning back to Mitchell and fixing his gaze on the man. "You're finished. I'm not going to let you do this."

For a moment, the perpetual sneer lurking beneath the surface of Mitchell's expression faded, and genuine confusion was splayed across his face. "Do what?"

"Take over. Destroy Black Fedora. Wipe out what Ron and I have worked for years to create. And our father before us. You'll deny this conversation took place. I get that. But that's not going to stop me from fighting you till I win or I'm dead."

"This is comical." Mitchell snorted.

"Yeah. Hilarious. Stupid for me to be fighting it now because it's already done, right? Papers are as good as signed."

Mitchell glanced around as if looking for hidden cameras. "You're doing some kind of corporate-punking thing, right?"

"I'm not laughing." Brock jabbed a finger at Mitchell. "I don't care what it takes, you're going down. I'm going to expose you. Everyone in your company, everyone on your board is going to see the truth. I know you have a partner, and he or she is very good at covering their tracks. But I'll find them too."

Mitchell didn't respond except to frown at Brock in puzzlement and give a tiny shake of his head.

"What is your problem, Mitchell? We were never friends, but we were never enemies either. And what about Ron? You have no problem slitting the throat of a man who has never done you harm."

Mitchell strolled over to a large weathered

log and sat, his elbows resting on his knees. He started to speak twice, and stopped both times. Finally he sighed and spoke words that sent ice down Brock's back.

"Either you have taken up acting unbeknownst to me and are giving me an Oscarworthy performance, or you are losing it — have lost it — and need some serious help."

No. It couldn't be. But it was.

"What are you saying?"

"Why are you doing this, Brock? I seriously don't get it."

"Doing what?" Brock's heart shuddered.

"Did someone hit you on the head? You have amnesia? Do you truly not understand who my partner is?"

At that moment Brock knew. There wasn't a shred of doubt in his mind. "No, it's not. It can't be."

"Uh, yeah, it can. It is. You came to me. You developed the plan. You convinced me it's what you wanted to do to Ron. Any of that coming back to you?"

Brock shuddered. "I wouldn't do that to him."

"Are you seriously trying to turn your back on this?"

"I didn't do it."

"That's entertaining." Mitchell snorted again. "You going to deny you've been the mastermind behind this?"

"That's exactly what I'm going to do."

"You know, Brock ol' pal? I've made my mistakes in the world of business, but getting hamstrung by a partner with cold feet isn't one of them." Mitchell reached into his briefcase and pulled out a tablet. After a few seconds, he turned it around and shoved it in Brock's face. "For your viewing pleasure."

The video was grainy due to the low light, and the sound of the voices was low, but there wasn't a shred of doubt it was a conversation between Mitchell and him.

"I want to take him down," Brock heard himself saying.

"Why?"

"My reasons." Brock rubbed his neck. "I simply want to know if you'll help me and what cut of the action you'll require."

"Don't worry, if we do this, I'll figure out a way to be fairly compensated."

"I'm sure you will."

"I'll develop the time line." Mitchell held out his hand. Brock hesitated, then took it. "But what happens to your brother?"

"He works for me. I win."

"No love lost, eh?"

Mitchell stopped the video. "That enough? Of course this couldn't ever be used in court, 'cause I didn't get your permission to video our little chats, but I think showing it to Ron would be enough."

"That wasn't me." But as Brock said the words, he admitted there were moments when he would have done this to Ron. Maybe not in the material world, but he'd done it to his brother hundreds of times in this mind.

"Still not convinced?"

"If I did it, I can undo it."

"Nah, not going happen. I have way too much skin in this game to pull out now."

"It has to be undone."

"You're sounding nuts again. I've crawled out on the skinny branches with you on this one, and nothing is going to stop it from happening at this point. The papers are as good as signed. The company is mine, and you're going to get your cut. You wanted to take Ron out, your wish has been granted. I'm not going to let you dance to the end of the pier, tumble into the water, and try to take me with you."

Brock sat in his home office that night determined to find a way out of the mess, but despair lapped at his mind and grew deeper by the minute. If he found a way to stop Mitchell, Mitchell would show Ron what Brock had done, and no amount of talking to Ron would convince him otherwise. His explanation would sound ludicrous. It was ludicrous.

But even though his brainstorming continued to hit the proverbial brick wall, Brock drilled down even harder. There had to be a way. Just before three a.m., the utter futility of the exercise struck him like a gong, and he was the bell. Brock slammed his laptop shut and shoved himself away from the desk. He leaned back and moaned as the papers filled with his scrawls filled his vision.

Brock went outside, sat on the edge of his walkway and slid his legs over the edge where his feet dangled just above the water, and began to pray.

Lord, I give it up. All of it. Full surrender. Black Fedora. Karissa, Tyson. My competition with Ron. All my idols. Only you. Only you. For my validation, it's you. For my worth, it's you. For my hopes, dreams, future and past. It's you. And if this is the life I'm destined to live, I accept it. Only you . . . only you.

He sat back, and a peace and a Presence he hadn't known this deep for years overwhelmed him. He soaked it in for an age in the stillness of the early morning. As the sky began to turn gray, he wandered back inside to fix himself breakfast. No point in sleeping. He wouldn't dream, and he needed to get in early to work. God willing, he'd still find a way to save the world. Well, at least save his brother. And Black Fedora.

Brock massaged the back of his neck as he got out the eggs and once again scoured his mind for the reason he couldn't dream. Maybe it didn't matter at this point, but he still wanted to know the answer. It made no sense. He'd been able to slip into lucid dreams almost at will. Maybe not every time he tried, but close to it. But his ability had crash-landed without his doing anything differently. Nothing different . . . except.

He spun and stared at his coffeepot. No way. It couldn't be that stupid and that simple. But he had no doubt it was. Everything, all of it, continued to be tied back to Black Fedora. Brock put on a pot of coffee. Strong coffee. The caffeine wouldn't touch him. But it would in some crazy way let him reach into the world of dreams.

When the pot gurgled to its conclusion, Brock rose and slowly poured a full cup of coffee. He smiled down at the dark liquid then raised it to his lips and took his first sip. Minutes after finishing his second cup, and seconds after sliding into the embracing folds of sleep, Brock began to dream.

And he knew it. A lucid dream. Hope rose inside like a fountain finally released after years of waiting, because he knew what was coming: his final chance to make things right.

CHAPTER 47

October 22, 1989

Brock expected to find himself standing outside Java Spot, or inside the coffee shop, or sitting at his usual table about to start another conversation with his younger self, but he wasn't in either place. He was inside a stadium — a deafening roar from the crowd told him it was a big one. The Seahawk coats, hats, and jerseys told him it was Seattle's.

Brock tried to move, but his feet felt stuck. He stared at them in surprise and fear. He wasn't in control. So if this dream wasn't under his direction, but he still knew it was a dream, who was running it this time? His subconscious? Or something else?

"Can I help you?"

Brock looked up. A gentleman he guessed to be in his late sixties with wispy white hair sticking out from under his Seahawks hat smiled at him. The usher name tag pinned to his dark-blue shirt read Sarge.

"I don't know where I'm supposed to go."

"I know how you feel." Sarge chuckled. "When we grew up the stadiums were a little smaller. You could navigate them a bit easier."

"We?"

"Well, I'm guessing I'm a few years further down the trail than you, but not more than ten or fifteen, I'm thinking."

"I'm fifty-three."

"Yep, gotcha by fourteen." Sarge smiled. "So you don't know where you need to go."

"I mean I'm not in control this time —" Brock stopped himself. Nothing he said to the man would make sense.

Sarge took two steps toward him. "Do you mind if I take a quick look at your ticket?"

"What ticket?"

"The one in your hand."

Brock gazed at his hand as if it were someone else's. Clutched between his thumb and forefinger was a Seahawks ticket. He raised it slowly, but before he could get a good look at it, Sarge slid it from Brock's grasp.

"Okay, let's take a look." The usher peered at the ticket for a moment. "Righty O, you're almost there. Just head down to your right another three tunnels, head through 'er, and your seat will be on the left, seven rows up."

Brock glanced again at Sarge, who gave him a crooked grin. "You need me to take you up there?"

"No. I'm good." He gave Sarge a quick salute, which made the older man laugh.

Brock lifted his foot — no problem now — and took a few steps down the concourse. He tried to wake himself as he moved, but it didn't work. So what now? Might as well get to the seat and try to enjoy the game until his body or mind or both decided to release him back to the waking world.

As he stepped through the end of the third tunnel, the crowd roared so loudly the stadium rumbled under this feet. Brock gazed at the big screen. Seahawks touchdown. Wait. The stadium didn't look like CenturyLink Field. And there was no sky overhead. As he stared at the ceiling of the stadium, he realized he had to be in the Kingdome, demolished in March of 2000. So this dream had taken Brock to a place in time at least fifteen years back, long before Paul Allen's Microsoft money would build a state-of-the-art stadium for the Hawks.

Brock trudged up the stairs till he reached row seventy-eight. He glanced at his ticket, then at the empty chair five seats in. That would be his. The man on the far side of the empty chair was turned, his attention downfield, so the back of his head was the only part of him Brock could see. Still, something about him seemed familiar. The action on the field died down, and the man turned and sat down, his face now in profile. Brock gasped.

It was Brock's father.

He turned and his eyes locked onto Brock's, but only for an instant. There was no recognition of who Brock was, but why would there be? Brock swallowed and rubbed his head hard. Wow. Regret and pain and longing all surged up from the deep part of his soul. The chance to talk to his dad again. This was a gift, orchestrated by God. Had to be.

Brock shuffled past the four people in the seats between him and his father, then sat down next to the man he'd longed to sit down with one more time. Brock's father nodded at him, then turned his attention back to the game. But a second later he turned back with a puzzled look on his face. "Do we know each other?"

"No." It was partially true, maybe completely true. The Brock Matthews his dad knew was not the man sitting next to him now. The Brock Matthews of today had

420

changed.

"I'm Donald." Brock's dad extended his hand. "What's yours?"

"My name is —" What should he say? His real name? Make one up? His dad wouldn't recognize him with his fifty-three-year-old face, so why not tell the truth?

"Yeah?"

"It's Brock."

"Really." Brock's dad gave a tilt of his head. "That's one of my sons' names."

"Good to meet you." The words felt thick coming out of Brock's mouth.

Donald leaned back in his chair and folded his arms. "Wish I could say it was good to meet you."

"What?" Brock let out an embarrassed laugh.

"Nothing personal, you know? I'm sure you're a good man. But you see, that son of mine I just mentioned? He was supposed to be sitting where you are. I bought the tickets, asked if he wanted to go. He said yes, and I was looking forward to the day together. But he obviously decided to scalp the ticket instead, and here you are. A little money worth more than a little time with your dad." Brock's father turned and gave a halfhearted smile. "But kids are born to break your heart, you know?"

Brock only nodded. He of course hadn't scalped the ticket, but he was too fearful his voice would crack if he spoke.

"In all fairness, I've blown it my fair share with him. And in his tween years? Not good. Never really got healing from that. So I can't say I blame him for blowing me off. Thought things were getting better between us, and they are, but apparently not enough for today. No worries. There's always tomorrow. Step at a time. Life isn't over yet. I'll get my chance, he'll get his, the good Lord is going to work it out for us."

Brock glanced at the date on his ticket and it became even more impossible to speak. October 22, 1989. His dad would live only three more weeks. Life was over for the man sitting next to him, and his father had no idea. Brock closed his eyes and swallowed.

"I hope he works it out with you."

"I'm telling you, he will. Gotta have faith. Gotta trust. Gotta hold onto the evidence of things not yet seen. I might have figured out the important things later in life than I wanted to, but I've got 'em in my back pocket now."

"What are the important things?"

"Simple." Brock's dad turned, zeroed his gaze on Brock, and leaned in. "My God.

My wife. My two sons. After that, nothing else comes close. You know?"

Brock did know. But he'd figured it out too late.

A roar from below turned their attention to the field, and for a few minutes Brock and his dad focused their attention on the behemoths in the blue-and-white jerseys. When the play stopped for a TV timeout, Brock turned to his father.

"I have a son, so I get it — they can't see life from our perspective. I'm guessing he's already feeling bad about not coming. I bet he really regrets it. He's probably already called your cell to apologize."

"My cell?"

"Your cell phone."

Brock's dad gave a puzzled smile. "You mean like a car phone? I've been reading about them. Supposed to be the next big thing. I doubt it'll ever catch on for the masses. Too expensive. Who is going to pay seventy-five cents a minute to talk on the phone in your car? But you said it like everyone has them. Are you into advanced technology?"

Stupid. Few people had cell phones in 1989. And no one carried them.

"I think a day is coming where cell phones will be as common as cars."

Brock's dad grinned. "Okay, if you can predict the future, can you tell me what I need to say to my son to jump-start our relationship?"

Again, Brock feared his voice would betray him, but he plowed ahead anyway. "I don't know about the future, but I know what I'd say to my dad if I could go back in time."

"Wouldn't that be wild? To go back and tell your dad the things you were too stupid to figure out in your youth?" Brock's dad shook his head. "That would be gift. So what would you say?"

Brock swallowed and turned his attention to the field as he spoke. "I'd tell him I was blind and couldn't look past the times we locked horns and tossed each other to the ground battered and bleeding. I'd tell him how much I looked up to him and hated him at the same time. I'd tell him I finally realized that he was dealing with all the broken parts of his past when he was trying to be a dad to me. I'd tell him how much I miss him, how much I love him, and how I wasted the years we were given."

Brock paused as one more thing he wanted to tell his dad filled his mind. But how could he say it without sounding extremely strange? The only way was to change the names and sport to protect the innocent and hope the message still got through.

"The last thing I'd tell him is about the time I went to baseball camp when I was young. The leader of the camp humiliated me in front of all the other kids, and then told me I had no talent for the sport. So I gave it up but wish I hadn't, because it was the thing my dad and I had together. I'd tell my dad that was the reason I gave up baseball. It wasn't a rejection of him."

When Brock finished he risked a look at his father. Tears had formed in his dad's eyes, and Brock pulled his gaze away because his eyes were welling up too. Silence rose between them, but it seemed to draw them together like a magnet. Finally, Brock's dad spoke.

"I know your dad would have given anything to have heard those things."

Again they sat in silence, and again, Brock's dad was the one who broke it.

"Can I tell you something?"

"Sure."

"Is it strange that I'm telling a complete stranger things about me and my son?"

"No, not at all."

"Okay then." Brock's dad folded his hands across his lap and seemed to be studying the program lying between his feet on the concrete. "A lot of people don't believe in signs. I do."

"Sounds like you didn't get the one you were looking for."

"Nope. Not this time." He glanced at Brock with a sad smile. "This game was going to be the spot of my big reveal. The plan was to give my son a gift that I think would have changed his life. That was my plan. Maybe even God's plan. But apparently not Brock's plan. And I think you gotta have all parties buying in for a plan to work. Manipulation Nation isn't a country you want those you care about to live in."

Brock sucked in a quick breath. A gift? He couldn't stop himself from asking the question, even though it was inappropriate.

"What was the gift?"

His dad gave Brock a curious look. "I'm probably going to keep that to myself. It's like blowing out a candle on your birthday cake and then telling folks what you wished for. And who knows, maybe the wish will come true someday."

"But you're going to find another time to talk to him, right?" Brock's pulse raced. For some reason his life seemed to hang on the answer.

"Yeah, probably." Brock's dad shrugged. "Actually, probably not. This was the moment, you know? If I believe the moment is now, then when this moment goes, the moment is gone."

"You need to ask him again." Brock tried to keep his voice steady. Part of him wanted to tell his dad exactly who he was, but there was a high chance that would end the conversation cold. His dad wouldn't buy into the idea that Brock had traveled into the past to have this conversation. Who would? He hadn't even been able to convince his younger self.

"Why's that?"

"Maybe this time he'll take the gift."

"Yeah, maybe." Brock's dad shrugged. "Maybe next year at this time."

"No, it needs to be soon."

"Who did you say you were, mister?"

A slew of responses ricocheted through Brock's mind, but none of them would be the right response, because he'd already cracked the ice under his feet with too many familiar questions. Soon he would be sinking into icy water.

"No one."

"Then I think it best if we move onto other subjects, don't you?"

"Yeah, probably a good idea."

The conversation was over. Brock had blown it, and he knew trying again would only make things worse. When the game ended, his dad stood, gave a vacant smile, and extended his hand.

"Good luck with your son, Brock."

"Good luck with yours."

The moment Brock's dad walked out of sight, the colors of the stadium and seats and players swirled together and the dream faded, then blinked out. But Brock didn't wake up. He rocketed straight into another dream, where he found himself at Java Spot staring across the room at himself.

CHAPTER 48

Brock restrained himself from sprinting across the room, eased over slowly instead, then stood at the table till his younger self looked up.

"Hey, Future Me, long time." Brock motioned at the chair across from him. "Sit. Catch me up."

"What's the date?"

"September 27."

"What year?"

"Hoo, boy." Young Brock shook his head and grinned. "Nineteen eighty-nine."

"There's a Seahawks game on October 22 between the Seahawks and the Broncos. You have to go to that game."

"Have to?"

"Yes."

"With who?"

"Your dad."

Young Brock smiled again and turned to Morgan, who was twenty feet away at his usual counter position, engaged in conversation with a young lady who took repeated sips of Morgan's drink.

"Hey, Morg-Man. Guess what my pal is telling me?" His younger self pointed at Brock. "Next month I have to go to a Seahawks game! With my dad. That'll be a blast, no doubt."

Morgan offered a confused smile, then returned his focus to the woman. Brock waited till his younger self turned back and stopped grinning.

"Please, just go to the game."

"Not gonna happen." Young Brock shook his head.

"Why not?"

"You're kidding, right?" His younger self stood and pushed his chair in. "Sorry, gotta run, F. B."

"No. I'm not kidding. If you only do this one thing, go to that game."

"Listen." Young Brock leaned on the table with both hands and drew his face close to Brock. "Do you still believe you're an ancient version of me?"

"Yes."

"Then like I said a number of times before, if you really are me, you know my dad and I aren't the best of pals. We weren't the greatest pals in days past, and it's on

430

the high side of likely that we're not going to be pals a year from now, or ten years, or twenty years. Going to a Hawks game isn't going to change that. I can wait a while to see how things go."

"No you can't. He's going to die of a heart attack just weeks after that game."

His younger self's countenance grew dark. "Don't say stuff like that. Not funny."

"It's going to happen."

"I think we're done here." Brock's younger self stood and slipped into his coat.

"I'm not here to anger you, Brock. I'm here because I dreamed about being at that game with your dad moments ago, and I talked to him and —"

"Even if you are who you say you are, and he's going to die, how am I supposed to get to that game? He loves the Hawks. So does Ron. Those season tickets are for the two of them. The Hawks are their thing. I've never been invited. And I'm not about to ask."

"Because you can't risk your heart being hammered again."

"Shut up."

"He's going to invite you. Trust me."

"Trust you?"

"Yes."

His younger self raised his eyebrows. "Even if he invited me, I wouldn't go. Fak-

431

ing my way through three hours at a football game would not be the way either my dad or I would want to spend a Sunday afternoon."

"Part of you desperately wants exactly that. And he wants a relationship with you more than you can imagine. But he doesn't know how to tell you. At that game, he's going to try."

His younger self jammed his hands into his pockets and pressed his lips together as he stared at Brock.

"I can see it in your eyes. You almost believe me — that I'm you — and somehow we're able to communicate with each other across time. I'm not saying I understand it either, but I know it's real."

"Yeah, you had me for a time, but I'm not subscribed to that magazine anymore."

Heat filled Brock's face. It wasn't going to work. "I proved it to you. The basketball story, the one no one knew —"

"There were more than thirty people there. I don't know why and I don't know how, but you somehow tracked one or two of them down and got the story."

"I didn't. No one knew about the conversation outside the gym with just you and the coach. No one could have overheard it."

"Maybe they did. I was eleven. I wasn't

checking to see if anyone was within ear-shot." Young Brock pointed at Brock. "I don't know what you're trying to do, but we're finished. Don't talk to me again. Go live out your weird beliefs with someone else."

His younger self rose and strode across the room toward Java Spot's front door.

"Brock!"

He didn't turn.

Brock rose to go after himself, but before he could take two steps, the coffee shop vanished.

CHAPTER 49

June 16, 2015

When Brock woke the next morning he didn't open his eyes right away. He needed a moment to accept the fact that when he looked around his world, he would see nothing different. No change for the better. No radical reversal of his circumstances. Because his younger self wasn't going to the game — correction, hadn't gone to the game — years ago.

But it was okay. He'd surrendered, and the peace he'd felt when he'd done that remained. He would survive in this time line because there wasn't any other choice. He would live his life as it came and would continue to try to have a relationship with Tyson. And until Karissa remarried, he would try to win her heart back. Lost cause? Waste of time to try? No, because God was the God of hope, and because this journey had given him the chance to give up his idols, and he had chosen well.

He took a deep breath, threw back the covers, and opened his eyes. His pulse immediately spiked. Not his ceiling above. At least not the ceiling in the houseboat. He whirled in bed, first to the right, then to the left. Definitely not the houseboat.

It took a few seconds, but then it struck him. There was a nightstand on the other side of the bed. With a hand lotion and lip balm on it. Not a man's, so not his. A woman's. He took a slower look at the room. A couple's room, not a single man's room.

No. He wouldn't let his heart hope. He glanced at the clock on his nightstand. Seven a.m. He concentrated his ears on the bathroom. No shower. That meant no Karissa. Not good. So where was he? Still dreaming? No way. By now he knew the difference.

Clearly he was back in his old home, but with whom? Sheila? Someone else? Brock roused himself out of bed, pulled on a pair of sweats, and stumbled across the hallway and into his den. The moment he stepped through the doorway he stopped cold. Where his Alaska photo should have been was a picture he'd never seen.

Brock shuffled over to the wall next to his

desk, lifted the photo off the wall, and collapsed into his leather chair.

"Impossible."

He held the framed picture in both hands, ran his thumb over the glass, and studied the photo. His dad and a twenty-seven-year-old Brock stood together in the Kingdome, arms around each other, the Seahawks field in the far background.

"He went." Brock's body went limp. "The kid went. I can't believe it."

But he did believe it. The evidence was staring back at him with an intensity he didn't know what to do with. He didn't need to read the short note scrawled on the photo to remember the date, but he did anyway. October 22, 1989. Underneath the date was a short note from his dad that broke a fissure open in Brock's heart: *Great day, great son. Love, Dad*

Tears rose in Brock's eyes and he didn't try to stop them. For whatever reason, his younger self had gone to the game. And whatever gift his dad had wanted to give him must have been given. But whatever the gift was, it wasn't the gift Brock was soaking in right now. That gift was the crossing of the chasm between him and his dad, which must have begun that day.

Brock closed his eyes and let the truth sink

in. Peace had come for his dad and him. The cold war was over. Not in this moment; the battle had ended long ago. But for him, the report from the field had just come in. He couldn't imagine anything sweeter. He sat and studied every line in his dad's face and embraced the warmth that spilled out of his father's smile. Both of them radiated hope, and it was obvious from their expressions that both longed for the Living Water to drench the parched land inside of them. Brock smiled as he accepted the reality that the water had come.

He sensed movement in the doorway but didn't look up. Brock begged God for it to be Karissa, or at least Tyson, but believed it was too much to hope for.

"Good morning."

The sound of her voice seemed to raise his head by magic. It was her. Not in a dream, but in the flesh. Karissa, her robe wrapped around her lithe figure, her eyes still as bright as when they'd first met. The animosity toward him was gone. This was her. Dream girl returned.

"Coffee's ready." She turned and strolled away toward the kitchen.

"Wait!"

Karissa poked her head back into the doorway. *"Oui?"*

He stood and started to speak, but couldn't find the right words. "I . . . I've . . ."

"You all right?"

"I've missed you." He fought back tears. "So much. And I am so madly, deeply, profoundly in love with you."

She frowned at him.

"I just need to tell you that."

"Okay." Karissa gave him a puzzled smile.

He went to her and held on so long she started to laugh.

"Wow, I know it's been a long time from last night when we went to sleep till this morning . . ."

"Don't ask." Brock released her from his arms and kissed her on the cheek with as much tenderness as he knew how to give. "How are you and I?"

"Not sure I understand the question."

"I'd give up anything for you. For your hopes, your dreams, for whatever makes you come alive."

"Why do you say that?" She frowned. "You've done that all our lives together."

Amazing. He'd changed.

"So our relationship, there's wind in the sails?"

"Wind in the sails?" She tilted her head. "I like that analogy. Most of the time there is." She gave him another quick hug, then turned toward the kitchen. "You coming?"

"In a minute."

She nodded and strolled away. The soft pad of her footsteps down the hardwood hallway faded. Part of Brock wanted to sprint into the kitchen and ask her a thousand questions at once. Was Tyson okay? Was Black Fedora still about to go under? Did he even work there? But another part of him didn't want to face the possibility the answers would slay him.

Yes, Karissa was back — and it seemed things were good between them — but that could be an act. They'd faked their way through their relationship for years. Maybe this was just another scene in their performance. After all he'd been through, facing that possibility was monumentally difficult.

He rose and forced himself through the doorway of his den and down the hall. No doubt now. He was back in the original house where his wild ride had started. But the pictures on the walls had changed. Where was the photo of the redwoods? In its place was a picture of Karissa and him in kayaks up at Ross Lake. He remembered the indecision they had before going on that trip. Ultimately they chose to go to the redwoods. In this version of his life, they obviously went to Ross Lake instead.

Brock clumped down the stairs, stopping for a moment on each one as he studied the other small changes. The instant he turned the corner, he zeroed in on Tyson's traditional spot at the kitchen counter. Not there. Sorrow squeezed his throat. Brock staggered into the kitchen and looked at the place he'd always kept his keys. They were there. At least one thing was the same. Next to his keys lay his wallet. Two out of two.

Before he could find anything else to ground himself, his cell phone rang. Caller ID told him it was Ron.

"Ron! It's Brock."

"I hope so, since I'm the one that called you."

"Right, sorry. Just having a strange morning." He eased over to the kitchen table and sat.

"You can tell me about it when you get here." His brother's voice was neutral. No clue what their relationship was like. "Are you on your way?"

"On my way where?"

"Funny. Hoping you can get here a few minutes early. I want to go over the details of the buyout one more time. This thing has to be done clean."

"It didn't get fixed." Brock's body went cold. "Everything at home seemed . . ."

"What? What didn't get fixed? What are you talking about?"

"I'd started to hope."

Karissa sidled up to him to top off his coffee, but he hadn't taken his first sip.

"Hope for what? There's nothing to fix."

"I promised you I'd fix it, but it didn't work."

"Yeah, you already said that. So I'll ask again, fix what?"

"The whole thing."

"Are you asleep? Is this my brother or some alien who stole his cell phone?"

"I'm sorry, Ron."

"Have you had your coffee yet?" Ron didn't wait for an answer. "Get your coffee. Get your head together, and get your posterior in here."

"Okay."

"You all right?"

"No."

"We'll talk when you get here."

"Wait!"

Ron's exasperated sigh sailed through the phone. "I gotta go."

"Just answer one question."

"Sure."

"Is Black Fedora going to survive?"

"What?" Another sigh. "Just get in here, Brock."

"Am I an owner in the company?"

The line went dead and Brock slipped his phone into the pocket of his sweats. *It doesn't matter. It doesn't matter.* He kept repeating the line to himself, but it didn't help. He'd promised Ron. And he'd broken the promise. He stared at Karissa's puzzled face and was about to speak when he caught movement out of the corner of his eye.

"Hey, Dad." Tyson clipped across the floor in jeans and a dark-blue collared shirt that covered a well-sculpted body. His hair was cropped short and his eyes were bright. He pointed at Brock as he strode toward the door at the other end of the kitchen that led to the garage. "See ya."

"Wait." Heat swept Brock's body. "Your hair is . . . and you're here. You're not . . . you're not . . ."

"I'm not where?"

"There. You're here."

"Did you take a weird pill this morning, Dad?" Tyson lifted a pretend bottle to his lips. "Or hitting the sauce?"

"No, it's just that . . . I didn't think you were here."

"Yeah, still here." Tyson pointed at the floor. "For about ten more seconds. Then I'll be headed there." He pointed east. "For school."

"Come here."

"I gotta go, Dad." He glanced at his cell phone. "They're in the habit of starting class on time."

"This is important." Brock marched over to Tyson and took him in his arms. "I love you, kid."

"Uh, okay. Sounds good."

Brock let Tyson pull away but still held him by the shoulders. "I know I haven't said that enough. And I haven't told you what an outstanding son you are. But that's going to change."

"Back atcha." Tyson nodded once and gave a half smile and stared at Karissa like Brock was crazy. "Can I go?"

"And we're going backpacking this summer."

"Sounds not good. I'm so outta shape."

Brock laughed as Tyson spun and loped into the garage. "Love ya, Mom."

"Me too." Karissa smiled at Tyson, then turned to Brock and winked. As soon as the garage door shut behind Tyson she sashayed over to Brock. "What in the world prompted that?"

"A dream."

"One of those lucid dreams you've been reading about?"

"Something like that."

She took him around the waist and squeezed. "Don't worry about Tyson's reaction."

"I'm not. It was better than expected."

Karissa let him go and went to the kitchen counter. "How soon do you need to head for the office?"

Brock balked. "Oh wow, I gotta get going."

"Any time for a little breakfast? I don't teach till ten this morning, so I have time if you do."

"Teach? You're a teacher?"

She frowned. "Okay, professor of speech pathology and ASL if you want to get technical."

"Unbelievable."

"Thanks for the pep talk."

"No, I mean . . . I can't explain."

"How about if you try over breakfast?"

"No time. I'll grab something at the office." Brock turned and strode across the kitchen.

"Latte for the road?"

"Without question. Triple shot. Maybe a quad."

"I'll put your concoction together while you get dressed."

"Thank you!" he called out over his shoulder as he jogged back up the stairs.

Brock took a three-minute shower and was shaved and dressed in seven. The thought kept pounding through his mind that if things were solid with both Tyson and Karissa, then why was Black Fedora still a mess? He half jogged back into the kitchen and looked for his latte.

"In the microwave." Karissa looked up from her laptop and smiled. "Ready for a twenty-second boost just to make sure it will burn your mouth on the way to the office."

"Perfect." He returned her smile, did a rapid shuffle across their hardwood floor, and pushed the button.

As he waited he glanced at the counter. Everything here looked the same as it did days back, and Brock started to relax. Wait. What in world was that? A cookbook lay open on the counter next to the stove. It was dog-eared in multiple places, and multiple pages were warped from apparent spills and food-laden fingers. It wasn't one from his collection, and neither Karissa nor Tyson cooked, so who would have been using it?

"When did you take up cooking?"

"I didn't. What are you talking about?"

"This." Brock pointed at the cookbook. "Someone has put this book to a lot of use."

"Remember that person who left for school about fifteen minutes ago? The one you hugged for the first time in years?"

"Tyson is cooking?" Brock frowned and ran his fingers over the pages of the open book.

"Are you all right?"

Brock called up his inner actor and prayed it was semi-convincing. "Yeah, I mean of course I know he's cooking, I just didn't realize he was cooking that much."

"That much? He's been working on it almost every night, and on the weekends too." Karissa put down her tea and sauntered over to him. "And you've been in the kitchen with him most of the time. So tell me what's going on with you. Real answers. Your acting stinks."

"Nothing, I'm just . . ."

"Just what?"

"I'll try to explain it to you someday when we have a lot of time, when your imagination can handle it."

"Oh, now you have to tell me." She grinned.

"I will. I promise. Tonight."

"Pretty high compliment that he wants to follow in your footsteps." Karissa straightened his shirt.

"He does?"

Brock's cell phone vibrated. A text from Ron. HOW CLOSE ARE YOU? WE START AT 9 SHARP.

Whoops.

"Gotta go." He turned to take a last glance at the cookbook to see what dish Tyson was working on. Eggs Benedict. Brock leaned and took a quick scan of the recipe. Exactly like his own. He shut the book to see who the author was. The instant the name registered in his mind, Brock's arms went limp.

"Wha— what is this?" He held it up for Karissa to see.

"A cookbook."

"With my name on it."

Karissa put her hands on her hips. "Yes. It's fairly common for the author of a book to put their name on it."

The blood rushed from Brock's face and his body went weak. "I don't understand."

"Have to say, you're acting a little strange this morning, love. You better have convincing answers tonight as to why."

Brock's cell phone buzzed again. HELLO? He texted Ron back, COMING.

"I gotta go." He tossed the cookbook onto the counter and jogged out the door.

CHAPTER 50

As Brock tore up 405 on the way to the office, he called Morgan.

"Yeah. Talk."

"Do you follow Jesus?"

"What?"

"Are you a Christian?"

"Hello, McFly. You were there, Brock-O."

Relief filled Brock.

"Did you give me a book on lucid dreaming?"

"There's a point to this, right?"

"Did you?"

"No, but I have one I can let you borrow."

"We have a lot to talk about." Brock pulled off 405 on his way to Black Fedora. "And I'll tell you all about it in the days to come."

Seven minutes later Brock arrived at the office and rushed into the elevator in the parking garage. He reached the seventh floor three minutes after that and strode toward the conference room. He glanced at his watch. Two minutes till nine. No time to jet into his office and see if he could pick up any clues on the state of the company. No time to put his head together with Ron. And Brock definitely needed the meeting more than Ron did.

Yes, from what Ron said, the buyout was still happening, but he would still be flying utterly blind on all the details. No chance to save the company when he had no clue where all the players were positioned on the chess board. And there was no way he could stall signing at this point.

"Thanks for getting here early." Ron strode down the hall and clapped Brock on the shoulder. "But no worries, we'll figure it out. Just tell me if you're leaning yes or no."

"Your hand." Brock pointed at Ron's right hand as heat rushed through him.

"Yeah, I have one on the left as well." Ron gave a questioning grin.

"You're still golfing."

"And you're not getting out of playing with me in the scramble tournament next week, so don't try."

"I won't."

"So yes or no on the buyout?"

"What do you mean yes or no? We don't

have a choice."

Ron gave him another puzzled look and pushed open the conference room door. "They're all in the lobby, but I told Michelle not to send them up till I give her the word. So talk to me, yes or no? And from what you've been saying this past week, no is not an option for you, right?"

They stepped into the conference room as Brock tried to formulate an answer that would draw out a hint of what Ron was really asking. But any thought of responding vanished the moment Brock spotted the posters on the walls. Every few feet was a six-by-four poster, eight posters in all. Four of them featured Ron. Four of them featured himself. At the top of the first poster in huge letters was the line, Cuisine to Live For. At the bottom in a smaller font was Brock L. Matthews Opens His Newest Restaurant April 23.

The poster next to his was one of Ron. At the top was the Black Fedora logo. Ron sat surrounded by fourteen flavors of Black Fedora coffee. His arms were spread, a huge grin across his face. An easel in the corner of the room held a smaller poster of Brock standing over a lavish island stove with a ladle in hand. Spread out on the counter next to the stove were three labeled dishes:

450

Tuna Scallopine with Parsley and Pome-
granate Seeds, Lobster Bisque Soup, and
Eggs Benedict. The top of the poster said,
The Latest from the Fertile Mind of Master
Chef Brock L. Matthews.

"You look like a zombie. What are you
staring at?"

Before Brock had a chance to respond,
Ron shook his head. "I get it. I agree. I
asked Carla not to put the posters up — I
know you don't like being the star — but
she said it would make a good impression
on the folks coming in. And since she's the
VP of Marketing, I respect her opinion, and
you have to admit, she's much wiser than
me and maybe even you in that area."

Brock turned to Ron and tried to say
something remotely intelligent, but what
came out was, "I don't own Black Fedora."

"What?"

Brock said it again, this time a whisper.
"Black Fedora isn't my company."

"Technically, no. But you own the company that owns Black Fedora, so technically
yes. I'm assuming there's a point to this
feigned ignorance?"

Brock's mind spun like a gyroscope. He
hadn't gone to business school. He took
another path. One his dad saw for him, the
gift he couldn't remember receiving. Brock

451

stared at Ron and couldn't stop shaking his head.

"That was dad's gift to me. It had to be."

"What gift? What are you talking about?" Ron turned his head to the side and narrowed his eyes. "You realize you're not making any sense, right?"

"I went to culinary school. That was dad's gift to me that day at the game, right? He paid for culinary school, didn't he?"

"Brocklee, we don't really have time for a history lesson. We need to let —"

"What'd you call me?"

"What?" Ron laughed.

"Don't call me that."

"You're definitely not doing well." Ron took Brock by both shoulders and shook him playfully. "I've been calling you that for twenty-seven years. Now all of a sudden you don't like it?"

"I like it when you call me that?"

"Ever since I graduated from college."

"We're friends. We have a good relationship."

"Yeah, I sure think so."

"And we're solvent." Brock glanced around the room. "More than solvent, aren't we? And we're not meeting with these people because we're on the verge of bankruptcy . . ."

"What did you eat this morning?"

Brock stumbled across the room till he reached a poster of himself kneeling beside fourteen or so children in what looked like Costa Rica. "We do relief work?"

Ron gave a nervous laugh. "Seriously, Brock, you need to stop screwing around and get ready for this meeting."

As if on cue, there was a rap on the door. It swung open and Michelle stood in the frame.

"Excuse me, gentlemen, your guests are here."

Behind Michelle stood three men and two women. But Brock could focus only on the man on the far right. Mitchell. And based on what Brock had learned about himself, his cozy relationship with Ron was about to be extremely short-lived.

Mitchell glanced at Brock, but there was no acknowledgement in his eyes of what they'd done. That's when the realization struck Brock. He'd planned the takeover with Mitchell in a different time line, not this one. Relief filled him and he strolled with Ron toward the group just inside the doors of the conference room.

"Welcome." Ron said and opened his palms as they reached their guests. "Good to see you all."

Ron proceeded to greet each of the party while Brock stared at Mitchell, trying to catch his eye. Brock was still flying blind, but at least he knew he'd fight signing the company over to Mitchell and crew, no matter how late the hour. But first, he'd listen, try to learn anything that might tell him where the negotiations stood. And he'd have to trust that this moment was not random, that it was orchestrated by Someone far greater than himself.

Brock moved slowly around the table. Mitchell was on the far side of the group, engaged in an animated discussion with Ron, so Brock greeted the other members of Mitchell's consortium. Brock produced the required smiles and pleasantries, and one by one they moved to grab a cup of coffee from the serving table at the back of the room before settling into the chairs around the conference table.

"Brock Matthews. Wow." Mitchell's voice snapped Brock out of his contemplation. "It's been a long time since high school, hasn't it, Brock?"

"It has been a while."

He studied his old rival's eyes — a mixture of defiance and arrogance — and the slight upturn of his mouth, and heat rose inside Brock. There was no question. He instantly realized that they were still coconspirators in this reality. Why? It made no sense. Hadn't he changed everything?

Mitchell turned slightly so his back was to Ron and the rest of the group and whispered under his breath. "Nicely played, amigo. We are about to score major Saint-Tropez for the celebration, huh?" He stuck out his hand. Brock took it and squeezed hard.

"Good to see you again after all these years." Brock gave a grim smile.

"Wow, you been working out." Mitchell pulled his hand out of Brock's. "That actually hurt."

"Good." Brock winked at him and relished the peeved look on Mitchell's face.

Then, inexplicably, Brock felt a sliver of peace. He didn't know the details, but the overall scheme was as clear as an alpine lake, and he could see straight to the bottom where a layer of silt covered the truth. A layer Mitchell created, and Brock was just as culpable. But it didn't matter who was to blame. All he cared about was the truth.

During the next twenty-five minutes, Mitchell and his team laid out their plan for buying out both Cuisine to Live For and Black Fedora. There were no holes. The money, the trajectory going forward, all the elements were perfect. The plan was diamond solid. The shares they were offering were of far more value than the two companies were worth. No wonder Ron was pushing them to say yes.

Once Mitchell and company made their final statements on why the buyout made sense, they began discussing the details. Questions and clarifications went back and forth for ten minutes before Mitchell waved his pen at Ron.

"So, do we have a deal?" Mitchell glanced around the room. "I know we'd need to work out the rest of the details, but in principle? Is this going to happen?"

Ron glanced at Brock before giving Mitchell a slight nod. "You need three yeses. You have mine. You have our CFO's. Brock?"

"I need more time."

"No input? No comments? Anything to add? What are we missing that would allow you to give an answer?"

An idea shot through Brock's mind. Was it possible? Would he find the files in this time line? Maybe.

"On second thought, yes, I do have something to add. But before I'm sure, I need to check a file in my office."

"What?" Ron grimaced. "Let's get this done. You've had weeks to analyze this deal from every angle. This meeting was supposed to be more of a formality than a negotiation. What do you need to check in your office?"

Brock stood and glanced at his watch. "I'll be back in five minutes."

He strode from the room, slightly surprised he was about to lay his own head on the chopping block, knowing the ax would fall hard.

CHAPTER 51

Brock burst into his office, woke his computer, and did a search for Project Gilgamesh. Half of him wanted it to be there, half didn't. More than half didn't. Because if he found it, there was no going back. He would have to confess, and he would destroy his relationship with Ron.

He thought it would take ten minutes to find the recordings. It took three. Another thirty seconds to find the one that would make the biggest explosion when he detonated it in the conference room. He transferred the file to a flash drive and shoved it into his pocket.

Brock strode down the hall back toward the conference room intent on pulling open the door, striding inside, and lighting the fuse that would blow up, but when he reached the door he stopped, his hand clutched too tightly around the knob. Was this the right move? If it wasn't, too late now.

He pushed the door open and marched into the room. The buzz of small talk died and all eyes in the room focused on Brock. Ron gave him a look that said, *This better be good.* Brock gave a look back that he hoped said it would be.

He pulled the flash drive from his pocket and wiggled it, then slipped it into his laptop. "This recording would never hold up in a court of law. I doubt the other party knew I was recording it. So this is merely a personal confession."

Ron stood and put his hand on Brock's arm to stop him from hitting play. "What are you doing, bro?"

"Setting myself free. I meant to have this conversation with you later, but now will work." Brock gently lifted his brother's hand off his arm. "All growing up, the only thing I wanted to do was beat you. I thought you and Dad were against me. Thought Dad didn't love me. And those things fueled my obsession to win at all costs. But it isn't true. You've been a good brother. And I don't have to win any longer. I've thrown that idol into the fire."

The auburn-headed woman named Teresa spread her hands on the table. "I think we're all really liking this family-reunion hour, but what is going on?"

"Blind eyes now finally see." Brock turned to face Ron full-on. "I betrayed you. It doesn't matter if I knew it or didn't know about it in this time line. It's inside me. There are dark places in my soul, and the only hope for those shadows is God's grace, God's mercy. I can't do any of it on my own. I've finally figured that out after fifty-three years of trying. So I'm throwing myself on his unquenchable mercy, that unquenchable grace. It's all I have, and for the first time in my life, it's all I want."

Brock hit play on his laptop, turned, and ambled toward the poster of himself holding up his eggs Benedict. Humpy Dumpty and his pals were about to take a fall.

"You say you've figured out how to do this." On the recording, Brock's voice sounded tinny and far away.

"It'll be simple," another voice said. Mitchell's. "The timing is perfect for us to make an offer. Black Fedora and Cuisine to Live For are exploding, but that means limited cash flow, right? So over the coming months, we form a dummy corporation. Buy up dummy shares and when the buyout happens . . ."

"I'll have control of both companies."

"You say you want to win the competition? Finally put your little brother in the position he should be? This will do it like a guillotine falling on his neck."

"And you'll get?"

"When the two companies go public six months later, I will be an extremely wealthy man."

The sound of two hands slamming down on the conference table made Brock spin. He didn't have to guess who the sound came from. Mitchell stood with enough force to knock over his chair. He took two strides toward Brock's laptop and brought his hand down on the computer. The entire table shook. Brock's and Mitchell's voices were silenced.

Mitchell whirled and jabbed a finger toward Brock. "I'm going to take you down so far you'll be looking up at Hades."

"Sounds good." Brock glanced at the smashed keyboard of his laptop. "Give me a call."

"Mitchell." Teresa stood and took two precise steps toward him. Her voice was just about a whisper. "Look at me."

Her tone told Brock everything he needed to know about her. Mitchell was not their leader. This woman was. She held her upturned palm toward Brock, then drilled

Mitchell with her gaze.

"Is there any defense you'd like to give to counteract what I just heard?" Her voice remained almost too soft to hear. Brock couldn't tell if she was enraged or deeply pleased.

"Yes, it's true." Mitchell returned her look with eyes full of scorn. "But this move would put serious coin in your coffers."

"Well done." She nodded three times, then strolled around the table with a smile on her face. She held out her hand to Mitchell, who took it. She shook it once, then let go and smiled again. "Yes, very well done."

"So . . ." Mitchell cocked his head. "You're okay with not knowing about this? We're good?"

She turned to Brock and Ron. "I pride myself on being an excellent judge of character. I rarely miss. But obviously this time I did."

She turned back to Mitchell. "You fooled me." She stepped back to the table, gathered her papers, and walked over to Ron.

"My deepest apologies. I should have seen this coming." She extended her hand to Ron, glanced at Brock, then fixed her gaze back on Ron. "I'll be in touch."

She sauntered out of the room, followed

by her four companions and finally Mitchell. Before leaving, Mitchell stopped and zeroed his gaze on Brock.

"Why'd you cave? This is what you say you've wanted your entire life."

Brock didn't answer.

"At least tell me, was it worth it? You've just destroyed your reputation, probably both companies', and your relationship with your brother. So was it worth it?"

"Yes. It was worth it."

The moment the conference room door clicked shut behind Mitchell, Brock turned toward his brother. "Forgive me."

Ron closed his eyes and bit hard on his lower lip. He started to say something to Brock, but then turned and strode out of the conference room.

"It was the best of meetings; it was the worst of meetings."

It was the only way to describe to Karissa what had happened in the conference room at Black Fedora. He'd set himself free and saved the company but at the price of his friendship with Ron. And he wouldn't believe God brought him this far just to destroy his relationship with his brother. So he would trust and take one moment at a time.

Karissa and he sat on their veranda talking as they watched the lights of Bellevue and Seattle come alive against the encroaching night sky. He told her every detail about the past weeks and ended with the confrontation in the conference room. After answering her numerous questions, they sat in silence for a long time till Karissa took his hand and squeezed three times.

"Do you find it amazing that I believe you?"

"I'm just glad you do."

"Things with Ron will be okay."

"You think so?"

"I know so." She squeezed his hand again. "Any regrets?"

"If I start counting them I don't know if I'd be able to stop."

"How can you say that?" Karissa put her other hand on Brock's.

"You mean because everything supposedly turned out better than I could ever dream of it becoming?"

"What do you mean supposedly?"

"It's bittersweet, that's all."

"Why?"

Brock sighed. "It sounds so ungrateful to say this, after the change God made in me and the life I now see in front of us, but there's so much of my life — this time line

— that I don't remember." He sat up and turned toward her. "I don't remember any reconciliation with my dad. All I know is what a photo tells me. Apparently Ron and I became friends somewhere along the way, but I don't remember any of it. The times cooking with Tyson? Just hearsay. My life with you? I didn't get to watch you step into your dreams of being a teacher and make it real. And so many other things." Brock slumped back in his chair.

"Anything else?"

"Tough to discover there are places inside me dark enough to do what I did to Ron."

"Yes, it would be." Karissa ran her fingers along the back of his hand. "But even with that, would you trade this life?"

"No, of course not. I'm just venting. Like I said, being ungrateful. I'm simply realizing I didn't live this life."

"That's not true." Karissa turned and took his face in both her hands. "You did live it. Just as you lived out the dark parts inside, you lived out the good ones as well. And you'll discover more and more of it as you taste the fruit of having been a tremendous dad and an extraordinary husband. Plus, you were always quite attentive with the camera and video camera. I'm guessing you'll find a great many files to explore that will fill in the gaps in your memory."

Brock pulled her close and kissed her. "You're my wind."

"And you're mine." She rose and stepped toward the doors leading to their bedroom.

"Where are you going?"

"I'm going to give you some time alone."

"How did you know I need that?"

"I think I might know you just a little."

An hour later Karissa returned.

"Enough time?"

"Perfect."

After a swath of silence, Karissa asked the question Brock had been praying about off and on from the moment he left Black Fedora.

"What are you going to do about Ron?"

"I'm going to talk to him. Tell him about my bizarre existence during the past weeks. I have to believe he'll believe. But I'll give him a few days to cool down."

Karissa gave a sly smile, then turned away.

"What?"

"Nothing."

"Tell me."

"No."

Before Brock could ask a second time, his cell phone rang. It was Ron.

"Tomorrow morning we're going to my cabin."

"We are?" Brock stared at Karissa.

"Yes. I already talked to Karissa about it. She's good, so you're good. I'll pick you up at nine."

Ron hung up without waiting for a response.

Karissa looked up from under her eyelashes. "Who was that?"

"As if you didn't know."

Her smile grew.

"Want to tell me what's going on?"

"No, I don't."

"When did he talk to you? Is that the real reason you left me out here by myself for an hour?"

Karissa kissed him on the forehead. "Have a good time with your brother, okay?"

June 17, 2015

At ten the next morning, Ron and Brock pulled into Anacortes; at ten twenty they drove onto the ferry that would take them to Ron's cabin on Orcas Island. By the time the ferry reached the San Juan Islands, the sun had torched the morning fog, and light reflected off the water like jewels. Lopez Island slid by on Brock's left and he stared at Spencer Spit, the spot where years ago

he'd gone on a perfect scouting trip with his dad before the dark years came. Twenty minutes later they landed on Orcas and began the drive toward Garden Lane.

The road was full of switchbacks, but it wasn't till Brock's ears popped that he realized how high they'd climbed.

"Are we going to continue to pretend what happened in the conference room didn't happen?"

"No." Ron glanced at Brock. "As soon as we get there and settle in, we'll talk."

After five minutes and three more switchbacks, Brock broke the awkward silence.

"Your place is up a ways."

"On top of the world." Ron gave Brock a puzzled look. "But you've only been here a dozen times, so I suppose it's easy to forget that."

"I'm getting old." Brock tapped his head.

He'd never been to his brother's cabin in his life before the dreams started, but soon he'd tell Ron his entire story, and pray he believed it.

As they turned a corner thirty-five minutes after leaving the ferry, Ron's cabin came into view. Not huge, but he guessed at least two thousand square feet. The home was painted Eddie Bauer green, with huge picture windows framed with dark wood on either side of the maple front door.

"Welcome back to my escape."

Ron slid his key into the lock and pushed the front door open. He motioned for Brock to step inside first. High ceilings — ten feet he guessed — gave the home a majestic feel, and the rich brown color of the walls made Brock feel like he was stepping into a luxury hunting lodge.

Ron's voice came from behind him. "You can take your usual room at the top of the stairs. Why don't you get settled — I have some things I need to take care of first — then come join me in the den."

"Good. I want to take a shower before we get down to business."

"This weekend isn't about business, bro. I'm believing it will be all pleasure."

Brock nodded and tromped up the stairs. All pleasure? Convincing Ron he hadn't really tried to bury him with the buyout wouldn't be a pleasure. He didn't need a shower, but it was the best excuse he could think of to steal a few moments of prayer before they talked.

He reached the room, walked in, and set his overnight bag down next to the bed. The room was simple but elegant. A polished desk made of redwood, a picture of Cannon Beach on the wall over the bed, and a door that led into a bathroom on the right. Two nightstands on either side of the bed and a small clothes bureau were the only other items of furniture in the room.

Brock went to the window that overlooked the bay. Spectacular. Then he prayed for a few minutes about the time he was about to spend with Ron. God would be in it, no question, but that didn't quell the butterflies making like ninja warriors in his stomach.

He clomped to the bottom of the stairs and ambled down the hallway till he found Ron's den through the last door on the right. The walls were paneled with mahogany, and a set of bookshelves ran the length of the wall to his left. On the right side of the room sat a large desk, and the angle of the sun sent columns of light across it. The far opposite end of the room was dominated by two overstuffed chairs, which looked out on the bay through a massive picture window. Ron already sat in the chair on the left with a drink in his hand. As soon as Brock sat, Ron handed him another, then raised his glass. Brock didn't join him.

"I don't get it. Where is the scene in this play where you come after me for what I almost did to you? Where you denounce me as your brother?"

"It's okay." Ron set his drink down and

470

zeroed his gaze on Brock. "It's all forgiven."

"How? Why would you —"

"Yesterday Karissa called me. Told me everything."

"And you believed her?"

"I did. Because it finally made something done long ago that made no sense, make total sense now."

"I don't understand."

"You will." Ron grinned. "Right now."

Ron stood and strolled over to the picture hanging on the wall to the right of his maple desk. A picture of a sailboat on the crest of a wave, the sky above it cobalt blue. Wind in the sails that would carry it forever. The perfect illustration of where Karissa and Brock were now. Ron pulled the photo back and revealed a small safe behind it.

"This is why I believed her."

"Because of what's inside."

"Yes. And because of the picture."

"Did Karissa tell you about the conversations she and I've had about sailboats recently?"

"No, but your reaction tells me God is in this." Ron reached for the lock. "Do you like the classic behind-the-picture hiding place? It's so cliché it makes the perfect spot. The place no one would look. Nice 'Purloined Letter' feel to it I think. Although any thief who did look would be disappointed at what's inside."

Ron spun the lock forward, back, and forward again. The safe clicked and the door swung open with a soft squeal. Apparently the safe hadn't been opened in a long time. Ron didn't block the view, so Brock easily saw the contents. Not what he expected. The only thing inside was a thick manila envelope. His brother pulled the envelope out and held it in both hands for a moment before shutting the safe door and swinging the photo back in place. Then he settled back into the chair next to Brock and laid the envelope across his legs.

"Before I give you this, would you like to know where I got the photo?" Ron pointed back over his shoulder.

A slight smile grew on Brock's face. "Are you kidding?"

"Good, because I can't give you the envelope without telling you where the picture came from."

"I see." Brock crossed his legs and tried to figure out what the enigmatic look on Ron's face meant.

"No you don't, and what I'm about to say probably won't make your vision any clearer. Plus it might be a little hard to believe. I know I still find it hard to believe."

"Try me."

"All right." Ron put his hands and elbows on the armrests of his chair and leaned back a few inches. "In the spring of 2006 I was given the photo and the envelope at the same time. I was also given the safe. The person who gave me these items made me swear on my father's grave that I would do three things. First, guard the envelope as long as I lived. Second, tell no one about the envelope. No one. Not even the slightest mention of it, even to the person who gave it to me. And third, when the time was right, I would give the envelope and the contents to you."

Ron stopped and paused as if giving Brock time to assimilate the information.

"The third requirement was of course the hardest to comply with, simply because I had to be the judge of when the time would be right. And now that the moment has arrived, I hope I've judged rightly, and this is indeed the correct time to tell my short side of this story."

"What's inside the envelope?"

"I have no idea." Ron tilted his head. "Can't say I haven't been tempted to look at times over the years. But I never succumbed to the temptation."

"You still haven't told me who gave you

the photo and the envelope."

"No, I haven't."

Ron leaned his head back till it touched the back of his chair. He closed his eyes for so long Brock wondered if he'd fallen asleep.

"Who gave them to you?"

Ron opened his eyes, leaned forward, took hold of the envelope, and set it on the coffee table between them, laughter about to break out on his face. "You did."

CHAPTER 52

"What?" The blood rushed from Brock's face. First Mt. Pilchuck, now this. "I gave you the envelope? Me? And the photo? Are you kidding?"

Ron shook his head slowly, then glanced back in the direction of the picture. "I have to confess I almost broke the third rule the first time you stepped foot into this room back in 2009, just three years after you gave me the packet, looked at the photo, and asked me where I got it. I almost laughed but then realized you were probably testing me — to see how strong my promise to you was. But over the years I realized that for some strange reason you truly didn't remember that you yourself had taken the photo, framed it, and given it to me.

"So as much as you've been waiting for this day to come, so have I, because as you can understand, I'm supremely curious as to why you forgot, and if whatever is inside that envelope can answer that question. And now you know why I believed Karissa's story about what has happened to you over the past four weeks."

Ron leaned forward slowly and with one finger slid the envelope on the coffee table closer to his brother. Brock pulled in two breaths before reaching forward to take the packet. He lifted it off the table, took hold of the string that held the flap closed, and unwound it like it was a gold strand he was in fear of breaking. The rapid-fire pulse of blood through his temples seemed to drown out all other sounds.

As soon as he opened the flap, Brock slid the contents into his hands. On top of a thin leather journal lay a letter. On the bottom was a copy of the photo that hung in front of the safe. He glanced at Ron's questioning eyes, then began to read.

July 22, 2006

Dear Brock,

What should I call you? Old Man Brock? Future Me as I did so many times when we were together? It's odd writing to myself, but I suppose I'm not writing to myself — but to the person I'll become. Have you thought much about that? How the experiences in the past are simply memories of events that define who we were then, not who we are now? I'm guessing we've both learned we are not the same person in the present that we were in the past — or the days to come.

When you first appeared in Morgan's coffee shop in the summer of 1985 I of course didn't believe you. Who would? But over time I entertained the possibility that God was doing the impossible. And if you're reading this letter, then you were who you said you were, and God did indeed make the impossible happen.

As you've no doubt figured out by now, I took your advice and went to the Seahawks game. Dad told me he'd enrolled me in the New England Culinary Institute and had paid the entire tuition and housing in full. He took me by both shoulders and said, "Pursue the dream, Brock."

He'd seen my feeble attempts at cooking during my teens and early twenties, dreamed of what I could become, and acted on it. That meant the world, more than words could ever accomplish. And it started a reconciliation between us.

I graduated with honors from culinary school, and after slogging it out in San Francisco, Austin, and New York restaurants for ten years I opened my own, and that's when things took off.

But my greatest accomplishments are being a good husband to Karissa, a good father to Tyson, and loving God with all that I am.

I'm going to give this letter and a special photo to Ron on my 44th birthday. I'll tell him to give you these things when God's Spirit tells him the time is right.

> Yours for eternity,
> Brock Lee Matthews

Brock folded the letter, slid it back into its envelope, then picked up the journal and leafed through the pages. The first twenty or so pages were notes from his times with his younger self. Strange to see dates at the top that were more than thirty years old, yet in his time line they'd happened only days ago.

Brock looked up, but Ron was gone. Brock slid the journal, the photo, and the letter back into the envelope and rose from his chair to go find him. He found his brother out on the back deck sitting in one of six chairs that surrounded a gas-powered fire pit. An assortment of cheeses, olives, and fruits sat on a plate atop the pit's thick marble frame.

"Since the great Northwest doesn't often serve up days as fine as this one, I thought we should move our discussion out here. Drink in as much of the day as we can before night steals the light once again."

"When did you put together this spread?"

"While you were reading whatever was inside the packet."

The land in front of them sloped off at a forty-degree angle, leaving an unobstructed 180-degree view. Brock could make out what he thought was Shaw Island and Blakely Island.

"The view is stunning." He slipped into the chair next to his brother and focused on a sailboat moving across the water at least half a mile away. "Do you ever get tired of it?"

"Never. I still take the same picture time after time as if I don't have a hundred other shots already." Ron motioned toward a cold coffee drink sitting on the armrest of the wooden chair. "The ice is half melted, but I guarantee it will still taste pretty good."

"I'm sure it will." Brock lifted the drink and took a sip.

"It's all right?"

"Perfect." Brock took another sip, then set the drink down and turned to Ron. "Do you mind if I say something so sickeningly sentimental it will make your brain melt?"

"Not at all."

"I love you as my brother, but even more so as my friend."

Ron stood without speaking, raised Brock to his feet, and embraced him for what felt like hours.

Sleep came easily that night, and so did a dream that Brock would treasure forever. He sat once again with his father in the backyard he grew up in, but this dream wasn't the terrifying recurring nightmare that had haunted him. This was his dad from the Seahawks game just weeks before he passed away. His dad's eyes were tender, his hands folded across his lap. They faced each other, and the sun behind his dad's head had just risen.

"Are you controlling this dream, Dad? 'Cause I know I'm not."

"Not me. I think Someone else is."

The lawn around them didn't swirl, and the evening breeze was as light as if it came from a butterfly's wings. After a time his dad unclasped his hands, knocked the armrest of his chair twice, then gazed deep into Brock's eyes.

"There are so many things I've wanted to say to you for so many years, you know? Not sure why I waited." His dad sighed, but he didn't seem sad. "Yeah, I do know. The truth is I was too weak to come to you. Too much pride. Too ashamed of what I did to you in the days I wasn't in my right mind.

"The hardest part, thinking back, is knowing you were old enough to remember the man I was at the start of the dark years. Your brother wasn't, so there was never that wall between Ron and me that there was between the two of us."

Brock's dad gave a tiny shake of his head that reminded Brock of himself. "I should have fought harder to tear it down than I did. I know the clouds I created still block you from seeing the sun. And I've longed to see those clouds burned away by a sun so bright no darkness could overcome it ever again."

"It's okay, Dad." His dad turned and Brock looked at his father's face in profile. They had the same nose, the same chin, the same look of contemplation.

"I think it is, Brock. I really do."

His dad turned and stared deeper into Brock's eyes than anyone in his life had ever done.

"I love you, Dad."

"Me too, Brock. I'm so proud of you."

His father laid his hand on top of Brock's and held it tight till the dream faded and Brock fell into the arms of the best sleep he'd ever had.

CHAPTER 53

May 23, 2015

When Brock woke the next morning, he kept his eyes closed and basked in the memory of his dream from the night before, but the moment he opened them his heart rate spiked. He wasn't in Ron's cabin. He was home.

Brock lurched to the edge of the bed and sat with his feet on their tan carpet, staring out the window at a gray sky, trying to remember what must have happened. Why would Ron bring him back here in the middle of the night? Brock spun to look at the other side of the bed. Karissa wasn't there. He wobbled around the edge of the bed and called her name as he pushed open the bathroom door. Empty.

"Karissa?" He called her name at the top of the stairs and again when he reached the bottom. No answer. And no sign of her in the kitchen, the family room, or anywhere else in the house. It wasn't till he opened the garage door and found himself staring at her empty stall that the truth started to creep into his mind.

Brock spun and loped back across the kitchen. He took the stairs two at a time, strode back into their bedroom, and snatched his cell phone off his nightstand. Karissa picked up on the second ring.

"What do you need, Brock?"

"Where did you go this morning? And why am I here instead of Ron's cabin?"

"You've never been to Ron's cabin."

"No." Ice shot down his back. "This can't . . . where are you?"

"Do we have to go over it again?"

The blood drained from his face as the words sputtered out of him. "You're at your sister's."

"And?"

More chills washed through him. "It was real. All of it. I swear it wasn't a dream. It can't have been."

"What was real?"

Brock whirled and headed for the top of the stairs. He grabbed the railing on the way down or he would have fallen. His legs felt detached from his body as he watched his feet clomp down the steps as if they belonged to someone else. He staggered into his den, stared at the walls, and despair buried him. There was one picture of his dad and him in Alaska. One. And no picture at a long-ago Seahawks game.

"Brock, are you there?"

"We went three times, Karissa. Three."

"Where?"

"And we went to the game. I went! And you and I . . . we're so good now. So good."

"What are you talking about?"

He squeezed his head and didn't answer.

"What is wrong with you, Brock?"

"It can't have."

"Can't have what?"

"Can't have not happened."

"I need to go, Brock."

"Wait."

But the line went dead.

Brock collapsed into his desk chair as quick, heavy breaths puffed out of him. Had to think. Figure out what was going on. But he knew already what to do. He needed to talk to someone wise. Only one person came to mind. A friend who most likely would think he was crazy.

Chapter 54

Ten minutes later Brock was on his way toward Seattle's Lake Union. In another thirty he merged onto Western, which would put him at Beth's in five minutes — if she truly lived there and wasn't just a creation he'd concocted inside his dreams. He held little hope she was anything more than that, but he had to be sure. Yeah, he could've Googled her to see if she existed, but he needed to stand on her doorstep before he let his sliver of hope go.

A few minutes later, he pulled into the tiny parking spot in front of the houseboat he knew as Beth's. He reached into the backseat for the paper bag full of Black Fedora coffee.

As he approached the dark-red houseboat, a puff of wind made the wind chimes hanging from Beth's roof sing as if announcing his arrival. Brock knocked on Beth's door and whispered to himself, "If she lives here, this is going to be really weird."

A moment later, Beth's door swung wide. It was her. She stood before him in a flowing red-and-white kimono, her dirty blonde hair a mess, her smile drawing him in like a magnet.

"Can I help you?"

"Hi." Any semblance of an appropriate introduction vanished, and Brock stood with his mouth cracked open.

"You are?" Beth squinted at him.

Brock suppressed an urge to hug her, and a quick laugh puffed out of his mouth. "Sorry. My name is Brock Matthews."

"Wonderful." Beth's smile dropped a few notches. "And?"

"I'm sorry to drop in on you unannounced." He shifted his weight as her face turned into a frown. "I should try to explain —"

"It's not that." Beth waved her hand. "I feel almost like . . . do we know each other? We've met before this, yes?"

Brock glanced at the house next door, the one he'd owned in his dreams, and debated what to say. No. Not time for crazy yet. "I don't think so."

"No, I guess not. I just had the strangest sensation though." She shook her head and beckoned him across the threshold. "But come in. Come in and tell me why you're here. And you simply gotta tell me what you have in that big paper bag, 'cause I'm the curious sort and you wouldn't have brought that bag unless you meant to show me what's inside."

Brock smiled. This might turn out okay.

Beth led him to her living room, and Brock set the bag next to his feet and pulled out ten different flavors of Black Fedora coffee. As he handed each of them to Beth, her eyes widened.

"Are you serious?" Beth rubbed her hands together almost fast enough to start a fire. "I absolutely love Black Fedora coffee."

"I thought you might." Brock clasped his hands together and leaned forward. Might as well dive in. "Do you believe in fate?"

"Depends."

"I think we're fated to be friends, Elizabeth."

She stared at him and a shard of . . . what? Brock couldn't tell what flashed into Beth's eyes. A shrouded memory? Recognition? It left too quickly, replaced by that megawatt smile.

"No." Beth protested with both hands. "You can't call me Elizabeth. Or Lizzie. Or Liza. The only thing that will work for you is Beth." The smile again. "Okay?"

"Okay." Brock let a grin take over his face. "Beth it is."

"Now, why don't you explain who you are and why you're really here. And explain how you knew my name before I gave it to you if we've never met." She winked.

"That is a story indeed."

"I love stories."

"Fiction or nonfiction?"

"Oh boy, wind up the toys." Beth laughed. "This is going to be a good one."

Brock glanced through Beth's windows at two kayakers paddling past, then leaned forward, elbows on knees. "Let me just preface this by saying I'm not crazy, and —"

"Wait a minute, grab the horses, give a yank backward." Beth mimicked pulling back on invisible reins, then picked up a bag of the coffee Brock had just given her. "I know where I know you! You're one of the owners of Black Fedora, right? You're the guy who shows up in the TV ads from time to time." She grinned and clapped her hands together over her head. "I gotta celeb in my house. This is so sweet."

"Me? No, no, no." Brock waved his hands. "You're the celebrity, not me."

"Because I write a few columns every now and then that people maybe enjoy? Hardly."

She laughed and it filled the room. "What a wonderful surprise. Someday I should write about your phenomenal coffee."

"That would be incredibly generous."

"Just a chance to tell the truth." Beth winked. "Good to find out there's a decent man behind the beans."

Silence settled on the room as if Beth was giving Brock an opening to say why he'd come. He took a slow breath in, let it out slower, then dove in.

"This is going to sound a little nuts, Beth." Brock rubbed his hands together. "A lot nuts."

"Oooo, yes. Wonderful. I love outlandish tales."

"This is so far past outlandish there's no map."

"Oh my, now you really have my attention." She leaned forward and winked again. "What? Did we know each other in another life?" She laughed.

Again, Brock hesitated for a moment before diving into the deep end. "Yes. That's exactly right."

When he finished telling his story of the month, and what she had meant to him, Beth's expression flitted back and forth from one that said Brock was certifiable and she was about to leap for the phone and dial 911, to one that said she would choose to believe every word.

"Just so I'm clear. We're not on camera. This isn't going up on the Internet or anything like that, right?"

"No."

"Well then." Beth clapped her hands together and shifted on her couch.

"Still interested in being friends?"

"I have plenty of friends who are crazy, so you'll fit right in." She raised a flat palm over her head. "But I will say you are now the Mt. Everest of my loony pals. So I might need to call you Sir Edmund."

"Hillary?"

"Precisely. You say I was your great counselor, your own personal Yoda."

"But much more beautiful." Brock nodded. "You changed my life."

Silence filled the room again.

"So what do you do now with the fact nothing in your life has changed?" She leaned forward as her face grew as serious as he'd ever seen. "The fact you're stuck with all the same problems you had when your dreams began? The fact that what happened to you was only in your head?"

"I was hoping you could tell me. Where to go from here. Show me how to figure this out."

"What about talking to this doctor friend of yours?"

"A good man, but he's more about the head, and right now I need someone who is more about the heart. And nowhere more than when it comes to Karissa. I need someone with heart to show me how to win her back. Life without her . . ." Brock pulled in a breath and held it for a time before releasing the air.

"I can't show you anything, Brock." Beth leaned back on her couch. "All I can do is guide you toward what you already know. Then pray your eyes will open wide enough to see what you already know to be true."

"Then what do I already know?"

"You're much wiser than this." She shook her head and gave a thin smile.

He asked again, fervor growing in his voice. "What do I already know?"

Brock waited for her to answer, but she stared at him, the slight smile still on her face, and he thought she wouldn't respond no matter how long he waited. But finally she did.

"Let me ask you once more, Brock, my precious new friend." Beth tapped her forefingers together. "How do you deal with the fact none of what happened to you was real?"

"It was real." Brock blinked as the realization swept over him.

"Yes. I think it was."

"It doesn't matter that it didn't happen in the physical world."

"No, it does not."

"It doesn't matter because I'm not the same man."

"No, I don't believe you are."

Brock stood and a smile grew on his face that turned into laughter. "I shouldn't feel this way."

"Why?"

"Because nothing has changed."

"And yet everything has changed." Beth's smile matched his own. "Now go after her."

Brock tried Karissa three times before reaching the Evergreen Point Floating Bridge, and three times the call went to voice mail. No matter. He'd be at his sister-in-law's house in fifteen minutes. Plenty of time to make two phone calls at the top of his priority list. Brock prayed and dialed the first number.

"Hello?"

"Ron, it's Brock."

"Yeah, I figured that one out."

"How are you?"

"Peachy. You?"

"I've never been better in my entire life." He glanced at the sailboats harnessing the wind on Lake Washington.

"Really." Ron's voice was flat, but he followed up with the requisite question. "Why's that?"

"I want to tell you all about it, but on one condition."

"Okay."

"We do it tomorrow morning on the golf course."

Ron went silent for a solid five seconds. His voice was a millimeter warmer when he spoke again. "You're kidding."

"No."

"What are you doing, Brock?" Ron's sigh filled Brock's phone. "Your plan to go back and talk to your younger self and fix things didn't work? So you're going to try to soften me up to give you more time before I sign?"

"No. No agenda. Just two brothers out on the course together. No company talk. I promise."

"Yeah?"

"Yes." Brook reached the end of the bridge and crossed into Bellevue.

Ron went quiet for so long Brock almost broke the silence. But then Ron spoke.

"You found something, didn't you?"

"It doesn't matter. Truly."

"Did you?"

"Yes," Brock said.

"You know who hacked into our accounts."

"There's someone probably worth checking into."

Again silence from his brother.

"All right," Ron finally said. Then so softly Brock wasn't sure his brother spoke the words. "Eighteen together. That'd be okay."

"And, bro?"

"What?"

Brock nodded to himself before speaking. He needed to say this. "Do you remember our favorite toy from when we were kids?"

Ron didn't answer for a good ten seconds. When he did, his voice was half its normal volume. "Captain Action, right?"

"Yeah."

Again, a long pause before Ron spoke. "What about it?"

"We need to talk about the Code. I need to ask you to forgive me. And I need to tell you a story that will blow your mind."

As he hung up, Brock glanced at his watch. Twelve minutes till he would stand in front of Karissa and give his confession. Plenty of time to make one more very important call.

CHAPTER 55

Brock dialed Sheila's number and prayed she'd pick up. What he wanted to say wasn't the kind of thing to leave in a message.

Three rings and no answer. *C'mon.* She picked up on the fourth. Relief. And nerves. But this was right.

"Hello?"

"Sheila? It's Brock." He hesitated then added, "Matthews."

She laughed. "I don't need the last name. I don't even need the first."

"How are you?"

She was silent for a few seconds. "Before you say anything, I have to apologize. I never should have sent that e-mail. I'm so sorry, it's just that —"

"I found the note."

"What?"

"The note," Brock said. "The one you probably wondered if I'd ever find. I went into my attic the other day and found the lion and unicorn drawing. For some reason I turned it over and discovered what you wrote under the paper on the back."

"Oh wow."

"Yeah."

He listened to the hum of the phone as he struggled to get his next words right. "Sheila? You'll always have a piece of my heart." He paused. "That's a good thing. A wonderful thing. We were great together and brought each other so much joy. That will never be taken away. And that's not just a good thing, but a very good thing."

A nervous laugh came through the phone.

"You okay?" Brock said.

"More than okay." Through the phone he heard her draw a deep breath. "I needed to hear that. Really needed to. Thank you."

"Good-bye, Sheila."

"I'll miss you, Brock."

"Me too."

Two minutes later, Brock pulled into his sister-in-law's driveway and for a few moments watched her neighbor prune her trees. He needed to do the same for his yard. Maybe in a few days. He had a plan for tomorrow. If a miracle happened and Karissa would agree to go along with it.

Karissa's sister turned when he opened his car door. "Hey, Brock."

"Is she here?"

"She's out back. Come on in."

"Thanks." Brock hesitated.

Karissa's sister cocked her head. "You okay?"

"No. But that's exactly why I'm here."

Brock shot up a silent prayer as he moved through the house to the sliding glass door at the back. He hesitated for a moment, then slid it open and stepped onto the patio. Karissa sat cross-legged in a lawn chair gazing straight ahead. If she'd heard him, she didn't give any indication.

"Karissa?"

She didn't answer.

He eased over to Karissa and sat in the chair beside her.

"Hey."

Again, no answer.

He gazed at her profile, more in love than he'd ever been. "I never saw you. Not like I should have. But I see you now."

"Okay." She continued to stare straight ahead.

Brock sat next to her for a few moments in silence. Then, "It's true. Deeper than you can imagine."

"No, Brock."

"And I don't tell you often enough how stunning you are."

"I said, don't." Karissa pulled her arms across her chest. "I need a month, a few weeks at least to figure some things out."

"You truly stagger me. So beautiful. Inside. Outside. All of you. Such a treasure."

"I said —"

"I need to ask for a crazy favor but I swear it'll be the last one I ask for till you tell me I can again. After this, I won't call, I won't come over here. Nothing till you're ready."

"What's the favor?" She moved her head farther away from him.

"I want to take you somewhere for the day tomorrow. And I want to tell you the most amazing story you've ever heard."

"Where?"

"To a place where we can start over. From the beginning."

"What are you talking about? The beginning of what?"

"Us." Brock leaned toward her, just a few inches. "Tomorrow morning I want us to go to the Birch Bay Waterslides."

"That is crazy." Karissa shot him a weary glance. "You want to go water sliding? Are you kidding? They're probably not even open yet."

Brock raised both hands. "I'm not suggesting we get anywhere near the water. I just want to stand in the spot in that park-

499

ing lot where I first met you and I knew you were my *density.*"

The hint of a smile played on the corner of Karissa's mouth. "That density which brought me to you." The smile faded.

Brock slid his hands on top of hers. "I'm not the same man."

"So you say." She pulled her hands out of his.

"No. I'm not going to tell you about it. I'm going to show you every day for the rest of our lives together. And the slides are where I want to start."

"I don't know." Karissa sighed. "I'd need time to think about it."

"For as long as you like."

"I tell you what." She looked at him longer than a few seconds for the first time since he'd sat down. "I'll let you know in the morning about going to the slides. But don't get your hopes up. Even a little."

That night they slept twenty-three miles apart, which was a good thing because the moment Brock went to sleep, he slipped into a dream he wouldn't want interrupted.

CHAPTER 56

June 12, 2001

"Hello, Future Me. It's great to see you."

Brock found himself staring at the younger version of himself sitting five yards away in a canvas chair in the center of Farrel-McWhirter Park in Redmond. Sunshine. Slight breeze with the hint of autumn in it. Perfect day. But something was . . . different. Was it . . . there, that was it.

"You're older." He grinned at not-so-young-anymore Brock and took a few steps forward.

"Yeah, it's been a few years since you came back to see me." Young Brock smiled and patted his chest. "Still looking pretty decent for thirty-nine though. Don't you think?"

"You look great."

"So do you. I see it. First time I've seen that kind of peace on your face."

His younger self motioned to the empty

chair next to him. Brock ambled over to him and sat.

"What happened to my future?"

"Surrender. Full surrender. Great freedom. Great joy. And much more."

"I'd love to hear all about it."

Brock told his younger self everything that had happened since they first met right up till he entered this dream. Young Brock nodded his head throughout the story, his eyes bright. When Brock finished, his younger self cocked his head, a look of contemplation on his face.

"So was any of it real?"

"All of it was more real than anything in my life has ever been."

"Yet nothing has changed. You've gone back to where you started."

"No." Brock smiled and shook his head. "Everything's changed. Everything. Because I've changed. I'm not the man I was. I'm the man I see has already come alive in you. I'm discovering my true self and no longer living out of the lies about who I thought I was. The one who gets his validation from what he does is dying. The one who gets his validation from who he is, from who God sees he is — that's the man who is alive now."

"And Karissa? Will she love you again?"

"I don't know. But it doesn't matter."

"How can it not matter?"

"It is truly an amazing thing to fully surrender to the living God. To completely give yourself over to the Spirit living inside you. Maybe that's what dying to self means. Where you're not worried about being loved, but how well you can love another."

"And you're ready to do that for Karissa as long as you live."

"I'm ready to do it at least for today. And I'm not going to worry about the day after that till it gets here. Jesus said each day has enough worries to deal with. I agree. I'm going to live in the now."

"Explain that."

"Our choices lead us to life or lead us to death, and as I now vividly know, what we do in our present certainly affects what we become in the future. But in the end, there is only now, only this moment in which to live. The future does not exist. So I will live now. The past is gone and cannot be retrieved, so I will live now. There is only the present. So I will live in this moment."

His younger self nodded, closed his eyes, and seemed to be soaking the power of the sun into his whole being. "I have a hope for you, deep down where hope cannot be thwarted. A hope that your future will be blindingly bright, that the sails will unfurl and the wind will dance in hard from the south."

Brock rose and his younger self opened his eyes and followed the lead. They smiled at each other.

"This is going to be a little weird and yet make all the sense in the world. I love you, Brock. You've set me free." He grabbed himself in a bear hug and held on till the dream faded and Karissa's voice called to him from the edge of sleep.

CHAPTER 57

May 24, 2015

"I'll go."

Brock opened his eyes to find Karissa standing in the door frame of their bedroom dressed in black jeans and a white blouse. He blinked hard to pull himself awake.

"What?"

"I'll go to the waterslides."

"Really?"

"I want to hear this story."

She turned away without smiling, but it didn't matter. Her answer sent Brock's heart soaring.

By nine thirty they were sailing up I-5 under a blue sky peppered with white clouds.

"You ready to tell me your amazing tale?"

"Yes." Brock glanced at her, then turned back to the road. "But it's insane."

"I'm ready for a little insane. Part of me is insane for not staying at my sister's."

The words bit, but not hard, because he could tell she didn't really mean it.

"Promise you won't think I'm crazy?"

"Yes."

When he finished Karissa was silent for three miles. Brock would let her sit in her contemplation as long as she wanted. As they passed the Arlington exit she extended her hand and offered it to him. Brock took it and held it tight. When they reached the outskirts of Mt. Vernon, she broke the silence.

"Can I make a suggestion?"

"Anything."

"Maybe ask Tyson on a backpacking trip? Maybe see if you could start cooking together?"

Brock nodded. "I'm going to make up a list of 'meals' that he and I can share together. Meals like taking a cooking class. A backpacking trip. Going to a Seahawks game, dirt biking. Appetizers like a movie night, video game night, go to the driving range together."

"You don't dirt bike or golf."

"Gimme a break . . . I'm brainstorming here." He smiled.

"I like it." She squeezed his hand. "Tyson will too."

"I hope so."

"I know he will," Karissa said. "Mind if I get a few tunes going?"

"Good call."

She reached into the backseat to search Brock's case of CDs. She came forward with it a few seconds later and rummaged through it before pulling out a CD cover and holding it up. "How 'bout Steve Miller?"

Brock glanced at the CD cover and a bolt of adrenaline shot through him. Impossible. Utterly impossible. He sucked in a quick breath and the words sputtered out.

"Where did you get that? Whose is it?"

"What are you talking about?"

He glanced at the CD again, thinking his eyes might have deceived him the first time.

"Look at the cover!" Brock tried to steady his breathing. "Where did you get that CD?"

"What do you mean?"

"Don't you remember? I owned the early version. I never bought the . . . but when I was on the PCT in my dream I told Young Brock to —"

"Buy the *Young Hearts* CD that came out in 2003." As Karissa spoke the words, the CD case slipped from her hands. She turned her body toward him. "Oh my gosh. What are you saying?"

"I'm not dreaming. I know I'm not. So

how could . . . ? Impossible."

Karissa just laughed and smiled as wide as Brock had ever seen.

"How . . . this is impossible," Brock repeated. What else was there to say?

"And after all you've been through you still don't think God can handle the impossible?"

"So was it real?" Brock's body flushed with heat. "Part of it? All of it?"

"You know what?" Karissa picked up the CD and gazed at it. "I don't think this is the last piece of evidence we'll find."

"But . . . that story . . . my dream-world story ended. It's over. What is God doing?"

Karissa took his right hand off the steering wheel in both of hers and kissed his fingers. "I think he's telling us our story and the restoration of so many things isn't ending. It's just begun."

A NOTE FROM THE AUTHOR

Dear Friend,

Usually it takes me a while to appreciate my novels. I see all the little flaws that remain when the story is finished. Eventually I come around, but not for a while. But not this time. As I read the book for the final time (trying to find any remaining typos and words that needed to be fixed), the story captured me and I found myself reading it as a reader, not a critical editor.

I suppose that's because Brock's story is my story. There's a large part of me that wishes I could go back and fix the things I did wrong. Part of me longs to tell the twenty-three-year-old James L. Rubart all the things he should have done differently.

But in the end what I truly yearn for is redemption. A second chance. For the Lord to open my eyes to how I can change right now, in this present moment. And he has done that for me, and continues to do that just as I know he will do it for you. I don't believe anything in our lives is too far gone for the Lord to bring restoration.

All we need to do is surrender to his unquenchable grace and love, and step deeper into the story he is still writing for us in every moment.

To your freedom,
James L. Rubart
June 2015

ACKNOWLEDGMENTS

To (my wife) Darci, for coming up with the entire premise that inspired this story and being my rock through the always arduous journey called writing a novel.

To my editor Amanda Bostic for being courageous enough to tell me the first version of this story just didn't work (she was so right!), helping me figure out the next version, and being an amazing friend through that challenging process.

To Erin Healy, my editor, who I'd heard was legendary for her skill at shaping a story and who exceeded the reputation.

To Ruth for once again being a first reader of the first draft (the only person who has read every first draft of all of my novels) and for making me feel so good when she said how much she loved it.

To Ron for giving me wonderful ideas for the story, giving me the name *Black Fedora,* being an insightful first reader, and being such an incredible friend during the insane time of my life that came while writing this story.

To Susie and David Warren for their staggering brilliance in shaping the plot of *Five Times*. You two are awesome.

To Allen Arnold for walking beside me like a true brother every step of this novel's journey.

To Jesus for taking me through the fire and for taking the shadow of the first version of this story and turning it into one I believe he will use to set people free.

DISCUSSION QUESTIONS

1. Which character did you relate to most in *The Five Times I Met Myself*?
2. What themes stood out to you in the story?
3. Throughout the Bible God uses dreams to perform powerful works in people's lives, as he did in Brock's life in this story. Have you ever had a dream that changed your life?
4. Had you heard of lucid dreaming before reading *The Five Times I Met Myself*?
5. Even if you hadn't heard about lucid dreaming, do you now realize you've had this kind of dream? If yes, what was it like?
6. If you had the chance to go back and talk to your younger self, would you do it?
7. If you did go back, what would you want to tell yourself?
8. Have you ever had a dream where you were younger? What did it feel like?
9. Beth became a tremendous friend to

Brock. Do you have a friend like her? Are you a friend like that to someone?

10. At the end of the story, Brock realizes while in one way nothing has changed, in another, everything about his life has changed. Have you had an experience that made you feel that way? What happened?

11. Brock has to face the truth that he tried to get his validation from his company — but that the only true validation in his life can come from his relationship with God. Have you tried to get your validation from things or people other than God? Why do you think we do that?

12. Brock experiences great freedom when he finally surrenders everything he is to the Lord. Have you experienced that type of surrender and that type of freedom? Do you think it happens once, or do we need to continue the act of complete surrender on an ongoing basis?

13. In the final pages of *The Five Times I Met Myself* we get a hint that some of the things that happened to Brock were more than just in his mind. Did you like that idea? Not like it? Why?

14. At the end of the story, Brock is determined to change his relationship with Karissa, Tyson, and Ron. Are there relationships in your life you'd like to change? If

there are, are there things you can do to accomplish that?

ABOUT THE AUTHOR

James L. Rubart is a professional marketer and speaker. He is the author of the bestselling novel *Rooms* as well as *Book of Days, The Chair,* and the Well Spring Novels. He lives with his wife and sons in the Pacific Northwest.

Website: www.jameslrubart.com
Twitter: @jameslrubart
Facebook: JamesLRubart